ADVANCE PRAISE FOR
DIANA GROE AND *MAIDENSONG*!

"Ms. Groe is a fresh new voice in romance.
Dramatic and stirring, *Maidensong* will
leave you clamoring for more
of Diana Groe's work."

—CONNIE MASON,
New York Times Bestselling Author
of *A Taste of Paradise*

A LOVE TOO LATE?

Bjorn's hair was bound back out of his eyes. A look of dogged concentration was etched on his rugged face as he swung the heavy double-bladed ax. Rika knew in that moment that she loved him. Loved him with every fiber of her being, with every breath in her body, with every drop of blood coursing through her veins.

And she knew just as certainly if she died without letting this man love her, she might as well die right now.

Maybe it didn't matter that tomorrow or next week or next month they'd reach the end of this journey and be parted. A Pecheneg arrow could find either of them at any moment. Life was nothing but a series of good-byes, anyway. No one was promised tomorrow. But they did have now.

As if he felt her gaze, Bjorn turned her way.

"Rika?" he said uncertainly, unable to hear her words over the roar of the great waterfall behind her.

She took a step toward him, but made it no farther. The soft bank beneath her feet had been eroded by the constant hammering, and all it took to send it plummeting downstream was the slight addition of her weight.

Her eyes and mouth flew open wide in shock, and she disappeared into the mists of the falls without a sound.

MAIDENSONG

DIANA GROE

LEISURE BOOKS NEW YORK CITY

A LEISURE BOOK®

May 2006

Published by

Dorchester Publishing Co., Inc.
200 Madison Avenue
New York, NY 10016

ISBN 0-8439-5710-7

Visit us on the web at www.dorchesterpub.com.

MAIDENSONG

PROLOGUE

The babe wailed again.

"There, lamb," Helge whispered as she sponged the last of the slick fluids off the enraged little body. Flickering light from the central fire kissed the newborn and danced across the smoke-blackened beams of the longhouse.

The old midwife sighed. However difficult the babe's entry into the world had been, she was at least a healthy child, perfectly formed with all her fingers and toes and a crest of coppery hair plastered to her damp head.

"Hush you, now," Helge coaxed.

The wrinkled little face puckered and the newborn shrieked as if Loki, the trickster godling, had just pinched her bottom. Helge wrapped the child snugly in a cat-skin blanket, crooning urgent endearments.

"Shut the brat up," Torvald said, his voice a broken shadow of its usual booming timbre. All the souls sheltered in the longhouse went expectantly silent. As if she sensed menace in the air, the child subsided into moist hiccups.

"Will you not hold your daughter?" Helge offered the small bundle to Torvald. "She's a fine child, fair and lusty."

"No, I'll not." Torvald swabbed his eyes. "She's killed my Gudrid. I'll have naught to do with her." When he looked at the mewling babe, his face was a mask of loathing. "Put her out."

Helge flinched. "But, my lord—"

"Don't argue with me, woman. Am I not chief over my own house?" Torvald's gray eyes blazed with a potent mix of fury and grief. "I said, put her out."

Helge's shoulders sagged. She couldn't remember the last time a healthy child had been exposed. But Torvald was master, so there was nothing for it but to do his bidding.

Still, it didn't seem right to consign the babe to *Hel* empty-handed. It was bad enough that she'd go unloved and unmourned to that shadowy, icy place. Even worse, she'd arrive there as a pauper.

Helge laid her little charge on the bedding, and untied the thin strip of leather from the dead woman's slim neck.

The pendant was a simple little amber hammer, its only distinctive mark a tiny purple orchid trapped forever in the glowing stone. Perhaps Thor would mark the child for his protection if she met her death wearing his talisman. It wasn't much, but it was all Helge could do for the mite.

She bundled herself against the cold and left the longhouse bearing her whimpering burden. The stiff hairs in her nostrils froze with each breath.

The thought of leaving the child for the wolves made Helge's chest constrict smartly. She decided to let the sea take her. It would be clean and quick. There'd be less chance of hearing the child's keening death wail on the wind. And the unhappy little soul would find it harder to trouble those who'd disowned her with malicious tricks later, as some malevolent ghosts were known to do.

Snow crunched underfoot as Helge trudged down to the shore where the fjord was choked with ice. Armed with an ax she picked up as she passed the woodpile, Helge carried the babe as close to the edge of the floe as she dared.

"Good-bye, little elf," Helge said as she placed the newborn on the smooth, cold surface. "Thor keep you, for I cannot."

She brought the sharp ax down with a thwack. The brittle ice shattered in a jagged line and separated from the main body of the floe. Helge gave it a nudge with the ax handle.

She watched with a gathering heaviness in her chest as, bobbing and dipping, the tiny bundle on the ice sheet floated out with the tide.

CHAPTER 1

Every dog in the settlement howled as if the world were ending. Rika peeked out a crack in the privy door. Rough men, armored in hardened leather, herded people and livestock to their dragonships moored at the quay. So far, none of the raiders had thought to check the cesspit. She and her foster brother, Ketil, were safe enough for the moment.

"Father's out there." Ketil's round face was streaked with dirty runnels where tears left their tracks.

"I know, I know." Rika bit her lip, trying to think what to do next. She hoped to catch a glimpse of the old skald's flowing white hair and multihued cape. "Where can Magnus be?"

And why, oh, why did he ever drag us from the Danish court?

Smoke wafted toward them. The flames were closer now.

"Come." Rika grabbed Ketil's big hand and pulled him behind her. She darted across the muddy lane, slipping and going down, then scrambled back to her feet and skidded into a stable. Rika stopped, frozen in midstep. A small gasp escaped her lips.

Her mind refused to make sense of what she saw. Magnus lay facedown on the ground, his skull cleaved open. The soggy gray porridge of his brain oozed out, a thousand nights' stories spilling into the straw-covered dirt.

"Oh, Father." Rika dropped to her knees beside him, clutching at her chest. A sob constricted her throat and stung her eyes. She had to remind herself to breathe.

She'd only been a small girl the first time she'd heard Magnus Silver-Throat tell the tale of *Ragnarok*, the Doom of the Gods. The death of Odin and his co-horts of Asgard had always seemed the most horrific, the most obscene thing she could imagine. Until now.

Ketil turned Magnus over gently. "All will be well," he kept repeating, trying to ease Magnus's brains back into his skull. "I didn't dream it, so all will be well."

"No, Ketil." Rika roused herself and pulled him away from Magnus's body. "All will never be well again."

Ketil's simple face crumpled. He howled his grief like one of the damned in *Niflheim.* In a harsh world, only Magnus had seen a reason for Ketil's gentle soul to live. And now Magnus was gone.

Rika wrapped her arms around her brother and rocked him, letting him cry. It didn't matter who heard him. Nothing mattered anymore.

A shadow fell across the stable doorway, sending a chill rippling over her. She looked up, the heaviness in her limbs making even that simple movement difficult.

A tall man blocked the way, his drawn blade still dripping red. His sword arm was bared and leather leggings were cinched to his muscular thighs. The mail hung over his short tunic proclaimed him a raider of substance. Rika felt sure the dark stains on the man's clothing were not his own blood.

His gaze raked over her slowly, and he flashed his teeth at her. A predator's smile.

"What have we here?" His strong-boned face was clean-shaven, as much a rarity among Northmen as his dark eyes. "A little mud-hen with an overgrown chick."

Ketil roared, got to his feet and plowed toward the man, arms flailing. The raider stepped aside and tripped Ketil, sending him sprawling into the mud outside the stable. Then he whacked Ketil's bottom with the flat of his long broadsword as a light reprimand.

Rika scrambled to cover her brother with her own body. With every bit of the skaldic art Magnus had taught her, she willed the man to obey her.

"No! You will not hurt this boy." Even though Ketil was nine years her senior, to Rika he would always seem the younger and in need of her protection.

"Looks like I'm wrong." The man drove the point of his sword into the ground and leaned on the pommel. "Not a mud-hen after all. You're more like a she-wolf, aren't you?"

"No, I'm a skald." Rika straightened to her full height. She considered herself tall for a woman. She'd been able to look Magnus eye to eye for some time, but she still had to look up to meet this man's mocking gaze.

"And you are a murderer," she said with a boldness that surprised even herself. "You've killed the finest skald ever to grace a hall. Behind you lies Magnus Silver-Throat, the bravest and best—" Her voice crackled with grief.

An emotion that might have been regret flickered across the man's angular face and he glanced over his shoulder at Magnus's corpse. "That's the Silver-

Throat?" His lips tightened into a hard line. "I've heard of him."

"And thanks to you, no one will ever hear him again." Rika spat the words, swiping at her eyes. Only the need to keep Ketil safe stopped her from flying at this dark barbarian in a shrieking rage.

"I didn't kill him." The raider eyed the old skald lying on the stable floor. "But one of my men surely did."

When he tugged off his leather helm, a shock of raven hair fell to the man's shoulders, a sharp contrast to his pale Nordic skin. He pulled a horn-handled knife from the sheath at his waist and placed it in Magnus's hand, wrapping the cooling fingers around the hilt.

"Here, friend," he said softly. "Drain a horn for me in the Hall of the Slain." Then he strode to the neighboring house, already ablaze, and plucked out a firebrand. The raider tossed it into the open stable door and waited for a few moments to be sure the flames caught.

Ketil dissolved into sobs again and Rika stooped to comfort him. She felt numb and heavy, as though the air she moved through was thick as water.

"It can't be real," Ketil insisted. "I would've dreamed it if it were real. I'd tell Father and we'd go away."

A furrow appeared between the man's dark brows. "What's the matter with him?" He narrowed his eyes at Ketil. "Is he soft-headed?"

"It's better than being hard-hearted." Heat rose in Rika's cheeks. Anger, *ja*. That was something she could let herself feel.

"Can he work?"

"He's strong, if that's what you mean." She fisted her hands at her waist. "If someone shows him what to do, he'll work the likes of you down to the ground."

"Good," the raider said. "We've no room for useless eaters. Come then, both of you."

"We're not going anywhere with you." She crossed her arms over her chest, determined to stand her ground, however shaky she felt inside. "We are a troupe of skalds, lately come from the King of the Danes and are not subject to capture. We've only been here in Hordaland for a week."

"Then it's too bad you left the Danes. Maybe you are what you say, but I only have your word for that, don't I?" The man's face hardened like an oak in winter. "Whatever you were before, you are now thralls. You belong to the Jarl of Sogna."

"And I suppose you are the jarl," she sneered.

"No, that would be my brother, Gunnar Haralds-son." One corner of his mouth jinked up in a grim half-smile. "I'm Bjorn the Black. The second son."

He raised the tip of his sword toward Rika and Ketil, motioning for them to march to the quay. Bjorn's eyes glinted at her, unfathomable as obsidian and just as hard.

"We're done talking, little she-wolf. You'll walk willingly or I'll drag you, but either way, you're coming with me."

Blood pounded behind her eyes. Rika grabbed Ketil's hand and led him toward the waiting longships. She nearly retched at the scent of searing flesh in the smoke-filled air, but she strode with her head high. The daughter of Magnus Silver-Throat would not show weakness before this blood-soaked raider.

For the first time in her life, Rika wished that she'd been born a man. So she could kill Bjorn the Black.

"I suppose you call yourself a hero and imagine a saga will be composed about your exploits. All you are is a murderer and a thief," Rika railed at Bjorn, hoping to shame him.

She knew baiting the man was foolhardy, but only her focused hatred of Bjorn the Black kept her on her feet. She couldn't be silent. Words had always been her only weapon and the white-hot rage boiled out of her, whether it was wise or not.

"Are there no more monasteries on the Isle of the Angles?" Her voice bordered on shrill. "No more fat Frankish towns for you to plunder that you must stoop to murder of your own kind?"

"If I were a murderer, your big friend here would be joining Magnus on his pyre," Bjorn said with icy calm. "I've done no murder. I did what had to be done. I lift my hand only against those who oppose me. And as for being a thief, it's no theft to take back your own."

When they reached the ship, Bjorn turned to face the smoldering village. The survivors huddled in miserable clumps.

"People of Hordaland! We've fallen upon you because of your raid on Sognefjord last month." His deep voice reverberated on the mountainside. "The Jarl of Sogna has a long arm. In his name, we've taken back the livestock that was stolen and punished the guilty. Don't make the mistake of trying us again. The men of Sogna will not stand for it."

Bjorn thrust his sword into its scabbard and bound a sniffling Ketil's hands together with a leather strap. When he turned to tie Rika, she jerked away from him.

"Fine sentiments, Bjorn the Black." She fired the words at him like arrows. "And what of the innocents you punished with the guilty?"

"I advise you to give me your hands, girl." He met her frosty stare with one of his own. "And see you give me no further cause to bind your mouth as well."

Rika clamped her lips together, giving him no excuse to gag her. She submitted to the leather strap Bjorn knotted around her wrists, glowering at him when he pulled it tight. Then Rika climbed into the swaying longship and hunkered near the prow. She wanted to put as much distance as possible between herself and that dark-eyed fiend.

His crew bent to the work and hauled away. Once
the vessel was far enough from land, they shipped the
oars, locked the mast into place and hoisted the big
square sail. A stiff breeze filled the woolen cloth and
the ship came alive, lifting in the water despite its full
load. The keel of the dragonship sliced through the
gray swells, the waves dividing like the wings of an ea-
gle on each side of the craft. It rode lightly on the sea,
as though at any moment it might rise and take flight.

Rika had always loved sailing with Ketil and Magnus in their little coracle, the sharp scent of the sea
and the cries of gulls wheeling overhead. Her whole
life had been one long voyage, interspersed with pleas-
urable stays as welcome guests. At Magnus's side, she
was greeted with something akin to awe. The old
skald's mantle was broad, easily covering his little family of foundlings. Even the lack-witted Ketil was sheltered under its protection.

Now that part of her life was at an end. In the prow
of the dragonship where the sea spray would obscure
them, she let herself weep silent tears for the only father she'd ever known.

A few tears fell on her own behalf as well. Rika had
tumbled from the high status position of the old
skald's daughter to the hopeless condition of a thrall.
She was now the property of some faceless jarl and
might expect even worse treatment than the captured
livestock.

Ketil curled up beside her to sleep, as he often did in
a rolling ship. His pale eyelashes quivered against his
ruddy cheeks. Rika's chest tightened. Ketil was so big
and strong, but inside he had but a child's heart and
mind, easily hurt and confused. How could she hope
to protect him in their new and bewildering circumstances? She had no idea, but she knew she must try.
Right alongside her father's tutelage in the lore and

legends of the Norse people, Magnus had taught her loyalty.

Oh, Father! Why had she argued with him that morning? And over so trivial a thing. Magnus had insisted she try harder to memorize the *Havamal,* the sayings of Odin. The sagas of heroes were more to her taste than the homilies of the One-Eyed All-Father. Now she'd happily learn a thousand of them if she could only take back her harsh words.

A prickle started at the nape of her neck and tingled down her spine. She turned to seek the source of her unease. At the far end of the dragonship, Bjorn the Black stared at her from his seat at the steering oar. She'd felt his eyes, hot and intrusive on her skin. They were darker than a bog and more menacing. She was forced to look away.

Rika was usually good at reading people. As a performer, she had to be. She'd seen desire in men's eyes before, but this was different. She couldn't decipher the meaning of his intense gaze. The dead stare of Bjorn the Black was more like the look of a wolf stalking a hapless kid who'd strayed too far from the rest of the flock. In spite of the sun on her shoulders, she shivered.

Surely someone in the settlement where they were bound would've heard Magnus perform. Perhaps they might also recognize her and Ketil. This whole misunderstanding could be laid to rest. She shot a glance from under her lashes at Bjorn, who now strained to keep his ship out of the pounding surf. Perhaps she'd even be able to charge him with murder before the Lawspeaker and demand a *wergild* for the life of her father. Someone must be held accountable for the death of so great a personage as Magnus, and Bjorn was clearly in charge of this murderous raid. With any luck, she'd even see the blackguard banished.

She swiped away her tears. Her lips flattened into a hard line, along with her resolve. Her dream of being recognized as a skald in her own right suddenly seemed a small matter indeed. But seeing justice done to the man responsible for her father's death was the best reason she could think of to keep breathing.

The setting sun slid beyond the curve of the water. Before the brief twilight deepened into the short Scandinavian spring night, Bjorn ordered the flotilla to pull up as close to the land as the sailors dared. The cliffs were too steep to beach the armada for the night.

Bjorn grappled with the heavy anchor stone and heaved it overboard. "Break out the *nattmal,* Jorand," he said to the flaxen-haired youngest man on board.

As Jorand passed out the spartan meal of flat barley bread, dried fish and wrinkled cloudberries, Bjorn stepped around the crew to check on his captives.

"Hold up your hands and I'll free you to eat," he said to Rika.

Scowling, she lifted her hands to him, but said nothing. "What? No cutting remarks?" Bjorn cocked his head at her.

"Out of insults already, I see. You must not be much of a skald after all." He ignored Rika's uplifted wrists and freed Ketil's hands instead.

"Anything I might say would stir your wrath, Bjorn the Hero, vanquisher of defenseless women and unarmed old men." Rika's tone was smooth as butter, making her words all the more biting. "However, if it pleases the great jarl's brother, I'll compose a saga about his restoration of livestock to be remembered for the ages. You'll be known as Bjorn the Boarbringer, savior of lost pigs everywhere."

When a couple of his crew chuckled, he silenced them with a frown.

She slid her gaze toward the sailors, who had erased the grins from their faces. "Ah! I see it is not only bound captives who must be careful with their mouths around you."

"Seems you're giving no heed to yours, girl." Bjorn knelt beside her and lowered his voice. "I don't know why I should bother explaining it to you, but this was a matter of honor. What a man has, he must hold. If he won't protect what's his, he deserves to lose it. We couldn't let the raid on our farmsteads stand. More would be lost than livestock the next time."

"*Ja*," she answered, dry-eyed and staring, the image of her father facedown in the straw swimming before her. "More was definitely lost."

Bjorn seemed to see the same grotesque vision. "It's a sad day that sees Magnus Silver-Throat dead, if that's indeed who he was. But you know as well as I that it's something that couldn't be undone. We wear our fates around our necks like you wear that little hammer."

He reached out a broad finger to stroke the amber pendant nestled in the slight indentation at the base of her throat. When she shrank from his touch, he pulled back his hand.

"The way of Magnus's death was decided long ago," Bjorn said. "It just happened that one of my men delivered it to him."

Rika narrowed her eyes to slits. "And for that, I'll never forgive you."

"I'm not asking you to," Bjorn said. "I'm only trying to untie your hands so you can eat in comfort." He worked the knot free and pulled off her bonds.

"I'm surprised you trouble to feed us." Rika rubbed her tingling wrists.

"If you're weak or sickly, you're of no use to the jarl. You'll find I look out for all of my brother's interests," Bjorn said. "But perhaps I should warn you that Gunnar's not as tolerant a man as I. If you irritate me, I'll just bind your mouth."

"What?" Rika's eyes flashed. "Will the mighty jarl

carve out my tongue and eat it with his herring and
turnips for *nattmal?*"

"No. Something much worse than that." Bjorn
handed her a generous portion of fish, bread and
berries. "He'll set the Dragon of Sogna on you. His
wife, the Lady Astryd."

This time, Bjorn's crew laughed heartily and loud.

"No!" Ketil thrashed beside her in the dark. She
wrapped her arms around him, trying to quiet him before he roused the wrath of any of the raiders snoring
in their *hudfats,* the leather two-man sleeping sacks.

"Hush now, Ketil," she whispered. "It's just a
dreyma."

Ketil subsided into soft sobs, his great body still
shuddering. "Don't let it happen."

She bit her lower lip, thinking he spoke of Magnus's
death and imagined it only a dream. "Some things
can't be helped," she said softly. "Father is gone, and
we can't change it."

He pulled back from her, blinking. "I know that. I
just don't want you to go, too. They're trying to send
you far away to a big, big city with a wall where the
sun burns so hot. And they won't let me go with you."

"It's only a dream." She pressed her palms against
both of his cheeks. "No one will separate us, brother. I
won't let them."

Even as she promised, she wondered whether she'd
be able to keep her word. A thrall had no say in where
she was sent, but Rika had no intention of remaining a
slave. Almost in reflex, she put a hand to the amber
hammer at her throat. If she'd been destined for servitude, surely Thor wouldn't have allowed Magnus to
save her from the icy water as an infant.

Magnus had always been Odin's man. But even
though the stoic All-Father was a favorite of skalds,

Rika could never warm to him. From her birth, she'd belonged to Thor, whose passions burned white-hot and dissipated like fading lightning. Of all the gods in the Nordic pantheon, the Thunderer was the least capricious and cruel to his devotees, and judged most likely to save them in a tight spot.

A fresh wind stirred the sea, sending its chilly breath rippling over them. Ketil shivered beside her. "I'm cold."

"Here you are." Rika pulled the green wool cape from her shoulders and tucked it around her brother. It wasn't big enough for the two of them.

"Go back to sleep, Ketil." She crossed her arms over her chest, hugging herself against the wind. In a short while, his deep, even breathing told Rika that Ketil had slipped back into his childish slumber.

Ketil's nightmare troubled her more than she wanted to admit. Magnus had been devoted to truth-telling above all else, so he was never evasive about how she'd come to be his daughter. He told Rika that one of Ketil's dreams had led them to the precise spot where she'd been abandoned on the ice. Her brother hadn't had another episode of prescience since then, so Rika discounted the tale as the fancies of a doting father with a vivid imagination. Now with Ketil's *dreyma* of a looming separation, she wondered.

The moon rose, cold and distant, over the steep cliffs and crashing surf. The silvery light was just bright enough for Rika to make out Bjorn the Black in his leather sleeping sack by the steering oar. The man's eyes flashed at her, fiery and threatening, like the feral predator she knew him to be. When he stood and walked toward her carrying his *hudfat,* her shivering had nothing to do with the wind.

"Get in." He stepped into the bag and held it open for her.

She glared up at him. "I'll tie loom stones around my neck and drown myself before I become your bed-slave."

"Don't worry. I don't intend to rut you," Bjorn said. "Not in a bobbing longship with two dozen other men around."

When she still didn't budge, his lips twitched, whether with irritation or amusement, Rika couldn't be sure.

"Rape isn't to my taste," he explained. "I prefer my women willing and a good bit cleaner than you are at the moment, little she-wolf." He stroked a patch of dried mud from her cheek.

It was spring, but the breeze sliding over her felt more like winter's icy breath. Rika didn't want him to see her quiver, but she couldn't help herself.

"There's no profit to you to spite me in this," he said. "I only want to see you warm, I swear it."

Her chattering teeth decided the matter and she climbed into the supple leather sack with the black Viking. The *hudfat* was designed for sharing bodily warmth so she stopped shivering in only a few moments. The big man seemed to radiate as much heat as a roaring central fire in a longhouse.

Earlier, he'd removed his mail shirt and the blood-stained tunic beneath it, leaving him smelling only of fresh sea air, tinged with honest male sweat. It was a strangely comforting combination. Even though he was her enemy, his warmth made Rika drowsy. She settled back against his chest as she sank toward exhausted sleep.

"Why did you do that?" his voice rumbled in her ear.

Every hair on her body stood at full attention. She should've known better than to trust him.

"I was cold. You promised only to warm me," she reminded him. "Nothing else could lure me into your bed."

He snorted. "There are those who could assure you that my bed is not such an odious fate, but that's not what I meant." Bjorn jerked his head toward Ketil. "Why did you give him your cloak?"

"He's my brother," Rika answered simply. "We share everything. That's what families do."

"Very touching." His voice was hard. "But not very practical when there's only one cloak."

She turned to look at him. The lines and planes of his face were as stony as the granite cliffs they sheltered under. "Wouldn't you share a cloak with your brother?"

Bjorn's dark eyes flickered down at her and then back up to scan the sea again. "I wouldn't have to. My brother would just take the cloak."

CHAPTER 2

By midmorning, the small fleet turned inland up a waterway Magnus's little troupe had never visited. *Sognefjord*. Rika had sailed past the wide inlet dotted with rocky islands numerous times, but for some reason, Magnus always made an excuse not to swing into this particular fjord. Her hope of finding someone who'd heard her father perform sank like an anchor stone.

They stopped at settlements along the steep sides of the inlet to drop off a cow here, a pair of pigs there. Rika couldn't help noticing that many of the *karls'* farmsteads had a neglected air.

A roof was caved in at one place, part of the longhouse open to the sky, with nothing being done to right the situation. Several plots of land that by rights should have been sprouting barley had yet to be sown with grain.

This was more than the ravages of a raid a month gone. Something caused a rot in the spirits of the inhabitants of the fjord, leaving them careless with their holdings.

Perhaps Magnus had been right to avoid Sogna.

Sognefjord seemed to go on forever, winding its way into the heart of the land. Rika was forced to spend another two nights sharing a *hudfat* with the hard-headed, hard-bodied leader of the raid.

She'd never slept so closely entwined with anyone, let alone a strange man. His warmth was a blessing, but she stiffened, prickling with apprehension, each time his body shifted. She wasn't able to fully relax until exhaustion drained her. What irritated her most was the fear that she might begin to enjoy his breath on her nape or the feel of his hand, heavy on her waist.

The wind died as they traveled farther from the open sea, and Bjorn ordered the mast down and the oars out. With each heaving stroke, Rika's heart fluttered. Whatever was wrong with Sognefjord waited for her at the end of the voyage.

She glanced at Bjorn. He stood at the steering oar, his dark hair streaming in the wind, his eyes narrowed to slits against the glare of sun on the water. His arms bulged with the strain of keeping the longship within the correct channel to avoid submerged rocks.

Rika frowned at him, puzzled. From his cryptic remark two nights ago, she judged there was no love lost between Bjorn and his brother, the jarl. Yet by raiding in the name of Sogna, he did his brother's bidding at the hazard of his own life and those of his crew. Why?

Some men loved killing. Bjorn must be just such a bloody-minded man, she decided. Yet he also seemed to be a man of his word. Even though she'd wakened to feel his hardness pressed against her backside as the big man slept spooned around her in the *hudfat,* he made no advances toward her. He kept his pledge only to warm her body. Still, his arousal proved Bjorn the Black's restraint wasn't for lack of interest in women.

"Like him, don't you?" The young man called Jorand

evidently caught her looking at his captain. He grinned at her between strokes of the long oar.

"Of course not." Rika jerked her gaze away. "How can I like my captor?"

Jorand's lips twisted into a knowing smile. "No woman I've met can spend a couple of nights curled up with our Bjorn and not come away liking him."

"Consider me the exception." She stared straight ahead.

"Don't worry." Jorand rocked forth and back with the oar. "He's always favored redheads. He'll protect you when we get there."

Protect me from what? Rika wanted to ask, but Bjorn bellowed an order, interrupting them.

"Jorand!" His voice was amplified by the water around them. "Stop flirting with the pretty thrall and take down the dragonhead. We're almost there."

"See, what did I tell you?" Jorand winked at her. "He likes you." The young man scrambled up the narrow prow to remove the grotesque serpentine figurehead. No point in frightening the land spirits on their home ground.

When the ship pulled up to the wharf, Rika realized what was wrong with Sogna. All the wealth, all the choice livestock, all the best building materials had been amassed in one place to create an unusually sumptuous longhouse and compound for the Jarl of Sogna. The *jarlhof* was massive, with several extra rooms jutting at right angles from the long main hall. On the flat plain before the jarl's house, scores of fighting men engaged in a mock battle, honing their skill.

"Supporting that many retainers would tax the coffers of a king," Rika murmured to Ketil. "No wonder the farmsteads along the fjord look so depleted."

They disembarked and marched up to the longhouse, trailing Bjorn the Black and his crew. As they climbed the steep path up from the water, she held

Ketil's hand to steady her pounding heart. She forced herself to smile up at her brother. It helped quell the dizzying sensation of being totally powerless for the first time in her life.

"Welcome home, Brother." Once inside the long-house, a raucous voice boomed toward them. It wasn't as low or as resonant as Bjorn's, but it filled the space.

Rika scanned the long hall. It'd been freshly scrubbed for spring with new rushes strewn about the stone floor. Light shafted in through the smoke holes spaced at intervals along the spine of the high roof. Earthen benches lined the sides of the hall, but instead of situating the jarl's seat in the middle, near the central fire, Bjorn's brother was ensconced in an ornate chair flanked by pillars on a dais at the far end. Rika recognized the deviation as a Frankish influence in the design of the great hall. Raised seating—even for nobility—was not typical in a Norse *jarlhof*.

Fires burned at the many hearths and a carcass roasted over each one, tended by a young girl with a basting gourd. After days of dried fish and flatbread, the savory aroma made Rika's mouth water. The Jarl of Sogna must set quite a table to attract and keep the host of fighting men in the yard.

A serving girl approached Bjorn with a long drinking horn brimming with golden mead. He lifted the horn toward the dais in salute and then drained the entire contents in one long swallow.

"You need to find a larger horn, Brother." Bjorn swiped his mouth with his forearm.

Bjorn's crew guffawed and congratulated each other on the drinking prowess of their leader. Rika stood quietly, a combination of irritation and dread curling her lip as she waited to see what it was she needed protection from. Other than him, of course.

"You've had a successful raid?" Gunnar asked.

"We retrieved every head that was taken from us."
Bjorn glanced at Rika. "And picked up a few other
things as well."

The whole crew marched the length of the hall until
they came before the jarl's great carved chair. Entwined serpents writhed in bas-relief up the pillars on
each side of the jarl. Rika noticed the same double-
serpent motif embossed on the shields hanging on the
walls. The Jarl of Sogna's device, no doubt.

At first glance, Rika thought the two brothers
couldn't be more different. Gunnar's coloring—white-
blond hair and pale gray eyes—marked him as the exact opposite of Bjorn the Black. But when she looked
more closely, Rika saw a resemblance in the brothers'
strong features. But while Bjorn's mouth was full-
lipped and smacked of sensuality, Gunnar's thin one
had a cruel twist to it.

Jorand dropped the bale of cloth he'd balanced on
his broad shoulders. Another member of Bjorn's crew
spilled out the contents of a leather bag. Pewter house-
ware, silver brooches and armbands, along with a
goodly quantity of hack silver clattered to the stone
floor. Another bag filled with carved amber was eased
to the ground. Six fur bales joined the rest of the
spoils. The jarl's eyes glinted with calculating avarice.

"And new thralls, I see." Gunnar's gaze slid over
Rika and Ketil and the handful of other unfortunates
Bjorn and his men had captured. His pale eyes returned to Rika and his tongue flicked out to wet his
bottom lip as he studied her from head to toe. "You've
done well, little brother."

The slight twitch of Bjorn's shoulders told Rika he
didn't much care for that appellation.

"How can I reward you?" Gunnar asked.

"I'll take those two for my own." Bjorn pointed at
Rika and Ketil. "For my men, we'll take half the spoils
here."

"Agreed. None of the livestock?" Gunnar asked.

"We returned the livestock to the *karl*s they belonged to on the way in," Bjorn explained. "They were stolen property and couldn't be counted as spoils."

A muscle ticked in Gunnar's left cheek. "I'll be the judge of that in the future." His gaze flitted back to Rika. "Now that I think on it, your reward seems overgenerous. You can have one thrall."

Bjorn looked at Rika and Ketil as if considering which of them would profit him most. "Then, I'll take the girl." He arched a brow at her. "I've need of a bed warmer."

"You can have that anytime just by crooking your finger at the serving girls," Gunnar said.

"Not in my house, you won't." A woman's voice came from behind them. The group of men parted to allow the jarl's wife to enter the circle. "Some here may wish to forget it, but this is a respectable *jarlhof*." Rika shifted uneasily as the woman, who could only be the dragon Bjorn had mentioned, skewered her husband with a sizzling glare.

Lady Astryd was dressed in a kirtle and tunic of rich blue and yellow. Her honey-blond hair fell in heavy braids to her thickening waist, and her head was covered discretely with a fine kerchief. The keys of her office dangled from the gilt chain above her distended belly. The woman's complexion glowed with her pregnancy. At least something in Sogna was fruitful, Rika thought.

Astryd stopped in front of Rika and gazed at her mud-spattered clothes. "My girls are cleaner than this one, I'll grant you," she said, turning to give Rika her back. "Why don't you just let her work for me, and your brother will find you a wife to warm your bed," she said to Bjorn. "There are plenty of houses that wish to ally themselves with Sogna, even through a second son."

"When I'm ready for a wife, I'll find one myself."
Bjorn folded his arms across his chest. "Besides, I've
grown attached to the muddy little thing." His crew
chuckled. "My men and I risked ourselves and our
ships in the service of Sogna. Shall it be said that such
a simple request was denied?"

Rika glanced from the jarl to his wife. An undercur-
rent of frustration and rage crackled between the noble couple. Astryd seemed to follow her husband's
gaze, and her face hardened as she caught the look the
jarl cast toward Rika. The matter was decided.

"Very well, you shall have her by night," Astryd said.
"But there's no reason why she can't work for me by
day. Come along, all of you," she ordered the entire
group of thralls. "No one eats here unless they earn
their bread with hard labor."

She clamped a firm grip on Rika's wrist and
dragged her from the hall. When Rika cast a glance
back over her shoulder at Bjorn, an infuriating smile
was on his lips.

Young Jorand was wrong, she guessed. Bjorn the
Black didn't like her at all. He certainly hadn't lifted a
finger to save her from the Dragon of Sogna.

"My lady, please stop." Rika trotted to keep up with
Astryd's swinging strides. "There's been a mistake, a
terrible miscarriage of justice, which I'm sure you'll
set right."

When they burst out of the longhouse into the midmorning sunlight, Astryd wheeled around to face
Rika, hands fisted on her hips. "What are you babbling
about?"

"Just that there's been a misunderstanding." Rika
gulped a quick breath. "My brother and I were taken
because your men thought we belonged to the settlement at Hordaland. We don't, you see. We are traveling skalds, and as such, we aren't subject to capture
and enthrallment."

Astryd cocked a pale eyebrow at Ketil, her cold gaze
sweeping over the young man's pleasant, vacant expression. "Oh, *ja,* I can see that your brother is much
in demand, no doubt. Recite for us, you great towering
slug," she ordered.

Ketil's half-smile changed to panic and he backed
several steps away. "I don't . . . no, it's not me. Rika's
the skald. Father always said so."

"Very well." Astryd turned back to Rika, crisscross-
ing her arms over her chest. "Let's hear the skald.
What shall it be, I wonder? Thor and the Frost Giants? Freya and the Brisingamen necklace, perhaps?
That's one I understand quite well, being overly fond
of jewelry, myself."

She eyed the silver brooches holding up Rika's kyrtle. The craftsmanship was finer and the design more
subtle than the gaudy ones at her own broad shoulders. Astryd circled Rika, running a jeweled finger
over the fine quality of the cloth beneath the caked
mud. Rika froze like a hare that sees the shadow of a
hawk hovering overhead.

"No," Astryd decided. "How about something easy?
Let's have a bit from the *Havamal.*"

Inwardly, Rika groaned, but she straightened her
spine and took her stance. *Breathe,* she ordered herself.
At first, no words tickled her tongue, and then, like water pouring over a precipice, they all came at once.

"A flame leaps to another. Fire kindles fire. A man
listens, thus he learns," she rattled off all in one
breath. "The shy . . . stay shallow." Rika's voice trailed
away. Her eyes flitted from left to right, but no more of
the sayings of Odin appeared in her mind.

Astryd's lip curled. "Not your finest moment, was
it?"

"Please, you don't understand. I'm a very fine skald.
I know all the sagas, truly I do." Even to her own ears,
Rika didn't sound very convincing. "I've been working

on the *Havamal,* but I just don't know it all yet." Was that Magnus's gentle laughter she heard in the back of her mind?

"I believe you are a very clever girl with a quick tongue and possibly a decent memory." Astryd squinted at her in frank appraisal. "But you're no skald. No doubt you've heard one or two and thought to imitate them to avoid thralldom. But if you were a student of the *Havamal,* you'd know that there's nothing you can do to change your fate." Astryd's blond brows knit together. "All you can do is meet it with courage."

The lady's eyes gleamed when she saw the amber hammer at Rika's throat. The hammer was simple but elegant, and Astryd's pursed lips told Rika she thought it far too fine for the neck of a slave.

"You can start by giving me that little bauble you're wearing," the Dragon of Sogna said. "Thralls have no possessions of their own, you know."

Rika bit her lip as she slipped the thin leather strip over her head and placed the hammer in Astryd's waiting palm.

The Lady of Sogna directed her attention to the whole group of new thralls. "Take off your clothes, all of you. You're no doubt infested with lice and fleas." Astryd turned to the serving girl who'd brought the horn of mead to Bjorn. "Inga, burn their clothes and get them all something more fitting to their new station."

So this is how it starts, Rika thought. In order to make them into slaves, they first had to strip away who they were. She slipped her garments over her head, determined it would not matter to her. In her mind, she would clothe herself with the dignity of her art. Her bare skin didn't quite get the message though, as gooseflesh rippled over her despite the sunshine.

After Ketil pulled his tunic over his head, Astryd took the garment from him and ran the fine fabric through her fingers. It was soft and supple as water compared to the stiff linen she herself wore.

"Save the clothing of these two." Astryd ordered her serving girl as she pointed to Rika and Ketil. "I may find a use for their garments, after a thorough cleaning, of course."

Rika's cheeks burned. The men at swordplay looked on and jeered, as she and the rest of the thralls were paraded, still naked, to the ironworker. A circle of ugly gray metal was bolted around her neck, a dismal replacement for the little amber hammer.

At least now if I decide to drown myself, I won't need loom stones, she thought. Rika had already cheated the waves once. She wondered whether giving herself to the sea constituted meeting her fate with courage, but then she thought of Ketil. No matter what happened, she couldn't choose to take the water, for his sake.

Inga gave them all shapeless garments of coarse undyed wool. Though Rika was grateful to cover her nakedness, the rough cloth chafed against her skin and rubbed her nipples raw.

Then Astryd reappeared with her shears. She seemed to take perverse delight in snipping off Rika's waist-length hair in uneven chunks, hacking and sawing at her thick tresses. Magnus had never allowed anyone to cut her hair. It shimmered like a sunset rain, he always said. As the long locks fell to earth, Rika squeezed her eyes shut, willing herself to remember Magnus brushing her hair when she was little. He always smoothed out the snarls she got into. How she wished he were there to smooth her out of this one.

She ran a stunned hand over her shorn head. Her father would be heartsick if he could see her now. Relieved of its weight, her remaining hair curled snugly around her ears and across her forehead.

Then Astryd sent Ketil to work felling trees with a

group of other male thralls. Rika was tasked with scrubbing privies. The harsh soap, a combination of lye mixed with ash and fat, reddened her hands and made her eyes burn. After she finished that chore, Astryd ordered Rika to join another group of women who were processing yarn by dragging it through a shallow vat of cow urine.

As Magnus's daughter, she'd never so much as assisted with meal preparation before. Her days had been filled with practicing the countless tales her father never tired of teaching her. She mastered the secret art of runes and could carve them with skill in wood or stone. The lilting tunes she coaxed from her little bone flute were admired in many a hall.

But now, she was only a drudge. And Astryd seemed intent on foisting all the worst jobs of the household on her during her first day of servitude. She caught the woman glaring at her more than once, but Rika schooled her features into a bland mask. If the Lady of Sogna thought to break her spirit with drudgery, Rika was determined Astryd would fail. She would not allow the Dragon to see the pain in her blistered palms. Or her blistered heart.

Besides, she knew the real villain wasn't Astryd. Oh, the Lady of Sogna was unpleasant and bossy and a true virago when crossed, but she wasn't the one to blame for Rika's misery.

That honor belonged to the man who'd dropped her into Astryd's grasping clutches. That toad-eating, louse-bitten, unfeeling waste of skin—Bjorn the Black.

CHAPTER 3

Rika clamped a hand over her mouth, not believing her eyes. The Dragon of Sogna had dressed for *nattmal* in Rika's fawn-colored tunic. It'd been scrubbed clean, but every seam in the fine garment bulged. Perhaps the heir to Sogna growing in her belly was to blame, but Rika thought Astryd looked like too much sausage meat stuffed into too small a bladder.

The lady stopped in front of her. "You have something to say?"

"No, my lady." Rika forced the smirk from her face. "Except . . . that color suits you." She guessed the Lady of Sogna must be desperate indeed if she thought dressing in Rika's clothing would turn her husband's wandering eye back to her. Rika could almost pity Astryd, if not for her shorn head and throbbing hands. But Magnus had always said desperate people are dangerous people and the Lady of Sogna was no exception. Rika expelled all the air from her lungs in relief when Astryd moved on.

She sent Ketil into the great hall with Surt, a thrall he'd worked with all day. Slaves were allowed to eat after the fighting men had been served, but Rika couldn't think of food. All she wanted was to wash the reek of privies and cow urine from her tired body. She decided there'd be no better time to sneak into the steam bath than when everyone else was feasting in the long main hall.

After slipping into the bathhouse and lighting the fire to warm the stones, she stripped off the scratchy tunic. Rika scrubbed it while the room filled with heat. She might have to put it back on damp, but at least it would be clean.

When the stones for the steam bath were hot enough, she poured a dipperful of pine-oil water on them, releasing a soothing cloud of steam. She kept adding water till the small room was filled with milky-white moisture. Then she felt her way to the smooth wooden benches.

Every pore in her body opened. When she was covered with a glistening sheen, she fingered along the wall and found the birch switches left there. Rika used one to scrape off the sweat and dirt. She was ready to dash into the next room where a cool bath barrel waited for her to rinse, when she heard the stamp of booted feet at the threshold. She skittered back up the benches, climbing into the farthest corner.

"Someone has started the bath for us already."

Rika recognized Bjorn's rumbling bass through the pine-scented cloud. Another dipper of water hissed on the heated stones. She pulled her knees to her chest and made herself as small as possible, trusting the thick steam to hide her.

"That's the story of my life, little brother. Everything is always handed to the Jarl of Sogna on a new trencher."

Bjorn didn't respond to Gunnar's taunt. Rika heard the swish of clothing being peeled from the two men's bodies, the scrape of leather boots toed off against the stone floor. She made out hazy flesh-toned forms and realized they'd see her too, if they happened to glance her way. She could only hope they wouldn't notice her if she kept still.

"Come now, little brother. Jealousy doesn't become you."

"Jealousy isn't what I'm feeling right now, but if you want the truth, the title of jarl doesn't become you much either, Gunnar." If Rika had to guess, she'd have said she heard barely bridled anger in Bjorn's even tone.

"That's a bit more candid than I'm used to." Gunnar's laugh didn't convince her that he found Bjorn's remark funny.

"I expect it is," Bjorn said. "When I'm gone, you allow no one near you who'll dare tell you the truth." Bjorn's voice sounded closer now and she felt the stair-stepping benches sag with the weight of the men as they settled on the lowest level. At least, Thor be thanked, they'd turned their backs to her.

"You've filled our father's hall with mercenaries who'll say anything you want for the privilege of sitting at your table," Bjorn accused.

"Indeed I have."

"But why?" Rika heard frustration in Bjorn's voice. "I wasn't gone that long on the walrus hunt, no more than a couple of months, but I come home to find the whole fjord miserable over your horde of men. What good are they? They didn't even fend off the raid last month. My crew cleaned up the mess for you. Again."

"We weren't here when the raiders came," Gunnar explained. "You see, little brother, if you want to be a leader of men, you must realize that they need some play as well as work. I'd taken the men inland to hunt. Besides, the raiders only hit the outer farmsteads. They didn't dare come all the way in to Sogna. No harm done."

"No harm?" Bjorn demanded. "Ask Gimli Bluenose and you'll get a different tale. The raiders took his milk cow but left her new twin calves to starve. We brought back the cow, but nothing can bring back the calves. Every *karl* in Sognafjord has a similar story. How could you allow it to happen, Gunnar? As jarl, you can't stand by and let the land be raped by strangers."

"Ah, the land." Gunnar's voice was oily and taunting. "Even though you hunt and trade and go viking with the best of them, you always did have dirt under your fingernails, didn't you, little brother? Or wanted to?"

Bjorn ignored the jab. "I'll admit I'm land hungry, but you're neglecting your holdings, and you just can't. The farmers look to Sogna for protection. You can't abandon them like that."

"You forget yourself, Brother. Don't tell me what I can or cannot do." Rika heard Gunnar's tone frost over, colder and sharp-edged. "Are you not my sworn man still?"

In the silence that followed, Rika heard the steady drip of condensed moisture pattering from the ceiling beams to the stone floor.

"*Ja,* Gunnar, I'm still your man," Bjorn finally said. "I'm no oath-breaker."

"Good. Then listen and know my mind, little brother." Gunnar's voice dropped and despite the heat, a shiver ran over Rika. What would the jarl do to a thrall who'd heard his secret thoughts?

"The world is changing," Gunnar said. "We can take a few lessons from the Franks. Why should I be content with just Sogna? I need the men who eat at my table to expand my holdings. I inherited the fjord from our father, but when my son is born, he'll have more to look forward to than I did."

"There's never enough for you, is there?" Rika detected the bitterness of a second son, who inherited nothing but what his own two hands could bring to him.

"If you were in my place you'd realize that in order to keep what's mine, I must be strong enough to increase it. For the good of all," Gunnar added quickly.

"But to feed your mercenaries you're taking more from the farmsteads than the law allows," Bjorn argued.

"Law, what law?" Gunnar spat out the word like a bitter berry. "In Sogna, I am the law. You've spent too long hunting in the frostlands, Bjorn. When men of talent arise, they can't be bound by law."

"Is that you talking or did Astryd plant those words in your mouth?" Bjorn asked.

Gunnar was silent for a moment, but then he hissed through the steam. "I'm going to pretend you didn't say that. Listen to me, little brother, and I'll leave you with one last thought. The Danes have a king. Why shouldn't we?"

Rika felt the bench flex under her as one of the men stood.

"And why shouldn't it be me?" Gunnar asked. Rika heard him pad to the door that led to the cooling barrels of tepid water in the next room.

How she longed to plunge into one of them herself. She'd been in the steam far too long and sweat tickled down the length of her spine. A drowsy, languid feeling sapped her strength and just holding up her head felt like too much effort.

The room began to clear, but she was unable to make sense of the formless blobs and colors that swam before her. Her eyelids fluttered, stinging moisture dripping from her lashes. She made herself focus. Dark hair. Bjorn still hadn't left the bathhouse.

She forced the hot, moist air in and out of her lungs,

her head lolling. Shadows gathered at the edge of her vision. A slow spiral pulled her into the irresistible tug of blackness. She winked out like a candle flame pinched off between two fingers.

When her head slammed into the wooden bench with a thud, she didn't feel a thing.

Rika came to herself with a start, disoriented and gasping at the water. She was up to her chin in one of the cooling barrels, the excess liquid surging over the sides and splattering onto the stone floor. Bjorn stood over her, a deep furrow between his dark brows.

"You're awake." His eyes blazed. "Good. When you threatened to drown yourself to avoid my bed I thought you were just bluffing. If you really are trying to kill yourself, you've made a pretty good stab at it. Another stunt like this and I may even decide to help you with it myself."

Rika's eyes started to roll back in her head, but Bjorn grabbed the nape of her neck and splashed water on her cheeks. "No, you don't. You're not getting away that easily."

Her eyelids fluttered and then she focused on his face.

"Have you any idea what the jarl would've done to you if he'd been the one to catch you spying on him like that?"

"I wasn't—" Rika gulped at the fresh air.

"You had no business being in there. What you heard wasn't intended for just anyone's ears."

"I'm not just anyone. I'm no one." She swallowed the hard knot in her throat. "You've made me a thrall. I know no one here. Who could I tell?"

"That's what I'd like to know." He leaned toward her, hands on the edge of the barrel.

"I wasn't spying." Her voice had a catch in it. "I just wanted to get clean."

His gaze swept over her and she remembered with a jolt that she was naked.

She hugged her forearms across her chest and tucked her knees up to shield herself from him. Her chin quivered. She'd lost her father, her freedom, and now the last trace of her dignity. A tear trembled at the base of her lashes and then slid down her face.

Bjorn cupped her cheek with his rough hand, smoothing away the tear with his thumb. Rika was too numb to pull back from him. His touch was almost gentle. Then he turned away from her and strode across the room for a towel.

Rika decided that if he could look on her nakedness, she could stare at him as well as he scrubbed himself unself-consciously with the cloth. His chest was dusted with dark hair. Years of living on the sea had bronzed his exposed flesh and sculpted his muscles into hard masses. A livid scar snaked across his ribs on the right side. Even with that flaw, Rika conceded that Bjorn was well-made.

When he propped a long foot up on a bench to run the towel down his heavily muscled thigh and calf, Rika's gaze was drawn to his sex dangling between his legs. She'd seen statues of Frey, god of increase, with his outsized phallus proudly erect. The quiescent Bjorn didn't look so dangerous.

He pulled another towel from the stack of fresh ones and strode back across to her barrel.

"Get out." He held out the cloth for her. "You're looking a little . . . cold."

Rika followed his gaze to her bobbing breasts. Her nipples had puckered into hard pink pebbles. She stood and snatched the towel, wrapping it around herself. Just before she climbed out of the barrel, she noticed a startling change in Bjorn's male member. It swelled and rose, as though possessed of a life of its own. He looked as though he might indeed have modeled for the statues of Frey, potent and virile. Definitely dangerous. She slid her widening eyes away from him before he caught her staring.

Too late. To her surprise, he laughed.

"Don't worry. I still don't intend to force you, if that's what troubles you." Bjorn closed the distance between them. He leaned toward her with a long arm braced on either side of her, pinning her against the wall. "Even though losing the dirt is a real improvement, my little mud-hen."

"Stop calling me that. I'm not a mud-hen," Rika said. "And certainly not yours."

"What shall I call you then? She-wolf?"

"I have a name."

"And you've yet to tell it to me," Bjorn said. "Though I gave you mine at our first meeting. Who are you?"

She straightened and mustered all the dignity she could when wearing only a towel. "I am Rika Magnusdottir."

"Rika." He caressed her name as he ran a hand over her close-cropped hair. "Who did this to you, my Rika?"

She cringed under his touch, a small swelling lump leaving her head tender. "Who do you think?"

"Astryd, of course." Bjorn leaned closer and inhaled her freshly washed scent. "I'm sorry she cut your hair. I didn't think about that when I let her take you. It was a thing of rare beauty. But 'twill grow back."

"If I'd known my hair pleased you, I'd have hacked it off myself. I think it must be good for a thrall not to possess any beauty." She forced herself to meet his eyes. "If it keeps her from the unwanted attention of her master."

"I didn't say you weren't beautiful." Bjorn frowned. "You twist my meaning."

"And you ignore mine."

"I let you work for Astryd today for a purpose." Bjorn traced one of his fingers along her jaw line. "I figured that if you had to choose either serving that dragon or serving me, I'd win the contest."

He caught up one of her hands and uncurled it. Bjorn shook his head at the rough, reddened skin. A blister festered at the base of each finger. He pressed a soft kiss into her palm. "You were not made for hard labor, little one."

"Better hard labor than your bed-slave."

"And how would you know enough to make that choice?" Bjorn clasped her palm to his bare chest, covering it with his warm, dry hand. His face hovered near hers. "You'll find my bed is full of delights you haven't imagined yet. You see, I've found my pleasure is only complete in giving an equal measure to my bed-mate. And that means you have to be willing." His eyes widened, urging her to tumble into their black depths. "You don't know enough to choose between me and hard labor. Why, I haven't even kissed you yet."

Rika felt his heart pounding beneath her palm. Her breathing went shallow as she pressed herself against the rough planks of the wall. She backed away as far as she could, but his face advanced steadily toward hers. His breath was warm and moist on her lips.

She couldn't let it happen. Rika turned her head away and squeezed her eyes shut. If the beast was going to kiss her, he'd have to force her. But closing her eyes didn't make him vanish.

She heard his uneven breathing. Smelled the clean scent of his male flesh. Felt the tickle of his hair against her bare shoulder. The solid thump of his heart under her palm sent a message up her arm and she felt her own heart match his quickening rhythm. A strange stirring ruffled through her belly, clenching her gut, and sending alarming signals to her skin. A shiver rippled down her body, but she didn't feel cold. She felt warm. All over.

Rika slitted her eyelids and sneaked a peek at him. Bjorn was just looking at her, intent and sure of himself. One corner of his mouth ticked upward. He reminded her of a great tom cat waiting at a crack in the wattle-and-daub, body tensed and ready to pounce. The only trouble with that picture was that it made her the mouse. No, she'd have none of that.

"What are you trying to prove?" She opened her eyes wide and shoved against his chest. "That you're bigger than me? Stronger? That you can take me whenever you like whether I will it or no?"

Bjorn stepped back half a pace, stunned by her outburst.

"We both know all those things are true." Rika hurled the words at him. "For all your fair speech about pleasuring, we both know that while I wear this collar, you hold all the power. But there is one thing you don't control. My hatred of you. I despise you, Bjorn the Black. And if you take me unwilling, I'll hate you all the more with every rutting thrust."

For a long moment, Bjorn did nothing. Then he cupped her face with both hands and planted his lips on her forehead. A dismissive kiss, like one bestowed on an errant child. He turned away from her and stalked over to his pile of clean clothes.

"Get dressed, Rika." His voice was flat. "You've naught to fear from me. I'll not bed you till you beg me."

The tightening in her gut loosened. She breathed a sigh, but she didn't feel relieved. Her insides still writhed like a ball of snakes, first surging in defiance, then wilting in confused disappointment. But she squared her shoulders and glared at him. "In that case, I'll die a maiden."

His dark gaze slid over her, a slow, deliberate search. "That would be a terrible waste."

CHAPTER 4

When Bjorn and Rika entered the great hall, the meal
fires had smoldered to glowing embers, producing just
enough heat to keep the soapstone kettles warm.
Torches burned at intervals on the walls, making the
long room even brighter than during the day. Scores of
burly fighting men swilled mead and gnawed on dripping haunches. Loud conversations buzzed all around
Rika, men swapping insults and bawdy songs. A fist-
fight erupted in one corner.

Rika passed Ketil, who was seated next to Surt. Her
brother had a bowl set before him, filled with a thick
porridge of cracked grains and seasoned with a big
dollop of butter. At least the thralls of Sognefjord ate
well. Ketil smiled, lifting a hand to wave at her. She
started to join her brother, but Bjorn caught her arm.

"Your work is not yet done, Rika," he said. "You're
to fill my trencher and don't stint on the portions. I'm
a man of great appetite." His tone left no doubt that
his appetite included more than food.

She gave him a mock curtsey. "As you wish, *master*."
The word dripped venom as it slid through her lips.

One corner of his mouth twitched, but he seemed willing to let her insolence pass unremarked.

She retrieved a wooden trencher and bowl, then made the rounds of the cooking fires. By gathering the choicest offerings she'd give him no cause to rail at her publicly. She filled his bowl with nettle soup, her own mouth watering at the thought of fresh greens after the long winter. Then she selected half a fat chicken cooked in beer, a meat pasty, two gulls' eggs, honey-glazed root vegetables, and rye bread that she slathered with elderberry preserves. The trencher groaned under the weight of the portions.

"Here now," one of the lighting men said, stopping her with a hand on her hip. "You're a pretty thing. Isn't this the redhead we saw today at the ironmongers, Kormack?"

"Leave her alone, Canute," his friend said. "She belongs to the jarl's brother."

"Then let her say so." Canute's mouth twisted under his heavy blond mustache. He ran his hand down the length of her thigh. "Do you belong to Bjorn the Black?"

"He thinks so." She directed her gaze toward the dais where Bjorn was seated beside Gunnar. "Why don't you ask him?"

Canute swiveled his head around and met Bjorn's scowl. The intense dark eyes sent a clear warning. It reminded Rika of the wild-eyed glare of a stallion to another male who'd come sniffing around his mare. Bjorn claimed her from across the room. Canute jerked his hand away, evidently deciding not to challenge the jarl's brother.

"So he does." The big blond man's laugh sounded forced. "What do I care? There are plenty of serving girls in Sogna."

At least Bjorn's interest would spare her from being molested by any of the other men in the hall. She lifted

her chin and wound through the knots of people to
the dais.

"Your *nattmal,* master." She slid the soup bowl and
trencher before him.

"You're forgetting something," Bjorn said.

"What?" She stared at the heaping trencher. There
wasn't room for anything more.

"Ale." He handed her a hollow cow's horn. "Dark
ale."

She snatched up the horn and turned sharply, mut-
tering things under her breath. Things Bjorn decided
he probably didn't really want to hear.

He watched her as she elbowed her way around the
room to the barrels of ale. Her long-limbed body
moved with fluid grace when she had room to
lengthen her stride. He could see tension in the set of
her shoulders and grim determination in her bow of a
mouth. She had spirit. He had to give her that. Still, he
wasn't used to being turned down by women, and it
stung his pride that this one rejected him. And with
such vehemence.

But if there was one thing a second son had to learn
in life, it was patience. Gunnar had given Bjorn charge
of his land and the land demanded patience. Patient,
back-breaking toil to clear the trees and plough the
fields. Patient sowing of the seed and waiting for Frey
to send the rain and sun in proper mix. Patience to wait
for harvest and save back the best part for seed the
next spring. Even as he worked his brother's holdings,
he yearned for his own. But Bjorn could be patient.

Like having his own land, Rika would be worth the
wait. He was sure of it.

"Dark ale, just as you requested." Her pale green
eyes glinted at him with the opalescence of a pair of
icebergs. And just like those treacherous floating ob-
stacles, Bjorn reminded himself the most dangerous

part was always under the surface. She turned to go, but he gripped her wrist.

"No, Rika," he said as though explaining to a child who was trying to skip away from her chores. "You are not finished yet. I need you to hold the horn. I can't eat and hold it at the same time and if I set it down it will all spill and then you'd have to clean it up." He shrugged at her. "Save yourself more work. Sit."

"I'd rather join my brother."

"And I'd rather you sit here with me." Bjorn smiled as he said it, but it was an order nonetheless. He wondered whether she'd defy him openly. He watched a string of emotions—indignation, ire, and finally resignation—flit across her face. She sat. A worthy adversary, he judged, and one who knew how to pick her fights.

"Besides, given the way you feel about me, you don't really think I'm going to eat this without a taster, do you?" Bjorn grinned at her. "Thor only knows what kind of poison you've seasoned this with."

"What a charming idea," Rika said. "I wish I'd thought of it."

He sliced off a generous bite of the glistening chicken and held the piece to her mouth.

"I can cut my own food." Rika ignored the meat on the point of his knife.

"Ah, but can I trust you not to try to carve out my heart while you're cutting your meat? I don't think I'll chance it." He lifted the bite toward her again.

She narrowed her eyes at him and opened her lips to receive what he offered. Bite by bite, he fed her the most delectable part of his supper and offered her the nettle soup to enjoy on her own. She drank from the same horn of ale as he and used the same spoon.

When the trencher was empty, Bjorn wiped his mouth on his sleeve. "Did you get enough to eat? Is there anything else you'd like? Some honeyed fruit?"

"If you meant to show me favor in this, you failed miserably," Rika said, her jaw clenched. "When I was a little girl, I watched a man try to gentle a kestrel he'd captured by hand-feeding it. Now I know how that hawk felt."

Bjorn shook his head. "You've missed my purpose entirely. I want to assure you that you will lack nothing with me. I will treat you well." He tipped back the horn and drained the last of the ale. "I had not thought of it, but now that you mention it, that is the best way to tame a wild hawk. So, how did the man fare with the kestrel?"

"The bird bit his thumb off," Rika said, one russet eyebrow arched, the hint of a smile playing about her lips.

Bjorn's laugh started in his belly, rumbling and deep.

For just a blink, Rika was tempted to laugh with him. He seemed not to take himself too seriously and she appreciated that in a man. But then she remembered that he considered himself her master, and that was something she took very seriously indeed. She wouldn't banter with Bjorn the Black or even be pleasant if she could help it.

From the corner of her eye, Rika noticed Lady Astryd's face growing redder by the moment. She looked piqued that Rika was sitting at the main table, even though it was only in the role of a servant.

"Husband," Astryd said, her voice forced and loud. "Did you know that our hall has been graced with the presence of a renowned skald? Come, Rika." Her sly smile would have melted butter. "Give us a bit of the *Havamal* like you did for me earlier today."

Gunnar looked at Rika expectantly. A skald in residence added to the reputation of any hall. "Is this true, little brother? Have you taken a skald captive?"

Bjorn leaned back on his bench and gave Rika a

questioning look. "That's what she claims, but I've yet to hear her recite. Judging from my own experience, I'd have to say she's more scold than skald."

Rika frowned at him, but he just smiled back at her, clearly enjoying her discomfort.

Astryd's blue eyes went dark. "Show us your gift, girl," the jarl's wife urged, running her finger along the thin leather at her neck where the amber hammer rested. It was a not-so-subtle reminder to Rika that she had nothing the Lady of Sogna could not take from her. "Something from the *Havamal*, if you please."

Panicked, Rika looked at Bjorn. The smile left his lips and he reached out to stroke her arm.

"Your choice," he said in a husky whisper. "I won't make you perform if you don't want to. Not ever. Say the word and I'll end this."

Rika squeezed her eyes shut. Why the *Havamal*? Why couldn't that horrible woman ask for anything else but that? They'd never believe she was a skald now. She drew a deep breath, taking the air in all the way down to her hip bones just as Magnus had taught her. It cleared her mind and helped her focus.

Then she heard him inside her head.

CHAPTER 5

It was Magnus's voice, rolling and clear, declaiming the most dramatic piece of the sayings of Odin in full force. Then, just as clearly in her mind she heard Magnus repeat the advice he'd given her hundreds of times: *"Rika, you must believe that you have power over everyone within the sound of your voice."*

She could do it. She had to.

In a fluid motion, Rika stood. She lifted one arm in a gesture that suggested she had tapped into a powerful source from above. The other she outstretched toward the crowded hall. She waited. She knew she was just a thrall in a shabby, ill-fitting garment, but in her mind, she saw herself robed in silk and gorgeously arrayed in a fabulous multihued cape.

The skaldic gift—Magnus had always assured her she had it. Being a skald was more than possessing a prodigious memory and a pleasant voice for recitation with skill. The best of the Nordic bards were also blessed with the ability to crystallize an image and send it to their listeners so that it formed in their minds as well. If she could only trust herself enough, open herself enough, her audience would see what she saw and she would feel what they feel. It was time, she decided, to see if the mantle of Magnus Silver-Throat had indeed passed to her.

Whether the men in the hall saw her as she imagined herself, she couldn't say, but one by one the raucous voices fell silent.

"Hear, O People of Sogna!" Her voice, low and musical, filled the great hall with a power that surprised even her. She inhaled deeply and went on. "I know an ash tree, whose outstretched limbs and deep roots pass through all the nine worlds, and Yggdrasil is its name."

A low murmur rippled through the hall. She'd struck a chord by starting with the unifying Life of the World Tree, the life that binds all the spheres together.

"Come with me, and we will journey along the mighty branches of the World Tree to far-off lands," she urged. Almost to a man, her audience leaned forward.

"We start in Agsard, that holiest place, home of the gods and of Valhalla, hope of every valiant heart, where the brave may live in joy." She caressed the words and thought she sensed the pulse of her audience ticking upward. "The All-Father joins us there. Odin, the One-Eyed, the wisest of all. He marches beside us, desirous of bearing us company on our journey through the worlds, for he has an appointment, a grim task ahead of him."

Brilliant as a lightning bolt and sharp as a blade, she felt the connection. Beyond the bond of a performer and her audience, the mystic umbilical bridged between them. Rika felt a delicious shiver tickle down their spines, and if any in the hall were still eating, they laid their knives on the benches, the better to listen.

"Next we fare to Aelfham, where all manner of pleasure abounds and the Fair Folk who dwell there are gilded with light. But human hearts can bear only so much exquisite joy. Our stay must be brief, but as we leave that enchanted world, the ethereal music of the Light Elves echoes in our ears." Rika's voice floated over the hall, dulcet-toned and airy. From the corner of her eye, she saw Gunnar's jaw sag with desire.

"Odin urges us to haste and we stop in Vanaheim, home of the All-Father's brother-god, Frey. Mighty god of strangled sacrifice, Frey, the Horned One, knows that all life springs from death, just as a seed must die before the abundance of harvest can ever be."

Solemn nods greeted this pronouncement.

"The branches of Yggdrasil take us to the fiery edge of Muspel, first of all worlds, but we dare not enter that bright, hot place. The border is guarded by one with a flaming sword, who waits for the dreadful day when he is loosed to burn the whole world with the unending fire."

Rika scanned the sea of rapt faces. Did they feel the heat and smell the sulfur belching from that white-hot sphere of molten rock?

"The thick trunk of Yggdrasil runs through the beautiful realm of Midgard, this very Middle Earth, the homely land of all the races of men," Rika said simply, as her audience relaxed a bit with the familiar. "Midgard, where the lives of mortals run their course and each man's mettle is tried by his fate."

Rika lowered her arms and shifted her stance as the mood of her tale took a darker turn.

"Odin warns us past the land of Utgard, hidden high in the sky-mountains, where giants and trolls burrow in foul caves bestrewn with the bones of unwary men. We shun the evil world of Svartaelfham, home of the maggot-bitten Dark Elves. And let us not wander into Hel, that cold hall reserved for the dead by sickness and old age. The welcome there is Scarcity and the dish served at *nattmal* is Hunger."

She pursed her lips, and slanted her eyes at her audience. "For tonight, Odin has doings in Niflheim, where ice-bonds lock the limbs and all lust is stilled in nothingness."

Cold fire flashed in her eyes as she thrust her hands toward them. "Hear the sayings of Odin as he hung upon the World Tree, Yggdrasil's frozen root in the dark domain of eternal winter. Hear the words of the Wise One as he plundered Niflheim to bring us mortals the secret of runes. I give you," she paused, "the *Havamal*."

Every eye in the hall was trained upon her, transported to the misty realm of Niflheim, that accursed place of ice and shadows.

> *"I know that I hung*
> *On the windswept tree*
> *For nine whole nights."*

She started softly, wringing every bit of meaning from each syllable, each percussive consonant and sibilance. Rika's lips moved, but the crowd seemed to hear Odin, the All-Father describing his own sacrifice.

> *"Pierced by the spear*
> *And given to Odin*
> *Myself to myself*
> *On that Tree*
> *Whose roots*
> *Nobody knows."*

Her voice grew stronger, rasping with agony, the tension in her arms showing how the frigid bonds had held the Wise One fast.

> *"They gave me no bread*
> *Nor drink from the horn."*

Her audience shifted in their seats guiltily. Every full belly in the hall churned at the thought of Odin's hunger and thirst.

"I peered into the depths . . . "

Rika's eyes widened in terror. She seemed to actually see Niflheim, the runic symbols etched on icy slabs before her, enshrouded with ghostly phantoms of mist. She heard several gasps around the hall as her listeners caught the same horrific image.

"I grasped the runes . . . "

She clutched at the invisible lettering, her voice edged with hysteria.

"Screaming I grasped them—"

She jerked violently and stutter-stepped backward half a pace, toppling, as it were, from a branch on the World Tree in that icy realm far away. She whisked her audience with her along the gnarled trunk of Yggdrasil, back to the warmth and light of Midgard in one blinding moment.

"And then fell back."

Rika finished in a whisper that circled the hall and echoed off the hardened leather shields hanging on the walls.

Silence hovered over the hall so potent that no one wanted to break the spell. Rika had taken them on a dizzying sojourn through the nine worlds, to Niflheim and back, and her listeners could scarcely draw a breath.

"By all the gods," Bjorn swore softly. "Rika, you *are* a skald."

She turned to Bjorn and gave him the first real smile that had graced her lips since she'd discovered Magnus facedown in the straw.

"Rika, Rika." Young Jorand started the chant and a couple of the nearby fighting men joined in. The cry was taken up around the hall, accompanied by scores of fists pounding on the benches. "Rika, Rika."

She raised her hand to silence them before starting on the Saga of Sigurd. The joy of her art sang in her veins, flooding her with power and charging her body with so much energy, it seemed to flash from her fingertips as she gestured.

Bjorn leaned forward, the better to watch her face. He'd never seen the like. And to think he'd believed he could take this woman captive. As he listened to her weave another spell with words, he realized that he was the one who was in real danger of being captured.

CHAPTER 6

He was drowning. Again and again, the waves closed over his head, dragging him down. He gulped for air, but got a mouthful of salty water instead. Yanking off the mail shirt, he kicked back to the surface. The tips of his fingers bumped something solid. Ice. Panic rose like bile in the back of his throat.

Bubbles escaped his lips and skittered along the underside of the ice sheet, seeking a way out to the world of light and air. He followed them, searching for the opening he must have slipped through. The freezing water stung his eyes. He pounded the ice with his fist, but it was too thick.

His lungs burned, screaming for oxygen. They threatened to burst out of his chest, red and pulsing like a gory blood-eagle. He'd seen it once, a man's lungs ripped through his ribs and spread out like spongy wings across his dying back. A vicious death reserved for the vicious crime of patricide. Now he knew what it felt like.

He began to sink, his sodden clothing pulling him into oblivion. The frigid water retarded his movements and lack of air disconnected his mind from his flailing limbs. He was bound for *Hel,* with no chance of Valhalla. An ignominious death by drowning would not lure the Valkyries to bear him to glory. His eyes closed as he stopped struggling and accepted his fate.

Suddenly, he twirled in the water and he snapped open his eyes to see what had disturbed the current around him. A flash of green scales and cold, reptilian eyes swished by him. *Jormungand,* the World Serpent. The monster turned in the dark water and headed straight for him, gigantic maw gaping, ridged with a thousand flesh-tearing teeth.

He used the last bit of air in his lungs to scream.

The strangled cry woke Rika from a deep sleep, and in the dark, it took her a moment to remember where she was. Bjorn the Black's bed. But surely the piteous sound she'd heard couldn't have come from that beast.

"No!" He thrashed about, tearing through the furs and blankets that made up his bedding. One of his hands found her at the far edge and pulled her in close.

Rika realized he was still asleep and she shook him with no gentleness at all. "Wake up," she said sharply. "You're dreaming."

Bjorn jerked, chest heaving, holding her as tightly as if she were a life rope. He inhaled deeply. Rika felt his heart galloping in his chest.

There was nothing amorous in his embrace, so Rika didn't struggle. His body shuddered once. The fearsome raider was more like a small, frightened boy now, and she wondered what phantasmal image could've reduced him to this weakened state.

"A dream," he repeated. "It was just a dream."

"Do you want to tell me about it?"

"No," he said with force. "I don't need to relive it again."

She felt his barely suppressed tremble and, for just a

moment, she pitied him. "Sometimes, when Ketil has a bad dream, it helps him to tell me about it," her voice rasped.

"That's all I need," Bjorn muttered. "Now you rank me with a half-wit."

Rika pulled away from him and sat up. "My brother is a kind and gentle person, a pure spirit who wouldn't hurt anyone. The day hasn't dawned when you're good enough to be 'ranked' with him." Her voice had a raw edge.

"Ah, Rika, I suspect you don't like me. You've been very subtle, but it's beginning to sink in." He sounded weary. "What's the matter with your voice?"

"It's just tired. I've never told so many tales in one night before, but they wouldn't let me stop."

She had recited for hours, sagas and eddas one after the other, the long room alternately ringing with laughter or gone silent with hushed expectancy. Bjorn must have seen her sway on her feet from exhaustion because he'd stopped the storytelling by lifting her over his shoulder and carrying her bottom first out of the great hall.

Once they were in the privacy of his small room, she'd protested that she wouldn't stay with him. She'd be no man's bed-slave. He pointed out that her only other recourse as a thrall was to sleep in the main hall with all of Gunnar's retainers. When she realized that her choice was fighting off fifty men or just one, Bjorn won the argument.

"A drink would help," she said, massaging the soft skin at her throat. Rika pushed back the bedclothes and started to get up, feeling her way.

"I don't think that's such a good idea." Bjorn swung his long legs over the side. Rika heard him grope for his fire-steel, flint and tinder. He struck a spark and lit the wick of a small clay lamp. The faint light glowed on his face as he turned back to her. "Not dressed as you are now, anyway."

The scratchy tunic Astryd had forced on her made her skin miserable, so he'd given her one of his own. It was soft and spacious, and even though the cloth retained a bit of his scent, she was grateful to have it. But it hung only to her mid-thigh. Rika caught him eyeing her bare calves, so she pulled her long legs up under the fabric and hugged her knees to her chest. Bjorn was right. If she ventured into the hall where the men were sleeping dressed like this, no one would believe her if she later cried rape.

"I'll fetch you some ale," Bjorn offered as he tugged up his leggings. He took the lamp to light his way and slipped out of the small room.

Huddled in the dark, she tried to puzzle out this bewildering man. Bjorn was a contradiction with feet. He was gruff and tender, fearsome and frightened, swaggering bully and willing servant. How was she to make sense of someone who blew so hot and cold? She never knew from one moment to the next which face he'd present to her. He made her feel strangely off-balance.

It was easy for her to hate the hardened warrior. The small frightened boy was something else altogether.

He came back with a long horn, brimming with the dark liquid that Rika thought tasted like warm bread.

"Oh, you've brought far too much," she protested. There was a small clay night jar in the corner of his room, but she couldn't bring herself to use it, and a trip to the privy was out for the same reason that she couldn't get her own ale. She'd have to wait till morning.

"Drink what you can, and I'll finish the rest. Maybe the ale will help me sleep." He held the horn out to her. "Please gods, a sleep without dreams," he said under his breath.

She took a small sip and let the familiar bite of the ale steal down her throat. It soothed her inflamed vocal cords and warmed her belly.

"Thank you. That helps." She sipped once more and handed the horn back to him.

He took a large gulp, his dark eyes never leaving hers. "We're both wide awake," he said, lifting the horn slightly. "We need to finish this before I can lay it down. How shall we pass the time, I wonder?" He sipped the ale this time, as he arched a brow at her.

Rika slid over and leaned against the wall, tucking her legs under her. Whatever he had in mind, she was sure she wouldn't like it.

"I know." His voice was a soft rumble that reminded her of a great cat's purr. "You can tell me more about yourself."

"You wouldn't believe me when I did try to tell you."

"I'm inclined to believe you now. I've never heard a more powerful skald than you, Rika."

"Maybe I don't want you to know any more about me," she said, crossing her arms over her chest. "You'd just use the knowledge for your own ends."

"You're probably right about that." He chuckled. "How about a story, then?"

"Another story?" Her shoulders sagged with weariness.

"Not as a skald, Rika. You've performed enough for one night." Bjorn offered her the horn again, but this time she declined with a shake of her head. "Just a simple tale told between friends when one of them has had a bad dream."

She started to argue that they were not friends, but then she remembered that as her master, he could be demanding so much more of her at that moment. A story seemed a harmless enough request.

"What kind of story?" She reached for the horn and

took another small drink. "What's the best cure for an evil dream? An epic battle? An adventure?"

"No, nothing so grand. Something soothing, I think." He moved over and leaned up against the wall beside her, stretching out his legs across the bed. "How about a maidensong, a love story? Surely you know one."

She knew several, in fact, but none that she wanted to tell to a man in his bed.

"They are forbidden in some realms, you know," she said. Magnus had warned her when he taught them to her that skalds had even been put to death for daring to compose love stories. A maidensong was powerful, as love was the most powerful force in the world. And sometimes, the most destructive. "Love stories hold as many dangers as pleasures."

"I'm inclined to risk it."

In the flickering lamplight, his smile was as intoxicating as the dark ale. She forced herself to look away.

"Come, Rika. Give me a maidensong."

She ran through the stories in her head and finally hit upon the least erotic tale in her repertoire.

"Very well, then," she said. "You shall have the tale of Ragnar and Swanhilde, a pair of doomed lovers."

"Doomed lovers," he repeated, pulling a long face. "Why does that not surprise me?" When she scowled at him, he waved his hand at her. "Please, go on."

"Ragnar fell in love with Swanhilde, a comely girl from the Hebrides, and she loved him in return. He asked for her and her father thought well of Ragnar, so the match was made. In due time, they married and he took her away to his home on a windswept crag overlooking the sea."

"He had land, then?" Bjorn tipped back the horn.

"*Ja*, it was a bridal gift from Swanhilde's father." Rika yawned, fighting the urge to lean against his warm shoulder. "And Ragnar built a keep for her with a high tower, so she could watch the ships coming and going."

"What was the land like?" His voice was soft and thoughtful.

"That's not an important part of the story."

"Pretend it is, and describe it for me." He closed his eyes and Rika suspected he was imagining his own land, had fate not made him a second son.

"It was a goodly land, fair and rich. The sun and rain fell upon it in equal portions, as sorrow and joy should fall upon each life."

"Mmmm." He sounded pleased. Then his eyes popped open and he turned to look at her. "No stones?"

"No stones," she assured him. "And every seed that fell to the earth returned a hundredfold."

He closed his eyes again, clearly satisfied. "It sounds a delightful place. They were happy, then?"

"Oh, *ja,* all that first winter they drank deep from the horn of love and found delight in each other." Since he'd closed his eyes, she felt safe to study his profile. Dark lashes rested against his high cheekbones. She found herself drawn to his full-lipped mouth and forced her gaze to move on. Straight nose, firm jaw, *ja,* all his features were pleasing. She had to give him that.

His was a strong face, an honest face. He was fine to look upon, she decided. Her heart did a strange little flop in her chest and she wondered suddenly what might have become of them if she hadn't met Bjorn over the body of her father.

He opened his eyes.

"Then came the spring." Rika quickly picked up the thread of her story and resolved not to look at Bjorn by lamplight again if she could help it. "And it was time for Ragnar to join his brothers and go viking."

"After the spring planting, of course," Bjorn said, a smile tugging at the corners of that dangerous mouth.

"*Ja,* of course." She smiled back, in spite of her best intentions. "But Swanhilde was desolate. 'How shall I know how it goes with you?' she cried. 'You could be wounded or fall ill.' Ragnar, being a clever man, devised a way for them to send messages at a distance. He made two white flags and two black flags and gave her one of each. 'Watch for my dragonship in the channel, and if all is well with me, my white flag I'll fly. If you fare well, drape you your white flag over the keep so that my heart may be eased also,' said he."

"'That sounds a good plan." Bjorn breathed deeply, tension draining from his body. It seemed the evil dream was receding in his mind.

"It was, at first," Rika said. "When weeks turned to months and Ragnar came not home, but only sailed by from time to time, Swanhilde's heart grew hard toward him. For she reasoned, when men go viking, they leave their hearts behind and take their bodies with them. She wondered if Ragnar had forgotten her in the arms of an English girl. So she decided to test him."

"Oh, this is never a good thing." Bjorn shook his head.

Rika pursed her lips in reproof and then continued. "When she saw his dragonship approaching, she draped the black flag over the keep and hurried to the water's edge. There she laid herself down and told her maid-servants to weep over her as if she were dead."

"Hmph!" Bjorn raised a dark brow at her. "Definitely not a good thing."

Rika ignored him. "Ragnar saw the black flag from afar and jumped into the sea, swimming with mighty strokes to beat the ship to shore. He staggered from the water and saw his love lying there, dead, as he supposed. A *berserkr* cry burst from his lips and he drew his dagger. Before anyone could stop him, Ragnar stabbed it into his own heart and fell down, dying."

"I just knew testing the man was not a good idea," Bjorn said with a small smile of vindication on his lips.

She rolled her eyes at him. "Do you want to hear the end of the story or not?"

"*Ja*, please."

"Swanhilde jumped up—"

"Knowing she'd done wrong," he said.

"*Ja*, knowing she'd done wrong," Rika mimicked, "but there was no help for it. Ragnar was already gone. She pulled the dagger from his chest, kissed his cold lips, and—"

"His lips wouldn't be cold yet," Bjorn interrupted.

"Would you like to tell the story next time?"

"No, please go on." He leaned back, obviously enjoying himself. "I'm sorry I interrupted you."

"She pulled the dagger from his chest, kissed his cold lips," Rika repeated. "And plunged the knife into her own heart."

"Ah, nothing like a pair of dead lovers to cheer a body up," he said, grimacing at the irony.

"You're the one who wanted a maidensong," she reminded him.

"So I was. Thank you, Rika. I think I can sleep now." He offered her the ale one last time and when she shook her head, he drained the horn. "You know what Ragnar and Swanhilde's problem really was, don't you?"

"I imagine you'll tell me."

"Timing."

When Rika screwed up her face at him, he went on. "If Swanhilde had just opened her eyes a moment sooner, the tragedy would've been averted. Timing is everything. It changes the course of a battle. It determines whether a crop will fail or thrive. There is a proper time for everything under the sun. If a moment slips by for something to happen and it doesn't, that moment will not come again."

He set the empty horn on the floor and then leaned toward her. "And I think the moment has come for me to kiss you."

She shrank back. "But what of your oath?"

"Not to bed you till you begged me?" he asked, moving ever closer.

"*Ja,* that's the one." She was sure the whites must show all the way around her green eyes.

"It still stands," he said softly. "I only want to kiss you, Rika. One kiss. It's such a simple thing. Don't make it difficult. Remember Ragnar and Swanhilde. If we let the moment pass, it may never come again."

"Just one kiss?" Her voice tremored a bit.

"Say you won't fight me. One kiss and I'll blow out the lamp and trouble you no more," he promised, shrugging his broad shoulders. "For tonight, at least."

"Very well." Rika couldn't believe the words coming out of her own mouth. Magnus had been right to warn her of the unusual power of a maidensong. "One kiss."

A smile blazed across his face.

As though she was as delicate as Frankish glass, Bjorn cupped her cheeks in his hands. He closed the distance between their mouths, stopping just before their lips touched. His warm breath swirled over her, tinged with the rich scent of ale. One of his thumbs traced the soft outline of her mouth as his gaze swept over her face and settled on her eyes. She felt herself being pulled into his dark depths and squeezed her eyelids shut.

His lips covered hers in a caress as soft as a whispered endearment. He moved his mouth, lightly probing, as though waiting for her answer, patient, but insistent. When her lips parted softly, his tongue slid into her with the same caution and thoroughness he'd use to sound an unknown harbor.

Rika could scarcely breathe. Her mouth sent some kind of undecipherable signal to the rest of her body, both frightening and exciting at the same time. Her skin tingled in anticipation of his touch. Their kiss deepened and it was as though a spark had been struck. Fire danced through her limbs and settled to smolder in her belly. All rational thought faded in the oblivion of his kiss, and the only truth in the world was the dizzying sensation of his mouth on hers.

Bjorn cradled her shorn head in his palm as his other hand slid down her neck. Her skin shivered beneath his fingers. His hand brushed lightly over the iron collar.

The hateful ring of metal yanked her back to reality. What was she thinking? To this man, she was no more than a possession to be used, like his bloody sword or humble piss pot, and cherished far less than his dragonship.

And to think she'd been enjoying his company, mooning at him with calf's eyes, and worst of all, answering his kiss. How could she have forgotten Magnus? Her father's blood was on Bjorn's head. Guilt clawed at her. Rika put both palms on his chest and shoved with all her might.

At least he had the wit to look surprised.

"There," she said. "You've had your kiss." She turned her face to the wall and drew herself into a tight little ball.

Bjorn was silent for a moment and then blew out the lamp. "Good night, Rika. May you sleep without dreams."

Of course she would. All her dreams were dead.

CHAPTER 7

When Rika woke again, Bjorn was gone. He'd lit the small lamp and left it burning on the wooden trunk for her. Without it, the windowless room was black as a moonless night. A trencher of bread and a salty wedge of cheese waited for her beside the lamp. She searched every corner, but her scratchy tunic was gone.

Loki take the man! He knew very well she couldn't venture out of his small cell in the short tunic she was wearing. He'd imprisoned her without so much as a bar on the door. She snorted in disgust, picked up the cheese, breaking off a small chunk with vehemence, and popped it into her mouth.

Bjorn's room was just a rectangle of space off the main hall of Gunnar's longhouse, without a smoke hole or fire of its own. His bed was made of built-up earth on one side of the room, covered with a straw-tick, and then piled with furs and fine woven blankets.

The one piece of furniture in the room was a heavy wooden trunk, which he used to store his clothing and personal possessions. A round, hardened leather shield leaned against the opposite wall. It was heavily scored with slashes from glancing blows Bjorn had taken in battle or raiding. *Pity the shield had caught them all,* Rika thought.

A long broadsword, safely tucked into its shoulder baldric, stood balanced next to the shield. She wrapped her fingers around the hilt and tried to lift the blade. She quickly realized it was too heavy for her to wield, and she soon gave up the effort with a disgusted grunt. She'd have to find some other way to make Bjorn the Black pay for Magnus.

The room was tidy, clean-swept and, like its owner, spartan. The only item that seemed out of place in that masculine space was a small bone flute on the wooden chest. She wondered whether he could play it, or if it was a remembrance of some sort, a trophy of his conquest of some witless female perhaps. The fiend.

The door swung open suddenly, and the fiend in question peered in.

"You're awake. Good." Bjorn strode into the room with a bundle of clothes in his arms. He dropped them on the bed beside her. "Here, you can put these on. Do you know how to ride a horse?"

"*Ja,* I can ride," she said as she sorted through the clothing he'd brought her. The tunic was a soft, creamy cloth the color of ripened wheat, with a kyrtle of deep forest green. She fingered the twin silver brooches sparkling up at her. They were every bit as fine as the ones Magnus had bought her. Thoughts of her father made her turn from them in disgust.

"We usually sailed to the places Magnus performed, but he liked to ride back into the less-settled areas, too," Rika said.

"A skald as renowned as Magnus wouldn't have to travel to out-of-the-way places." Bjorn helped himself to some of the bread. "I'd heard from one of our traders that he was at the court of the Danes."

"We were for quite a while on and off, but Magnus

could never bear court life—all that posturing and preening. So we'd head for the wilds." She wiggled out of his short tunic while keeping herself covered with the blankets. If he thought she was planning to undress in front of him, he was sadly mistaken. "Besides, sometimes he collected a new tale in the hinterlands, so he always felt it worth the trip. And Magnus used to say that all people need a skald, not just the powerful. Our sagas and eddas make us who we are as a people and keep us strong."

"There's no doubt you put heart into Gunnar's hall last night." His dark eyes crinkled with admiration. "There hasn't been that much laughter here since my father was jarl." Bjorn's voice trailed away as if following the wisp of memory.

"Has he been gone long?" she asked. Her own loss still pierced like a blade, yet she recognized pain in his drooping shoulders.

"A little over a year," he said. "So much has changed, sometimes it seems even longer."

Rika would not allow herself to sympathize with the pain of the man who took her own father from her. She disappeared completely under the bedding and after several moments of tussling with the tunic and kyrtle, threw back the blankets fully clothed.

Bjorn frowned at her. "That's a lot of trouble to go through just for dressing. It's not as though I haven't already seen you naked."

"I was unconscious at the time, so that hardly counts." She ran a hand through her close-cropped hair. It was so short she didn't even feel the lack of a comb. "I was not raised to be a bed-slave, so I'm not likely to conform to your lewd notions of how one should behave."

"Pity," he said under his breath.

Rika scowled at him, but she supposed she should be grateful. Little comments like that made it easier for her to hate him as he deserved. Last night, when he'd awakened from his evil dream, disoriented and afraid, she'd been tempted to see him as just a man, not as the brute she knew him to be.

In the light of day, she wondered whether he'd made up the whole incident, feigning a night terror just to weaken her resolve. Remembering his soft kiss made her lips tingle and her chest constrict strangely. She shook herself to ward off the unwanted sensations. It puzzled her that her body could react so independently from the wishes of her head. Her lips didn't recognize Bjorn as the enemy. The kiss had been a mistake. That was a certainty. Now that she knew how crafty he was, she'd be doubly wary.

"Where are we going?" she asked. "I was hoping you would let me see my brother for a bit today. I need to make certain he fares well."

"Today we ride up the mountain," Bjorn said. "And your brother is already on his way there. I'll make sure you see him."

"Are you sure I'll not be missed here?" Rika asked archly. "Perhaps you should confer with Lady Astryd. There may yet be a privy somewhere I haven't scrubbed."

"I've already spoken to Astryd." Bjorn popped a pinch of the cheese into his mouth. "You'll be scrubbing no more privies. The skald of Sogna shouldn't be wasted on drudge work. From now on, you'll attend me, day and night."

"I might've preferred the privies," she muttered as she fastened the buckle on her new leather boot.

They crossed the jarl's compound to the stables. There they mounted a matched pair of chestnut geldings and plodded out of the settlement, past the iron worker's and tanner's sheds, past the lush cultivated lands and up a narrow trail into a fragrant pine forest.

The air was crisp, and Rika tugged at the brown woolen cloak Bjorn had draped over her shoulders.

Several tree trunks they passed had been gnarled by wind and extreme age, shaping them into oddly human figures. With knotholes for eyes and gaping mouths unevenly bearded with moss, they were trolls in the wood, indeed. A light wind ruffled through the trees, setting them swaying in a macabre dance. Rika decided she'd rather not be in this wood by moonlight.

"Where are you taking me?" she asked. Snow-kissed air washed down from the high summit, and she pulled her cloak tighter.

"To the new fields," Bjorn said, a heart-stopping smile on his lips. The sunlight glinted blue highlights on his dark hair. When he went out of his way to charm, she had to admit Bjorn was devastatingly appealing.

So must Loki appear when that shape-shifting godling has a fool to bedevil, Rika reminded herself. She tore her gaze from her captor, trying to ignore the way her insides tightened with excitement.

Bjorn gestured up the trail. "There's a nice level spot up there. Once we clear the trees and pull up the roots, we'll double our tillable soil. We can plant more barley and rye. There are more people living in Sognefjord now than ever in memory. And people need to eat."

"But why do I need to see it?"

"The extra tillable land is important to the whole settlement," Bjorn said. "I thought skalds were interested in the lives of the people, not just in entertaining them." When she gave a grudging nod, he continued. "Anyway, it's also important to me."

"And why should that interest me in the least?" she snapped back at him, wishing she could drive his kiss from her mind.

"Because I will it," he said, his dark eyes narrowing at her. Then he looked around and inhaled deeply.

"The land gives us all we need if we care for it. Rika, I brought you here to show you the things that mean something to me. How else can I persuade you that I am not the ogre you think me?"

"How indeed, since that is impossible." She glowered at him with her best frown, the one that'd sent several would-be swains in far-flung settlements scurrying back to their local sweethearts. "I'll never forget that you are responsible for my father's death, even if it wasn't directly at your hand. You waste your time, Bjorn the Black."

"It's mine to waste," he said with deceptive lightness. "But when I kissed you last night, I did think you were almost of a mind to forgive me for a bit."

Heat surged into her face. He had felt it then, that brief flicker of a moment when her body had betrayed her, opening to him, tumbling into him as gently as a stream into the fjord, and she responded to his kiss. She burned with the shame of it.

"You spoke of a proper time for all things last night," she said grimly. "The time for us ended before it began. When my father died."

He dug his heels into his horse's flanks and spoke no more as they continued to ascend the steep trail into the thick forest. Soon Rika heard the resounding thwacks of axes on trunks and the rasping thrum of the long two-man saws. Before she could see them, she smelled the dying trees, perfuming the air with the pungent aroma of the heart of pine.

They broke through the dense woods into a clearing, where men and teams of horses strained to uproot the broad stumps left by the woodsmen. Sweat darkened the chests of the horses as they bent to the will of their equally sweaty masters.

Bjorn slid off his horse and put a shoulder to one of the more stubborn stumps. The thick muscles in his biceps bulged with effort, as he grunted beside the other workers.

"Get up, now!" he bellowed as the whole crew of men and equines strained together. The long, snaking roots finally released their hold on the earth and wrenched free, pointing skyward in surrender to man's will. A cheer went up from the gang of workers.

Bjorn vaulted up onto his horse's glossy back with the sturdy grace of a born horseman and chirruped to the gelding to walk on. He glanced sideways at Rika, but she riveted her gaze away, determined not to let him catch her paying any attention to him. She scanned the field instead.

"You said Ketil was here." She lifted a hand to shade her eyes. "I don't see him anywhere."

"He'll be working with an ax someplace. He told me this morning he likes to chop wood," Bjorn said as he looked for Ketil at the far end of the field. "He's a strong one, your brother. I asked Surt to watch out for him, but he said Ketil seems to know his way around a blade with a handle."

"That he does. Ketil will chop up a tree just for the pleasure of stacking up cordwood." It irritated her that Ketil should be talking to Bjorn. It was one thing for her to spar with their captor. Especially since she had no choice in the matter and the wit to be wary of him, but Ketil wouldn't know a grass snake from an adder. Her gentle brother always accepted everyone at face value. He'd be easy prey for someone like Bjorn, who could turn anything Ketil said to his own advantage.

"There he is." Bjorn stretched out a long arm and pointed at the young man in the distance, who was flailing at a towering pine. He nudged his horse into a trot and Rika followed.

When they were near enough, Rika cupped her hands around her mouth and cried out Ketil's name.

He stopped chopping and looked around. His sweating face broke into a wide grin when he saw Rika. He buried the ax head in the trunk he was working on and lumbered toward her.

A brisk wind whipped across the open field and caught the treetops, sending them swaying back and forth. Ketil's tree shuddered and cracked and, in a sickening surrender, slowly started to come down.

"Run, Ketil! Run!" Rika screamed.

Ketil glanced over his shoulder, but instead of running to the side to avoid the falling timber, he kept running straight as a plumb line in the same direction the tree was toppling. Rika's throat constricted as panic rippled over her. Ketil would never clear the treetop in time.

Bjorn dug his heels into the gelding's flanks, bolting into a gallop. He closed the distance between him and Ketil in only a few heartbeats. Rika watched, hand clasped over her mouth, as Bjorn leaped from the back of his mount and plowed into Ketil, shoving him aside just as the giant trunk came crashing down.

Rika gasped as Ketil rolled to safety. But the jarl's brother disappeared under a solid avalanche of boughs and needles.

CHAPTER 8

Men swarmed over the fallen tree like bees around an upturned hive. Rika slid off her horse and ran to Ketil, afraid to look lest she see Bjorn's crushed body under the pile of shattered timber. Tears coursed down her cheeks.

Shock, she told herself. Relief that Ketil was safe, surely. The choking knot at the back of her throat couldn't be for Bjorn the Black, the man who'd enslaved her and altered the course of her life forever.

Ketil's friend Surt slithered in among the boughs of the fallen pine. After a few moments, he crawled back out from beneath the mess of limbs, rubbing a hand across his grimy neck. "He still lives, but . . ."

Rika didn't wait to hear more. "Why are you just standing around?" Her voice held all the commanding power of her art. "Cut him out. Surt, show the others where he is so they don't damage him further."

Rika took charge of the recovery, encouraging here, railing at them there, until finally the last section of the trunk pinning Bjorn to the spongy ground was lifted.

His eyes were half-closed and an egg-sized lump

swelled at one temple. Bjorn's arms and chest were
laced with countless small punctures and slashes. A
limb as thick as Rika's wrist stood upright in the heavy
muscle of Bjorn's thigh, quivering like the shaft of a giant's arrow.

Surt grasped the limb and started to pull it out.

"No, wait!" a young man commanded. Rika recognized him as Jorand, the gangly youth with an easy
smile she'd met on Bjorn's dragonship. Now his face
was drawn with concern. "The limb is stopping the
flow of blood. If you pull it out, he'll bleed to death before we get him down the mountain."

Jorand stripped the leather sweatband from his head
and cinched it around Bjorn's thigh above the wound.
"I need some cloth."

Rika picked at the hem of her soft new tunic. She
started it unraveling and then ripped a long section of
fabric from the garment.

Jorand nodded his thanks and motioned to Surt to
remove the limb. Black blood surged from the deep
wound, followed by a flow of bright red, proof that
Bjorn's heart still pounded in his chest. Jorand packed
the wound with Rika's cloth and bound it tightly.
Through it all, Bjorn never moved so much as an eyelash.

As the men loaded Bjorn's body onto a waiting
travois, a feeling of dread settled on Rika. In the short
time she'd been there, she'd learned from the serving
girl Inga that the Jarl of Sogna was not known for his
mercy. Thralls had no rights, even if they hadn't done
wrong. What might Gunnar Haraldsson do to the
thrall responsible for his brother's death? She pulled
Surt to the side.

"Take Ketil and hide him until . . ." She couldn't finish the thought. Her throat tightened at the possibility
that Bjorn might die. "Just hide him until I send word."

Surt nodded and slipped away from the main body

of men with Ketil in tow as Rika and the others started back down the mountain. She trudged beside the travois, watching the color drain from Bjorn's face with each step.

Runners fled ahead of them to announce the accident and make what preparations they could. By the time the travois pulled into the grassy area in front of the longhouse, Astryd was ready and waiting, doctoring being the province of the lady of the house. Bjorn was carried to his airless little room and Rika tried to follow, but Astryd blocked her way.

"Stay out of here," she ordered, her lip curling. "He no longer needs your services, perhaps for good."

"But I want to help," Rika said.

The Lady of Sogna slapped her across the cheek with a stinging blow.

"Thralls do not talk back to me. Do as you're told or it will be the whip for you next time," Astryd said. "Now fetch me some raw spirits. Then help Inga boil water."

Face burning, Rika ran to the brewing shed for the alcohol Astryd needed. She delivered it to Bjorn's room but still wasn't allowed inside the door. Then she helped Inga scrub the large soapstone kettle at the central fire and hauled water from the stream to fill it.

Jorand came out of the room once. He glanced Rika's way, a grim set to his lips, but he didn't say a word. He drew out a leather pail full of the boiling liquid, still refusing to meet her eyes, and disappeared back into Bjorn's room.

Finally, Astryd's bulging belly filled the doorway. "He asked for you," she said with disdain.

Rika scurried past her. Bjorn was stretched out on the bedding, his leg bandaged tightly, a red stain still seeping through the cloth. His eyes were completely closed now, in what might have passed for natural slumber except for his pallid complexion. Rika saw his chest rising and falling shallowly. The lump on the side of his head was turning a royal shade of purple with yellowish undertones.

"Bjorn," Rika whispered as she knelt by his bedside and took one of his callused hands in her own. His hand was cool and his fingers didn't respond to her grip.

"He'll not answer you," Astryd said. "He's slipped away again. He may wake up. He may not. Only the *Norns* know."

The *Norns,* the three weavers of all human lives had undoubtedly calculated the length of Bjorn's skein and decided his fate long ago. If he'd reached the end, and the *Norns* were determined to snip him off, nothing could stop it.

"I've done all I can for him." Astryd shook her head. "Pity that he should meet such a death. A warrior like Bjorn should go out with glory, not shriveling in his bed."

Rika wanted to say that Bjorn had done something glorious. No one else of noble blood she'd ever met would've risked himself for the life of a thrall, but she couldn't voice the words. Astryd would not believe saving Ketil from his own blunder was a heroic act, and if the reason for Bjorn's accident ever came to the lady's sharp ears, it would only endanger her brother.

"Jorand, undress him," Astryd ordered. Then she turned to Rika. "Bathe him and dose all the punctures with this." Astryd handed her a small bowl filled with a noxious-smelling paste.

"And then what?" Rika's eyes widened. She'd never been in a sickroom before, let alone nursed someone who'd been grievously wounded.

"Sit with him and tend to his needs," Astryd said.

Jorand cut away Bjorn's clothing to avoid moving him any more than necessary. Then the young man spread a thin blanket over his captain to cover his nakedness. Without a word, he gathered up the scraps of fabric from Bjorn's tunic and leggings and filed out after the Lady of Sogna. Rika was left alone with Bjorn.

She lathered up a small cloth and began washing the spatters of dried blood from Bjorn's arms and chest. His tunic had offered little protection from the scrapes and jabs, but she patiently removed slivers of wood and gently cleansed the abraded skin. The ointment Astryd had ordered her to doctor him with was pungent with ammonia. It made her eyes water and she almost envied Bjorn his oblivion as she dabbed some on each scrape and puncture wound.

When she reached his waist, her gaze was drawn to the narrow ribbon of dark hair that started at his navel and spread downward. What if he were damaged in his most sensitive male part? Holding her breath, she drew the blankets down.

He seemed to be intact, with no injury she could see. She stood there for a moment just looking at him, the mysteries of a man becoming clear to her. What an odd combination of strength and vulnerability Bjorn was, and nowhere more obviously than in the tangled thicket of dark hair between his legs.

She'd seen him fully engorged and aroused, and the disturbing image had flashed through her mind unbidden several times since. It was hard to believe this soft, limp tissue was the same organ. Gooseflesh rippled over the darker skin on the bag of his seed and she was startled out of her study of him. Guiltily, she drew the blankets up to his chin and folded back the bottom edge to soap and doctor the hurts on his well-muscled legs.

Tend to his needs, Astryd had said. Rika soon discovered the needs of an unconscious man were few. She held a wet cloth to his temple, willing the lump to subside. She rearranged the blankets over him and tucked them around his feet. When she could think of nothing else to do, she perched quietly at his side on the bedding, with one of his hands in hers.

He had strong hands, broad fingered and lightly peppered with dark hair. A little bit of dirt had collected under his nails and she used a knifepoint to clean it out.

She searched his face. The hard lines around his eyes etched by years at the steering oar battling the wind and waves had relaxed and he looked years younger. His skin was so pale, with an unhealthy undertone, almost gray. She put a hand on his chest to feel the great muscle of his heart constricting under her palm. The rhythm seemed steady, if a little fast.

"Open your eyes, Bjorn," she whispered. Her stomach twisted like raw wool on a spindle. Why should she care what happened to this man? Wasn't he the enemy? The blood of Magnus Silver-Throat might just as well drip from his hand. The hand she held gently, even now. As she willed him to wake, part of her heart damned her for a traitor.

"Poor little brother." The voice behind her made her jump to her feet. She was so intent on Bjorn, she wasn't aware that Gunnar had slipped into the room, silent as a cat. "He must be dying. If you sat on my bed, I'm sure I'd rouse."

Gunnar's voice had a greasy quality, like a slick of whale oil on the waves. She didn't like the way his gaze traveled over her body.

"He hasn't wakened?"

"No, lord," Rika folded her hands before her, keeping her eyes cast down. When he took a step toward her, crowding closer than he should, she reflexively moved back. Before she knew it, he had her cornered.

"Nowhere else to run, my little skald," Gunnar said, his pupils fully dilated, making his pale eyes nearly as dark as Bjorn's, black holes ringed with icy gray.

"I'm not your skald," she said. "I belong to your

brother." The words sounded strange to her ears, yet if it would protect her from the jarl, she would readily admit to being Bjorn's property.

"That's an odd turn now, isn't it?" he said, still crowding close. "Ever since we were boys, Bjorn has always wanted what I have. He wants the land, you know. Always, he's wanted the land."

Rika didn't say anything. She didn't dare meet Gunnar's gaze, so she studied the plank floor trying to control the tremble that threatened to take her.

"He's always been eaten up with envy," Gunnar continued. "Seems strange that now I'm envious of him." The jarl leaned toward her and inhaled deeply, nuzzling along her neck, where the wisps of her shorn hair curled around her ears. Her breakfast of cheese and bread curdled in her stomach.

Gunnar placed a possessive hand on her waist. "But of course, even though Bjorn can never have what's mine, there's nothing of his that didn't come to him through my good graces. You were mine by right. I think I may just decide to take you back, Rika."

"Bjorn might have something to say about that," she said, schooling her face not to show the panic she felt rising. Bjorn the Black may have had compunctions that guarded her against rape, but she doubted that his older brother was troubled by any pangs of conscience in that regard. The salacious gleam in his eye convinced her of it.

Gunnar tossed a dismissive look over his shoulder at his brother, who lay pale and drawn and still as death. "I don't hear him objecting."

She tried a new tack. Ducking under his arm, Rika managed to get away from the corner. "Have you considered the danger you bring to yourself?"

"I see no danger," Gunnar said. "You're not big enough to fight me, and Bjorn is in no mood to."

"But what of the danger of bedding a skald?" Her

mind worked feverishly, as her feet managed to keep her out of his grasp. "I'm a gifted poet. Suppose as a lover, you suffer in comparison to your brother and I compose a little ditty about your . . . inadequacies?"

"I'll cut out your tongue." The hard glint in his eyes and the set of his thin lips told her it was not an empty threat.

"And how would you explain that to the men who expect to hear me each night at your table?" She sidestepped to avoid his grasp. "I promise you I would only have to sing it once and my words will dog you for the rest of your days. It will be too deliciously scathing not to repeat. Whether they sing it in your hearing or not, you'll be forever known as Gunnar Short-Sword to the men you want so desperately to lead."

He stopped for a moment as if weighing her words. "Of course, that supposes that you will not be pleased with me." Then one pale eyebrow lifted and he strode toward her with purpose. "But I think you will be."

He feinted one way and when she dodged the other he caught her and crushed her to his chest. Gunnar plastered his lips to hers, driving his tongue against her teeth to force her mouth open. He bruised her with the force of his kiss. She pounded his chest and shoulders, trying to get away. When he finally released her mouth, she gasped for breath.

"Let me go, you worthless crust of lint from a beggar's navel," she railed at him. "Filth from Loki's unwiped arse! Limp-sworded, pea-balled troll!"

Gunnar laughed deeply. "Very good insults, but you'll sing a different tune once I slip my 'sword' into you." He fumbled with the front of his leggings. "You see, it's not limp at all. Or short."

"No!" She didn't care who heard her, though with the foot-thick walls, she feared no one would.

"Let her go, Gunnar." The voice was ragged, but it was Bjorn's.

The jarl whirled to face his brother. Bjorn was propped up on both elbows, his face a white mask of fury. Murder swirled in the reddened whites of his dark eyes.

Gunnar laughed uneasily. "Come, little brother," he said. "Don't distress yourself. What's a wench, more or less, between us?"

"If you don't take your hands off her right now, you'll find out."

Gunnar narrowed his eyes at Bjorn. "Stop talking like a madman. You're weak as an old woman. You're in no position to stop me."

"If you try to take her, I swear on our father's grave mound, I will beat you bloody." Bjorn raised himself stiffly to a full sitting position. His face set like granite, he swung his legs over the edge of the bed and rose to his feet, leaning to keep most of his weight on his good leg. The muscle in his left cheek ticked. Naked but determined, he confronted his older brother with both fists closed tightly at his sides. "As you can see, maybe I am in a position to stop you after all," he said through clenched teeth.

Gunnar glared at him, then back at Rika. He made a low noise of disgust deep in his throat. Rika wondered how the jarl would explain a fight with his injured brother just then. Besides, Bjorn had the pain-deadened look of a *berserkr*. He was as dangerous as a wounded bear.

"She's probably not worth the bother." Gunnar turned on his heel and stomped out of the room.

When the door closed, Bjorn weaved a little, then collapsed shakily back onto the bedding. Rika hurried to his side to help ease him into lying down.

"You've started bleeding again," she scolded, as she

lifted his legs back into the bed. She ripped another section of cloth from her hemline and bound it tightly around his thigh.

He settled into the bedding, letting her fuss over him without protest. After she tucked the blanket across his chest, his belly jiggled with a small chuckle. When his mouth turned up into a broad smile, Rika noticed for the first time that a deep dimple was carved into one of his cheeks.

"Limp-sworded, pea-balled troll," he said softly before he drifted off again, this time just settling into a light sleep.

Rika hoped it was a sleep without dreams.

CHAPTER 9

"Healing is not a footrace," Rika reminded him. "You can't force your muscles to mend themselves in little more than a week."

"I'll never heal if I let you turn me into a slug-a-bed," Bjorn said, allowing a sly smile to steal over his face. The woman was a walking distraction. He might yet be an invalid, but she stirred his blood just with her nearness. Bjorn tossed the blanket back in invitation. "Unless you intend to give me reason to stay here."

She frowned. He longed to kiss away the deep furrow creasing her brow. "You know better than that," Rika said. "I'm still not your bed-slave. I just want to see you well, and you're not helping matters. It's time you admit that there are some things even you can't control."

Bjorn shook his head and pushed himself all the harder, but only time would fill the deep gouge in his thigh with muscle and flesh. The swelling at his temple was gone, though Rika told him the skin was still washed with deep indigo and yellow.

Bjorn kept to his room lest the true extent of his weakness be known. He stood for longer periods each day, pacing the length of the small space with sweat pouring down the sides of his face from the effort. Once, the leg buckled under his weight and he went down hard on the plank flooring.

"You're going to start bleeding again," Rika chided. "You need a walking stick."

"You'll not make me a cripple, girl." He scowled at her, but when she helped him back into his bed, he relented. "Perhaps a staff might be useful, for a little while at least."

When Rika asked him, Jorand was happy to honor the request. He took time out from working on his klinker-built longship to cut and sand a staff for his captain.

Each day Rika slipped out of Bjorn's room only long enough to fill his trencher and empty the night jar. After *nattmal,* she was hounded into leaving him for the length of time it took her to tell the restless horde of men a story and then Jorand escorted her back to Bjorn's side.

She carefully avoided both Gunnar and his wife.

A week went by and the true tale of how Bjorn met with his accident had not reached the jarl's ear. The incident was cloaked in a conspiracy of silence because Bjorn had committed such an unusual act. Even the ones who'd seen him shove Ketil to safety didn't know what to make of it. Privately, men thought it strange that the jarl's brother would risk himself for a mere thrall, and a simple one at that. The fact that Bjorn had done so had a curious effect on the men of Sogna. They rightly reasoned that, in a tight spot, the jarl's brother would do the same for them, and that knowledge made them eager to serve Bjorn in a way that had eluded Gunnar, who only knew how to lead with threats and coercion.

Rika sent word to Surt and Ketil came back to the *jarlhof* after a week of huddling in the woods, none the worse for his scare. Her brother was returned to her. And she owed his life to the man she held responsible for Magnus's death.

Her insides twisted every time she tried to unravel this hard knot. She'd vowed to hold on to her hatred of Bjorn till the man turned to dust, but every day she found herself smiling at him and aiding him with a willing heart as he struggled to recover. Only at night, while she listened to Bjorn's deep rhythmic breathing, an image of her father formed in her mind and the guilt overtook her. Loki himself had never devised a more convoluted puzzle.

"And how are you feeling, my lady?" Helge ran her gnarled fingers over Astryd's tight belly. The child inside distorted her skin as it fought against the small confines of the Lady of Sogna's womb.

"How should I feel, you old fool?" Astryd said crossly. "Like I'm about to burst. I can't get any bigger. When will the child come?"

"He'll come when he comes," the old midwife answered, chipper as a sparrow. She'd dealt with too many irritable pregnant women to let anything one might say upset her. "I've birthed more than I can count, and no one can tell for sure when a babe will decide to come. But I'd say it's good I arrived today. If you're still swollen in the morning, I'll be surprised, so I will. Your husband did well to summon all his *karls* to his table. My master Torvald never travels without me these days since I doctor his gout, so it was lucky for you we were called."

"A canny jarl might have wanted all the landholders in the fjord here when his son is born, so they can acclaim my issue the rightful heir to Sogna." Astryd sniffed with disdain. "The truth is that Ornolf Bloodax

returned from Miklagard with a shipload of trade
goods, so Gunnar wanted all his *karls* to come to the
jarlhof to trade. The man can't think past either his
pecker or his pocket."

Helge clucked her tongue against her teeth. So there
was profit to be made for the Jarl of Sogna. The fact
that the general summons had yielded an experienced
midwife as well was just a happy accident. If Gunnar
indeed put the clink of coins above his wife's safe de-
livery of an heir, Helge spared a moment to pity Lady
Astryd in her choice of husbands.

She pulled down the Lady of Sogna's tunic and
grabbed her hands to help her sit up. When she did,
the old midwife's gaze fell on the amber hammer at
Astryd's throat. She blinked twice. Before she could
stop herself, Helge reached up and grasped the amulet
to look at it more closely.

It couldn't be, and yet there it was. Many amber
hammers had been fashioned, but there couldn't be
two little talismans of Thor with a tiny orchid in them
just like the one that had belonged to her long-dead
mistress.

"Little Elf," she whispered, as she felt her wrinkled
face going pale. How many times over the long years
had the memory of that pitiful bundle of fur on the ice
stolen into her dreams and woken her with a guilty
start?

She remembered it all with knife-sharp clarity. The
babe just wouldn't stop wailing. . . .

Astryd grabbed the hammer out of Helge's hand.
"What's the matter with you, old woman?"

"Begging your pardon, my lady, I'm sure," Helge
said as she ducked her head deferentially. "But where
did you get that amber hammer? It's such a pretty little
thing, so it is."

"One of the thralls was wearing it when she first
came here," Astryd admitted. Her face contorted to a

snarl. "Far too fine for the likes of her, but she's a cheeky thing. Styles herself a skald, though for all that, the hussy is nothing more than a bed-slave to my husband's brother."

Helge helped Astryd struggle to her swollen feet. "And where might I find that thrall?"

"In Bjorn the Black's chamber, no doubt," Astryd said. "But you'll see her tonight. She amuses the men with silly tales, though what they see in her performance is a mystery to me."

Helge wondered whether she'd recognize Little Elf when she saw her.

That night, for the first time since the accident, his little brother felt up to joining the crowd in the great hall for *nattmal*. Gunnar gritted his teeth while the assembly greeted Bjorn with cheers. His brother leaned gently on his staff as he and Rika made their way to the dais.

"I didn't know we had such an old man in our midst," the barrel-chested Canute said loudly as Bjorn limped by. Gunnar smiled at the insult.

Quicker than Gunnar expected, Bjorn shifted all his weight onto his good leg. He brought up the tip of the staff and punched the butt end into Canute's gut. When Canute doubled over from the blow, Bjorn whipped the staff around and whacked him soundly on his broad backside, sending him sprawling.

"If you're as slow as that, Canute," Bjorn said with a satisfied grin, "it looks like we have more than one old man in this hall." He extended a hand to the fallen warrior.

Laughing heartily, Canute clambered to his feet and clasped forearms with his vanquisher. "It's good to see you up and about, Bjorn the Black. But I thought all weapons except a meat knife were supposed to be left at the door."

In that gruffly generous statement, the symbol of

Bjorn's weakness was elevated to the status of a weapon. Gunnar made a low growl of annoyance in the back of his throat. His little brother's progress toward the dais was slowed by the congratulations and well-wishes of the fighting men he passed.

Gunnar watched the procession through narrowed eyes, distrustful of the deference his brother received. Something would have to be done about that. And soon.

When Bjorn reached the end of the hall, the great bear of a man seated next to Gunnar stood to greet his youngest nephew with a rib-cracking embrace. Uncle Ornolf's bald pate shined, though the ring of iron-gray hair at the sides of his head grew long enough to brush his shoulders. His clothing was an odd mix of furs and exotic silk.

"Bjorn, my boy!" Ornolf's voice boomed loud as the crash of a glacier calving.

"Uncle!" Bjorn's eyes glittered with pleasure. "Why was I not told you were here?"

Ornolf ogled Rika and a knowing smile waggled the ends of his bushy mustache. Their uncle always did have an eye for the wenches and Gunnar had to admit the skald was looking particularly fetching this night. Though, of course, she would stand out on any night.

"Perhaps because I thought you might be busy elsewhere." Ornolf's gaze swept her again approvingly. "And to good purpose, too, by the looks of her."

"Rika, this is my Uncle Ornolf." Bjorn turned to pull the skald toward the older man. "He's Sogna's most profitable trader and a demon in a dragonship. My father and he opened the trade route to the far south when they were young."

"Bah! You make me sound a doddering graybeard," Ornolf complained.

"Graybeard you must admit to, but anyone who's crossed blades with you would never call you doddering," Bjorn said with obvious affection. "Ornolf, meet the new skald of Sogna."

"A skald? I shall look forward to hearing you." Ornolf bowed his head and sketched a gesture that was purely Eastern, though the smile left his lips. He seemed to have noticed the iron circle at Rika's neck. He stared at it, his wiry brows nearly meeting over his hawkish nose. When she arched a russet brow at him quizzically, he recovered himself. "Forgive me, I've been in Miklagard for the past year, trading with an Arab there. No doubt I've picked up some of his effete manners. Sit down, Bjorn, before you fall down. We have much news to catch up on."

Rika made Bjorn comfortable and filled a trencher with his favorites. Gunnar noticed the way her face flushed with color while she fussed around his brother.

Gunnar couldn't remember the last time a woman had fluttered around him like that. Even before her pregnancy had turned her into a waddling cow, Astryd had ceased to stir herself on his behalf.

The skald leaned toward Bjorn and whispered something to him. When he nodded, she turned and glided away. Rika moved across the hall in a flowing stride, another new tunic and kyrtle his little brother had given her draped around her. Her limbs were loose and graceful as a long-necked crane. Gunnar's hard glare followed her.

When Inga came to refill his horn with mead, he stopped her with a hand to her wrist.

"What is our skald doing over there with that big thrall?" Gunnar asked. Rika had seated herself close to the blond giant and was patting his forearm.

"Oh, my lord, that's her brother, Ketil," Inga said. Gunnar tightened his grip on her wrist, signaling that he expected more information. "He's a bit simple, but very sweet and a hard worker. Rika is devoted to him and he adores her. I've never seen a brother and sister so close."

"Have you not?" He released her wrist and extended his empty drinking horn to her, while he studied Rika and Ketil. How was it he'd missed the connection between the two of them? Gunnar narrowed his eyes at them.

There was no family resemblance between them, so that certainly explained his oversight. They sat with their heads together, sharing a joke that ended in the simpleton rocking with laughter. And by the look on the skald's face, even though the big thrall was obviously a half-wit, she cared for her brother deeply. Interesting, and most definitely useful.

"Just what I like to see. A close family always does the heart good, doesn't it?" Gunnar said as he waved Inga on to fill his uncle's horn.

In a dark corner in another part of the hall, another pair of eyes marked Rika as well. The sadness in them was matched only by regret.

"Gudrid," Torvald said softly. If Helge hadn't warned him, he'd have been certain he was seeing the ghost of his beloved wife instead of the daughter he'd abandoned long ago.

CHAPTER 10

"I've never laughed so hard in my life," Bjorn said as he collapsed back onto his bed. "The way you told that story about Thor and Loki—"

"Dressing up as women to get Thor's hammer back from the frost giants?" Rika interrupted as she unfastened the side buckles on his leather shoes and slid them off, her fingers brushing the tops of his feet. Yet another part of this man she found fair and appealing. Her gut clenched with guilt and another oddly unsettling emotion she couldn't identify. She slid her gaze away.

"It was better than a feast. Just thinking about it makes my ribs ache." He chuckled again low in his belly.

Rika smiled as she struck the fire steel to light the lamp. Once it was lit, she closed the door on the noise of carousing from the main hall.

"I could see the whole thing," he said. "And some of it I really didn't want to see. I can't imagine two uglier women and now I'm stuck with them in my head." He shook his black mane as if that would expunge the horrific spectacle of the Thunderer in woman's guise. "How in the world do you do it?"

"Do what?" she asked.

"Put pictures in other people's heads, whether they will it or no?"

"Who knows? You might be able to do it if you tried," Rika said. "It's really quite simple. First, I see it clear and complete in my mind, and then I *think* it to my listeners. It just takes practice and a little something else."

"What's that?" He lifted his arms to assist her in easing him out of his tunic. They'd developed a rhythm between them as she cared for his needs.

"The gift. Magnus used to say that without the gift, it's all just words." She dipped into a deep mock curtsey. "That, Bjorn the Black, is why they call it art."

"Let me try it then." He caught her wrists and pulled her in close to stand between his knees. "Tell me if you can see the picture that I think to you."

She looked into his eyes and found herself caught by the intensity of his gaze. An image shimmered. What did she see in his eyes? Desire? Certainly. Desire was always there when she caught him looking at her.

A shape wavered in her mind, but refused to come into sharp focus. She frowned and shook her head.

"I'm sorry. I can't see anything. What were you thinking?"

His hands rested possessively on her waist and pulled her closer. "Just that I want to kiss you more than I want to take my next breath."

"Oh." Her heart did a strange little jig in her chest. "Maybe you should close your eyes and think a little harder."

A smile spread across his face as he followed her instruction, squeezing his eyes shut. "If you think that will help." His grip tightened on her waist.

Rika tried to steady herself. During his recupera-

tion, they'd been as close as this many times, but just
knowing that he wanted to kiss her now made her insides quiver. She realized with a twinge that it was a
shiver of anticipation.

Since the accident, she'd struggled with her growing
tenderness toward Bjorn. It was just the natural result
of nursing someone, she tried to convince herself. Pleasure at seeing her patient recover. Now, looking down
at his handsome face, she wasn't so sure. She was
drawn to him with a force as strong as a surging tide.

This man had led the raid when her father died.
He'd totally destroyed her world. She should despise
him with every bit of her being. There were so many
reasons to hold herself from him, but at this moment,
Bjorn was simply a man who wanted to kiss her.

And she wanted to kiss him back.

She lowered her mouth to his. They fit together with
a naturalness that felt like a homecoming. His lips
were firm and warm and lightly tinged with the sweet
aftertaste of mead. His mouth moved over hers, setting her senses spinning, drawing her into him. After a
few moments, she pulled back gasping.

"I think it's working," he said softly. He leaned forward and took her mouth again. He kissed her simply,
gently, as though the slightest pressure might damage
her. Unhurried, he tasted her as if he found her inde-
scribably sweet.

When he started to draw back, Rika shocked herself
by groaning into him, urging him to stay. In response,
he began an exploration of her mouth with his tongue.
She draped her arms around his neck.

His mouth was a wonder, a chamber of delights
she'd only just begun to discover. When she timidly
slid her tongue into it, he gripped her tighter. She
peeked at him, and found his expression almost
pained. Did it hurt him to want her so?

At last, he released her lips and pulled her close

against him. "Rika," he breathed into her ear, his lips charting a course along its curve until he took the soft lobe gently between his teeth.

A small gasp escaped her lips and she surrendered herself to his mouth. He traced a row of feather-light kisses down her neck as his hands worked the clasps of her brooches. Before she knew it, the kyrtle slid off her shoulders and down to the plank floor. Rika couldn't find a reason to care. The longing for his touch was fast becoming unbearable. His hands found her breasts, stroking them with light circles through the soft fabric of her tunic. She arched her back instinctively, like a cat demanding a more thorough petting, straining against the thin cloth that separated them.

He stood, tugging up her tunic, and she lifted her arms so he could pull it over her head. He dropped it in a heap on the floor behind her. It seemed so natural and yet her bare skin prickled.

She reflexively cradled her breasts with one arm while she cupped her sex with the other hand, partly to shield herself from his hot gaze and partly to comfort the bewildering ache.

"No, my Rika." His voice was husky, as he teased her hands away and placed them on his own shoulders. "It pleases me so just to look at you. There's a picture I won't mind having stuck in my head at all. You're all fair, and fine and . . ." He cupped one of her breasts, thrumming the tip with his thumb, sending a jolt from her nipple to her womb. "So soft."

Bjorn settled back on the edge of the bed and pulled her close. He buried his face between her breasts, then one by one, claimed the hardened tips with his mouth. His broad hands roamed over her bare skin, his callused palms inducing shivers.

Rika could scarcely draw breath. Words were her life, but none came to her mind just then. Only a swirl of sensation. Only white-hot need.

When his hand found the cleft between her legs, she cried out and stepped back. "No, please."

"You're right." His breathing was ragged, but he managed to stand. "We should be equal." He tugged down his leggings and stepped out of them. "All I am is yours, Rika."

He took her hand and guided it to his thick, swollen shaft for her to explore. She let the smooth skin slide through her palm, hard and hot. He swayed toward her, eyes closed, chest heaving. She gently cupped the bag of his seed, now drawn up tight under her touch. She stroked the twin lumps with her fingers, before re turning to his hardness. When she gripped him firmly, a shuddering groan slipped from his mouth as if she'd clearly tested the limits of his endurance and he could stand no more. Bjorn's arms swung around her, clasping her to him.

He found her mouth and plundered it this time, taking her with a fierceness tinged by desperation. She answered his kiss, hot and hungry, letting her hands slide down his muscled back and clasp his tight buttocks.

He lowered her to the waiting bedding and eased down beside her. His mouth was everywhere, nipping and licking, stoking the fire in her till she burned. She heard someone moaning. It took a moment to realize it was her.

He ran his fingers over her flat belly and down into the moist depth of her. She shuddered as his fingertip grazed a point of exquisite pleasure.

"Beg me, Rika," he urged. "Release me from my vow. Beg me to bed you." He lowered his body onto hers. His lips trailed upward, hopping over the iron circle around her neck to find her mouth again.

Suddenly a word leaped into Rika's mind. *Bed-slave.* The iron collar burned her skin. What was she thinking? He had said they were equal, but that was a lie. They'd never be equals as long as the iron weighted her neck. She couldn't allow him to take her willingly. Not as long as she wore that hateful symbol of her thralldom.

She clamped her legs together and crossed her ankles, struggling under him. Finally he realized that she wasn't answering his kiss and released her mouth.

"No." She shoved against his chest. "No, I will not beg. I will never beg you for anything, Bjorn the Black."

He stared down at her, not believing what he was hearing. She wanted him. He knew it for a certainty. But she wouldn't have him, not even when her body was screaming for release as loudly as his. Stunned, he rolled off her.

She sidled quickly to the far wall and curled up, making herself as small as possible. He still ached for her, a low throbbing that would rob him of sleep till it wore itself and him out. Her arousal hadn't been feigned. Could she really cast aside desire that quickly?

He stared at her for a long time in the flickering lamp light. So, she despised him still.

"Oh, Rika, will you never forgive me?" he whispered, then blew out the lamp.

CHAPTER 11

The wood just wouldn't cooperate. Bjorn had sanded all day and still it warped the wrong way when he tried to fit the strake to the crosspiece.

"You may as well admit it," Jorand said. "You're a good captain. You can make a new field dance and sing with a bountiful crop. And there's no one I'd rather have at my back in a tight spot, but you're no shipwright." He grinned smugly. Jorand was fast becoming a master woodworker. The fact that Bjorn never would be in no way dimmed his captain's worth in the young man's eyes. "A man can't be good at everything."

"And sometimes, he's good at nothing," Bjorn said with disgust, his gaze following Rika's swinging strides back to the longhouse. She'd brought him water and changed the bandage on his thigh. Then she scolded him for standing too long, as though he were an errant three-year-old. He sensed no tenderness in her concern, just irritation that he'd aggravate the wound and further slow his healing, making more work for her.

"Well, we all have a knack for something," Jorand

continued cheerfully as he rasped the adze over a long piece of oak.

A knack? Was that what it took to make a woman love a man? Bjorn treated her kindly. He kept his vow not to take her unwillingly, though only the gods knew what it cost him. Lying beside her in the darkness, listening to the sweet sigh of her breathing, awash in her scent, brushing up against her softness, the ache of not bedding her was fast becoming nightly torture. He even took a wound the Fates had meant for her brother. How many different ways could he show her how he felt about her? He'd done everything but come right out and say it. Bjorn plopped down on an upturned cask.

Was this love he felt? It was certainly a hopeless burning that left the shallow lusts of his past pale by comparison. More than just bedding her, he wanted Rika's heart, her mind. He wanted to fill her as completely as she consumed him. He wanted all of her.

Inn makti murr—the mighty passion. Bjorn had heard of it, of course. The madness that could take a man's mind and turn it into a bowl of mush over a woman. He just never expected it would happen to him.

He watched as Torvald, a respected *karl* and one of his father's oldest friends, stopped Rika and spoke a few words to her. Her laughter floated down the steep path and grated on Bjorn's ear. What had that old man said to her? Why couldn't she laugh like that for him?

Torvald ambled toward him, down to the beach where the ships were lined up in various stages of completion. Some would be sturdy broad-breasted *knorrs*, destined to haul livestock and settlers to new farmsteads in the Hebrides or the Faroes. Some would become the lithe, shorter tradeships used to navigate the shallow inland rivers, easily ported, yet strong enough to survive white water and haul goods to far away Miklagard, the great city of the south.

And some would be *drakars,* the warships that left death in their wake and brought riches to the men bold enough to go viking in the shallow-drafting vessels. But Bjorn knew Gunnar didn't intend the new dragonships for raiding. No, the jarl would use the *drakars* for his personal war, his own dream of uniting the fjords and carving out a kingdom for himself.

The world was changing, Gunnar had said, and perhaps he was right. The time might come when the fjords would need to unite to stay strong, but Gunnar was not a strong leader. The way he had mismanaged and depleted Sognefjord had proven to Bjorn that his brother was not the man to hold all Northmen in his thrall. Such thinking was a violation of Bjorn's oath of fealty, but it niggled at his brain anyway, a disloyal thought as persistent in the daytime as the recurring nightmare dogging his dreams in the dark.

Bjorn didn't think the fjords needed a king. The Christians were ruled by kings, but Northmen had the law. The law made them free. It settled disputes. It demanded justice, meting out prescribed punishment that suited the offense. From what little Bjorn had heard of kings, the justice they dispensed was far from even-handed. A bribe here, a favor there, and a king could elevate or destroy his subjects at his whim.

Bjorn could accept whatever fate dealt out for him. He felt less sanguine about the will of a king, especially if that king were his brother.

"Bjorn the Black," Torvald said. "I've been looking for you."

"And I'm looking for a reason to stop working, so I'm glad to see you." Bjorn clapped his hands to brush off the sawdust. "No doubt Jorand will be happy to see me elsewhere since I'm no good to him here. Walk with me, Torvald. My leg is stiffening up."

A sharp embankment rose to Bjorn's right, the sparkling water of the fjord rippling on his left. Bjorn limped down the rocky beach, using his staff more as a walking stick than a crutch. He carried it only because Rika insisted. And besides, he didn't want to fall in public if the leg should give way again.

"Why did you seek me?" Bjorn asked.

The old man paused for a moment as if unsure how to begin. "I want to make a trade with you," Torvald said. "A young man like you can always find a use for silver and I've a stash buried on my farm from back when I went viking with your father. The hoard is big as a head of cabbage and all finely worked. No hack silver."

"The *Sea-Snake* isn't for sale," Bjorn said. His ship was his only possession worth that much, though why Torvald would even want her was a mystery. The old man was still strong of limb, but his remaining days of raiding were certainly few. Perhaps Torvald was seeking a battle death, like old Einar Blood-Eagle who had ringed his neck with gold to tempt an attack. The ploy was successful, and the ancient warrior died with his sword singing. While Bjorn could appreciate the reasoning, he didn't want to see the *Snake* go down in a reckless quest for Valhalla. "I won't part with her."

"It's not the *Sea-Snake* I'm after," Torvald said. "It's your skald. I've a mind to buy her."

An echo of Rika's laughter resounded in Bjorn's mind, and he narrowed his eyes at Torvald. "She's not for sale either."

"I know the silver is at least ten times her *wergild,* were she a free woman," Torvald said. "You needn't worry for her. I'd treat her well."

So that's how it was. The old man wanted a young body for his sagging bed. Bjorn's eyes burned in their sockets at the thought of Rika with another man.

"No," Bjorn said evenly, trying to keep his anger in check for his dead father's sake. But part of him wondered why Harald had ever claimed this randy old goat as a friend.

Torvald stopped walking but Bjorn plowed on.

"My holding," Torvald called after him. "Would you take my land for her?"

Bjorn froze. Torvald's land was some of the richest in the fjord, fecund and level, easily worked. The old man offered him his dearest dream. At least it had been before Bjorn met that green-eyed, redheaded elf-maiden disguised as a mortal.

"No," he said forcefully and walked on.

"She's too good to be your bed-slave." Torvald's voice was edged with frustration.

Bjorn rounded on him, crowding up to stand eye to eye with the lanky karl. "But not too good to be yours, old man?"

Torvald made a noise of disgust and his pale face reddened. "You mistake me. I don't intend on taking her to my bed. I would free her. She isn't meant for thralldom. Rika belongs to herself."

"You're right in that," Bjorn admitted, a little of the steam of his anger dissipating.

The way Rika carried herself, the way she served without submission, there was no question of his actually owning her. In the legal sense, he supposed he did. He could take her body if he chose, beat her for any reason or no reason. A master could even kill his slave and no punishment would fall on him. When he captured her in Hordaland, he might've taken power over her body, but Bjorn wanted her heart. And that he'd have to earn.

"I will not part with her." Bjorn was adamant.

"But you dishonor her." Torvald's gray eyes blazed with smoldering fury and he balled his fists at his sides.

Bjorn glared at the man. "What I do with my own is

none of your business. I don't know why it should matter to you, old man, but I do her no disservice. Rika is yet a maiden." He turned and stalked away, calling back over his shoulder. "Ask her yourself if you wish, but trouble me no more. I will not sell her to you."

On the embankment above Bjorn and Torvald, Gunnar and Ornolf listened to the exchange below. Gunnar shook his head and spat on the ground.

"Hmph!" Gunnar said. "Makes you wonder just who is thrall and who is master, doesn't it?"

Ornolf looked down the beach after Bjorn. Gunnar thought he detected a combination of approval and sympathy in his uncle's sharp eyes. "Your brother seems to have lost his heart."

"Or his head. Torvald better not offer his land to me in exchange for Astryd unless he's prepared to take the carping witch. I'd make the trade in a heartbeat," Gunnar said. "My little brother is a fool to waste time and energy over so trivial a thing as a woman, and a thrall at that."

Rika's refusal still stung, and he wasn't one to forget a slight. Part of him was mollified by the fact that the infuriating woman had rebuffed his brother too, but Gunnar was a strong-willed man. Opposition to his will raised his hackles like the hair on a dog's back. Male or female, he was determined to dominate.

"Speaking of women," Ornolf said, passing a hand over the back of his neck. "The Arab has a request."

"He isn't trying to sever our trade agreement, is he?"

"No, Abdul-Azziz is more than pleased with our goods. Furs and amber are considered quite exotic in the south, and he can't get enough walrus ivory."

Gunnar chuckled. It amazed him how distance and novelty made such ordinary things desirable. "It was a good day for Sogna when you and father made that first trip to Miklagard all those years ago, even if the great city is halfway to Niflheim."

"Some have ventured farther," Uncle Ornolf said. "Sven Long-Bow of Birka claims to have seen a city of marvels in the midst of a vast wasteland where a man might find all the wealth of Midgard. He called the place Baghdad. But he had to make a long journey on the back of a cursed camel to get there." Ornolf's lip curled. Gunnar knew how his uncle detested any mode of travel but by ship. "Constantinople—Miklagard, I mean to say—boasts a fine port. It's rich enough for my blood. It was another good day for Sogna near a dozen years ago, when I met Abdul-Azziz there and struck a pact with him. Each time I return, you find yourself a richer man, nephew. This last trip doubled your wealth in silver and brought Sogna much gold."

"So what does Abdul-Azziz want?"

"He wants a more permanent alliance with Sogna," Ornolf said. "One cemented by marriage, after the custom of his people. He wants you to send him a Norse wife."

"I thought he had a wife," Gunnar said.

"To speak the truth, I think he has half a dozen, but in that respect the Arabs are more civilized than we." Ornolf smiled slyly. "Our women may tolerate a concubine in the house, but not another wife willingly. Abdul's little harem is aflutter with dark beauties who won't have any say in the matter if another is added to their ranks."

Gunnar pulled at his lower lip. "The problem is whom do I send? I have no sister to marry off and no daughters yet. Though don't wish any for me till Astryd births my son." He held up a hand as if to ward off the specter of a girl-child. "I suppose I could send Inga or one of the other serving girls. They're all comely enough."

"It will have to be a girl of some importance and un-questioned virtue or the Arab will be offended," his uncle said with surety.

In the fjords, slights and insults often required bloodshed before satisfaction was declared. Ornolf always claimed that in the case of preserving personal dignity, his Arab trading partner was even more exacting than a Northman.

"Perhaps one of your *karls* has a daughter that might suit."

"I'll think on it," Gunnar said as his gaze followed his brother's halting progress down the beach. He and Bjorn hadn't said three words to each other since Bjorn stared him down over that redheaded thrall. Bjorn might have voiced disagreements with him privately in the past, but that was the first time his little brother had blatantly defied Gunnar's will—and over something as inconsequential as a wench.

What if Bjorn decided to assert himself on weightier matters? How many would follow him? That was yet another situation that required Gunnar's attention. "What other news have you from the southern fjords?"

Ornolf's mouth turned down beneath his heavy mustache, as if knowing Gunnar would not be pleased with what he had to say. "Halfdan is amassing men," Ornolf said. "He draws them like ants to honey and each day more swarm to his table. Already he controls Raumarike and looks to gobble up his neighbors as well. Some say they may fall willingly because Halfdan is well-loved by his people."

Gunnar made a growling noise in the back of his throat. "I need more men, more silver and more time," he complained.

"Right now, you are overmatched. We'd be wise to avoid a direct confrontation with Halfdan. Have you considered allying yourself with him?" Ornolf suggested, his tone as conciliatory as he dared. "Perhaps an offer to foster his son or to arrange a marriage between your houses once your own child is born?"

"Why should I go cringing to him?" Gunnar's pale eyes frosted over. "The Norse will have a king, you've said so yourself. That king will be me, and after me, my son. I will have it so, Uncle."

The older man cast a sideways glance at his nephew. Gunnar had always had a will of iron and a black temper to match. Ornolf looked back down the beach where his dark-haired nephew leaned on his staff. More than once, he'd wished the fates had switched the birth order of these two boys and given Sogna to Bjorn. He drew men to him naturally. Ornolf knew Bjorn's crew would trail him blithely into Hel, singing as they went.

"That is why you will return to Miklagard within the month," Gunnar said.

Ornolf closed his eyes. The way to Miklagard—Constantinople as the inhabitants called it—was a long, weary one. Not only was the journey fraught with danger, but upon arriving in the sprawling city, one had to navigate intrigue as well. Ornolf had hoped to winter in Sogna before attempting another trek south. He'd planned to offer a steadying hand to his nephew the jarl and persuade him to a more peaceful road. Strange, how the older he got, the sweeter peace sounded. Perhaps Ornolf had spent too much time in the voluptuous south. Fair weather and fine living made a man soft.

"We have enough trade goods," Gunnar continued. "My little brother got lucky in the frostlands, so we're well stocked with walrus ivory and furs. We took a fair cache of amber in the Hordaland raid. There's more than enough to make a trip worthwhile. If Abdul-Azziz is seeking a permanent bond with us, let us not keep him waiting."

"But what of a bride for him?" Ornolf asked, wondering what his devious nephew was scheming this time.

"You just make what preparations you must for your trip," Gunnar said, the corners of his mouth curving into a calculating smile. "Leave that little detail to me."

CHAPTER 12

The old midwife Helge had been wrong. It was a full week before the heir to Sogna decided to be born. On a mizzling day, when the sky and water competed to see which of them could be grayest, the Dragon of Sogna was finally brought to childbed.

She did not believe in suffering in silence.

Astryd's shrieks rattled the timbers of the longhouse and sent her serving girls scurrying about with no more purpose than a bunch of lemmings on a trek to the sea. Despite the rain that fell like cold, wet needles, Gunnar fled the longhouse to hunt, most of his fighting men trailing him gratefully.

As Rika predicted, Bjorn pushed himself too hard and his wound reopened. He was forced to sit around the great hall listening to Astryd's overblown moaning. And Rika was forced to sit with him.

"I had no idea sound carried so well through wattle-and-daub." He looked wild-eyed at her over the chess set on the table between them. "Is it always like this?"

"How would I know? There's not much call for a skald in a birthing room." A long wail reverberated toward them. "Thor be thanked," Rika murmured with the callousness of a maiden.

Hearing Astryd's groans made part of her glad she had not given herself to Bjorn. Childbed was no light matter. But another part of her replayed that night over and over in her mind, reliving his kisses and the shivering ecstasy of his hands on her, till her lips and skin tingled, and she was left wondering what further delights she'd denied herself. What was it about this man that seemed to tie her up in knots? Even now, his steady gaze was enough to set her pulse dancing.

Bjorn turned his attention back to the ivory and jet pieces before him. Uncle Ornolf had brought him the intricately wrought chess set from Miklagard. Once Bjorn found out that Rika knew how to play, he insisted that she teach him. It proved more challenging than Bjorn expected. He was considered a master of *hnefatafl*, the Norse board game of strategy, but the wide variety of moves and gambits in chess would take time for him to learn. He fingered the figure with a cross on its top that Rika told him was called a bishop, and then slid the piece over to threaten her white queen.

"How do you expect to learn if you ignore my advice?" she asked, swinging her king's knight around and knocking his bishop from the board. "You're not paying attention."

"That's because it doesn't make any sense." There were far more white pieces than black left on the board. How was it possible that a woman could out-strategize a man?

"When I learned to play while we were at the *Dannevirke,* I was taught that the game is modeled after a Christian court," she explained. "There's the ruler and his consort." Her fingers danced over the board and slid down the side of the king. "You're just not thinking about it in the right way."

It was a wonder he could think at all as he watched her pale hand stroke the chess piece. He remembered those slim fingers, cool and smooth on his own heated flesh.

"The bishops represent their religion." She waggled the piece she'd just captured in his face and then tapped the mounted figure. "And the knights are their fighting elite."

"That's the one piece whose movement makes sense to me. It's a flanking action, just like cavalry swooping in from the side when a battle is at fever pitch," Bjorn said. Of course, he'd also stood up to a frontal charge with nothing but a long spear propped up before him to drive into the horse's chest. But he supposed it would complicate the game even further to allow the knight another type of motion.

"And the castle is their stronghold." Rika balanced a fingertip on the crenellated top of the piece.

"Which is a foolish playing piece because castles never move," he said.

She ignored his complaint. "Then there are the pawns, the hapless foot soldiers, which Christian kings spend like so much cordwood on a bonfire."

"But why should the queen be able to move about so freely while the king moves just one square at a time?" Bjorn positioned his remaining knight to threaten her queen. "I begin to think this is a woman's game."

"But isn't that how the kings conduct their battles?" Rika asked. "Magnus always told me that they sit astride great steeds on the top of a hill and direct the battle from a distance."

"*Ja,* that's true, but it does them no credit," Bjorn said, his gaze tracing possible moves on the variegated board. "How can a man call himself a king if he won't lead at the head of his men when they must pass into harm?"

"Speaking of harm," she said, a satisfied smile on

her lips as she slid her white queen into a menacing position, "your king is in jeopardy. Check."

"And so is your queen," Bjorn smiled as he toppled her with his knight and lifted the vexing piece from the board.

Her castle roared across the table and knocked his king on its side. "Checkmate. Bjorn, you have to pay attention to your king instead of going after my queen all the time."

"I can't help that I'd rather chase a woman than worry over a man." He raised an eyebrow at her. "Let's try again. One of these times, I'll beat you."

As they reset the game pieces, Bjorn caught her sneaking peeks at him from under her lashes in quick, unreadable glances. He'd trade a year in Valhalla to know what was swirling in this woman's head. From the birthing room, Astryd wailed again and loudly cast doubts on the parentage of her absent husband.

"You had another bad dream last night, didn't you?"

He frowned. "I didn't think I woke you."

"You have them often, Bjorn. Sometimes, more than once a night." She leaned forward. "Are you sure you don't want to tell me about them? Ketil—" She broke off what she was going to say. "I just think it might help you to talk about it."

"I don't know why it would," he said gruffly, folding his arms across his chest, trying to seem intent on the chess pieces but not really seeing them.

"But it might, and I think you're being selfish."

He looked up at her sharply. "How is that?"

"After all, the dreams are interrupting my sleep, as well as yours," she said.

He shifted uncomfortably in his chair. The dream terrified him, true enough, but lately he'd been even more afraid of seeming a coward in her eyes. Last night, he thought he might have even rebuffed her angrily in the throes of the nightmare, but when he fully came to himself, she seemed to be asleep. Was it feigned? Part of him was tempted to share this private terror with her, but he was already a cripple just now. How could a man admit weakness and yet remain a man?

"Please, won't you tell me?"

When he met her direct gaze, the warmth in her green eyes made him want to trust her.

"All right, girl, all right. If only to put a stop to your nagging. You're worse than a leaky roof." He pushed back from the chessboard and dragged a hand over his face. "It's always the same dream." If he related the facts baldly, perhaps none of the panic the dream gave him by night would creep into his mind by day. "I'm underwater and I can't get back to the surface."

"Why?" She made her opening move, sliding her king's pawn forward two spaces.

"Sometimes ice blocks my way and sometimes it's as though there's a hand that comes down into the water and holds me there." He mirrored her chess move with one of his own. "I run out of air and start to sink." Bjorn's voice trailed away.

"Go on."

"*Jormungand,*" he whispered, not able to meet her eyes. "I see the Great Serpent."

Rika covered her mouth with her hand. "An evil dream, indeed. No wonder you shake—"

"Then I wake making a fool of myself." He exhaled noisily in disgust.

"But no wonder you cry out. The World Serpent is terror enough when we're awake." Rika reached across the small table to touch his forearm. "It's not foolish to feel fear, Bjorn. It's human."

"A brave man feels no fear."

"Nonsense. I don't care how daunting the act, unless you fear, you've done nothing brave." Rika paraded her bishop to a new position. "It takes no courage at all to face something you're not afraid of. Fear is a requirement for true bravery."

Bjorn rolled that idea around in his mind, grateful for the fresh insight. Perhaps he wasn't the coward he suspected he was becoming. He nodded slightly. "You may be right about that."

"Of course I am. Now we just have to discover why you dream of drowning and seeing the serpent," she said as she studied the positions of the chess pieces with obvious satisfaction. "It's your move."

"The first part is easy enough." He inched another pawn forward. "I nearly drowned as a boy. I couldn't have been more than five or six winters. It's one of my earliest memories."

"That's awful." She captured his pawn with her bishop. "How did it happen?"

"Gunnar and I were out in a little coracle." He leaned back, threading through his memories to that young time. "We'd been climbing the cliffs for gulls' eggs all day and were headed back home. I remember we got into an argument about who found the most eggs. He's about five years older than me, and in my childish eyes, he was practically an adult. So I had to lord it over him that I'd managed to scale more cliffs and find the most eggs. We are brothers, after all, and brothers fight. Sharp words turned to yelling and then"—Bjorn grimaced both at the gap in his memory and his lost pawn—"I don't recall exactly how it happened, but suddenly I was in the fjord and sinking. I couldn't swim."

"That would certainly explain part of your dream," Rika said. "Then what happened?"

"Gunnar pulled me out," he said quickly. "Again, the how of it is fuzzy in my mind, but my next clear memory is of my hand clasped on his arm, then me clambering over the side, and collapsing in the coracle. My brother saved my life. And even child that I was, I knew I owed him. I swore an oath of fealty to him right there in the boat and then repeated it later in our father's hall. We have our differences, Gunnar and I, but I'm still his man." He grinned at her sheepishly. "And to this day, I still can't swim a stroke."

"Then you *are* a brave man, Bjorn," she said. "If I couldn't swim, I wouldn't set foot in a boat."

He smiled at her and then took her bishop. She hadn't seen the danger. Perhaps the key to besting her lay in distraction.

"How strange . . ." Rika's voice trailed off to a whisper.

"My taking one of your pieces isn't all that unusual," he said defensively.

"No, I mean your near drowning," Rika said. She paused and gnawed her lip. "Someone meant me for the water, though I don't have any memory of it."

Bjorn cocked his head at her.

"I'm not Magnus's natural daughter," she confided, with an odd catch in her voice. "He and Ketil found me on an ice floe. 'My Pictish princess,' he used to call me, because I was so blue when they first fished me out."

Bjorn shook his head. "Whoever abandoned you was a fool."

She gave him a sad little smile and raked her fingers over her cropped head. "I like to think of it as a gift. Otherwise I wouldn't have had Magnus." Her chin wobbled a bit and she didn't meet his eyes.

Bjorn sensed how much it cost her to tell him those things. He knew she still blamed him for Magnus's death. So why did she look so . . . guilty? *Ja,* that's what he saw on her. When she looked back up at him, her face was pale and drawn. Guilt. He suddenly felt it, too.

"Rika, I wish . . ." Only weaklings wished for the impossible, yet he knew he'd be willing to give up even his hope of having his own land if he could somehow give Magnus back to her. Still, her expression puzzled him. Why would she feel guilty unless she was starting to feel something for him? *Ja,* that was it. It had to be.

She sighed deeply and moved another pawn. "Anyway, back to your dream. Your near drowning happened a long time ago. Have you always been plagued with this dream?"

Bjorn frowned. "No. Now that I think on it, I really hadn't thought about the mishap for years."

"When did the dream start then?"

He tented his hands before him. "Just last year. After my father died."

When she raised a quizzical eyebrow at him, he continued. "My father was still an active man, even though he'd seen nearly fifty winters. He always liked to hunt alone, said it steadied him to have just his own company now and then. He'd get away into the mountains to bring down a buck or two. When his horse came back to the stable alone, we set out to find him."

"An accident?"

"No," he said. "Murder. He'd been set upon by someone, but he'd put up a fight. His sword was nicked deeply, but not bloodied." Bjorn dragged a hand over his face. "The worst of it was . . . the death wound came from behind. A coward's wound."

Rika bit her lower lip. "And you think your father tried to run away from the fight. It might not have happened that way. Things are not always what they seem. But it seems clear that your father's death triggered your dream somehow," she said. "Now, what meaning can you see in the image of Jormungand?"

Bjorn leaned back and laced his fingers behind his head, studying Gunnar's symbol on one of the many shields hanging on the walls. Entwined serpents. He frowned at the image, then shrugged. He'd called his beloved dragonship the *Sea-Snake*. It seemed both brothers had an affinity for the fearsome creatures and he wondered whether Gunnar was plagued with similar nightmares. He didn't even want to think about the clammy, reptilian visions that haunted his sleep. "You're the skald. You tell me."

"In the sagas, the World Serpent is linked with both treachery and destruction," she said, her eyes flitting up and to the right as she mentally scanned her repertoire. "Jormungand helps destroy the gods at Ragnarok, but the serpent is also killed in the last battle, so that's an encouraging thought."

Bjorn narrowed his eyes and studied the chessboard. Treachery? Why would he dream about that? Then suddenly he saw an opening on the game board. She'd left her king exposed. He whipped his queen out and moved her into position.

Bjorn leaned back, triumphant. "Check and mate."

CHAPTER 13

"Parry and thrust," Ornolf bellowed as the blades rang with the force of their meeting. Bjorn backed across the compound, his body balanced and loose. If the wound in his thigh troubled him, no one could tell from his deft movements.

"Now turn and upward thrust," Ornolf yelled.

Bjorn whirled and jabbed his sword point back under his arm toward his uncle. It was fortunate that the seasoned warrior knew the thrust was coming and jumped out of the way.

"*Ja,* that's it," Ornolf said, swiping the perspiration from his gleaming pate.

"Ingenious." Bjorn turned back around and clamped a hand on his uncle's shoulder. "First you distract your enemy by showing him your unprotected back and then he meets your sword tip with his gut. The Arabs must be a cunning race."

"That they are," Ornolf said, panting with the exertion of showing Bjorn the new sword tricks he'd picked up in the south.

Abdul-Azziz, Ornolf's Arab trading partner, was

also an accomplished fighter, as merchants frequently had to be in a land where caravans were considered easy pickings by the desert bandits. The Arab enjoyed mock sparring with Ornolf, who matched him for age if not for size. Northmen towered over the populace where ever they roamed. Still, the dark little man was cunning with his long curved blade and generous enough of spirit to share his knowledge with his large Nordic friend.

"Always remember you must to turn back quickly to defend against a last blow," Uncle Ornolf said. "A dying man can kill you just as easily as a healthy one."

"Little brother!" Bjorn heard Gunnar calling him from across the yard.

"Thank you, Uncle. I'll remember." As he and Ornolf ambled toward Gunnar, Bjorn cast about for a safe subject of conversation with his brother. Bjorn had no intention of apologizing for his defense of Rika, even to the jarl, so they'd effectively ignored each other for weeks. "How is my pretty little niece today?"

Gunnar's face screwed into a scowl that suggested he'd just swallowed bad herring. "Probably puking and soiling every cloth within her range. I suppose she'll be useful in about thirteen years when I can marry her off, but for now I'm keeping my distance." Bjorn knew his brother was still furious that Astryd had presented him with a girl-child. "And besides, she looks like a gnome."

"All babies look like that at first," Bjorn said charitably. "Rika says little Dagmar will be more comely with time." *And with hair,* he thought less charitably.

"Rika, *ja,*" Gunnar said. "You've hit upon the very thing I wanted to talk to you about." He put a brotherly arm around Bjorn's shoulders and led him away from the yard where the fighting men were taking their exercise.

"What about her?" Bjorn asked suspiciously, his hands balled into fists. He wasn't yet ready to discuss her with Gunnar. He could still see Rika's wild eyes and hear his brother's voice hoarse with lust.

"Is it true what I've heard? She refuses to bed you?" Gunnar lowered his voice.

"Where did you hear that?"

"Never mind. A jarl has ways of knowing things that don't need to concern you," Gunnar said. "Is she still a maiden?"

Bjorn was tempted to lie. It was none of Gunnar's business, but he'd never kept anything from his brother. He saw no reason to start now. Bjorn's shoulders sagged. "*Ja*, she is."

"What's wrong with you, little brother?"

"Just because I won't force a woman doesn't mean there's anything wrong with me." Bjorn shook off Gunnar's arm. "I don't see you leading Astryd around by the nose."

"Ah, a wife is another matter entirely, trust me on that." Gunnar sighed. "Now a thrall, her wishes shouldn't concern you particularly."

"But they do," Bjorn admitted. "In truth, brother, I would marry her."

"Marry? Now it's certain that Rika is not just a gifted storyteller, but a sorceress as well," Gunnar said, clearly alarmed. "We know almost nothing about her. She could easily be a practitioner of *seid* craft." He made the sign against evil for even mentioning that most malicious of dark arts.

"That's ridiculous," Bjorn said. "Magic can't account for me wanting to wed her."

"She's bewitched you with some runic spell. How can you even think it?" Gunnar shook his head. "She's a thrall and your bed-slave. That woman is meant for one thing only—your pleasure, and believe me when I tell you that marriage is not conducive to a man's pleasure."

"It's like to be my only hope." Bjorn grinned wryly.

"But consider what you do to the house of Sogna, to marry so far beneath you? By Loki's hairy toes, she's a thrall, little brother."

"Only because I made her so," Bjorn said. "Actually, I never met a woman who believes herself so far above me." An image of Rika in the bathhouse, naked and defiant, brought a smile to his lips. "She may just be right in that."

"Hmm. Do you know what I think?" Gunnar slid his tongue over his teeth. "I think you should free her."

"Free her?" Bjorn backed a step away. "Then I'd lose her entirely."

"I don't think so. I've seen her watching you when she thinks you don't see. There's a look on her face that I wish a woman would cast toward me."

Bjorn narrowed his eyes at Gunnar. Did the jarl still wish Rika would look his way? He suspected his brother thought the fiery redhead would easily be worth Astryd's ire. Yet Gunnar's words gave him hope. Rika held herself aloof from him, but did she secretly want him?

"You think she'd have me if she were free?" The tone of his voice was pathetically hopeful, even to his own ears. Bjorn winced at his words.

"*Ja,*" Gunnar assured him. "If she were a free woman, she'd fall into your arms like a ripe plum. It seems to me that she only withholds herself now because she chafes under the iron collar. As a skald, she's a proud woman. She's like a fine kestrel that needs to fly free, but will be happy enough to settle back on your wrist of her own choice."

First Torvald and now his own brother. Bjorn had been told that Rika needed to be free by no less than two men. Three, if he counted the counsel of his own heart.

"You're right, Gunnar," he said. "I'll free her tonight after *nattmal.*"

* * *

"Tell it again, Rika," Ketil urged as he lugged most of the weight of the large bucket they toted between them.

Rika smiled at him and launched into her second telling of "Ketil the Bold." She'd known since childhood that Magnus and Ketil had found her on an ice floe. But to amuse her brother, she'd dreamed up an elaborate story about the event. In Rika's tale, Ketil was no longer just a young simpleton. He was a foreign prince, who wrestled her from the coils of Jormungand, that vile serpent whose body encircles the earth. In Rika's tale, he was Ketil the Bold.

Actually, Ketil's own story was much like hers. He too had been abandoned at birth, a fate that befell most infants whose vacant expression betrayed a faulty mind. Magnus had saved Ketil from a wolfpack just outside of Trondheim and always said he'd rescued the kindest soul Odin ever sent to Midgard.

As Rika told Ketil the fanciful story in which he played such a heroic role, she couldn't help wondering how she'd come to be adrift on the ice. Why had she been expelled? It was a hurt, a small keening ache, which never quite went away.

Yet, when she smiled up into her brother's beaming face, the ache retreated in the warmth of his unabashed love. Somehow, Bjorn had arranged for her to spend more time each day with Ketil, which delighted them both.

Ketil was doing surprisingly well. Surt had taken him under his wing and her brother's good-natured sweetness had won him easy acceptance among the other slaves of the house. Ketil's needs were few: kind words, plenty of food and a warm place to sleep. Since Ketil had difficulty making decisions anyway, he wasn't the least troubled by taking orders all day, as long as no one barked at him or scolded. He seemed genuinely happy.

"Rika, I would speak with you," Gunnar called behind them.

"Go on into the house with the bucket, Ketil," she said quietly. Unease ruffled through her whenever she heard the jarl's voice, especially when Bjorn wasn't around.

Ketil squinted at Gunnar for a moment and then heaved the bucket up. "Be careful. He's got bad eyes," her brother whispered before he turned to go.

She bit her lip, pondering Ketil's warning. Before that moment, she'd never heard him say a negative word about anyone.

Rika waited for the Jarl of Sogna to come to her, her hands folded demurely before her. "I have duties, my lord, that require my presence elsewhere, so I trust this will be brief."

Gunnar laughed. "What delightful impudence! You are indeed an ornament to my court." He circled around her, taking his time, as though measuring her. Satisfied, he stopped before her.

Rika knew he was trying to fluster her with his bold stare, so she returned his gaze coolly. They were in a public place. She had no need to fear him, she tried to assure herself. But just the same, she couldn't suppress a wish that Bjorn would appear suddenly around the corner.

"You want it brief? Very well," Gunnar said. "Brief it shall be. That large ox you were with just now is your brother, isn't he?"

"Ja." Her lips pressed into a tight line. It hurt her heart for anyone to demean Ketil. She wondered sometimes how people could look at her brother and not see his good soul, shining pure and clean through his childish eyes. "He is my brother."

"Very close, are you?"

"I'm all he has in the world, and he is all I have," Rika said simply.

"Good." Gunnar raised a speculative eyebrow at her. "I like close families."

"I'm glad to have gratified you, my lord, and now if you'll excuse me." She turned to go, but he snaked out a hand and grabbed her arm.

"Oh, no, you don't." Gunnar's voice was sharp-edged. Her brief flare of alarm seemed to excite him. "We're not finished yet." He pulled her close and she felt his sudden arousal, pressed lewdly against her hip. "I need to send a bride to my trading partner in Miklagard."

"I fail to see what that has to do with me." She wrenched herself away from him, rubbing her arm where his grasping fingers raised angry red marks on her pale skin.

"I intend to send you."

A nervous smile fluttered on her lips. "It's not wise to marry a woman off without her permission. Have you forgotten the tale of Botilla, whose family saw her wed without her consent, not once, but five times? All five marriages ended in maiming, murder or divorce," she recounted airily, trying to keep the mood light. Surely the jarl must be attempting some grim jest.

"Still, I will see you sent to Abdul-Azziz in Miklagard," Gunnar said with certainty.

"That would be rather difficult to do since I belong to your brother." When he circled her now, she turned with him to keep him in sight.

"But if you were free?"

"Then it would be even more difficult for you to bend me to your wishes, my lord," she said through a clenched jaw.

"I think not. Not as long as your brother belongs to me." A crooked smile stretched Gunnar's features unpleasantly.

"What are you saying?"

"Just that if you do not my will, then I have no

choice but to send your brother—Ketil, is that his
name?—your brother Ketil to Uppsala when the year
for sacrifice comes again." He tapped his temple
thoughtfully. "Why, that's just next summer, isn't it?"

Eight years ago, she and Magnus and Ketil, along
with most of the Northern population, converged on
the Sacred Grove. For nine days, people traded, drank
and brokered marriages. And at night they worshiped
Odin in the dark, leafy bower of giants next to the temple. The mighty boughs strained under the weight of
hanged victims of all sorts, horses, goats, fowl, and
men.

Rage quivered impotently inside her. "How can you
demand this of me when you know it is not in my
power to grant? I can't wed of my own choice as long
as I am your brother's slave."

"So you're saying that if you were free, you would
consent to the marriage?" Gunnar asked.

"*Ja,* I would," she said, her heart pounding. "To save
my brother, not to please you."

"I have your word, then." Gunnar all but pounced
on her. "If you were free, you would willingly go to
wed my trading partner in the south?"

"But I am not free."

"Humor me for a moment," Gunnar said. "If you
were free?"

"*Ja,* you have my word," she said warily. What was
the jarl playing at? It was a moot point as long as she
wore the collar. For the first time since it was bolted on
her neck, its weight comforted her. "If I also have
yours."

"What?"

"Your word to spare my brother, of course," she
said. "My consent would depend on your promise to
keep Ketil safe."

"Of course," he said quickly.

"If I went, then Ketil must come with me. Otherwise, how could I be sure you would keep your word?"

"How dare you doubt the oath of Sogna?" Gunnar's eyes narrowed to glittering slits. "If you were a man, you'd be dead now. I'll swear on any god you care to name. May Astryd never bear me a son if I break this bargain."

Neither of them said any more for the space of several heartbeats.

"But I belong to Bjorn. I am not free, and therefore this conversation is meaningless," she said, trying not to let him see how he'd panicked her. She knew now how the hare who escaped a lunge from the hawk felt; a piercing scream, a flash of feathers, and the scrape of sharp talons missing her by a hair's breadth. She controlled her tremble only with effort. "If you will excuse me, my lord, I have work to do."

She turned and strode away from him. Once she told Bjorn about Gunnar's threat toward Ketil, he'd know what to do.

"One last thing, Rika." Gunnar's voice curled around her ear and she froze. "A word of this conversation to Bjorn could seriously harm the health of your brother. I will see Ketil sent to the Grove, I swear it. And as for my brother—"

She whirled back to face him. It was as if he'd heard her secret thoughts.

"Bjorn has shown himself to be accident-prone of late. Should you feel the need to prattle to him about this, I fear another bit of bad luck might come his way. In fact, I'm sure of it. An accident is easily arranged for a price and I'm a very wealthy man. He'd not be likely to recover next time."

Gunnar walked toward her as he spoke, not stopping till he was nose to nose with her. Rika resisted the urge to step back.

"Not a word," he hissed. "Not ever. I have ears and

eyes all over Sogna, so don't think for one moment you could deceive me. Do you understand?"

She nodded, not trusting her voice to speak, as Gunnar shouldered past her into the longhouse.

CHAPTER 14

Bjorn bristled with nervous energy. He laid his plans with the same care he'd devote to besieging a city. Everything was in place for his assault on Rika's heart.

He hadn't been this excited since the day he took the *Sea-Snake* out for her first cruise. That was a watershed in his life. He was finally a man, in command of his own vessel, his own crew, and his own life.

Tonight would be another marker of sorts. The night he willingly surrendered his life to a woman.

Back in Hordaland, he'd been intrigued by her face and form and amused by her plucky courage in a tight spot. He thought she'd be a good diversion for a few weeks. He hadn't expected to need her so. He hadn't counted on falling in love with the soul and the wit, the woman behind those captivating green eyes.

As the drinking and eating wound down after *nattmal,* the men started chanting for Rika to begin her saga for the night. After dusty hours of hard work, it was the high point of their day, as much anticipated as a draught of sweet mead or a rich haunch of venison.

When she started to stand, Bjorn stopped her with a hand on her arm. He rose to his feet instead and raised his palms to silence the rowdy crowd.

"I don't have Rika Magnusdottir's gift for words, but I wish to speak," he said, his deep voice filling the hall easily. "She has been my thrall for the short space of a season now and never was a master less deserving."

A couple of the men shouted their ribald agreement and Bjorn smiled good-naturedly. In the far corner of the room, Torvald leaned back and steepled his long-fingered hands before him. He nodded in approval, as if sensing what was coming.

"I captured her in the raid of Hordaland, and in the time since then, she has captured me." He smiled down at her, his dark eyes soft and inviting.

Rika's jaw sagged. What was Bjorn doing? At the edge of her vision, she saw Gunnar, his cruel face alight with triumph. She had the sinking feeling that she was caught, like the unsuspecting fly that stumbles into a soft web and doesn't realize its danger till it feels the weight of the spider approaching. Without her conscious volition, one of her hands went to the metal ring at her throat, and trembled.

"That is why I am setting her free tonight," Bjorn shouted and motioned for the smith to come forward with his tools. A cheer roared up from the throats of the men in the hall.

"Bjorn, no," she pleaded urgently, but he didn't seem to hear her over the din.

The ironworker directed her to lay her head on the table while he placed his chisel at the nut holding her collar fast. The resounding strike rang in her ears, followed by another round of cheers. The weight of iron lifted from her neck, leaving her feeling naked, and so light she feared she might float away. Her vision wavered uncertainly, and she forced herself to take a deep breath.

Bjorn caught both her hands and raised her to her feet. "Rika Magnusdottir, I give you back yourself." He grazed her cheek with his knuckle, wiping away the tear that trailed down it. Bjorn raised one of her hands and kissed it.

"And if you will have me, I give you myself, too." He tugged her close. "Marry me, Rika."

"Oh, Bjorn." Rika inhaled raggedly, but there was no air in the smoky hall. She'd given her word to Gunnar, thinking it a debt she would never be called upon to repay. That calculating toad! He must have known Bjorn's plans when he accosted her that afternoon. And now she was caught, with no way to answer Bjorn's question.

An expectant silence hushed the hall. To a man, they leaned forward expecting to hear her happy acceptance of this surprisingly well-spoken proposal. Her throat constricted and no words came to her lips.

When she tore her hands away from Bjorn and bolted from him into the star-crusted night, the stunned silence gave way to murmurs of disbelief. Bjorn was quick to follow her.

"Rika, what's wrong?"

"Go away, Bjorn. I can't look at you," she rasped, tears stinging her eyes. "Not now."

He caught up with her and wrapped his arms around her. She struggled for only a moment and then leaned back into his embrace, savoring it, knowing it would be the last.

"Is it still Magnus? You know how sorry I am about your father," he whispered urgently into her ear. She trembled in his arms. "I will spend my life trying to make it up to you."

"No, Bjorn, it's not that." She felt the galloping thump of his heart against her spine. Her own threatened to leap out of her chest. She couldn't tell him the truth. Ketil would die a terrifying death and Gunnar had all but promised to murder Bjorn as well if she breathed a word.

Bjorn whipped her around and forced her to face him, cupping her cheeks in his big hands. "You just won't have me?"

"I *can't* have you, Bjorn," she said.

"What foolishness is this?" He lost patience with words and covered her mouth with his. She gave herself up to his kiss, surrendering her lips to his.

Then with a moan, she pulled herself away from him. "I cannot marry you. I am pledged to another. I gave my word."

"That's right," Gunnar interrupted. He stepped from the shadows, the stark moonlight dividing his face into dark and light planes. "Congratulate the skald of Sogna, little brother. She is to be the wife of Abdul-Azziz, our worthy trading partner in Miklagard. A match that benefits us all."

"You mean that benefits you." Bjorn turned to face Gunnar, his shoulders set. "You arranged this whole thing."

"Indeed I did," he said. "Rika and I had a nice little chat after you told me you intended to free her and she agreed to the match, didn't you, my dear?"

"She couldn't agree to anything this afternoon," Bjorn argued. "She wasn't free and you can't hold her to anything she might've said."

"Oh, but I do." Gunnar directed his icy gaze at Rika. "I still hold to our arrangement. All of it."

"Then defend yourself, Brother," Bjorn said through a clenched jaw. His sword slid from its scabbard with a metallic ring. "Because I am going to kill you."

Rika gasped. Magnus had always taught her that there was no more obscene battle than one between brothers. The fact that she was the cause of the rift added to her horror.

"I'll be happy to meet your challenge." Gunnar lifted

a haughty brow at Bjorn, but didn't move a finger to grasp his sword hilt. "However, before you become an oath-breaker and doom yourself to banishment on earth and *Niflheim* in the next world, perhaps you should be sure she's worth your trouble. First ask the lady now that she's no longer your thrall if she wants to keep her pledge of her own free will."

Bjorn hesitated. When he drew his sword, Rika knew he fully expected to fight his brother. The tension in his limbs proclaimed a deadly intent. Now his oath made him stop, as it should. Oath-breaking was as bad as killing a man by stealth instead of open challenge. A man who would go back on his word was worthless. When Bjorn seemed to weigh the risk and still raised his sword in defiance, Rika gaped in surprise.

"You will not force her to web the Arab," Bjorn said evenly.

"No, indeed I will not. We'll let the skald decide for herself." Gunnar turned to Rika. "It's up to you. Of your own free will, do you wish to marry Abdul-Azziz? I will abide by your decision and know what to do in any case." The surety of Ketil's death if her answer displeased him burned in Gunnar's pale eyes. And if she told Bjorn of the threat, Gunnar would arrange for his own brother to have "an accident" as well.

Bjorn's taut muscles relaxed as he turned to look at her. He'd been prepared to dishonor his oath for her, and she didn't doubt he'd fight his brother. Perhaps he'd kill Gunnar. Her heart surged with hope, then plummeted. Bjorn would be an oath-breaker, an outcast, perhaps even put to death by the Lawspeaker for his breach of fealty. Or perhaps he'd die before her very eyes this night, struck down by his brother's blade.

Rika couldn't speak. She looked at Bjorn, his face earnest and intent, his heart shining in his dark eyes, so hopeful. This was the man she could have loved all her life.

"Rika?" Bjorn's puzzled frown told her he couldn't understand her delay.

Her father was gone and her sweet, simple brother was all she had left. Ketil depended on her. She couldn't purchase her happiness at the cost of his life. She couldn't allow the man she loved to choose dishonor. She straightened to her full height and schooled her face into impassivity. A wall slid down behind her eyes, shutting off her heart from Bjorn's reach.

"Of my own free will, Bjorn, I choose to wed the Arab," she said without the slightest hint of tremor in her voice.

It was the most convincing performance of her life.

Gunnar stepped between them. "Did you really think a woman would be content with someone who just wants to be a dirt farmer?" Gunnar shoved her refusal into Bjorn's teeth. "When you think about it, it's not much of a contest, is it? A man of wealth and power or a man with only a ship to his name? Can't say I blame her."

The point of Bjorn's sword dropped.

"Come, my dear," Gunnar said, extending a hand to Rika. "We shall go announce your impending marriage to the hall and then you can amuse the men with one of your stories."

He turned back to Bjorn, whose massive shoulders drooped like his sword. "Rika shall be sent forth as if she were the honored daughter of the house. And as a demonstration of your renewed fealty to me and to Sogna, little brother, you shall escort her to her new husband." Gunnar congratulated himself on that little bit of cunning. He'd placated his trading partner, crushed a woman who'd spurned him, and rid himself of his increasingly popular brother in one bold stroke.

He snatched up Rika's hand since she'd made no move to take the one he extended to her. He gave her fingers a cruel squeeze as a reminder of her bargain with him for the life of her brother. As he led her back to the *jarlhof,* Gunnar called back over his shoulder to Bjorn. "And see that she arrives in Miklagard unspoiled."

CHAPTER 15

"Can't someone make that infernal child stop wailing?" Astryd demanded, as she settled back on her bedding. "It's bad enough she's a girl. Does she have to be loud as well?"

"She's just got a belly gripe, like as not." Helge scooped up the unhappy babe and patted her back.

The child stopped crying and emitted a small burp.

"There now, lambkin, there my dear," the old midwife crooned as she settled the little one into her tiny bed. "She'll sleep sweet now, I'd expect."

"What am I to do without you?" Astryd peered out from under the milk-white arm she'd draped across her eyes. "Are you really going, Helge?"

"My master is off for Miklagard, he says, so there it is." Secretly, the old woman was eager to get away from Astryd's moaning demands, though the idea of going all the way to Miklagard to escape her seemed a bit extreme. "Torvald wants a last adventure, so he does, and your husband needs a woman-servant to attend the skald to her wedding. Since I always travel with my master, it's a simple matter of untying two knots with one tug, so it is."

"Rika, again. That redheaded witch has been a scourge to me since my brother-in-law dragged her here. So haughty, so superior in her manner, and so damnably lucky." Astryd's face grew red with fury. "Our trading partner in Miklagard is fabulously wealthy. And now, to see that worthless thrall elevated to the status of daughter of the house and sent off in style to become the Arab's new wife—it's just too much to bear, Helge. The injustice of it grates on my nerves worse than that child's high-pitched whine."

The babe jerked in her sleep. Helge held her breath, but Dagmar didn't wake.

"I just wish Gunnar would consider the needs of his wife and child above those of a slave." Astryd pouted. "He's still angry because I birthed him a daughter, I know it. That's just how he is, spiteful and small."

"There now, my lady," Helge soothed. "Don't be troubling yourself. I expect you'll have a son next time."

"I wish I could be so sure."

"There are ways, my lady." Helge breathed a silent thank-you to whichever gods might be listening. This was just the opening she'd hoped for. "Back when I was a girl, there was an old wise woman in the next valley over but one, who always swore that wearing the hammer was bad luck for birthing boys."

"What?" Astryd's hand went to Rika's amber pendant at her throat.

"Oh, ja," Helge said earnestly. "If you want a man-child, you should start wearing an image of the Lady of Asgard, Freya. You know how particular the goddess is toward menfolk. She'd help you have a son, sure enough."

"Why didn't you tell me when you first arrived? There still might've been time." Astryd ripped the leather cord over her head. "Take this thing out of my sight!" she shrieked. "That vile skald. I swear she did this to me on purpose."

Helge slipped the leather strip over her own head and secreted the offending hammer down the front of her tunic for safekeeping.

"When will you leave, Helge?" Astryd sniffled and for just a moment, the old midwife could almost pity her and the helpless child left in her negligent care.

"Since it's a wedding party, we leave with the tide on Friday morn," Helge said. Marriages were always performed on the day of the week honoring Frey and Freya, the twin god and goddess of fertility and increase. Since the Jarl of Sogna had no way of influencing the actual day of Rika's marriage to Abdul-Azziz, Gunnar had decided to get the expedition off on a propitious foot by decreeing the date of their departure.

"But that's tomorrow. I shall be lost without you, Helge," Astryd whined and then her voice hardened into a harsh rasp. "But the sooner the better to be rid of that redheaded whore."

In her tiny bed, little Dagmar flinched at the sharp tone. She woke squirming and launched into a full-blown wail.

CHAPTER 16

The monotonous scrape of stone on steel just outside her door made Rika want to scream.

"Can't the man sharpen his weapon somewhere else?" she hissed, as she paced the small room, hands clamped over her ears.

There was nothing else she could do. Now that she'd been elevated to the status of a free woman and endowed with the distinction of representing Sogna in an advantageous match, Rika no longer had any official duties. She went to fittings for the truly splendid wardrobe Gunnar decreed for her, but other than that, she had nothing to occupy her time.

Bjorn had turned his small room over to her, so she at least enjoyed solitude, but each time she stepped out the door, she nearly tripped over his long legs. Gunnar had charged him with seeing her safely to Miklagard, and Bjorn took his job seriously, even to the point of sleeping lengthwise across her threshold. And if preparations for the trip called him to the *Sea-Snake*, he left young Jorand there in his stead. She couldn't even make a trip to the privy without an escort. In many ways, Rika was more a prisoner now than when she wore the iron collar.

Her gaze fell on the bone flute resting on Bjorn's wooden chest. She picked it up and put it to her lips. A hauntingly sad tune floated from the slender pipe, the exact reflection of her mood. When the last notes died away, she noticed that the rhythmic rasp on the other side of the door was stilled. Was he there even now, listening to the wistful, hollow sound of the flute? Could he hear how she longed for him?

Even though she saw Bjorn every day, it was as if he weren't really there. His face held that same flat emptiness she remembered from the Hordaland raid. A ruthless, dead expression. He was a man who no longer cared what became of himself or anyone else, as long as he did his duty to Sogna. Bjorn had shut down his heart, his body only working from force of habit.

And how was she any different?

The feel of his lips on her body came back to her unbidden and her nipples tightened into hard knots. He'd awakened her to such bewildering need. Even now, she sometimes woke at night, flushed from a vivid dream of his kiss, feeling Bjorn's hand on her, driving her to an aching fury from which there was no release. Every bone in her body yearned for that dark warrior. Why hadn't she given herself to him when she had the chance?

And now, she never would.

She put down the flute and opened her door. As she expected, Bjorn was there. He rasped the sharpening stone over the cutting edge of his sword with a swift, ringing stroke.

He looked up at her, not bothering to disguise the loathing in his dark eyes. "If it isn't the daughter of the house."

He was talking to her, finally. Rika hid her surprise. "I have a request."

"Your wardrobe is finished, the *Sea-Snake* is provisioned, and Gunnar is leaning on his karls as we speak, gathering enough silver to send a dowry for you that would beggar a king," he said baldly. "What more could you possibly need now?"

"I wish to see Ketil." She'd been putting it off, but they sailed with the morning tide. She could avoid telling Ketil no longer. "I need to explain things to my brother."

Bjorn scowled at her darkly as he slid the sword back into his shoulder baldric. "Wish someone would explain things to me," he muttered. Rika suspected that nothing about this turn of events made any sense to him. Surely he knew that she wanted him, cared for him as much as he did her, but she could offer him no reason for her choice. A jarl held the lives of both his thralls and his karls in the palm of his hand. Even Bjorn was guaranteed no safety on account of blood. Gunnar's threats shimmered in the air around her and she held her tongue.

"You do need to talk to Ketil. He asked for you this morning," Bjorn said. "Though explaining things seems to be a little out of your repertoire lately."

His tone might've been scathing, but this was the most he'd said to her since the night of his proposal. She decided to ignore the anger in his voice.

"Can you take me to him?"

"Delivering you where you wish to go is my duty, isn't it?" He motioned her ahead of him. "We'll have to ride. He's at the new fields again. But since I'm taking you all the way to Miklagard, I think I can manage to get you up the mountain."

At the moment, Rika was in favor of anything that would get her out of Bjorn's room. The tiny space smelled of him, undeniably male with a sharp, fresh tang of sea air. There was no ease for her in his room, and even less in his actual presence, but her conversation with Ketil couldn't be delayed.

She followed Bjorn across the exercise yard to the stable where he saddled the two sturdy-chested geldings. He helped her up onto the horse's back, taking care not to let his hand linger on her waist a moment longer than necessary. It seemed to Rika that he jerked back from her as though she were made of red-hot metal fresh from the forge.

They plodded together out of the settlement, up the steep trail to the new fields. When they crested the first rise, Rika pulled back on the reins and swiveled around to look out over the fjord. The water and sky were impossibly blue. The sheer sides of the land cupped the long arm of the sea, snuggling it in a deep green embrace. A stiff breeze rustled over her and Rika inhaled the crisp scent of pine. She sighed.

"What's wrong?" Bjorn asked, nudging his horse back down the trail to stop beside her.

"Nothing," she said. The beauty of Sogna made her chest tighten. "It's just this place. When you first brought me here, I hated it. Now it's hard to think of leaving. With Magnus, I traveled around so much, no place ever felt like home. I don't know why, but this fjord does. I can't believe that once we embark on Friday, I'll never see Sognefjord again. I was just wondering if Miklagard will have charms to compete with it."

"No doubt your new husband's wealth will be charm enough," he said dryly. She flinched at his words. "Don't fret yourself, Rika. The mighty city is a wonderment, never fear. It sits astraddle two great seas with a large wall to keep its people safe from harm. And from raiders like me."

"You've been there, then?" She pressed her heels into the gelding's flank and urged him up the path. It felt so good to be talking with Bjorn again, even if his resentment was still there, roiling under the surface.

"Once, when I was a boy." Bjorn pressed up the trail after her. "Uncle Ornolf took me with him. Made me want to keep traveling forever. It was the best adventure of my life." Rika heard a smile sneak into his voice.

"What was Miklagard like?"

"There's nothing I can compare it to," he said. "The city is so large it would take days to walk all the tangled rabbit warren of streets."

"Oh," Rika said, suddenly feeling very small.

"They don't build with timber as we do. The rich use stone for their magnificent houses. The poor make do with mud-bricks." Rika glanced back at him to see his face flushed with excitement as he remembered. "The market was something. It smelled like perfume and spicy foods and great piles of steaming camel dung all at the same time."

"Ew!" Rika laughed and was heartened when Bjorn laughed with her. "What's a camel?"

"You'll see. Goods from all over the world find their way to the bazaars of Miklagard—silks, spices, tin, silver and gold, gems that sparkle with such fire you'd swear they were alive. Anything can be had for a price. And the people . . ."

"What about them?

"You never saw so many different kinds. Greeks, Arabs, Jews, men from Abyssinia who are black as jet, Mongols. Uncle Ornolf was always after me to stop staring, though I must admit they stared back readily enough. Seems Northmen are considered quite exotic there." He chuckled softly. For a few moments, the fact that he was taking Rika to Miklagard to marry another man seemed to have slipped out of his consciousness.

"You sound excited to be going back," she said.

Reality crashed down on him with more force than

the falling pine. "No," he said soberly. "I could stand not seeing the great city again."

He urged his mount into a lunging scramble past her up the path. The muscles of the gelding's heavy flanks bunched and flattened with the effort.

Rika found Ketil helping to load a long, thick tree trunk onto a sturdy wagon. No doubt Jorand's clever hands would find a keel for a longship or two buried in the heart of the lumber. When Ketil saw her approaching, he wiped the sap off his hands onto his tunic and ambled toward her, a wide smile on his face.

Rika dismounted and ran to meet him, clasping him in an embrace. They sat down in the shade of a broad ash tree and talked happily with each other while Bjorn picked the horses' hooves a discreet distance away.

After awhile, Ketil's face grew serious. "I had a dream last night, Rika."

"What about?" She was almost afraid to ask. Suddenly she remembered Ketil's last dream. The night of Magnus's death Ketil had wakened blubbering that she would be sent away to a big city. "Was it about me going away?"

"No," he said with a shudder. "I was the one who went away." Ketil's voice dropped to a whisper. "To the place with the big trees and the dead things."

Ketil had been so upset eight years ago when they went to Uppsala with Magnus, the old skald had sworn not to go to the sacrifice again, never mind that it was practically mandatory for a devout Odin man.

Ketil's new dream solidified Rika's resolve. It was within her power to thwart this evil prediction. She would make it not be true.

"Ketil, that will not happen. I swear it," she said, sneaking a glance at Bjorn, who busied himself with the horses. She had to make certain she was not overheard. "I made a bargain with the Jarl of Sogna, and he has promised me that you will not go to the sacred trees at Uppsala."

"Really?" His broad face beamed for a moment and then crumpled. "But he has bad eyes, sister. How do you know he'll keep his promise?"

"I'm sure he will, because I'm doing something he wants in exchange," she said solemnly. "I told you I made a bargain with him. In return for his promise, I have to go away. Do you remember your dream about the big city?"

"*Ja,*" he said shakily.

"That's where I have to go."

"And they won't let me come with you," Ketil said flatly. It was not a question.

"No, you'll stay here with Surt." She forced a smile.

"Surt is my friend." He nodded slightly. Then a new thought struck him and he turned to her. "Will you come back?"

Moisture gathered at the corners of her eyes and she drew her lips into a tight line. "I don't know," she said honestly. "I don't think so."

Ketil put his arms around her and squeezed.

"You'll see me again," he said. "I'm sure of it."

She took his face in her palms and kissed him, once on the each of his cheeks and once on the lips. Then she leaned to touch her forehead to his for a moment, her eyes squeezed tightly shut.

"Good-bye Ketil," she whispered. Rika tore herself away from him and fled back to where Bjorn stood holding the horses.

Ketil waved at her and watched till she and Bjorn were out of sight. Her shoulders twitched and he knew she wept.

"Don't cry, Rika," he said softly. "You'll see me again. At the place with the big trees."

CHAPTER 17

Rika's route to her wedding would be a long one. Gunnar envisioned her progress as an ambassadorial entourage and decreed some of their stops. At his order, Bjorn sailed the *Sea-Snake* up the crevice of Viksfjord to Kaupang, the better to display the lavishness of Sogna's jarl to the citizens of that important trading center. Ornolf cast some longing glances at the fine soapstone kettles that would fetch a princely sum in Miklagard, but decided against them on the basis of bulk and weight.

From there, they negotiated the Danish archipelago and stopped at the Dannevirke to pay Gunnar's respects to the Danish King. Rika was welcomed warmly in the mighty fortress of oak and earth, but the joy at court over her coming wedding was tempered by the news of Magnus's death.

Royal courts swirled with gossip like a cesspool with slime. Now Bjorn understood why Rika said Magnus couldn't stay at one for too long. The sibilant voices hummed around him. Rika's demeanor was a bit glum

for a bride, they noted, but everyone knew how devoted she was to her father, so it was easily explained.

And wasn't the Jarl of Sogna a fine man to arrange
so advantageous a match for an orphan like Rika?
Gunnar's generosity was praised even as the court
evaluated his astuteness in the choice of a strong,
wealthy alliance. There was definitely a new power rising in distant Sognefjord.

When he overheard snippets of these conversations,
Bjorn clamped his lips shut. Gunnar's plans were suc-
ceeding. Again. But they'd have to do so without him
from now on. He was bound by his word to take Rika
from Sogna forever, but it would be no breach of his
oath not to return himself.

With the eye of a warrior, Bjorn studied the heavily
fortified ramparts of the Dannevirke. The earthworks
had held back the Frankish kings, and even Charle-
magne himself, from overrunning the Danes. Bjorn
was no stranger to battle and he'd decided the time to
support himself with his own blade was fast at hand.
Now that Rika was going to another man, even the
pull of the land had dimmed. Bjorn couldn't go back to
managing his brother's holdings, even if all he ever
won for himself was a foreign grave.

They were blessed with fine weather, and their next
port of call was Birka, the bustling trading port that
sparkled like polished amber in its inlet setting. A man
could walk from Sogna to Birka if he had to, crossing
the spine of mountains and dropping down into the
southeastern edge of the Norse peninsula, but Bjorn
couldn't imagine why anyone would want to trudge
that weary way when he could sail.

"Thank the gods!" Helge clambered out of the longship. "It's a fine thing to have solid earth beneath these
old feet."

"I don't mind sailing, but I'm glad to be ashore,"
Rika said as she watched Bjorn tying up the *Snake* at

the wharf. The ship would ride quiet there, thanks to a breakwater surrounding the sheltered lagoon.

"Can you attend Rika on her trip to the market?" Helge asked Bjorn. "I've got to find the herbalist and mix up some of Torvald's medicine or he'll be unfit to stand, so he will. Thor knows, you young people don't want to stand around and watch herbs ground."

"I'll go with her," Torvald said, as he frowned at the old woman and tried not to wince when he put weight down on his big toe. Pain from the inflamed joint must have shot up his leg, for he settled back down onto his sea chest. "Maybe Helge is right, just this once. But a bride can't walk unescorted in a strange town. You'll take her?"

Bjorn nodded sullenly.

Jorand helped his captain secure the ship, then sniffed the air appreciatively. The yeasty presence of a nearby ale house wafted over them. "Sailing is thirsty work. I'm tired of curdled milk and stale water."

"You'll have to wait for your ale till the second watch. We've too many goods on board to leave her unguarded," Bjorn said to the younger man. "After I escort the skald around the market, I'll come back and take your shift."

He hardly ever used her name anymore, Rika noticed. It was just another way of keeping the distance between them and she supposed she should be grateful, but it still stung. The way he said "the skald," with no more warmth than he'd use to say "the fur bale" or "the amber," made her feel like cargo. Just one more item for trade goods he was forced to carry. Which was exactly what she was.

Nevertheless, she straightened her spine and strode with her chin up, determined not to let him see that she felt the slight. As they walked up the planked path to the market, she noticed an oval fortress rising from a long bare rock just south of town.

"What's that?" she asked.

"A safe haven. A place to retreat in time of trouble," Bjorn said. "Birka is a rich town, too tempting for some to resist. If a fleet of dragonships heads into the lagoon, the merchants gather their goods and make for the fort." Bjorn met her eyes for the first time in days and she felt herself being pulled into those dark orbs. "You know what men are. When they see something they want, their natural inclination is just to take it."

Her pulse jumped under his steady gaze and she suddenly wished for a safe haven herself. If she let him look at her like that, soon he'd see that he wouldn't have to take her. She'd give herself willingly. If not for her bargain . . .

"There'll be no taking today," she said firmly. "The merchants here look like they expect silver in exchange for their goods, not steel."

"True," he said, nodding at the guards who roamed the streets in this home of a thousand souls. "Even the shopkeepers are armed. Birka has a good market. But if you don't find what you need here, we have a stop yet at Uppsala before we make for the mouth of the Dvina."

"Uppsala?"

"*Ja,* Gunnar was very particular about it," Bjorn said. "He was concerned for your religious sensibilities since you'll be so far from Odin's temple in Miklagard. He was sure you'd want to see the sacred grove once more since you're not likely to see it again."

It wasn't her religion Gunnar was concerned about. He wanted one last chance to remind her of the consequences to her brother if she violated her agreement.

"I was never one for Odin," she said. "I'd be just as pleased not to go to Uppsala."

"As you like," he said flatly. His frown told her he thought her eager to get to Miklagard and her new husband.

They passed a silversmith and watched while he poured the molten metal. Fascinated, Rika noticed that he was making both a hammer pendant and a Christian cross on the same stone mold. She fingered the jewelry that was already finished, letting the silver slide over her palm, cool and smooth.

"You make amulets for both Thor and *Kristr?*" she asked.

"Ja," the craftsman said. "In Birka, people worship Red Thor and the White Christ, as they choose. Old gods or new, we get along." A wry smile crossed the smith's face. "And I sell to both of them. Which can I sell to you?"

"I used to wear a hammer," Rika said, still missing the smooth, glowing amber. "But it seems Thor has deserted me, so I'll wear no god's emblem just now. Good day."

Bjorn looked at her sharply as they walked on down the main street. "Lost your faith, have you?"

"Misplaced it, I think," she said. "The gods of Asgard are all I know. I was weaned on their adventures, but lately they all seem pretty distant."

"When have the gods ever taken much interest in us, anyway, unless it suited their own purpose?" Bjorn said. "None of them have much use for a second son or a fatherless girl."

"You're right," she said. "But I used to feel that, well, that someone was watching out for me, making sure I was safe. I used to believe that someone was Thor."

"I'd think you'd still feel that way." He didn't bother to disguise the bitterness in his voice. "After all, you're about to become the wife of a very wealthy man. What more could you want?"

You! You stupid, stupid man! almost tumbled out of her mouth. Instead, she bit her lip and lengthened her stride. He matched her pace easily. They spoke no more till they rounded the next corner and Rika saw a building whose shape was foreign to her, spiky staves jutting at angles and a tall spire.

"What's that?" she asked.

"It must be the Christ's church," Bjorn said. "They'd just started building it ten years ago when Uncle Ornolf and I came through here. A little priest came from the south and won some converts so they erected this building to celebrate. Even Hergeir, the city prefect, defected to the Christ."

"Do you know much about their religion?" she asked.

"Not much," he said, his eyes taking on a hazy quality. "My first raid was on a monastery. All I know about Christians is that they die easily. They seem to care fiercely about their fancy books and silver chalices, but they aren't willing to kill to keep them. What do you know of their faith?"

"Just what Magnus told me," she said. "He spoke at length with a priest who'd come to convert the Danish king. Magnus said their Christ was a powerful skald. He told stories to teach his followers."

"Hmph," Bjorn said, clearly unimpressed. "Did he also say that their Christ died?"

"Yes, like poor Baldur," she said, thinking of the hapless son of Odin whose death by poison would herald the beginning of *Ragnarok,* the epic battle that signals the end of the world. "But Christians believe their Christ came back to life and lives forever."

"Not even the gods do that." Bjorn's gaze followed the tall spire to the cross on the church's top. "It's strange, isn't it? Those who worship Thor wear his hammer, the symbol of his strength, while the Christians wear a cross, symbol of their God's weakness."

"Magnus said they saw it as strength because it meant their forgiveness," she said.

"Forgiveness?" Bjorn scoffed. "A man has to bear

the weight of his own actions, good or bad. Only a weakling expects to be forgiven."

"Yet I seem to remember you asking me to forgive you," she said. "For Magnus."

Bjorn hung his head. "When it comes to you, I am weak," he admitted. "And I remember you telling me you would never forgive me."

She looked up at Bjorn. Many times since her father's death, she'd heard his voice in her head, admonishing, prompting, gently laughing, but now there was only silence. What would Magnus want her to do, she wondered. She could only follow her feelings. This was something she needed to do, both for Bjorn and for herself.

"I can only tell you now that I was wrong. From my heart, Bjorn, I want to forgive you." She reached out and touched his arm, his skin warm under her palm. His tight muscles relaxed as she felt some of the tension drain out of him. "But can you forgive me?"

"What do you mean?" He covered her hand with his own ever so gently, as if just to touch her was a gift.

She barely breathed.

"Can you forgive me for marrying the Arab?"

"I can if you repent of it now," Bjorn said urgently. "Are you turning to the White Christ with all your talk of forgiving? Christians are as full of repentance as they are forgiveness, aren't they? If you change your mind about this marriage you've agreed to, then the religion is beginning to have real appeal for me."

"No, I'm not converting," she said, sadness crackling her voice. No matter what, she couldn't risk both Bjorn and Ketil coming to harm for her sake. His warmth stole up her arm and almost made her knees buckle. It had been a mistake to touch him. She tugged her hand away gently. "And I can't repent of my agreement with Gunnar. But I do still want your forgiveness."

They stood frozen on the square before the Christ's church, merchants and shoppers bustling around them. Bjorn couldn't believe she would make such a request.

She was asking for the impossible. How could he forgive her for ripping his heart from his chest and stomping on it? Her sea-green eyes held a beseeching look of such intensity, he had to look away.

"You shall have to remain wanting," he finally said.

CHAPTER 18

In accordance with Rika's wishes, they didn't sail to Uppsala after all, but made straight for the mouth of the Dvina at the far corner of the Baltic Sea. Ornolf had left his light riverboat there in the care of a local tribe of Slavs. The cargo from the *Sea-Snake* was off-loaded and repacked for the smaller vessel.

The *Valkyrie* was a trim, high-riding craft, perfect for navigating shallow waterways and built to be hoisted onto a wagon for portage. A square sail could be run up when the wind was favorable and there were four oar ports for when it was not. It was small enough to be manageable with just four men, yet roomy enough to accommodate their cargo and the two women in comfort. Ornolf's pride in the *Valkyrie* was evident each time he laid a large-knuckled hand on the vessel.

Bjorn stood looking his last at the *Sea-Snake*. The bulk of his crew returning to Sogna bent to the oars and pulled her away from shore. Two dozen backs bent and flexed in rhythm. When they were out far enough, they shipped the oars and rigged the mast. A fair wind billowed her sail and she lifted, surging into the waves like a sleek porpoise. Bjorn followed the *Sea-Snake*'s progress with his eyes. He didn't think he'd ever see her again.

"Bjorn?" Rika stood beside him.

"What? Are we not speeding to your bridegroom fast enough for your taste?" he said, not tearing his eyes away from his receding ship.

"No, it's not that." Her tone flared briefly at his surliness, then softened. "I just wondered what was wrong. You look so . . . Are you well?"

"I'm fine," he said curtly. "Anything else?"

"I was also wondering about that." She pointed to a tall rune stone propped on the bluff overlooking the mouth of the river.

"A memorial of some kind," Bjorn said. "I can't read runes, so I've no idea what it says."

"But I can," she said, smiling. "There's just one word in the inscription that has me puzzled."

Bjorn sighed as he glanced once more at the *Sea-Snake* bounding out of his life, then turned back to gaze up at the stone *stele*. He'd always been inquisitive about rune stones, but since he couldn't decipher the characters, the carvings were nothing more to him than unusual patterns.

"Let's go see if we can solve your mystery," he said, knowing that the outline of the *Sea-Snake*, sparkles of spray capturing the sunlight in tiny prisms around her, would be forever burned on his mind.

As Rika and Bjorn climbed the little rise together, she cast sideways glances at him. His face was pale and strained. He looked like a man who expected to be drowned in a bog in the morning, but she didn't want to say so.

At the top of the hill, they came to the stone. A serpent pattern writhed over the rock. Along the Snake's body, runic letters were carved in slashing strokes.

Rika wrinkled her forehead as she concentrated on the lettering.

"What does it say?" Bjorn asked.

She touched the words as she voiced them. "Farbjorn and Edmundr set up this stone for their brother, Roald. He fared like a man after gold. Roald went far into Aeifor and so gave food to the eagles." Her fingertips lingered on a group of slashes. "What does *Aeifor* mean?"

"Always fierce," Bjorn said.

"Roald went far into always fierce? That doesn't make any sense."

"It does if you've been down the D'nieper," he said, the corners of his mouth tugging downward. "The Dvina is a pretty tame river, easy currents and shallow banks. We'll make good time till we come to the headwaters and have to portage. After we travel overland to Kiev, we start down the D'nieper. And that river is another thing entirely."

"How do you mean?"

"There are five cataracts between Kiev and the Black Sea. And the largest one is Aeifor." Bjorn shook his head. "More white water than I've ever seen and rapids that end in a fall five times higher than a man's head. If this Roald went into it, I think he did not come out."

Rika was silent. She had not considered until that moment that in saving her brother's life, she would be endangering others. "Is there no other way to Miklagard?"

"There is a western route. We could sail south of the Isle of the Angles, past the Frankish lands, around the home of the Moors and through the inland sea, but that would take much longer," Bjorn said, folding his arms across his chest. "And I'm sure you're in a hurry to meet your new husband."

She narrowed her eyes at him. She dreaded what

awaited her in Miklagard so much, she hadn't even allowed herself to think about the Arab. Even though Bjorn was behaving like a surly jailer, she was in no hurry to have him dump her into her new husband's harem. "Whichever route is safest would be my choice."

"There are hazards either way," Bjorn said. "A long ocean voyage has perils to equal Aeifor, and without the option of porting around them. You know I don't swim, so there's no chance of me running rapids anytime soon. Not when there are portage routes established all down the river. Don't worry, skald. I'll see you safe to your wedding. I promise."

How she wished he would say her name. When he called her by her title it was as though she had ceased to exist for him. Perhaps that was his point.

He reached out a finger and traced some of the runic lettering. " 'Wealth dies, kinsmen die. Cattle die and wheat too. But this thing never dies: word fame! Word fame never dies for he who achieves it well,' " Bjorn quoted the old proverb. "Long after you and I are dust, people will know of this Roald's journey into Aeifor. It's recorded here forever as a testament to him. To have a man's deeds remembered after him is the best he can hope for. It must be a grand thing to understand the mystery of the runes."

"I could teach you," she said.

He drew back his hand quickly. "I care not for magic." While it was not unusual for women to seek power through the dark arts, men who dabbled in *seid* craft were deemed effeminate and suspicious.

"It is no magic," she said. "It's just a craft, a tool if you like, for capturing words and freezing them in stone or wood. It's easy."

She slid close and reached for his hand, guiding him to run his forefinger through the grooves of the first rune. "The symbols are called the *futhark*, after the first few letters of the alphabet. This is the first symbol."

Together they traced the first letter of the name Farbjorn. She tried not to enjoy the feel of his hand under hers, warm and strong, but it was a losing battle. Rika was intensely aware of every detail of this man, down to the crisp dark hairs on the back of his hand. His flesh called to hers, blood to blood and bone to bone.

"It represents the *f-f-f* sound," she blew air over her teeth and lips, trying to ignore the way her insides tumbled about. "But it can also mean cattle or wealth. Each symbol has a double meaning."

"A double meaning?" He raised a brow at her and she suddenly realized that her breasts were pressed against his side. When she started to pull away, Bjorn turned to her, capturing her hand between his. "It sounds like a lot to learn."

"Perhaps it is," she said. His dark eyes dared her to look into them and she made the mistake of doing so. Swirling in those black depths was a passion, a turbulent fire, she'd only seen hints of before. She looked away feeling as if he'd scorched her. "But you said it's a long way to Miklagard and learning something new might help the time pass."

"*Ja*, it's always good to learn." Bjorn leaned a hand on the *stele*, pinning Rika between his body and the standing stone, close but not touching her. Still, a current of longing rippled between them, her skin fully charged. "And what can I teach you in exchange?"

His mouth was so close. All she need do was turn her head and he'd be on her. She closed her eyes tightly and a vision of their mouths on each other, probing, demanding, burst into her mind. Then she saw their bodies strained against each other, writhing hot and slippery, in a primal, rhythmic dance of lust. Her eyelids flew open and she looked up at Bjorn. He'd almost been able to send her an image that night in his room. Was he doing it now? Or was the vision a product of her own desire? She had no way of knowing for sure.

She ducked under his arm and slipped away from him.

"I know," she said, trying to keep her voice from tremoring. "You've been to Miklagard. Did you learn any of their tongue?"

"Some, but it's been a long time," he said. "Ornolf would be better to teach it."

"Maybe he could teach us both when you can't remember anything," she said, feeling suddenly relieved to think about another party in their tutoring sessions. She was sure Bjorn could certainly teach her many things, but none that a maiden on the way to her wedding should know. "After all, I don't want to embarrass Sogna by my ignorance."

"No, by all means, let's remember Sogna," he said flatly.

"It looks like the *Valkyrie* is ready to sail," she said, and started down the bluff to the waiting craft.

Bjorn watched her for a moment, the scent of her hair still in his nostrils. It was longer now, covering her ears and curling over her head like a coppery nimbus. He longed to tangle his fingers in those curls. He wished he could call the moment back, wished he'd kissed her, whether she invited him to or not. This whole trip was going to be excruciating. One long good-bye. He looked back at the standing stone.

"Maybe you were the lucky one, Roald," he said under his breath.

CHAPTER 19

Bjorn was right. The Dvina was a comfortable river. They sped upstream before fair winds, using the *Valkyrie*'s small sail to good effect. It also kept the men—Ornolf, Torvald, Jorand and Bjorn—from wearing themselves out rowing each day.

Occasionally Rika saw scattered bands of grubby, unkempt tribesmen on the riverbank, but when Bjorn and Jorand stood in the swaying boat with arrows nocked on the string, the natives melted back into the thick woods. Previous skirmishes with Northmen, who topped the locals by a head, proved a powerful deterrent to attack, even of so small a group.

By night, they pulled the *Valkyrie* ashore and camped alongside the gently rolling river. Around their fire, Rika taught Bjorn to carve runes on smooth pieces of wood. He showed himself to be a fast learner and she frequently found evidence of his practice on small scraps of kindling before she tossed them into the fire. He carved the names of each member of the group, then worked on the symbols to form nautical terms.

Bjorn's memory of the languages he'd heard when he was in Miklagard as a boy proved scattered. So each evening, Uncle Ornolf gave them all rudimentary instruction in Arabic as well as in-depth tutelage in Greek, the tongue of the educated all over the world.

"It is well not to let anyone know you speak their language at first," he warned. "Much information can be gleaned if your lips are closed and your ears are open. I've made many advantageous trades feigning ignorance."

"Enough study for one night," Jorand said, splaying his fingers on his knees. "All this learning is making my head swell."

"Ah, there's not enough between your ears to fill an old woman's thimble and you know it," Bjorn said, cuffing the younger man good-naturedly.

"You're probably right." Jorand grinned at him. "Rika, how about a story? After all these lessons, we've certainly earned one."

"Oh, *ja*," Helge piped up. "That's just what we need, so we do."

"Very well." Rika cast about in her mind for just the right tale. She glanced up at the black sky, where the stars congregated in a gauzy strip across the wide expanse. Just the thing.

"Look at the glittering stones in the sky," Rika said, her voice taking on additional depth and resonance. "And I will tell you the tale of Freya and the fabulous Brisingamen necklace."

Bjorn stretched out his long legs and leaned back against a fallen log. His fingers locked behind his head, the better to gaze upward into the endless night. Rika caught herself watching Bjorn covertly during the day, noticing the easy grace of his movements and the strength in his body. Now, while everyone's attention was diverted skyward, she could drink her fill of him.

"The goddess Freya is the Lady of Asgard, more

beautiful than the sun and so desirable that gods, giants, and men have all sought her favors. Some say she is wild, for Freya takes her pleasure with whomever she will. It is she who grants love to men and women. Unhappy lovers would do well to direct their petitions to her, for the goddess has a sympathetic ear for those who have lost in love," Rika said simply, trying to lay the foundation for the story.

Bjorn's gaze abandoned the night sky and wouldn't leave her face, his look questioning. She forced herself to turn away.

"But for all her lovers, Freya was devoted to the god Odur. It is said that though many enjoyed the delights of her body, only Odur held her heart," Rika said.

Bjorn's snort told her that he didn't think Freya's devotion to Odur was very strong.

"In time, she and Odur married. Freya gave him two daughters and Odur showered her with gold, which, as you know, is the one thing the lady covets greatly. Her life in Asgard was pleasant enough," Rika said as she looked up at the sky to avoid Bjorn's gaze. "But Odur was a traveler and once when he was gone, Freya took to wandering herself."

Rika made the mistake of glancing back at Bjorn across the campfire, the pulsing light on his rugged face. She was beginning to crave him with the hollow-bellied yearning of one who knows only hunger. Her gaze darted away guiltily.

"One day as Freya was walking along the border of Svartaelfheim, she saw four Brising dwarves. They were master craftsmen and had fashioned a necklace of such delicate strength, it was more dazzling than the night sky in its grandeur."

Rika peeked under her lashes at Bjorn to see him looking up again as all the rest were, each seeing Freya's necklace strung in pinpoints of fire against the black sky.

"Freya's heart would not rest until she had the necklace, so she offered them gold, for she had it aplenty, but they would have none of it. The only treasure the dwarves desired was the goddess herself. She must spend one night with each of them and then the necklace would be hers. Even though the dwarves were hideously ugly, such was the power and beauty of the Brisingamen necklace that Freya agreed to their demand. She would bed them all, one night of love apiece."

Rika's voice wove a spell over the group around the little fire, as they imagined the supremely glorious goddess engaged in lascivious acts with beings far beneath her. Only Bjorn tore his gaze from the heavens to watch Rika questioningly.

His soul shone through his dark eyes, pain-filled but with a glimmer that Rika thought might yet be love. When Bjorn looked at her like that, she had difficulty drawing breath. Her insides rioted and she felt warmth between her legs. Was it possible for a man to make love to a woman with only his eyes on her, hot and knowing? Part of her wanted to be as wild as Freya and fly across the campsite at him, begging him to bed her and Loki take the rest of the world.

"And then what happened?" Jorand prompted.

Rika shook herself slightly and refocused on the tale. "After the four nights of dwarvish love, Freya returned with the necklace to her home in fair Asgard to find that Odur had returned," she said, noting Jorand's disappointed frown. He must have been hoping for more salacious details. "Loving the dwarves had meant nothing to Freya, so she felt no need to tell Odur how she came by her new trinket. They were supremely happy together with Odur none the wiser."

"Isn't that just like a woman?" Uncle Ornolf said cynically.

"More like most men, if you ask me." Helge raised a wiry brow at him.

Rika continued with the tale. "But Freya's deception could not be overlooked. Loki, the trickster, is never satisfied that joy should reign either among the gods or here in Midgard amid the realms of men," Rika said. "Loki told Odur the price Freya had paid for her gorgeous new necklace and his heart was enraged. Odur stormed out and left Asgard to roam the wilds of the nine worlds forever."

Love betrayed is love lost. The theme was potent enough not to need any elaboration and Rika waited for her audience to absorb the sorrow of it. She knew the pain of it too well herself already.

Then she continued softly. "Freya still wears the Brisingamen necklace she bought so dearly, for it has great power, but nightly she searches for her lost Odur. As she travels through Midgard, the goddess weeps for her love, leaving golden tears behind her."

"A man might think more of those tears if he believed they were genuine," Bjorn said, looking sideways at her. "Favor that can be bought with baubles, no matter how fine, shows a certain . . . shallowness. Love without faithfulness, love without a life together is no love at all."

Rika's lips tightened into a thin line and she wouldn't meet his eye.

As Bjorn studied her, he wondered whether she was trying to tell him that Gunnar was right. She was marrying the Arab for his wealth. If that were truly the case, he knew he should despise her. But when Bjorn saw her chin tremble, he knew he would always love Rika, however she might shred his heart.

Rika's hand went to her neck, where the little hammer used to reside. "Men who find Freya's tears do value them highly." Her voice quivered. "They have become a glowing substance so prized we even bear some to faraway Miklagard. Freya's tears are what we call amber."

She paused for such a long time, her listeners shifted restlessly.

"The next time you wear amber, remember the woman who made a poor bargain and lost her love in the process," Rika said softly. Bjorn noticed she had said "woman," not "goddess."

"Rika, the time for you to wear amber is now," Torvald said. He drew the little hammer from the pouch at his waist and dangled it before her. "I heard you'd lost this and might want it back."

Astonishment kissed her face and she reached for the necklace, open-mouthed.

"How did you ever . . . ?" She looked at the hammer in wonderment. In the glow of the firelight, the tiny orchid trapped inside winked brightly. It was her necklace, without a doubt.

"I'm glad it pleases you," Torvald said, as he reached around her slender neck to tie the leather cord. "It belongs on the neck of a beautiful woman. It always has."

Bjorn slitted his eyes at the old man. What was he playing at? First Torvald wanted to see her freed, almost to the point of coming to blows with Bjorn, a man less than half his age and in his fighting prime. Now Torvald was giving her presents like a hopeful beau.

"Oh, thank you! How shall I ever repay you?" Rika gushed. When she wrapped her arms around Torvald, Bjorn mentally kicked himself for not thinking to retrieve the necklace from Astryd for her. She might have been embracing him instead of hugging the stuffing out of that old man.

"I thought your faith in Thor had dimmed," Bjorn said flatly.

"This isn't about faith," she said. "This necklace is

my one link to the past, my last remembrance of my father."

"Your father?" Torvald blinked.

"*Ja*, Magnus Silver-Throat," she said. "Perhaps you've heard of him. Magnus always told me I have worn this emblem since I was but a babe."

Bjorn saw a shadow pass over Torvald's face, a stricken expression that faded so quickly he couldn't be sure he hadn't imagined it. His distrust and dislike of the older man was growing by the moment. Bjorn still didn't understand why Torvald had insisted on coming on this long, weary trip. He'd seen well over fifty winters, maybe more than sixty. Occasionally, Torvald was nearly crippled when the painful gout in his foot flared up. He had no business on a trip of this length and they hadn't even reached the most dangerous part of the journey yet. Why would the old man push himself to make the voyage?

When he saw the warmth in Torvald's eyes as he gazed at Rika across the fire, Bjorn was beginning to think he knew why. And he didn't like it one bit.

CHAPTER 20

They reached the headwaters of the Dvina sooner than Rika would've liked. She enjoyed the relaxed travel up the placid waterway and the easy camaraderie of the party. But sometimes the tension between her and Bjorn was so thick, she was sure the others must feel it vibrating in the air around them. If they did, they gave no sign, and each night Bjorn's eyes sent Rika silent messages of desire.

Part of her knew it was foolish to extend the torment for them both. Yet another part of her was grateful for just one more day to spend in his company, to watch his muscles working as he bent to the oar, to hear his laugh when Jorand said something ridiculous, and to feel him caressing her with his gaze across the fire each night. She was storing moments, saving snippets of time forever in her memory, like her orchid trapped in amber. They were stolen treasures to be savored the rest of her life once the harem doors slammed shut on her.

The great city with its tall walls loomed larger in her imagination, but she was not there yet. She would wring every drop of joy and exquisite torment she could from each day.

Ornolf had trade agreements with a Slavic tribe at the river's end. In exchange for hack silver, they furnished a large wagon with a bowed box, designed to haul the *Valkyrie* overland to the town of Kiev. The price for this service was meticulously weighed out in silver and Ornolf snapped one of the coins with strange Arabic symbols in two to make the scales finally balance.

Each morning when Bjorn lifted Rika onto her horse for the day's travel, he slipped her a small piece of wood with his rune carvings from the previous night. Some days, he'd worked on the names of the members of the party, straining to make the sounds appear in proper sequence. Rika noticed that he had yet to get Torvald's name right. Other times he used the individual letters in their symbolic meanings to send a nonsense message that made her laugh. One morning he surprised her with a horn comb he'd carved, on which he'd inscribed "Rika owns this comb."

There was never much opportunity for them to have a private conversation, but the runes had become their method of secret communication. Since no one else knew runic writing, it was almost as if they had their own code. This morning when he pressed the wood into her hand, his palm lingered on hers a moment longer than propriety allowed for another man's bride, but she didn't pull away.

As they began their day's journey, Helge and Torvald rode in the wagon with Uncle Ornolf. She, Bjorn and Jorand rode sturdy horses. When the rest of the party was engaged in conversation, she sneaked a glance at the wood Bjorn had given her.

"Rika owns this heart," the inscription proclaimed.

Tears gathered at the corners of her eyes. A leaden weight settled on her chest. Why was she doing this to herself? She couldn't have his heart, didn't want it, she told herself angrily. His kisses came back to her against her will, and she remembered his mouth on hers, full of wanting and hers on his, accepting and demanding in return. She swayed in the saddle.

There was no chance for them. None. Gunnar and his threats against Ketil and Bjorn ensured that. So why was she playing the coquette, making eyes at him, laughing with him, torturing them both with what could never be?

Because it was all they would ever have, she answered herself. Because she was greedy for him and no matter the pain she caused him later, she had to have what little she could of him now.

When she squeezed her eyes shut to stop the tears, she could almost see Magnus's reproving face, mouth tight, one wiry brow arched. The old skald hadn't raised her to be cruel.

That would end right now. A cut from a sharp blade healed quickest. Bjorn might not see it as kind now, but later, when he forgot her in the arms of another woman, he would recognize the wisdom of her action.

Rika squared her sagging shoulders and dropped the rune stick so Bjorn could see her do it. When she heard it crack under the wagon wheel behind her, she didn't even flinch.

CHAPTER 21

The wedding party spent little time in Kiev, even though it was the only sizeable town they'd encountered for weeks. Though the settlement was laid out in the typical Norse plan with half-timbered paths winding through the narrow lanes, and peopled with tall, fair-haired folk, Rika still felt out of her element.

The trappings of home in this faraway place made her feel all the more homesick for the northlands. The town wasn't perched on the edge of the sea or in the sheltered inlet of a fjord. Instead, Kiev signaled the start of their journey down the river D'nieper, whose reputation for ferocity Rika was beginning to dread.

There was no space in the *Valkyrie* for additional trade goods, so Ornolf wasn't of a mind to linger in the market. And Bjorn had pushed the group to exhaustion each day, driving them to cover more *landmiiller* than Rika would've thought possible. He hadn't spoken to her or met her eyes since she purposefully dropped his last runic message to her. She supposed she should be grateful.

Rika climbed into the *Valkyrie* after Helge.

"I never thought I'd say this, but I'm happy to be getting back into the boat, so I am," the old midwife announced. "My bony backside has had enough of being jolted along in that wagon. The *Valkyrie* glides along pretty smooth by comparison."

Rika wondered whether the old woman was reconsidering that comment when they pulled back to shore later, just above the first cataract. It was called Essoupi, meaning "Do not sleep." The roar of water made normal conversation impossible. Rika couldn't imagine anyone would actually be able to fall asleep.

The D'nieper narrowed at that point and was clogged with mossy boulders standing midstream like little islands that sent the waters surging and leaping over them. Trying to shoot over the rapids in the center of the river would tear out the bottom of even so light a craft as the *Valkyrie,* reducing the boat to shattered splinters.

But if all the cargo was off-loaded first, there was a narrow lane along the high bank where the men could half-float, half-drag the boat without having to portage away from the river. After they passed through the white water, the men would hike back along the riverside path to retrieve the trade goods and carry them down to the waiting *Valkyrie.*

Once Rika and Helge were safely ashore with the barrels and fur bales stacked around them, the men stripped and waded back into the water around the vessel.

"Tie yourself onto the boat," Ornolf shouted. "That way if you slip, you won't be swept away. The rest of us can hold her till you find your feet. Feel your way over the rocks and we'll walk her down nice and slow."

Bjorn positioned himself at the far down-river side of the craft with Jorand on the bank side. Ornolf and Torvald took stations at each side of the stern. Rika watched as Bjorn strained, his back and arm muscles quivering with effort, to hold the *Valkyrie* from a headlong plunge down the river. He eased the boat along, waist deep in water, feeling his way over the slippery bottom of the D'nieper.

If the situation had been less precarious, Rika would've enjoyed the way Bjorn's muscles rippled and flexed under his skin. As it was, the slightest misstep could send them all careening down the rapids to disaster and Rika caught herself holding her breath.

A high-pitched wail made Rika turn her gaze upstream. A crudely woven basket bobbed in the center of the D'nieper, shooting toward the rapids. A tiny hand shot up from the wickerwork, grasping skyward.

"Oh, gods!" Her heart lurched. "There's a child in there!" Without hesitation, Rika jumped into the D'nieper and flailed toward the disappearing basket. The swift current dragged at her and pulled her off her feet, scraping her along the bottom of the river toward the men and the boat.

She heard Helge's scream and realized she was surging toward them. As the river whipped her past, Torvald let go of the *Valkyrie* and grabbed Rika around the waist. She felt him struggle to keep his footing, stumbling out of balance with her in his arms. She was sure the other three men holding the boat immediately felt the loss.

"What are you doing?" Torvald bellowed at her, shouting to be heard above the din of the water.

"There's a baby," she gasped, realizing someone from the Pecheneg settlement upstream must have sent the babe to its death.

"Let it go," he yelled and hoisted Rika up onto the bank.

"Torvald!" Bjorn's voice traveled over the roar of the water to them. "We can't hold her much longer."

The old man slogged back to his position, the deepening wrinkles across his forehead betraying the agony his gouty foot was sending to him. He reached the *Valkyrie* and pulled back on her with all his might, groaning with effort. Then Torvald tossed a look over his shoulder at Rika. She winced at the anger in his hard gray eyes.

What she'd just done had endangered them all, but it was for a babe. Someone had just abandoned a helpless child to a terrifying and violent death. Why? There could never be an answer that made sense to her. The old hurt inside her smarted afresh. Tears streamed down her cheeks, both for the dead child and for herself.

"There, little elf," Helge squatted beside her and put her thin arms around Rika's shaking shoulders. "My master's not really mad at you."

"I'm not crying about that," Rika said, wiping her nose on her wet sleeve. "It was a child, Helge." She could hear Bjorn bellowing orders to the others as they worked their way downstream. Now that there were four men on the corners of the *Valkyrie,* they negotiated the rapids safely, if slowly. She sniffed as she remembered the coldness in Torvald's voice when he yelled at her. "But he certainly sounded angry."

"Menfolk are like that sometimes," Helge said, as they both stood and followed the men's progress along the footpath overlooking the rapids. "They don't want us women to know they're scared, so they hide behind anger. Torvald was just afraid for you."

"He should have been afraid for that poor child," Rika said, hoping she wouldn't encounter a small corpse farther down the D'nieper where the water ran slower.

"I know how you feel," Helge agreed. "No one loves the feel of new babe in her arms more than I do, but think on it for a moment. We've got no nurse for a child, no way to feed it. And even if we did manage to save it, you couldn't very well greet your new husband with some other man's babe. I don't care how odd the folk in Miklagard are bound to be, I suspect some things are the same the world over."

"*Ja,*" Rika said sadly. "Some things are the same." No doubt unwanted babies were exposed to the elements by people of every race and tribe.

When the men finally pushed through Essoupi, Rika and Helge were waiting to help them tie up the boat. Bjorn hauled the *Valkyrie*'s prow onto the bank and secured her. Then for the first time in days, he looked directly at Rika.

"How did you fall in?" He raised his voice to be heard over the cataract. "Are you hurt?"

"No. And I didn't fall," she said. "I jumped."

"Why?"

"There was a basket with . . ." Somehow, she couldn't bring herself to finish the sentence. The child was lost, dashed to bits on the cold granite of Essoupi.

"Someone sent an unwanted babe down the rapids in a basket, and she tried to catch it before it went," Torvald answered for her gruffly. "All she did was endanger herself."

And us hung unspoken in the air.

An unwanted babe. Rika could see from his expression that Bjorn immediately understood how this dredged up the ache of her own abandonment.

"You're sure you're not hurt?" he asked her.

"Just a scrape or two, nothing serious." She could feel a warm trickle of blood snaking its way down her shin from a banged knee. It was nothing compared to the heaviness in her heart.

That evening around their fire, the mood of the party was subdued. When Jorand asked for a story, Rika declined, saying she just wasn't up to it.

"Don't fret yourself about the child," Bjorn said

softly. "Its end was quick and there was naught to be done about it. No doubt the Norns decreed it so."

"No," she said vehemently. "I don't believe that. Not any more. No trio of fate weavers in Asgard decided that poor babe's end. Its parents did. They are to blame for its death."

"There are a hundred reasons that lead someone to expose a child," Torvald said flatly. "Poverty, shame, grief—"

"None of it the child's fault," she interrupted.

"No, of course not," the old man said. "But whatever the reason, at the time, it seems the only sensible course of action. And the decision is almost always made in haste, in desperation, in the kind of madness only sorrow brings."

An image of the child's uplifted hand burned across her eyes. "It was so small, so helpless," she said.

"I know you feel for the child, but your pity is misplaced," Torvald said. "The child feels no more pain, but for the parents, the pain is just beginning."

"They deserve to feel pain—if they are even capable of it." Rika narrowed her eyes to slits. "How could you know what they feel?"

Torvald's sigh seemed to come from clear down to his toes. "'Tis a knowledge bought with bitter experience."

No one stirred around the fire. Only the rustle and click of insects and the hunting call of an owl interrupted the silence.

Torvald dragged a hand over his face and a faraway look filled his eyes. He seemed to have forgotten the group's presence, lost in his own private Hel. When he continued to speak it was barely a murmur. "A small ghost will dog them each day. Each passing year the questions come. Would she be walking now? How tall would she have been? Would she look like her mother or be cursed to look like me?" Torvald's eyes fogged over as he seemed to see a phantom child at different stages of growth. "What would it have been like to bear her on my shoulders, to feel her chubby arms around my neck?"

A small prickle found its way up Rika's spine as the old man looked at her searchingly.

"At least I finally know the answer to some of the questions," Torvald said. "Rika, you are the image of your mother."

CHAPTER 22

"What?" Rika couldn't believe what she was hearing. It was unthinkable.

"I said you look just like your mother." Torvald didn't blink an eyelash. "My wife, Gudrid. You've definitely got her way about you. If Helge hadn't warned me, I might've thought I was seeing Gudrid's ghost that first night I spied you in the great hall of the *jarlhof*."

Rika's eyes widened.

"She was a fair, saucy redhead just like you." Torvald's voice was firm. "I didn't need any other confirmation than my own eyes, but Helge knew it was you because of that little hammer. She saw it on Lady Astryd and asked how she came by it."

Rika's hand went instinctively to her throat.

"It belonged to my Gudrid. I gave it to her at our wedding," Torvald said as matter-of-factly as if he were discussing the weather or which crops to plant. "A simple little thing. In truth, not worth much, but in all her life, she never took it off."

"I put it around your neck myself, so I did, on the day you were born," Helge added. "I couldn't bear to see you leave us empty-handed, Little Elf, so I filched it for you."

"How can you just sit there and tell me this?" Rika asked, shocked.

"Because it's the truth," Torvald said. "I don't say it to be cruel. I'm not proud of what I did, and I have regretted it every day since."

"Your mother died birthing you, you see." Helge patted Rika on the forearm, trying to ease the sting. "And they loved each other dearly, your mother and the master. When she died, he went fair wild with grief."

"That's no excuse," Torvald said flatly. "Even then I knew it was wrong. And I bore the guilt of it every day. Then when I saw you at the *jarlhof*, I knew the gods had blessed me with a second chance."

"Just what is it you think you have a second chance at?" Rika asked.

"To know you," Torvald said. "To care for you as a father should."

"It would seem you've had little practice at caring," Rika fired at him.

"True enough," he said. When he met her livid green eyes, he realized that this conversation was not going as he'd hoped.

Perhaps he should have waited to tell her who he was, but her anger at the baby's abandonment that morning was only exceeded by his terror when he saw her flailing in the swirling waters of the D'nieper. If he hadn't managed to snatch her when he did, he might have lost her again and it would have been his own fault both times. Right after he tossed her to the safety of the bank, Torvald had decided to tell her the truth the next chance he got.

"After you were gone, there was little left in my life to care about," Torvald said. "For good or ill, my blood flows through your veins. I am your father, whether you will it or no, and it's finally time for me to start acting like it. I only hope I am not too late for your forgiveness."

No one spoke. Ornolf and Jorand hung on every word batted back and forth. The drama being played out before them was more potent than any story in Rika's repertoire. Only Bjorn felt the pain and anger emanating from her in scalding waves.

"Blood is all I ever received from you, and I'll never ask for more. A man saved me from the water where you sent me to die." Her voice was brittle as ice. "His name was Magnus Silver-Throat. He was a good man, a brave and gentle man, with a heart big enough to shelter a helpless babe and not think himself anything extraordinary. But Magnus *was* extraordinary. He was my father, the father of my heart, the only father I'll ever have."

She stood and stalked out of the circle of light to stand by the beached *Valkyrie*. Bjorn would have followed her, but he was sure she'd push him away as vehemently as she just shoved Torvald.

There was pain in Torvald's eyes as the old man watched her go. Suddenly it was clear to Bjorn why the old man had tried to buy Rika's freedom, even to sacrifice his land holdings for her. It was the reason behind Torvald's irrational decision to make this trip. He loved Rika as hopelessly as Bjorn did.

Bjorn flashed Torvald a look of understanding. Torvald had abandoned her as a father. Bjorn had robbed her of Magnus, the only father she'd had. The old man met his gaze. They were bonded somehow in that moment by their love for a woman they had each hurt deeply in their own way.

And she'd never let either of them forget it.

CHAPTER 23

They passed safely through two more cataracts the same size and ferocity as Essoupi, using the same technique of maneuvering the boat over the rocks by hand. The *Valkyrie* rode swiftly between the barrages, drawn inexorably by the rapidly falling water as it surged toward the Black Sea.

A distant thunder began to rumble.

"It's going to rain," Rika said.

"No." Uncle Ornolf shook his head. "That's Aeifor you're hearing. We're still a good way off, but the cataract is sporting enough to warn of its coming."

"It must be enormous," she said.

"*Ja,* that it is," Ornolf agreed, as he leaned on the steering oar to send the *Valkyrie* closer to the right bank of the river. "Bjorn, keep an eye out for that big hawthorn. The spot to put in and begin the portage is coming up soon. If we miss it, the river won't give us a second chance."

Bjorn nodded from the prow.

"Aeifor is so big, we must haul the ship overland for several *miiller,*" Ornolf explained. "It roars through a canyon, swirling and boiling, and ends in a fall of some thirty feet."

Bjorn leaned out over the *Valkyrie*'s long neck, making hand signals back to his uncle when he saw a shallow place to be avoided. "How were the Pechenegs behaving when you came through last?" he called back to Ornolf.

"Not as cordial as we might wish," his uncle replied.

Bjorn turned to Rika. "We must be wary. The Pechenegs are poor fighters in a clinch, but they're demons with a bow."

Rika nodded mutely as guilt hammered her. Yet another danger her choice forced upon them. "But don't you trade with the Pechenegs?" she asked Ornolf. "Won't they provide a wagon like the tribe who helped us for the portage to Kiev?"

"There'll be no wagon this time," he said. "We'll fell some saplings and push the *Valkyrie* overland on a movable skid road of pine. It takes longer than a wagon, but we'll manage it."

"Isn't that the start of the portage?" Bjorn pointed toward a slight opening in the thick forest in the shade of a broad hawthorn.

"*Ja,*" Ornolf said. "You've got sharp eyes. It's been ten winters at least since you made this trip with me. I'm glad you still remember the landmarks."

Ornolf turned the *Valkyrie*'s head toward the bank and beached her.

"Stay close to me then while we're on the march," Bjorn said to Rika.

She nodded mutely.

Ornolf kept watch for hostile tribesmen while Bjorn and Jorand pulled out their axes. They started felling trees to be cut into lengths to skid the hull of the boat across for the portage. Torvald and Helge busied themselves with setting up a temporary camp while preparations for the overland trek were made. Since

Rika's scathing rejection, Torvald had not attempted to draw her out in conversation or trouble her in any way. She sometimes felt he was watching her, but she never caught him at it directly.

Rika was drawn a short distance downriver, near where Bjorn hacked rhythmically into a ramrod straight pine. She wanted to look over the edge of Aeifor. She'd heard so much about this fierce cataract, she had to see it. The first glance snatched her breath away.

The pounding water grinding away at rock roared in her ears and mist rose around her like dragon's breath. Her skin was coated with the dizzying spray and pebbled with cold. The white water plunged downward into a seething cauldron the entire width of the river. The cataract seemed to go on forever, its fury not abated as it rounded a bend. Ornolf had told her that the river disappeared into a stretch where the banks rose on each side to form a narrow canyon for the roiling water to cascade through.

The restless energy tugged at her and Rika leaned closer to the edge. Thousands of kegs of water poured into the barrage in a never-ending dance of frenetic insanity.

She remembered the standing rune stone she and Bjorn had read at the mouth of the Dvina and spared a moment to think of the lost brother memorialized there. "Roald went far into Aeifor and so gave food to the eagles." To go far into Aeifor would be a journey to the next world, indeed.

The hypnotic pull of water drew her closer and Rika watched individual droplets leap over the rocks always different, but always in the same pattern. She began to notice hollow indentations in the granite, where the river had pummeled the stone into grudging submission.

Not even stone lasted forever. Eventually, she knew

the rocky bones of the Middle Earth would wear out
and be destroyed in fire. In Rika's cosmos, nothing was
eternal, neither her world nor her gods. The realiza-
tion made her feel suddenly very sad and very small.

The short span of seasons allotted to her and the
problems of her life were both fleeting, she realized.
Her hopeless feelings for Bjorn, her sacrifice for her
brother's life, a thousand winters from now, none of it
would matter. All she had was this one life, this one
moment. What was she doing with it?

She turned her back on Aeifor to look at Bjorn. He'd
stripped to the waist the better to free his arms to
swing the heavy double-bladed ax. His hair was bound
back out of his eyes. A look of dogged concentration
was etched on his rugged face and she knew in that
moment that she loved him. Loved him with every
fiber of her being, with every breath in her body, with
every drop of blood coursing through her veins.

And she knew just as certainly if she died without letting this man love her, she might as well die right now.

Maybe it didn't matter that tomorrow or next week
or next month they'd reach the end of this journey and
be parted. A Pecheneg arrow could find either of them
at any moment. Life was nothing but a series of good-
byes anyway. No one was promised tomorrow. But
they did have now.

Even though Bjorn was a hunter, he still had the same
instinct that tells a wild stag there are eyes on him. He
stopped the ax in mid-swing and swiveled around to
find the intent gaze that had sent a tingle to the base of
his skull. He expected a Pecheneg warrior looking
down a long arrow at him, but found Rika instead.

Something about her softly parted mouth was different. Her eyes were warm and hazy, the deep color of
tall summer grass, instead of their usual icy green. He
saw her lips move. He couldn't hear her over the riot

of Aeifor, but he could tell from the shape of her mouth that she'd said his name.

"Rika?" he said uncertainly.

She took a step toward him, but made it no farther. Not only stones were chiseled by the force of the water. The soft bank beneath her feet had been eroded by the constant hammering and all it took to send it plummeting downstream was the slight addition of her weight.

Her eyes and mouth flew open wide in shock and she disappeared into the mists of Aeifor without a sound.

CHAPTER 24

"Rika!" Bjorn bellowed her name and dropped the ax.

Ornolf turned his head just in time to see his nephew race to the edge of the cataract and leap in. Arms windmilling, Bjorn dropped out of sight. Ornolf didn't see the skald anywhere and his heart sank.

He and Torvald chugged to the crumbling spot on the bank just as two bobbing heads, one flame-red and one dark, disappeared around the bend in the river.

"What can we do?" Torvald demanded frantically.

"Nothing." Ornolf's voice was flat. He loved Bjorn like a son. "They're gone. If we're lucky, at the end of the portage we'll recover their bodies, but don't count on it."

He clamped a hand on Torvald's shoulder and led him away from the pull of the cataract before the old man followed his lost daughter into the water out of grief. Without Bjorn, Ornolf needed Torvald more than ever. Even without a bride to deliver, the Jarl of Sogna still had a load of trade goods for Abdul-Azziz that would not wait.

* * *

He was drowning. And this time not in some night phantom, but for a certainty.

The water closed over his head and he writhed against the force that dragged him down. Bjorn's lungs ached. Then his feet touched bottom and he propelled himself upward with a thrust. His head breeched the surface just long enough for him to grab a breath and see Rika fighting the water three arm-lengths away. It might as well be three *miiller*. He had no way to reach her.

The water grasped him and wrestled him down again, dragging him across the rounded stones on the bottom. In the flash of a moment, he looked up through the clear liquid to see the sun sending shimmering spokes through overhanging tree boughs. Then his back was dashed suddenly against a boulder and with the thud of the impact, all the air expelled from his lungs in a rush. Bjorn struggled against the urge to inhale, his depleted lungs screaming at him.

Arms flailing, he clawed his way upward to the world of light and sound. He broke through the frothing surface and dragged in a lungful of oxygen. Air had never tasted so sweet. Why had he never appreciated the simple miracle of breathing?

Rika was closer now, wide-eyed and gasping. Bjorn thrust out his arm, straining toward her. Their fingertips grazed each other, but couldn't latch. A swirling current spun her away from him as an undertow grabbed his ankles and yanked him down again.

The force of the water assured that there were no jagged surfaces to rip at him. The rocks in Aeifor were polished smooth, but that didn't detract from their hardness. No fist in all his fighting life had ever pummeled him like the stones of the D'nieper. He felt his flesh give, a blow to the shoulder here, a punch to his kidneys there, a glancing shot to his head that made his vision tunnel for a heartbeat or two. He had to get away before the river pounded him into raw meat.

He surfaced in time to see a huge boulder looming toward him, and he twisted in the water to meet it with his back. He braced himself for the impact. The rock knocked him across the current and into something soft. It took him a moment to realize that it was Rika. He wrapped both arms around her and held on as they disappeared beneath the water again.

Rika was limp and boneless. Her head lolled back onto his shoulder. With one arm, he pawed the water, clambering back to the surface.

The banks of the D'nieper rose menacingly on both sides and though there were fewer half-submerged boulders for him to avoid, the water ran swifter and deeper than ever. Even if he somehow worked his way to the side, there was no place to crawl out and no way to withstand the drag of the current as it drove them along.

The roaring in his ears grew louder. *The fall.* It was coming and there was no help for it.

He gripped Rika tighter as they neared the precipice. For a frozen moment, they seemed to hang on the edge and he saw the sky, blue and serene above them. Then down, down they fell in a rush, droplets of water airborne around them, crashing into the deep pool at the bottom, feet first.

Water swirled around like milk in a churn. They rolled helplessly, caught in the crushing circular wash that hollowed away the riverbed and, over the lifetimes of thousands of men, formed the fall. It was a pitiless force, not to be gainsaid by rock or tree or the strength of so puny a thing as a man.

Bjorn sank, his sodden clothing and the burden in his arms pulling him down. He recognized the lethargy stealing over him, draining his limbs of strength and his mind of the will to continue the struggle. This was the point in his nightmare where he gave up and let the water take him.

Let go, a whisper urged. *Accept your fate.* It all felt too hauntingly familiar. It was the last respite before the gaping jaws of Jormungand flashed from the darkness to rend him. But this time he wasn't alone. Rika was in the path of the monster as well.

No. If he were bound for Hel, he would go down fighting, not drifting aimlessly in the deep like a piece of flotsam. A rush of determination surged through him. He pushed off the bottom. He scissored his legs and clawed upward with one arm slicing through the water and the other tight around Rika's waist.

When he reached the surface, he dragged the air into his lungs with a rasping gasp. He rolled onto his back, pulling Rika's body on top of his. With her head resting on his chest, he sucked in another lungful of air, the heady draught sending strength back to his arms and legs.

The current took them again, gently this time, but Rika didn't stir. Bjorn saw that they were close to a small island in midstream and he flailed toward it. His feet found the rocky bottom, and he struggled to stand. Cradling Rika in his arms, he staggered to shore.

He laid her down on the long grass. Her skin was white, like the fine alabaster he'd seen in Miklagard long ago, and her eyes were open, but she didn't see. Panting, Bjorn watched her chest, praying for some sign of movement. Nothing.

"Rika, no!" he shouted. His father had revived a drowned comrade once. What had he done? Bjorn tried to remember. He shook her, then pressed hard against her breastbone.

"Breathe," he ordered.

He covered her mouth with his, willing her to rouse

to life. Her chest rose and sank. Then nothing. He filled her lungs with his own breath again, but she was completely still.

"No, not like this." His was voice edged with panic. "No, no, no!" With each chanted denial, he pressed down on her chest. "Come, Rika, cheat the water with me."

He fitted his mouth to hers again, to force his breath into her. Her lips were warm yet, but Bjorn sensed he was losing the battle with the death-dealing Norns.

"No!" He balled his hand into a fist and brought it down hard in the middle of her chest. Her body bucked with the force of the blow.

Then her eyelids fluttered. She closed her eyes and Bjorn could see movement under the thin skin as her eyeballs rolled in their sockets. Rika coughed and made a choking noise. Relief flooding through him, Bjorn turned her onto her side and pounded her back as she expelled the water from her lungs.

"That's it," he coaxed. "Get it all out."

When she finished, she rolled onto her back, gasping.

"Are you hurt anywhere?" he asked with urgency.

"I hurt everywhere," she said, flexing her muscles and showing him that her limbs all still worked.

Bjorn ran his hands over her arms and legs. Then he slid a hand up under her tunic to run his fingertips over her ribcage, feeling the curved bones beneath her smooth skin.

"Nothing broken," he said. "Nothing I can feel, anyway."

She reached up and placed a shaking hand on his chest. "Bjorn, you can't swim."

One side of his mouth turned up. "I think maybe I can now."

"You . . . you went into Aeifor after me."

He stretched out beside her and leaned on an elbow. "I saw my heart going down the river." He reached up and cupped one of her cheeks in his palm. A bruise was already beginning to form on the soft flesh. "My body had to follow."

"Oh," she sighed. Her mouth gaped a little and her chest heaved. "Love me, Bjorn."

"I do," he said, kissing her softly, and then pulling back to brush a strand of hair from her eyes.

"No, I mean *love* me. Right now." She grasped his shoulders with both hands. "I'm begging you."

"Rika, I don't want to hurt you any more," he said.

"I don't care if it hurts." She pulled his head down and kissed him hard. "I want to live, Bjorn. I want to feel, pleasure or pain, I don't care. I want to feel . . . everything."

CHAPTER 25

Rika pressed her mouth to his neck, tasting his skin, salty and warm. Beneath her lips, she felt his pulse quicken. "Please, Bjorn," she begged. "Show me how to love you."

He gathered her in his arms and she melted into his embrace. His hands slid over her skin, not clinically this time, not looking for broken bones, but languidly, trailing his broad fingers over the charged surface, sending shivers over her. She mirrored his movements, lightly tracing circles across his shoulders and then down his chest. She loved the feel of him, hard and hot under her probing fingers.

He found her mouth and poured himself into the kiss while his fingers worked the catches on her brooches. She helped slide off her kyrtle and pull her sodden tunic up, grudgingly releasing his mouth only for the brief time it took to yank the fabric over her head.

Warm and strong, his hands molded themselves to her bare breasts, kneading and caressing. A sunburst of sensation flooded through her, heating her blood, and sending it singing through her veins. Low in her belly, a small throbbing began, just the hint of an ache.

She tugged at his leggings and slid them down his hard thighs. He was ready, but when she touched him, he shuddered and pulled her hand away.

"Not yet." His voice was husky as he struggled for control.

He rolled her down onto the grass. It was cool and soft against her skin, the long blades tickling at her. She raised her arms over her head, as he began an exploration with his mouth, down the side of her neck, grazing her collar bone, and plundering her breasts.

She arched her back, thrusting the swollen tips toward him. Could he feel her surrender? She was his, totally and completely. Whatever he wanted from her was his to take. If he asked for her soul, she'd rip it out and hand it to him without a qualm.

But when he raised his head to meet her eyes, Rika could see that Bjorn was not intent on taking. His dark eyes glowed at her, his smile radiated love. From every pore, from every finger-width of his skin, he wanted to give.

And so he did. Waves of pleasure washed over her under the skilled art of his hands and mouth. He found and teased every tender spot, nuzzling her navel, running his tongue over the soft creases of her knees and elbows, exploring the dip of her back. As adroitly as he ever guided his longship through a storm, he led Rika through troughs and peaks of exquisite torment.

"What do you want me to do?" she asked between gasps when she felt his teeth graze her nipple.

"Time enough for that later," he said hoarsely. "This time is for you." His mouth moved down to the red crescent of curling hair.

She writhed under his lips. Moaned his name.

Clutched at his shoulders to pull him close. Her world spiraled down to disjointed elements. Hot. Slick. Need.

When he finally relented and entered her, she felt like a safe harbor, rejoicing as he slid in, welcoming him home at long last.

He bit his lip, straining to hold back, but she urged him on, and he thrust in, shredding her. Pain exploded in her mind. She didn't care.

He was hot and hard and strong. The wonder of holding him inside her was too much bliss for her to contain and she cried out at the joy of it.

They joined hands, fingers entwined as their bodies moved together, heart on heart, skin on skin. Slowly at first, then with gathering urgency, they surged into each other, like two turbulent rivers meeting at a wild fork, colliding and bruising, straining to become one. The line between pleasure and pain blurred, but all that mattered was the need.

Rika had no memory of cresting Aeifor's falls, but Bjorn felt the eerie sensation of time repeating itself as they hovered at the edge, and then plunged together in spasms of ecstasy. All sense of themselves burned away in a hot blast of fiery rending, their spirits shattered and stripped away.

Only one shining new being shivered between them. The soul they now shared.

CHAPTER 26

The warm sunlight teased Rika's eyes open. Something heavy pinned her to the ground. It took her a moment to realize that it was Bjorn. Before sinking into exhausted oblivion, he'd hooked a leg over her thigh and draped one long arm across her chest. His hand still cradled one of her breasts, claiming it possessively. Her nipple hardened in response to the nearness of his fingers.

Every joint in her body felt loose, as though she'd been stretched out on a Frankish rack. The bruise on her cheek ached and when she put a tentative hand to it, she winced. The tender skin was pulled taut. No doubt when she tried to move, she'd find other hurts, but for now it didn't matter.

She was alive.

And more joyously alive than she'd ever felt in her entire life. Feeling anything at all was a gift beyond measure. She'd not complain over a few aches.

Rika eased herself away from Bjorn, taking care not to wake him. She gingerly walked down to the water's edge and waded into the shallow eddy. The water was deliciously cool. She slid in up to her chin and let the river caress her.

A songbird trilled overhead, his mating call both piercing and sweet. The air around her was alive with the fresh scent of growing greenery.

How was it she'd never really paid attention to her senses before? Too wrapped up in stories and sagas, in the lives of gods and heroes, she supposed, to actually get involved with the real business of living.

No matter what happened now, she'd remember this day till she died. It was the day she came fully to life. *Please, gods, help me to remember it through the troubled times ahead.*

"Ho there, elf-maiden," Bjorn called to her.

She turned lazily in the water to see him sitting up, grinning at her. She wanted to plant a kiss on that devastating dimple in his cheek. Her heart skipped like a spring lamb.

"Are you hungry?" he asked.

Now that he mentioned it, the juices in her stomach began to swirl. *"Ja,"* she said, as she rose dripping from the water, delighting in the sun kissing her bare skin.

She saw his eyes darken as she walked toward him. He wanted her again. A surge of joy flooded through her as she knelt to kiss him. Perhaps he'd show her how to love him this time. Was it possible for her to give him delight with her mouth as he'd given her? An ocean of possibilities, a saga of epic proportions, delicious ways of loving this man surged in her imagination. She felt slightly light-headed. Rika slid her hands over his chest, feather-light across the deep purpling bruise on his shoulder, and then down to rake her nails across his flat belly. She loved the feel of his skin, smooth and warm with the hardened muscles just beneath the surface.

"Food first, my love." He snatched up her hand and pressed a kiss into her palm. "We need to keep up our strength. I'll set a snare, but for now, we'll make do with a bit of foraging."

He stood and stretched, his naked body glorious in the full sun, though Rika noted the mottled bruising on his legs and arms. Large indigo splotches marred one shoulder and the wild ride down Aeifor had branded him across the broad spread of his back. She knew by the ache of her skin that she was similarly marked.

Bjorn took her hand and led her to some nearby bushes, heavy with late berries the birds hadn't yet found. The fruit was drowsily sweet, but occasionally she found one whose tart flavor made her mouth water and her lips pucker. She and Bjorn made a game of finding the best offerings and popping them into each other's mouths.

Bjorn licked the juice from her fingers, sucking each one slowly. Her gut clenched with desire. How could he make such a simple action so erotic?

"You are desperately wicked," she said.

"It's good that you recognize that right from the start," he said, his eyes blazing at her. "That way in the winters to come you won't be shocked at the decadent little bed games I teach you."

The winters to come. If only it were possible. What joy she and this man would give to each other in a lifetime of loving. Part of her yearned to keep silent, to let this idyllic moment linger as long as it could. The part of her that remembered Magnus's strictures about truth-telling knew she could not.

She squared her shoulders and felt the pain in her joints afresh. "In the winters to come," she said evenly, "I will be the wife of Abdul-Azziz."

"That's foolishness." He popped a berry into his mouth, grimacing at its sourness.

"No, it's the truth." Her voice was flat.

The first prickle of unease ruffled his brow. "In case it's escaped your notice, my love, you're not exactly bridal material anymore. You are no longer a maiden, thank the gods."

"There are ways around that." She remembered overhearing the whispered panic of one young bride at the Danish court. An old midwife had advised the young woman insert a small blood-filled bladder just before coming to the bridal bed. Honor was satisfied, and the bridegroom none the wiser.

"I love you, Rika, and I believe you love me." Bjorn's face was pale and drawn. "There has to be a way for us to be together."

"No, Bjorn. I will always love you, but we have no future together." Tears trembled on her lashes. "I gave my word."

"So did I, but by bedding you I've broken my vow of fealty to Gunnar. Once I would've faced a snake pit rather than renege on my oath of loyalty, but that was before I fell under your spell." He looked at her questioningly. "Gunnar told me you'd bewitched me. Was he right?"

"Of course not," she protested. "I practice no *seid* craft."

"Yet our love is so strong it feels like magic," he said. "In truth, I care not, if only you stay with me, Rika. My honor is gone, but it's a small matter now," he said softly.

"I'm sorry," she said. "This is how it must be."

"No, I won't believe you mean to continue with this farce of a marriage to the Arab." Then she saw the light of an idea burst over his features. "We're dead. Ornolf will never suspect we survived Aeifor. I hardly believe it myself. We need never return to the North. No one will ever know differently."

"No, Bjorn." She placed a hand on his forearm. "No matter what, I must go on to Miklagard."

She saw his jaw clench. A small muscle worked beneath the skin of his cheek. When he turned to glare at her, Rika looked into the dark eyes of a stranger, a violent stranger. Somehow in the weeks she'd spent in his company, she'd forgotten that dead expression she'd first seen on his rugged face. It was back. He bared his teeth at her in a predator's smile.

"No one will have you but me."

He crushed her to his chest and savaged her mouth. She whimpered, but he seemed not to notice. His fingers clutched at her, her bruises making his ungentle touch even more savage. She cried out, in pain and shock. Even in the heat of passion he'd never hurt her like that. Never with intent to harm.

She struggled and managed to slip out of his grasp. She bolted away, not sure where she could run, but he overtook her in a few steps. Bjorn stumbled and he pulled her down on top of him. He rolled, pinning her beneath him.

"Bjorn, please," she begged.

He seemed not to hear her. He wedged a knee between her thighs and forced her legs apart.

"No one but me," Bjorn said fiercely. She felt his erection pressed against her inner thigh.

"Don't do this," she cried. If he took her in anger, pounding into her with rage pumping thought him, he'd punish her more thoroughly than all the stones of Aeifor.

"Don't make me hate you," she screamed.

He stopped.

The feral light in his eye dimmed and he saw her clearly. Saw the tears coursing down her bruised cheek. Saw her swollen lips. Worst of all, saw the fear in her eyes.

"Oh, gods, Rika." He pulled back with a shuddering sob. Bjorn rolled off her and turned away. His great shoulders heaved. "Forgive me."

Stiff and sore, she sat up. Rika reached out to touch him, to offer him comfort, but her hand shook so badly, she pulled back. Fear curled uncertainly beside longing. Magnus had warned her of the volatile power of *inn makti murr,* the mighty passion. When she begged Bjorn to love her, she never expected this all-consuming ferocity.

"Why?" he asked. "Why do you kill me by finger-lengths?"

Only her submission to Gunnar's will guaranteed her brother's safety. No one—except possibly Bjorn, who was in danger himself—would credit her against the Jarl of Sogna. *Ja,* the threat to Ketil and Bjorn still weighed on her, but nothing short of the whole truth would serve now.

"If I don't marry the Arab, your brother will send Ketil to Uppsala to be sacrificed in the sacred grove next summer. And Gunnar warned that if I told you of it, he'd arrange 'an accident' for you as well."

Bjorn turned to face her. "That's it?"

"*Ja,* isn't it enough?"

"Why didn't you tell me?" He sat up. "Do you think me so powerless? I can surely steal Ketil away to safety. You of all people should know that I'm a good raider."

"Because I wanted to protect you and Ketil. Even if you knew what Gunnar planned, you couldn't be vigilant forever. He would only need to be lucky once. And even later, when I thought maybe we could defeat Gunnar, it was for your honor's sake that I kept silent."

"For my honor's sake?"

"Oh, love, don't you see?" She ventured a hand on his forearm and he covered it quickly with his, as if he feared she'd pull it away. "If we flee north and take Ketil away, it will be known that you have broken your fealty to Gunnar. You would be outlawed. Banished at best, drowned in a bog at worst. You'd be damned to Niflheim in the next world for oath-breaking and you could never return home in this one."

"I'll never return to Sognefjord anyway," he said bitterly.

"You must," she said. The tip of her nose reddened and a single tear slid over her cheekbone. "For my sake. If I continue to Miklagard, as far as the world knows, your oath is still intact. The only way I can bear marriage to the Arab is if I know that you are there in Sognefjord, caring for the land and the people of the fjord, watching out for Ketil, living in honor, and I hope, with joy."

Her lips twitched uncertainly. Her chin quivered and he saw how she strained to hold back the tears. It was a losing battle. They fell just the same.

He opened his arms to her and was grateful beyond words when she came to them. Gently, he held her and let her cry, knowing as he did that the tears were for both of them.

Damn tomorrow, he thought savagely. For the moment, just holding her was enough.

CHAPTER 27

Bjorn had managed to snare a small coney that morning and its carcass now roasted on an improvised spit over their small flame. Grease drippings hissed in the fire, sending a savory aroma into the air. Days had stretched to more than a week as they waited on the island for Ornolf and the rest of the party to complete the arduous portage around Aeifor.

In that time, the lovers hadn't suffered any lack. Bjorn fished in the shallows with a makeshift spear and snared small, unwary prey. Rika dug for tubers and gathered other edible plants. The river that nearly killed them when they ventured into its angry cataract now provided for them well.

And they had "drunk deeply from the horn of love." Rika smiled, thinking of the poetic euphemism she'd used so often in the telling of a maidensong. She'd never guessed the horn of love was so intoxicating a brew.

By tacit agreement, they spoke no more of the future. They laughed and played in the shallows like children, then loved each other furiously with the guilty desperation of those who know their time is short. Sometimes they joined with heart-stopping tenderness and sometimes they took each other with the ferocity of mating wolves. Tomorrow didn't exist. All that mattered was the eternal now.

The rumble of Aeifor was constant, but Rika had learned to ignore it. When an odd scraping sound bounced off the tall pines around them, her ears pricked to it immediately.

"What is that?" she asked.

"It sounds like the *Valkyrie*'s hull," Bjorn said. "To make this portage, they've had to lay down logs in front of the prow and shove the boat over them." He demonstrated the action, sliding one palm over the other. "When they reach the end of the row of trunks, they go back and drag up the ones they've already hauled the boat over and lay them down in front. It's like building a plank road before you while pulling it up behind you as you go. It's a slow business and they've had to travel at least six *miiller* that way. Shorthanded, too," he added guiltily. "But it sounds like they're near the river now."

"Oh." Her heart turned to stone in her chest. "When will they get here?"

"Soon, my love," he said softly. His face suddenly became grave. "Rika, what if there is a child?"

She blinked. Truly, it was something she hadn't considered. But if a child hadn't been conceived on the island, it wasn't from lack of trying. Still, she had to go forward with the arranged marriage. Nothing Bjorn said convinced her there was any other recourse. It was the only way to ensure the safety of her brother and the man she loved more than breathing. She forced a smile.

"If I bear your child, it will be like a gift to me, Bjorn." For just a moment, she imagined the dark-haired, dark-eyed baby he might have planted inside her. "Is it not often said that the first child can come at any time, while the second always takes nine months?"

"This is no light matter," he said, clasping her hand urgently. "If you bear a pale-skinned child too early, the Arab will send you back to Gunnar without a nose. They are a pitiless people in this regard."

She blanched and then counted the weeks backward in her mind. Fortunately, her cycle had always been regular as the tide. "How long till we reach Miklagard?"

"Another three days down the D'nieper, then ten days to sail across the Black Sea to the Golden Horn," he said. "With fair weather, two weeks, no more."

"If there is a child, I should know by then," she said.

"Then promise me this." Bjorn planted a soft kiss on the inside of her wrist. "If there is a child, you will tell me. The world is bigger than you can imagine. There is yet time for us to run to a corner so remote we will never be found."

"But, my heart, you would be without honor. The North would be barred against you forever." Rika already accepted that she would never see the fjords again, and the knowledge lay like an anchor stone in her belly. She didn't want Bjorn to feel the same rootlessness, the same dull ache. "Sognefjord and your people, the land, everything you care about . . . it would all be lost to you. How can I let you sacrifice your oath for me?"

"I was willing to follow you into the river. Doesn't that give you an idea how little all those things mean to me when weighed against losing you?" The scrape of the *Valkyrie*'s hull was nearer now. Bjorn thought he could hear his uncle's voice bellowing orders.

"And what of my brother?"

What of me? What of us? Bjorn wanted to shake her, wanted to rail at her, but he knew it was a losing argument. She was convinced this was the only path through the snare Gunnar had set for her, and her resolve was set in stone. Whether these few days of loving her were a gift from the gods or a curse to bedevil him for the rest of his life he wasn't sure. But he would take this woman on whatever terms she gave him.

"One way or another, I will not let Ketil go to the trees of Uppsala," he promised. "Now upon our love, Rika, swear to me that you will tell me if there is a babe. It must change everything if you bear a child of mine."

"I swear it," she said. "I will tell you when I know."

"Then with everything I am, I pray that we have made a new little life together." Bjorn kissed her softly. He stood and walked wearily to the side of island closest to the noise of the approaching *Valkyrie*. He cupped his hands around his mouth and shouted to his uncle.

"I pray so too." He heard Rika whisper behind him.

CHAPTER 28

The wonder of finding Rika and Bjorn alive was almost more than the rest of the party could accept. Even though Ornolf saw what looked like his nephew on the island and heard his voice, he suspected at first that he was being visited by the ghosts of Bjorn and the skald. Once the pair swam across the D'nieper to join the travelers, it took a few days for even Jorand not to flinch each time his captain laid a hand on his shoulder, as if he feared that it was Bjorn's shade, not the man himself, come to drag Jorand back to Hel with him.

Torvald was just thankful to see Rika again, whether it was really her or not, even though she still treated him coolly. Only Helge professed not to be surprised.

"After all," the old woman said, "this isn't the first time she's cheated the water."

Helge knew Rika and Bjorn were real enough, but she did notice that her young mistress and the jarl's brother were much changed toward each other since their ride down Aeifor. Unlike the earlier part of the trip when she often caught them making calf's eyes

across the fire, now Rika and Bjorn studiously avoided
each other.

Just as well, the old woman thought. Nothing good
could come of wanting what a body couldn't have.

Bjorn had told Rika about the great city of Miklagard,
but despite his descriptions, nothing prepared her for
her first sight of the capital of the Byzantine Empire.
He'd told her of the Hagia Sophia, Church of Holy
Wisdom, with its amazing dome, but she never really
believed such a marvel could exist.

Until she saw it. The early morning sun glinted on
the curve of white marble. Its gigantic vault hovered
above a circle of arched windows as if it had de-
scended intact from the heavens and didn't deign to go
all the way down to the level of mere men.

Situated on a jutting peninsula overlooking the Sea
of Marmara, the great city flowed over seven hills. It
was a grand echo of Rome, whose glory its founder,
Constantine, sought to replace. The horizon was
spiked with countless spires and pillars, each topped
with a statue. Rika thought it looked like a village of
giants, frozen and mounted on tall columns.

As they turned north from the Bosporus into the
Golden Horn, the deepwater port of Constantinople,
Bjorn came up to stand beside her in the prow of the
Valkyrie. He tried to make the maneuver seem casual,
but his heart pounded just standing beside her. When
she wobbled a bit in the swaying craft, he put a hand
to the small of her back to steady her. She leaned ever
so slightly into his touch.

"Is something wrong?" he asked.

"It's just a bit overwhelming," Rika said, not letting
her gaze linger on him for more than the briefest
flicker. "It's a city of such obvious richness. Doesn't
that mark it for raids?"

"Miklagard is well defended," he said, stretching out

his other arm to gesture toward the high seawall. "On the land side, there's a ring of three walls, each one nearly twenty times higher than a man's head and so thick, no battering ram ever devised could punch through them."

The pale marble buildings glowed with a radiance nearly blinding in the sunlight, and she raised a hand to shade her eyes. They slid past the imperial shipyards, where the emperor's fleet was constantly expanded to the accompaniment of pounding hammers and rasping adzes.

"What about from the sea?" she asked.

"You've seen the seawall. It's heavily guarded, so a pirate would have to think twice before trying to scale it," Bjorn said, drumming his fingers absently on the *Valkyrie*'s pointed prow. The riches of Miklagard called to his Viking blood, singing a tantalizing tune of seduction. How could the city's defenses be breeched? It was a conundrum he'd given some thought already. "The harbor is guarded by a chain that the soldiers pull tight across the opening at the water level. They think they can keep anyone from sneaking in with that."

"What about sneaking out?" she asked, her voice cautiously neutral.

"Even with the chain up, I think I could get us out," he said with certainty. There'd been no opportunity for them to speak privately since rejoining the rest of the party at the base of *Aeifor*. Each day, Bjorn had covertly watched Rika, wondering whether she carried his babe in her flat belly. Hoping. He'd had no chance to ask if she knew yet.

"Do we need to get out?" He willed her to understand the true meaning behind his question.

Rika gazed at him squarely, and for the briefest moment, he saw moisture gather at the corners of her eyes, a slight quiver in her chin, and he knew. There was no child. She blinked hard and looked away from him.

"No," she said softly. "We don't."

As splendid as the city appeared, Rika was totally unprepared for its stench. Down by the harbor, she expected the reek of fish slime, but as they ascended the steep lane into a tangle of back streets, her nostrils were assaulted by the odor of rotting vegetables, trashstrewn doorways and raw sewage percolating from cracks in the terra-cotta pipes that carried most of the refuse out to the sea. The crowded tenements bulged with shabby occupants.

As they made their way upward, the character of the narrow lanes changed. No garbage littered their pathway in this newer neighborhood. The wholesome smells of baking bread, rich spices Rika couldn't identify, and heady incense greeted them. Merchants offering ripe figs and green olives, and carts filled with huge melons and a wild assortment of unfamiliar fruits lined the streets.

Bjorn stopped by a stall, haggling with the proprietor for a respectable time before he bought a loaf of soft, sweet bread. He ripped it into fairly equal portions and gave some to each member of the group. After the rough fare Rika subsisted on during the journey, the bread tasted like it had fallen from the table of the gods.

The merchants hawking their wares called out in a myriad of tongues—Arabic, Latin, Frankish, Persian, Mongolian and, of course, Greek. Rika couldn't help staring when she passed the African merchants, men as black as ebony in wildly colorful robes. She might've felt she was being rude, except for the way the buyers and sellers in the market stared frankly at her party as well. The Northmen dwarfed the people of

Miklagard and even she looked down on many of the men scurrying through the crooked lanes.

"So many people." Wide-eyed, Rika made a slow turn in the street.

"About a quarter of a million," Ornolf said. "And a full fifty thousand of them come from somewhere else. The whole world comes to Miklagard, my children." Uncle Ornolf spread his arms wide and breathed deeply. Rika suspected that part of him always longed for the wild beauty of the fjords, but another part reveled in this great city where so many lives met at its crossroads.

Rika thought she could pick out the natives of the city from the visiting merchants by their dress, Greek-style *pallas*. Most of the Byzantine men had neatly trimmed beards, but a few sported smooth faces. Not just clean shaven like Bjorn, but as hairless and soft-looking as her own. And their voices were pitched in her register as well.

"Eunuchs," Ornolf said when he saw her puzzled frown. "The third sex, the Byzantines call them. Neutered males." His lip curled derisively. "Hardly a household of repute has less than a dozen of them running it. We'll see some at Abdul's house. He uses them to guard his harem. Can't see why a man would allow himself to be mutilated."

"I don't imagine they do allow it," Torvald said.

"No, the poor wretches don't do the deciding," Ornolf admitted. "Usually it's the parents. They have the younger son castrated so he can serve in a government post or with an influential family. I guess I never told you, Bjorn, but I got a very tempting offer for you from an old Greek courtier when I brought you down here as a boy. Once he found out you were a second son, he became most insistent."

Bjorn glowered at him.

"He thought you were a very pretty little fellow."

Ornolf didn't bother to hide his smirk. "But I didn't think he'd want a knife in his ribs, so I decided not to sell you to him."

"A wise decision, Uncle," Bjorn said, jabbing Ornolf's shoulder with his fist. "Otherwise, it might've been your ribs with a knife in them."

Ornolf slapped Bjorn's back approvingly, but so fiercely the blows would've knocked most of the Byzantines flat.

They continued upward, passing under the two-story-high aqueduct that brought fresh water to Mikla-gard from the mountainous region beyond the walls. Wide, marble-paved thoroughfares opened onto colon-naded forums and ornate gardens with splashing foun-tains. Several small carriages clattered on the stone pavings, and the deep gong of bells from the city's many churches resounded off the palaces and government buildings. This was Miklagard—Constantinople—the throbbing heart of the Christian world.

In Rika's wildest imaginings, not even Asgard was as splendid as the imperial section of this city. But for all its beauty, Rika sensed the cold grip of treachery in the very air around her. She shook herself to ward off the fanciful notion.

Uncle Ornolf led them to the new hostel for visitors, known as the Xenon of Theophilos, to rest and refresh themselves. Later in the afternoon they visited the Zeuxippos, the opulent public baths next to the palace of the emperor.

"Can't meet your bridegroom looking like a travel-stained bumpkin," Ornolf said to Rika.

So with dread curling in her belly, Rika bathed in perfumed waters and donned the best tunic and kyrtle Gunnar had sent with her. Helge fretted over Rika's hair, which still only curled to her chin. She really didn't care what her prospective husband thought of her. Her only concern was how to make it through the next few moments without running to Bjorn and begging him to carry her away.

When she came out of the bathhouse and saw him, her knees nearly buckled. He was freshly bathed and shaved, but his dark eyes looked haunted. She forced herself to look away. He was already burned on her heart, the rumbling timbre of his voice, the feel of his hard muscles, the smell of his skin, the taste of his kiss. She only need close her eyes to summon him, but looking at him now could wreck all.

Ornolf led the way to the Arab's home. Bjorn and Jorand flanked Rika, with Torvald and Helge forming the rear guard. Rika sensed tension in Bjorn's body beside her. She felt his agony. It was in exact harmony with her own.

As they walked through the streets, Rika saw more than one dark-eyed woman gazing long and hard at the tall Northmen. From her peripheral vision she noted that Bjorn ignored them, looking straight ahead. But Rika knew he wouldn't be alone for long in this city. In time he'd surely forget her. The knowledge made her stomach lurch.

She glanced sideways and saw a muscle tick in his cheek. Rika recognized it as barely controlled fury. Why should he be angry at her? Didn't he realize she was only doing this for his sake? She no longer doubted he could keep Ketil safe, but by disrupting the alliance her marriage cemented for Sogna, Bjorn would be branded an oath-breaker, a man without honor.

He'd protested that it didn't matter, and maybe it wouldn't for a while. But sooner or later, it would. A life without honor was no life at all. They both knew that. And he would come to despise her for destroying him. His love for her would turn to hate.

She told herself she could bear living without him. She could even bear a loveless marriage to a stranger. But she couldn't bear Bjorn's loathing.

They reached the home of Abdul-Azziz, a three-story affair just off the main road that presented blank marble walls to the street. From this position, Rika could see only one tall set of double doors and no windows. Despite its opulence, the house had the look of a prison. Rika's courage nearly faltered.

Ornolf rapped soundly on the door and the opening swung wide to reveal a portly, bare-chested eunuch. His broad, swarthy face parted in a wide smile as he recognized Ornolf.

"A thousand welcomes, Northman," he said, graciously sketching the gesture of greeting and bowing to admit them. "My master will be pleased to see you again so soon."

Uncle Ornolf returned the gesture and smiled. "Many years and good ones, Al-Amin," he said in the time-honored tradition of Byzantines.

Rika knew she was expected to step forward, but her feet were leaden. She felt rooted to the spot. Once she entered this house, there was no going back.

Bjorn scooped her up into his arms and carried her over the threshold into the large enclosed courtyard.

"What are you doing?" She tightened her arms around his neck, barely resisting the urge to lay her head on his shoulder.

"Don't you remember? It's bad luck for a bride to trip on her new doorstep," he said loudly, then dropped his voice in an urgent whisper. "Even now, love. Say the word and I'll take you away."

Sharp-edged longing pierced her chest, nearly stopping her breath. There was nothing in the world she wanted more. Nothing except the life she wanted for him, a life of purpose and honor among his own people. A life he could never have if he broke his oath for her. She pressed a hand against his chest, feeling his heart pounding beneath it.

"I can't." Somehow, her mouth formed the words.

As she watched, the hopeful light went out of his eyes and the flat, dead expression returned. He set her down lightly and stepped back from her.

"Then good-bye, Rika." He turned and strode out of the Arab's house without a backward glance.

CHAPTER 29

Rika watched, motionless, as Bjorn turned on the far side of the courtyard door and strode forever out of her sight and out of her life. Ornolf gave an almost imperceptible nod toward Jorand and, on that tacit signal, the young man broke into a trot after his captain. The big eunuch closed the double doors behind Jorand, barring them with a massive piece of timber. Rika's first impression of the house as a prison rang more true by the moment.

"Please, come with me and refresh yourselves." Al-Amin led them into a vine-covered pergola in the spacious courtyard. He clapped his hands and maid-servants appeared bearing silver ewers filled with rosewater. "If you will condescend to wait here, I will inform the master of your coming." He bowed once more before turning to glide into the dark shadows of the house.

Rika followed Ornolf's example and splashed some of the fragrant liquid on her face. Perhaps it would help her to feel something. She had the eerie sense of watching herself from outside her own body, a strange detachment from the actions of her own limbs.

All she wanted to do was hide somewhere and cry until there was nothing more inside her to spill out. There were so many unshed tears pressing against the back of her eyes, she felt the tension in her face creep down her neck. If she once succumbed to weeping, she feared she'd never stop.

"Oh, mistress," Helge said. "Isn't this a fine place? I've never seen the likes of it, no I haven't."

Rika looked around. The Arab's house was more than magnificent. In her wildest dreams, not even Valhalla was this opulent. The size, the ornamentation, the costly building materials and fine appointments of the house proclaimed not only wealth but exquisite taste as well. Rika sniffed. However gilded and perfumed it might be, a cage was still a cage.

The house was designed in a large square surrounding the open courtyard, in which a riotous garden bloomed. Rika noticed that the lowest level of the three stories was devoted to stables and storage. The kitchens must be on that level as well, since she could smell the savory aroma of roasting meat and the yeasty scent of baking bread mingling with the homely scent of warm horseflesh and fresh straw. She heard water splattering into the base of a fountain whose flow disappeared into a low, white marble building in the center of the courtyard. Bathhouse, she surmised.

The boxy appearance the house presented to the outside world was softened inside by arches and sinuous curves. It seemed deceptive to Rika and she yearned for the straight lines of a longhouse. Inside the massive structure, every room on the second story opened onto a wide veranda. On the third level, the chambers had a window or a door with a balustrade that overlooked the courtyard. She saw no one at any of the openings, but she felt the oppressiveness of eyes on her. Her spine straightened.

Never forget who you are.

She hadn't heard Magnus in her head in weeks, but the old skald's voice was most welcome. Her mouth twitched. She would remember. A skald carried herself with dignity to generate the respect she deserved. Her heart was numb, and would likely never recover, but the poise of her art might carry her through the uncertain future. She hoped it would. It was all she had.

Abdul-Azziz leaned back into a cushion and popped a sweet date into his mouth. His young guest was enjoying himself, which was all to the good. Yahya al-Ghazzal, court poet from the Caliphate of Cordoba, had been sent as an emissary to the Byzantine court, and was thus worthy of Abdul's notice.

It was always beneficial to have an ear in those labyrinthine halls of power. If Abdul-Azziz could cultivate a friendship with al-Ghazzal, he would have a useful source of imperial information without having to pay for it openly. In his years of navigating the curious webs of Byzantine intrigue, Abdul had learned that this type of insider gossip was far superior to the drivel collected by paid informants. And if the supplier of information was unaware he was being used, far more profitable.

"How do you find court life?" He kept his voice neutral.

"Here or at home?" The fastidious young man dabbed at the corner of his mouth with a perfumed linen cloth.

"Either," Abdul said.

More than two decades ago, Abdul had come on a diplomatic mission from the same Moorish caliph. He found the rich city of the Christians to his liking and stayed on to build a trading empire of his own. The long tentacles of his contacts stretched eastward to the Indus for silks and spices, north to the icy fjords for amber and furs, and south to Africa for fabulous gemstones and ivory. Abdul could easily afford to sit back and luxuriate in his wealth for the span of several lifetimes without lifting a finger to increase it further. But he liked the game and he played it very well.

"Like our Saracen brothers, we fight with the Christians near us and trade with the ones who are far away," Yahya said. He selected a plump piece of roast fowl, drizzled with fruit glaze, from a delicate china plate. "The whole world is mad."

"And if it were not, what need would we have for poets to bring us sanity?" A little flattery often loosened a man's tongue quicker than the wine he used to ply non-Muslims.

"True." The younger man accepted Abdul's statement as his due. "Still, does it not seem odd that the Byzantines, who send men to fight against the Saracens in Jerusalem, trade and treat with the men of Cordoba, who are followers of the same Prophet?"

"Odd, yes," Abdul-Azziz said. "And for us, most fortunate. It gives us a clear field in which to trade here in Constantinople without having to compete with our Saracen brothers." He took a sip of iced pomegranate juice. The ice shavings were a decadent luxury he never denied himself, even though they came at great expense from the distant mountains. "What do you think of the imperial couple?"

"Oh, the Empress Theodora." Yahya rolled his eyes and clutched at his chest. "I wonder at the emperor's wit, allowing her to go unveiled. She is far more than a moon of beauty. She is the sun in full radiance. Anyone who's seen her up close could not fail to be captivated by her dark eyes. I confess myself lost."

Abdul-Azziz was mildly alarmed at his comrade's effusiveness. "Bridle your passions, my young friend, or they will be your undoing. Just because the Christians are foolish enough to display their women, don't think they will tolerate any indiscretion with them. Confine your lovemaking to poetry praising Theodora's charms and you will do well. And find yourself a wife while you're at it." He winked broadly. "Find yourself two."

The poet chuckled. "You're right. And your advice is such that I will happily follow."

A servant stepped discretely into the room from behind a stone lattice. He made a brief obeisance before Abdul-Azziz. "A thousand pardons, my master," Al-Amin said, his high-pitched voice severely at odds with his size. "The bridal party from the North has arrived."

"So soon?" Abdul frowned. "I didn't expect them till next spring. Very well. Show them in."

Al-Amin bowed and slid out of the room, graceful despite his bulk.

"You have personal business," Yahya said, wiping his mouth and starting to rise. "My thanks for this repast. I will leave you now."

"No, please stay." Abdul-Azziz put a hand on the young man's arm. "It is only the arrival of my newest wife. My trading partner to the north, a minor potentate in that frozen world, has sent me a bride to solidify our alliance. I have but three wives, so she will make the fourth."

"Ah, but I have heard it said you are a connoisseur of feminine delights and that your harem is full of beauties." The poet's tone was tinged with admiration and just a touch of envy. "Surely you already have more women than the All-Merciful allows."

"Truly, women I have in abundance, but wives? No." He shook his head. "Is it not most fortunate that while we who follow the Prophet are confined to just four wives, no limit is set on the number of concubines a man might enjoy?" A sybaritic smile creased his face.

"And of all the pleasures women can offer a man, the greatest, my young friend, is variety."

"Are the women from the north fair to look upon?"

"Who knows?" Abdul said. "The men are a strong, handsome race and devilishly quick with a blade. They are utterly fearless, but unbelievably coarse in their manners. I believe their trading representative, Ornolf, may even be illiterate."

"Uneducated savages," Yahya pronounced. "No match for a businessman with your acumen."

"They have not had the advantages of our education, it's true, but it is a mistake to underestimate them. They are shrewd traders. I confess that Ornolf has bested me a time or two in our negotiations," Abdul-Azziz admitted with grudging respect. It was part of what made the game worth playing. "You must stay and meet them. Perhaps it will amuse you to see what type of flower blooms in the cold north."

Rika wasn't aware of the eunuch's reappearance in the pergola till he spoke from the shadows. "The master is delighted by your coming. Please, walk with me."

They followed Al-Amin into the cool interior of the house, up a circular marble staircase and down a long veranda that was open on one side to the courtyard and dotted with doorways into various rooms on the other. Glimpses of polished onyx floors strewn with ornate rugs and costly mosaics flashed by Rika's eyes, making her feel light-headed. When the eunuch finally turned into one of the openings, she was relieved to be able to wait behind a stone lattice to allow her eyes time to adjust to the dimness.

Through the ornate stonework, she could make out two men reclining near a low table, laden with all manner of delicacies. One of the men was younger, inclined to pudginess, and, after popping a trifle into his mouth, he licked his fingers in an effete manner.

The other man was older, his dark hair and neatly trimmed beard shot with silver, but firm-jawed yet. He was probably considered handsome in a fierce, hawkish way. The lift of a dark brow and the calculating snap in his eyes told Rika she did not want this man for an enemy. Which was her prospective husband? It didn't really matter to her, but she recognized immediately that the elder man was the more dangerous of the two.

They followed Al-Amin into the room to be announced, Ornolf with powerful strides, Torvald and Helge toddling after him, clearly overwhelmed, and finally Rika. She held her head high, and reminded herself that her sacrifice was a small thing really, to ensure the life of her brother.

And the honor of the man she loved.

The younger man eyed her unabashedly and barely contained his snicker. The older man frowned and muttered something in Arabic. Rika couldn't be sure but she thought she caught the phrase "red Norse cow." Then the man pasted a smile on his face that didn't reach his eyes and stood to welcome Ornolf. Rika looked down at the little Arab. She topped him by half a head.

"Welcome, my old friend," Abdul-Azziz said, switching to the Greek he and Ornolf used to communicate with each other. "I had not thought to have the pleasure of your company for some time yet, let alone glimpse the rare northern . . ." he faltered for a moment, taken aback by Rika's appearance, "moon of beauty you have brought for me."

Abdul-Azziz's dinner guest failed to disguise his disdain when he gazed on Rika. He murmured a few words to his host which confirmed her suspicion that the Arab ideal of feminine beauty was epitomized by the petite, dusky morsels already crowding her future husband's harem.

Abdul gulped and stared up at her as if the sheer size of his new bride was enough to unman him. He whispered a biting retort back to his friend, a scathing remark about her unfortunate garish coloring and glittering pale eyes. Rika thought she caught him making the sign against evil with one hand. Obviously, when Abdul first suggested this union, he'd never stopped to consider that tall, pale Northmen must come from tall, pale Northwomen.

Ornolf balled his fists at his sides, Rika noticed. He must have heard the slighting remark as well, but he feigned ignorance, as he'd admonished them all to do at times. "The Jarl of Sogna is pleased to honor your request for a bride and has sent you a highly esteemed daughter of his house. Rika of Sognefjord." Ornolf waved a hand in her direction and she inclined her head to the Arab.

How interesting that he seemed not to want her. She was strangely comforted by the Arab's look of unease. It made her feel that she was not the only fly trapped in Gunnar's web. Perhaps this was her chance to break free. A small shivering started deep inside her. She hadn't felt it in a long time, but she still recognized it. Hope.

"Alas," Abdul-Azziz said. "An unforeseen complication has arisen that may preclude our arrangement."

"And what might that be?" Ornolf's tone was not sympathetic.

The Arab stared at Rika for a moment before collecting his thoughts. "A religious difficulty," he said. "I am, as you know, a follower of the Prophet and people of the North are notoriously pa— Your people are the devotees of many gods. Under the laws of my faith, I cannot enter into a marriage with an unbeliever."

"We've come a very long way for you to remember this difficulty just now." Ornolf glared down at Abdul-Azziz.

"My friend, you and I have established a long and fruitful partnership," Abdul said. "We have agreed on so many mutually profitable trades, I had simply forgotten that there would naturally be this difference between us."

"The jarl will be extremely displeased," Ornolf said. "He will no doubt look to find another trading partner. One who will be a man of his word."

Rika resisted the urge to smile. Gunnar would be livid. But it would not be her fault that the Arab failed to live up to his part of the bargain. Her pulse jumped. She and Bjorn could marry before they returned to Sogna in the spring.

"Do not be hasty," Abdul said. "You wound me, Northman. You know I stick to my agreements, even when you have gotten the better of me. I would willingly take this Northern flower as my wife, but how could I ask her to give up her gods and embrace my faith? It would be too much."

The quick flare of hope sputtered and died. Rika's first assessment was correct. The Arab was dangerous. With his well-crafted argument, he deflected all the failure of their union neatly into her lap. Gunnar would indeed be furious. At her. And Ketil would pay the price of his rage.

She had to do something to turn this back on Abdul-Azziz. Could she give up Thor and the rest of the gods? Magnus had taught her all she knew of them, but the court of Asgard seemed to have forsaken her. After all, they stood by and watched, amused no doubt at her present predicament, without lifting a finger to help her. She needed time to figure a way out. Suddenly renouncing the Nordic pantheon seemed a small hurdle.

"May I be given instruction in your faith before I decide whether to put aside my own?" she asked in flawless Greek. Ornolf's tutelage was proving its worth.

Abdul-Azziz jerked his head toward her, obviously stunned that she was able to follow their discussion.

Rika lifted a haughty brow at him. "When a 'red Norse cow' is moved to a new pasture, she must be given time to acquire a taste for different grass."

The young man seated behind Abdul snorted and nearly choked on a fig. Abdul ignored his distress and stared at Rika, clearly reevaluating her.

"With your permission, Ornolf." He bowed and pressed his fingertips first to his lips and then his forehead. "May I show this Northern moon the delights of my garden? You are welcome to observe us from the veranda to preserve her reputation, but by your grace, I would have private speech with her."

Ornolf looked askance at Rika, and when she nodded slightly, he agreed. Abdul-Azziz offered his arm and escorted her from the room.

They walked together in silence down the long veranda and through the cool marble stairwell. The sun had set behind one of Miklagard's seven hills, but the garden still retained some of the heat of the early autumn day. Abdul-Azziz stopped next to the fountain where the air was cooler.

Very astute, Rika realized. The patter of the water would also cover their words, protecting their privacy from any who might wish to overhear.

"You surprise me, Rika of Sognefjord," he said, wincing as though even the syllables of her name were harsh and jarring to his tongue. "In my experience, impudence and intelligence in a woman is not a likely combination."

"Then I would have to assume your experience with women is somewhat limited," she fired back. "You surprise me as well. I had been told that Arabs were a people of great courtesy and discretion."

A smile tugged at his mouth. "You have me at a disadvantage, then, for you had warning of me. No one told me that women of the North were so quick of mind and tongue." He gestured for her to sit on one of the elegant carved benches ringing the fountain. "You are certainly no cow and I cover my head with ashes for having presumed to say so. My profoundest apologies for an unworthy statement."

"Accepted," Rika said. "But I should tell you that I never despise someone who speaks the truth as he sees it. It's most refreshing."

He cocked his head at her, like a fierce tiercel surprised by the fight in the field mouse he'd planned to have for supper. "A woman who values truth is also refreshing. Tell me some truths about you, Rika of Sognefjord. Why do you wish this marriage to go forward?"

Rika weighed her answer. If she'd been hurt by his insulting comment, she might have been tempted to hurl the fact that she was in Miklagard only under the direct coercion. But her heart was still so abraded by Bjorn's departure, she couldn't feel anything, certainly not this little man's slight. Besides, it was better to spar with Abdul-Azziz than fend off his amorous intentions. She was grateful that he seemed as reluctant to wed her as she was him.

"Truth, like a rare spice, is sometimes best used sparingly. My reasons are my own, and I have not said I want our marriage to proceed." She gazed up at him with a directness that seemed to unnerve him. "I have only said I'd be willing to learn about your faith."

"If you were a man, you would no doubt have been a judge," Abdul said as he settled next to her on the bench. As the day dimmed to twilight, it seemed her strong features were less jarring to him. She suspected he liked her better sitting down. "For a woman, you have great subtlety with words."

"Perhaps you have just not spent enough time speaking with the women you know. And if I were a man, we would not be in your lovely garden having this conversation," she said. "But I should be comfortable with words. In my own land, I am accounted a fair storyteller and a poet."

"That explains much." A flicker of respect glowed in his eyes. "I confess that poetry touches this jaded heart of mine and gives me more joy than all my trading empire. I am truly honored in my trading partner's choice of a bride for me."

"Ah, but by your own words, it remains to be seen whether I shall be your bride," she replied smoothly. "The religious difference?"

"A situation I will endeavor to remedy immediately. I shall engage an imam for your instruction at once." His dark brows nearly met over his hawkish nose. "Libidinous adventures with women I've had aplenty. I've never encountered one that challenged my wit. Until now. Your lessons in Islam will begin in the morning. Will that satisfy you?"

"Very well," she said, then hurried on in a flash of inspiration. "Ornolf told us he cannot return to the North so late in the year. There will be ample time to give your faith a fair hearing over the winter. If I find I cannot convert or if I still find no favor in your eyes, I will leave with Ornolf in the spring."

Despite himself, Abdul smiled. "You have just extended our betrothal by several months. Skillfully done. Remind me not to talk trade with you. During that time, you and your party must be honored guests in my poor home. And you must share some of your tales of the North with me."

"I would be pleased," she said.

"Rika of Sognefjord, perhaps we can make a pact with each other." He stood and offered her his arm. "Let us agree always to speak the truth to each other and . . ."

"And what?"

"And always hope for the wisdom to know when to speak it sparingly." He shrugged in a self-deprecating manner.

Her lips parted in a thin smile. She could deal with Abdul-Azziz, but he would bear careful watching. "Agreed."

CHAPTER 30

Bjorn plowed down the street, giving way for no man. The well-dressed, perfumed citizens of Miklagard skittered out of his path. He wished he'd encounter someone who would challenge him. The longing to strike something was fast building to a fever in his blood. He heard quick boots steps behind him, but didn't turn his head. If it was a foe, he was ready. If it was a meddlesome friend . . .

"Where are we bound?" Jorand fell into step with him.

"To Hel, most like," Bjorn said sullenly.

"Then we'll need a drink to cheer us along the way," Jorand said, not at all dismayed. He looked up and down the main thoroughfare. "Not a decent tavern in sight. I doubt we'll find an ale to match the brew in Birka. What do the Christians drink, I wonder?"

"Let's find out," Bjorn said. From what he remembered from his boyhood visit, the bazaar district contained several thoroughly disreputable establishments that Ornolf had favored.

Night fell over Miklagard and the change showed

not only in the darkening sky but also in the character of the foot traffic in the twisted lanes. Honest merchants scurried to the safety of their homes, while cutpurses, prostitutes, and more than a few assassins for hire roused to ply their nightly trades.

The urge to fight coursed through Bjorn's veins. He wished he had more than just a few silver coins jingling in the leather pouch at his waist. He and the lanky Jorand presented too sturdy a front to tempt an attack for so small a return.

The tavern they came to was even more squalid than any he remembered, dark with a haze of incense to cover the more fetid odors. The place suited Bjorn's mood. He and Jorand discovered that the Christians drank wine, deep and red. Bjorn downed eight bowls of the sweet, strong concoction without feeling the slightest hint of a buzz in his head. Or the slightest numbing of the pain in his heart.

The woman he loved was determined to become the wife of another man. Not tonight and maybe not tomorrow, but soon. And there wasn't a cursed thing he could do about it.

"How can she do it?" The words slurred over Bjorn's thickening tongue. Maybe the red stuff was more potent than he thought.

"Practice, I imagine," Jorand said, eyeing the skillful undulations of the scantily clad dancing girl. He nearly touched his ear to his shoulder, tracking her movements as she contorted into a backbend and flipped her heels over her head. "Lots and lots of practice."

Bjorn snorted. Jorand was being purposely thick. But maybe Jorand was right. No good could come from talking.

Action. That's what he needed. Bjorn's gaze swiveled around the room. Two uniformed soldiers burst through the door and demanded service. They were armed with short Roman swords, and moved with the sturdy grace of men who knew how to use them. Bjorn smiled.

"Hail, defenders of the city," he staggered to his feet and gave them a mock salute. "Let me buy you a drink."

The soldiers were more than agreeable. The older one, a grizzled veteran with one eye and hard, ropey muscles in his shoulders and bull-like neck, leaned against the bar and took Bjorn's measure. "A Northman, are you?"

"That's right." Bjorn waved his empty wine bowl toward the serving girl and motioned for drinks for the newcomers. The other soldier seemed fascinated by the long broadsword in Bjorn's shoulder baldric. He was half a head shorter than Bjorn, but stockier.

"Your empire is broad." Bjorn tossed the girl a silver coin. "Where do you hail from?"

"You probably wouldn't know of it," the younger one said.

"Northmen have itchy feet. We are great travelers. Try me," Bjorn challenged.

"Paphlagonia." The veteran accepted a bowl of wine and hefted it toward Bjorn in thanks before taking a deep draught.

"Oh, *ja,* I know that province," Bjorn said. "On the southern edge of the Black Sea, lots of mountains." He also knew the region's principle exports were pork and mutilated little boys for the eunuch market in Miklagard. Crude rumor claimed the women of the region were so homely, the men preferred coupling with swine or newly made eunuchs to avoid their ill-favored females. There was even an old slur on Paphlagonia he remembered from his last trip, one able-bodied Paphlagonians considered a scathing reproach on their manhood. Would the insult still grate its citizens?

"Jorand," he bellowed across the room. "You'll

never guess who they've got guarding this fair city. A pair of pigs' arses!"

The older soldier dropped his wine and buried his fist in Bjorn's gut, doubling him over. The younger one leaped on his back, a beefy arm hooked around Bjorn's neck, trying to wrestle him to the ground. The insult was still potent, then.

Despite the wine swirling in his brain, Bjorn was ready for the onslaught. He slammed backward into a wall, knocking the wind from his assailant's lungs in a whoosh. The other tavern patrons scrambled out of the way. In the far corner of the room, Bjorn heard the enterprising proprietor laying odds and taking wagers on the outcome.

The two soldiers were upon him, raining blows on his chest and shoulders. Fists flying, Bjorn lashed out, blocking a few of their punches and landing more than few of his own with satisfying thuds. His blood was afire. The lust to maim and destroy roared through his veins. Pressure built inside him and exploded through his lips in a *berserkr* cry, fierce as a bear, feral as a wolf pack.

The soldiers reeled back, stunned by the unnatural sound. Evidently they weren't trained to attack madmen.

"Come, you pathetic little girls," Bjorn taunted.

They gang-tackled Bjorn and the three of them went flying, rolling over a tabletop and crashing to the floor. Bjorn caught a hobnailed boot to the kidneys as he struggled back to his feet. He grabbed both soldiers by the neck and knocked their heads together. They wobbled, but stayed upright.

The veteran barked an order to his friend, and they launched another assault. The fight boiled out the side door and into a narrow alley in a tangle of arms and legs. Jorand shouted encouragement to Bjorn and followed with the other onlookers.

Bjorn couldn't see out of his right eye. He swiped at it and his hand came back sticky with blood. One of their blows had split the flesh of his forehead.

"You want blood?" Bjorn roared. He drew out his broadsword in a fluid motion and sliced the air with the long murderous blade. "Let's play like we mean it."

Baring their teeth, the soldiers pulled out their swords with metallic rasps. They began circling.

Bjorn flexed his knees, waiting for the first lunge. Suddenly something cracked him on the back of the head. Pain exploded in his brain in a flash of bright light. He heard his own sword clatter to the cobblestones. Then he crumpled in a heap and knew only blackness.

CHAPTER 31

When Bjorn struggled to the surface, pain was there to meet him. He let himself drift downward again, wallowing in oblivion, like a boar in a mud puddle. Sometimes, he heard voices above him, some gruff, some laced with concern, but no meaning registered in his mind. It was the light that finally forced Bjorn to consciousness.

"Close the shutters, for pity's sake," he mumbled and burrowed beneath the covers.

"Sorry." Jorand ripped off the blanket. "You've slept all night and most of the day. You're not getting any prettier, so I thought I'd see if you'd gotten less mean with the extra rest."

Bjorn groaned. His mouth tasted like a Byzantine legion had tramped through on his tongue. Barefoot. When he tried to sit upright, his head threatened to detach itself and roll off his shoulders. He thought it might be an improvement.

"Mead and ale from now on." Bjorn raised a steadying hand to his temple. "Promise me you'll kill me yourself if I ever touch wine again."

Jorand chuckled. "The wine's not completely to blame for your head. Some of that's my doing, I fear."

Bjorn frowned at him. "I'm not up to riddling. What are you talking about?"

"Before you get angry, I think you should know I was under orders." Jorand shoved a plate of fresh bread and olives into Bjorn's hands. "Ornolf told me before we arrived at the Arab's house that I was to follow you last night if you tried to leave us. He's not stupid, your uncle. Nor blind."

Bjorn gnawed on the bread, hoping it would settle his stomach. "So does the whole world know me for a fool?"

"Not a fool," Jorand assured him. "Just a man in love. By the way, Ornolf is really impressed with the way you and the skald carried yourselves. He half expected the two of you to bolt."

"If I'd had my way, we would have."

"Anyway, you're past the worst now," Jorand said. "Ornolf told me to let you do something foolish if you wanted, but not something deadly. That fight last night was just what you needed, but when you drew your blade, I had to end it."

"You?"

Jorand grinned and snatched an olive from Bjorn's plate. "I had to repay the tavern keeper for the amphora I broke over your thick skull, but at least you're still in one piece."

Bjorn slanted his eyes at Jorand. He knew his friend expected thanks, but he couldn't bring himself to feel grateful. He was suffering from far more than the miseries of too much drink and a solid clout on the head. Truly, his body was whole, but his heart was a stone in his chest. Jorand was naive if he thought Bjorn had seen the worst of it already. Bjorn's pain was just beginning. The long stretch of years without Rika yawned before him. He chewed the bread slowly and swallowed it only on reflex, not tasting a thing.

"Where am I?" Bjorn looked down the long hall lined with pallets like the one he lay on.

"The barracks," Jorand said, pouring some slightly lumpy whitish liquid into a bowl for Bjorn to drink. "Argus and Zander were pretty decent once I explained things to them. Of course, the silver I crossed their palms with helped as well."

Bjorn raised a brow at Jorand, then winced. Even that little movement hurt.

"They're the soldiers you fought with last night." Jorand held out the noxious-smelling bowl toward his captain, urging him to drink. "You're the not the first man to lose a woman, you know. They understood."

Bjorn snorted and curled his lip at the bowl his friend offered. "What's that?"

"Goat's milk, two eggs and some other things you don't want to know about," Jorand said without the slightest sympathy. "Drink up. Argus says it'll clear your head."

Bjorn drained the bowl. "Ugh! They're still trying to kill me." He swiped his mouth with the back of his arm. "Why are we here? Am I under arrest?"

"No, nothing like that," Jorand said. "Seeing as you were so keen to pick a fight, Argus thought you could be tempted to join his regiment as a *tagmata*. That's what they call their mercenaries. He figured you might as well get paid for something you enjoy doing. He says there are already quite a few Northmen in service here."

Bjorn's ears pricked to some new sounds, the tramp of many hobnailed boots and the clatter of wooden blades meeting. He dragged himself to his feet and trudged down to the open doorway. Out on the expansive flat yard, men were drilling, sparring and honing their fighting skills against each other and against clever devices that simulated the random thrusts of combat. At the far end of the field, a cavalry unit practiced tight turns and goaded their mounts into rearing and slashing with their hooves.

The evil concoction of goat's milk seemed to be working. Bjorn's head felt surprisingly clear. Rika was as good as dead to him. The dream of his own land faded into the mists of his memory along with the rest of Sognefjord. Any softness or ease he might have enjoyed with Rika at his side melted away with it. Blood and grit and a violent death were all he could see ahead of him. As he watched the men in the yard, he felt a growing kinship with them. Battle. That was something he understood. This was where he belonged.

"They said the pay is only fair," Jorand said.

Grim-faced, Bjorn nodded. "It'll be enough."

With any luck, the years without Rika wouldn't be so long after all. Or so many.

CHAPTER 32

The scent of night-blooming jasmine was still heavy in the air when Rika opened the shutters. She leaned on the sill and inhaled. Nothing. The fragrance was sweet, but she could find no joy in it. It was as though a shroud had been draped over her heart and she knew neither pleasure nor pain. She wondered whether she'd ever feel anything again.

Rika scanned the courtyard below and found Ornolf and Jorand sitting under the pergola, heads together, speaking in low voices. Whether by a fluke of architecture or by design, every word floated up to her third-floor room. She wondered whether the other chambers in the women's quarters enjoyed the same covert advantage.

"So he has enlisted, then?" She heard Ornolf ask.

"Ja, he made his mark on the tablet yesterday afternoon."

"Probably just as well. He needs a change," Ornolf said. "And besides, the spoils of war can make a man rich. He'll make a fortune with his blade, no doubt. But we will have to find another man to make the trip

back north next spring. I don't want to portage around
Aeifor short-handed again. When will the regiment
leave the city?"

"Next month, Bjorn says. They go east to fight the
Saracens." Jorand raked a hand over his golden head.
"He's not seeking a fortune, though. It's a battle-death
Bjorn is after."

Rika's heart plummeted to her toes. She was wrong.
She could feel something after all.

Ornolf made a low growl of annoyance in his throat.
"Where have they placed him?"

"He's in the infantry now, but Argus told me the
commander would like to see him in the cavalry. Bjorn
has some skill with horses, as you know. Yesterday,
they were having trouble with a four-hoofed imp from
Loki who wouldn't submit to a saddle for anything.
Bjorn snatched the lead rope, hauled the horse's head
down and grabbed him by the ear. Then he whispered
something to the beast and it settled immediately.
Bjorn vaulted up on his back and paraded around the
ring once or twice, then he hopped off and tossed the
lead to the commander. The horse had the manners of
a prince after that," Jorand said. "Bjorn's made a reputation for himself as a horse master already, but members of the cavalry have to provide their own mount
and kit. Bjorn doesn't have the silver."

Rika heard the rattle of coins.

"See to it," Ornolf said. "The infantry is no better
than a meat-grinder for someone seeking death. At
least on horseback, he's got a chance of surviving if he
comes to his senses soon enough."

"Won't the jarl be upset at the expense?" Jorand
tucked the money away in the pouch at his belt.

"With the profit I'm making for him on this trip, I
think Gunnar can spare his brother a horse." Ornolf
snorted. "Compared to what he's taken from Bjorn, it's
little enough."

"Good morning, my lady." Al-Amin's smooth alto made Rika jump away from the window. She turned to see the portly eunuch set down a silver tray laden with fruit and bread. Then he smoothed down Rika's bedding with Helge following him around like an angry bee.

"I tried to keep him out, but he's a pushy one, so he is," Helge said. "In and out of a lady's bedroom without so much as a by your leave. It's not fitting, not fitting at all."

"Evidently, it is here, Helge," Rika said. "We are living in a new land. We must adjust to new customs."

When she reached an accord with Abdul-Azziz, he insisted on giving her Al-Amin as a body servant. Each of his wives had a eunuch of her own, in addition to maidservants to attend to their daily wants. Eunuchs offered the protection of a man's strength along with the asexual indifference that made them perfect for service in a harem. The fact that Abdul had gifted Rika with his own servant was seen as a mark of special favor, Al-Amin assured her. Either that, or a clever way of keeping a very close eye on her, Rika thought.

"After you have broken your fast, you will have your bath, my lady," he said.

Rika blinked. "I bathed just last night." Under normal circumstances in the Northlands, bathing once a week was considered sufficient for decent hygiene, especially in winter.

"You will find that here, it is customary to bathe twice a day," the eunuch said. "As you say, my lady. A new land. New customs."

After she ate some bread and a few tart slices of a fruit called an orange, Rika trailed Al-Amin out of her chamber toward her bath.

The third floor of Abdul's grand house was the exclusive haunt of women and their servants. In accordance with security needs, the long hallway around the square was on the outside wall, totally enclosed but for a few slits that a defender could use to loose arrows through without exposing himself. These slits also allowed air to circulate through the rooms with surprising efficiency. There was only one staircase leading out of the women's quarters, going down through Abdul-Azziz's personal suite of rooms on the second floor or up to the pleasant roof garden.

Abdul had taken her there on that first night to watch the moon rise over the city. She supposed he thought it would dazzle her to see the splendor of Miklagard at her feet. Maybe he even saw it as a conciliatory gesture, another sop to her bruised esteem after his unfortunate "cow" reference. Not that it mattered to Rika in the slightest.

She was sure she'd piqued his interest anyway. Not sexually, of course. He'd been forthright about his feminine preferences, but he seemed to see Rika as a mental challenge. She expected to see more of her fiancé in the future than she would have liked.

Helge bustled along behind Rika. "I still don't hold with bathing so often, mistress," she said, as they slipped into the sumptuous bathhouse. "Especially not with a man standing by gawking the whole time."

"Lady Helge, do not concern yourself," Al-Amin said. "I was fitted for this service long ago. I do not have a man's natural tendencies. My presence here is for my lady's protection and convenience, nothing more."

Helge raised a skeptical silver eyebrow at him.

"Most of the household staff is like me, but there are a few intact men who work in the stables. We would not wish for one of them to stumble into my lady's bath unannounced now, would we? Hence, my presence."

Rika undid her brooches and slid out of her tunic and kyrtle. Helge continued to scowl at the eunuch, clearly unconvinced.

"Still sounds unnatural to me," Helge muttered.

"Oh, it is," Al-Amin said with amazing frankness as

he extended a long arm to help Rika into the bath. "Most eunuchs are made, not born. The lucky ones, like me, were altered young. It is impossible to miss what one has never had."

"And the others?" Rika took a scented cake of soap from his hand.

Al-Amin shrugged eloquently. "I have heard that eunuchs emasculated after their tenth year, suffer the loss of their manhood greatly."

"Ah! I told you she was here." The new voice made Rika turn in the water toward the sound. An olive-skinned woman glided into the bathhouse dressed in a fluttering *palla,* so thin and ethereal it was as though she wore butterfly wings. She moved with the grace of a falcon in flight, her expression fierce as well. She stopped at the edge of the pool. "Stand up so we can get a look at you," she ordered.

Rika stared at her and the two other women flanking her. They were each attended by a bare-chested man dressed in baggy trousers, the same as Al-Amin. This entourage could only be the wives of Abdul-Azziz and their eunuchs.

"Are you addle-brained as well as big as a red Norse cow?" The woman's eyes were large, expertly enhanced with kohl, and glinted with a hard light.

The insult stunned Rika, but not as much as the exact wording. Obviously, someone had overheard Abdul's initial reaction to her and spread the word. Life in a harem was much like the Danish court. Rika made a mental note never to whisper anything she didn't want to hear shouted.

"What do you have to say for yourself?" the woman demanded.

"Only that in the North, introductions are a better way to begin a conversation than insults." Rika deliberately turned her back on the assembly and began lathering her outstretched arm. "If you wish to speak with me, please see Al-Amin to arrange a time that will be more convenient. You are disturbing my bath."

She heard the woman make a squeaking noise of frustration and stomp out, trailed by her coterie of followers.

"Well done, my mistress." Al-Amin expelled all the air from his capacious lungs. "Not many women would stand up to the head wife that way. In your country you must be a queen among women."

"Hardly," Rika said as she climbed out of the bath and allowed Al-Amin to drape a thick towel over her shoulders.

"It is well that Sultana knows you will not bend to her will, but beware of making an enemy of her," Al-Amin cautioned. "Her son, Kareem, is the master's heir. She will hold much power when he comes into his own."

Rika sighed. She really didn't care. Intrigue and plotting and lusting for power all seemed so empty. All she wanted was Bjorn, and since she couldn't have him, there was really nothing else in the world she cared much about. Perhaps love was actually a curse after all. Like the unfortunate late-made eunuchs, she would suffer all the more for what she had known.

But she'd never wish to undo her knowledge. She would never see Bjorn again, yet his face was there each time she closed her eyes. At night, in the first flush of waking from a dream, she almost thought she could feel him beside her. No matter what her future held, Bjorn would always be with her. She would grow old and feeble, but he would remain forever young and virile, frozen in her memory.

He'd become a soldier, Jorand had said. She made up her mind not to try to learn where he was, lest she hear that he had fallen in some battle. As long as she lived, he would, too. Magnus had always told her that the Lady of Asgard, Freya, looked with compassion on unhappy lovers and made a place for them in her great hall. Perhaps Bjorn would come to her there and they would love each other in the next world as they longed to in this one.

Yet here and now, she had Helge and Al-Amin to consider. Rika detested domestic politics, but she knew how to play the game. She would have to stir herself enough to make a comfortable place in this household for the sake of her servants. Perhaps she should begin by finding out who had repeated the "red Norse cow" comment to Sultana.

"Al-Amin," she said, as he helped her don a *palla*. The fabric was so thin Rika felt she was still naked even though she was fully clothed. "Someone must have put those words into Sultana's ear before they could come out of her mouth. Who do you suppose that was?"

"Ah, my lady is the soul of discernment," he said. "That very question was on my mind as well."

"As I recall, only my party and Abdul's dinner guest were present," she said carefully. "And you, of course."

His face went pale. "My mistress, you cannot possibly think that I—"

"I'm not sure what to think," Rika said. "I need to know where your loyalties lie. Do you serve me or Abdul-Azziz? Or perhaps you have some furtive arrangement with Sultana?"

"You wound me, my lady," he said with great dignity. "When I served Abdul-Azziz, it was with my whole heart. Now that he has given you my papers, I am yours to command. Perhaps my lady does not know the practice of naming among our people. My name is not Al-Amin for nothing."

"Forgive my ignorance." Rika bit back a smile at his indignation. He reminded her of a peacock whose feathers had been ruffled. "What is the meaning of Al-Amin?"

He bowed his head toward her, hand over his heart. " 'Trustworthy One.' "

CHAPTER 33

The *oliphant* blasted three times. The ivory horn's signal marked the end of the soldiers' working day. Sweat poured down Bjorn's body. He swiped the stinging moisture from his eyes and trudged off the drilling yard. Even though the mock battle was played out with wooden swords, a couple of his opponents managed to land some solid blows. A bruise that went clear to the bone purpled his right shoulder.

In the Northlands, brute strength and the ability to ignore pain usually won the day in hand-to-hand combat. His new comrades-in-arms were teaching him some different tricks. Bjorn learned to feint and counter-swing, using his opponent's own momentum against him. His lessons with Ornolf came back to him and he used one or two of those maneuvers to good effect. Even Argus, the tough one-eyed veteran Bjorn had brawled with, gruffly admitted that Bjorn might live through his first battle as a *tagmata* after all.

Blessed forgetfulness came upon him when his sword whistled through the air. The concentration required to keep his balance during the deadly dance kept thoughts of Rika locked away in a far corner of his mind. But once Bjorn was done for the day, she rushed back to him, piercing as the sharpest blade, sweet as honeyed fruit, and inevitable as the tide.

He drank too much each night. But never quite enough to dull the pain beyond a keening ache.

"Bjorn!"

Jorand strode toward him, leading a black stallion. The horse sidestepped, prancing skittishly, its large eyes bright with intelligence. Bjorn met them halfway across the yard.

"He's a beauty." Bjorn ran a hand over the withers and down the stallion's deep chest. "A fine animal. But what does Sogna's best shipwright need with a horse?"

"He's yours," Jorand said. "Ornolf wants to see you in the cavalry."

"I'll think on it." Bjorn's mouth tightened. He knew his uncle meant well, but he didn't want his interference. "Are you all staying at the Xenon?" He couldn't help himself. He wanted to ask if Jorand had seen her, if the wedding had already taken place, but he couldn't bring himself to form the words.

Jorand had sailed with Bjorn long enough to understand. "Ornolf and I are at the hostel, though we frequently visit the Arab. Your uncle says he can't be a guest in Abdul-Azziz's home and a profitable trader at the same time. Rika and Helge are at the Arab's house, along with Torvald. Abdul insisted on it once he learned the old man was Rika's father."

"So," Bjorn sighed. "It's done then."

"No. The wedding is postponed for a time," Jorand said. "A religious question, I guess."

Irrational hope surged through him, but he forced it down as Jorand explained how Rika had agreed to extend her betrothal to the Arab so she could learn about Islam.

"How does Rika feel about Torvald being there?"

Bjorn asked. "She never did warm to him after she learned the truth."

"I haven't seen her," Jorand said, guessing that was Bjorn's real question. "She keeps to her chambers in the Arab's house when Ornolf and I are there, after the custom of their women."

"She's held against her will?"

"Torvald says not." Jorand shook his head. "He sees her every day. She studies the Arab's faith with an eye to converting, but hasn't committed to it yet."

"Hmph!" His gut twisted afresh with longing. Having it done with or dragging out the agony—Bjorn didn't know which was worse.

Argus sauntered over to inspect Bjorn's new mount. "A worthy beast," he pronounced. "This reminds me. There's someone you both might be interested in meeting. A countryman of yours, a Northman, anyway. He just returned from maneuvers with his unit. Fenris the Walker, they call him."

"Why?" Jorand asked.

"Because we haven't found a horse big enough to carry him yet." Argus's one eye glittered with amusement. "I'll take care of this dark son of Satan." He took the stallion's lead rope from Jorand and led him toward the stables. "Fenris will be in the chow line, no doubt," he called over his shoulder.

Bjorn and Jorand had no trouble finding the big man. Fenris the Walker towered over the Byzantines around him and even topped Bjorn by half a head. A braided russet beard flowed over his barrel-chest and his beefy arms were bigger around than most men's thighs.

Bjorn and Jorand introduced themselves, enjoying the chance to let Norse trip off their tongues instead of the labored Greek they used most of the time in Miklagard. Fenris was ugly as a troll, coarse-humored and loud. Bjorn was just beginning to like the man when the giant pulled out a sword for him to inspect.

"Galata steel," Fenris said. "The sweetest blade I've ever owned. Try it."

Bjorn sliced the air in glittering arcs and then rested the flat of the blade on one finger just below the hilt. Perfectly balanced. "It's a fine sword," he said, handing it back to Fenris. "Even with the nick in the blade, the balance is still true."

"*Ja,* the pesky thing. It was too deep to grind out completely." Fenris slid the sword back into his shoulder baldric. "I got that nick in your part of the world too, in Sognefjord."

"Really?" Alarm bells clanged in Bjorn's brain. He noticed for the first time that Fenris wore a fine silver armband, not on his bulging bicep—Bjorn doubted that one big enough had ever been made—but on his forearm. It was cunningly designed to look like intertwined serpents with amber inset for the eyes. With a lurch in his stomach, Bjorn recognized it. He looked back up at Fenris, studying him intently. "I don't remember seeing you in Sogna and I think I would."

"Of course, you would." Fenris guffawed. "Not exactly inconspicuous, am I? I'm a Birkaman. I came overland into your forests, but didn't come down into Sogna itself." Fenris grimaced, making his features even more hideous. "We are all men who have sold our blades here, so I'll make no pretense. I was hired to kill a man in Sognefjord."

"Was that armband your pay?"

"It was." Fenris's eyes narrowed as he looked at Bjorn.

"The man you killed, who was he?"

"He was the jarl, Harald Gunnarsson."

Bjorn had only his wooden practice sword, so he reached for Jorand's real one. He yanked it out of his friend's shoulder baldric with a metallic scrape. Legs spread, knees flexed, Bjorn used a two-handed grip to point the long broadsword at Fenris's ample middle.

"Defend yourself, Fenris the Walker, for I am Bjorn the Black, son of Harald of Sogna. You killed my father and tonight you will feed the worms." He glanced sideways at Jorand. "Interfere this time and you're next."

Fenris sidestepped out of the line, his pale eyes never leaving Bjorn's. "Don't be too hasty, youngster. We're a long way from the Northlands and there's no need for you to start a blood feud over this. The killing was just business. Nothing personal."

"It was personal to me."

The Byzantine soldiers didn't understand the Norse words, but the tension in the air was palpable. An intent ring of onlookers formed around Bjorn and the Walker.

"So be it." Fenris spat on his palm and rubbed both hands together. Then he unsheathed the Galata again. "Shame to kill a man and his son with the same blade, but Odin be my witness, you force me to it."

Fenris's chest heaved and he released a cavernous roar that made all the Byzantines reel back. Quicker than Bjorn would have thought possible for a man of his girth, Fenris swung the blade over his head with a whoosh and brought it down.

Bjorn quickly raised his sword to meet the blow and, with a clang of steel on steel, the shock reverberated up Bjorn's arms to his shoulders. If he hadn't locked his wrists and elbows, Fenris would have cleaved him from nose to navel in one stroke.

The giant's blade slid off and flashed in a wide arc across Bjorn's chest. Bjorn jumped back, arms spread wide to avoid the slash, but a row of red beads bloomed on his skin where the tip of Fenris's sword sliced him.

Fenris rained down a hailstorm of blows, which Bjorn managed to parry, but only with grunting effort. The Birkaman fought without finesse, heaving one punishing stroke after another. With his brute strength, Fenris didn't need finesse.

Bjorn danced backward, trying to formulate a plan. He knew from the outset he was outmatched for size and reach, but he'd expected the bigger man to be slower. He wasn't. All Bjorn could manage was a shaky defense from the relentless hammering, and even at that, Fenris had nicked him in several places. Blood streamed from gashes on his shoulder and thigh. As sweat burned into the corners of his eyes, Bjorn realized with a tightening in his gut that he was in trouble.

He circled, trying to slow his breathing and stay out of the wide arc of death that surrounded Fenris the Walker.

"Come to me, boy," Fenris urged, his gruff voice almost kind. "You've fought well enough for honor's sake. I'll kill you clean and you'll be in Valhalla in time for *nattmal*. You can drain a horn for me there with your father."

His father. Had Fenris's hideous face been the last thing Harald had seen? Rage boiled inside Bjorn, but he shoved it down. If he didn't keep a cool head, he was lost. He couldn't win in a test of strength against Fenris. Bjorn's stamina was being leached away by the constant need to defend himself and he still hadn't so much as scratched Fenris.

Fenris tossed his sword from hand to hand, toying with him. Bjorn had to move quickly while he still had wind. It was time to meet his fate and all that was left to him was guile.

He dragged in a lungful of air and hefted his sword for another round. Bjorn bellowed his defiance in a *berserkr* cry and lunged, his blade sweeping the air in glittering swaths. Fenris met the challenge and soon had Bjorn giving ground once again.

The Walker delivered a ringing blow that knocked Bjorn off his feet. Panting, he struggled to his knees, his back to Fenris. The sinking sun projected the big man's shadow over Bjorn and he saw the dark phantom of death looming in Fenris's upraised arms.

In a flash, Bjorn whipped around and plunged his blade into Fenris's belly halfway to the hilt. Then he rolled out of the away as the Galata clattered to the ground and Fenris sank slowly, his fingers grasping at the steel protruding obscenely from his gut.

Bjorn rose to his feet and staggered back to his adversary. He grasped the hilt, slick with blood, and yanked it out of Fenris's flesh. The fetid odor from the wound told him that the big man's bowels were perforated. He would suffer much, perhaps for days, before death came.

Bjorn turned to go.

"Finish me, Sognaman," Fenris croaked.

"Like you finished my father? With a blade in his back?" Bjorn's eyes blazed, as much with shame at his father's cowardice as fury at his killer.

"Your father didn't run," Fenris panted. "He was a braw fighter, like you. In truth, he almost had me, but—" He shuddered as blood strangled his innards.

"What happened?" Bjorn knelt beside his foe.

Fenris lifted the arm that bore the entwined serpents. "The man who gave me this came out from his hiding place. He stabbed your father from behind as we were fighting."

"His name? Who paid you to murder Harald of Sogna?" Bjorn demanded as he gulped air. The fight had been close. If not for Ornolf's tutelage, Bjorn would be worm's meat already. He didn't want to believe the Birkaman, but he trembled with fury at his suspicions. "I need to hear you say his name."

"I never knew it," Fenris said with a grimace of agony. "He said it was cleaner that way. Come now and make an end. Don't leave me to die in a bed covered in my own piss."

Bjorn pulled out his knife and drew it across Fenris's throat in a quick stroke. The Walker half-smiled at him before the light went out of his eyes.

"Drain a horn for me in the Hall of the Slain, Birka-man," Bjorn said softly.

Suddenly the circle of onlookers parted and two officers grabbed Bjorn by the shoulders.

"Northman, you are under arrest for the murder of a fellow *tagmata*," one of them said.

As he was dragged away, Bjorn called back over his shoulder to Jorand. "Claim his sword and the armband. Take them to Ornolf. He'll know what to do."

Bjorn was sure his uncle would remember the armband. After all, he was the one who'd given it to Gunnar.

CHAPTER 34

Wind whipped over the headland. Behind her, Rika heard Al-Amin whimper about the cold. She scoffed under her *bourka*. What did these southlanders know? What they called winter here was more like a fresh day in early spring to her.

"Why must we come here each week, mistress?" he asked. "The statues in the Acropolis don't suffer from the chill, but I assuredly do."

"Stay home next time." She lengthened her stride toward the marble figure that drew her back to this place since she'd first seen it. It was a statue of Mars, his alert eyes turned to the Bosporus in an eternal stare. "Go back home now, if you like."

"My mistress torments me with thoughts of a warm brazier. The master would have me flayed alive if I should leave you unattended," he said. "You know this. I did not expect you to be so unfeeling, my lady."

"But you serve me, not the master," Rika countered. "I would not let him beat you. Stop whining and we'll visit the market for some pistachios on the way home."

"My lady is kindness itself." He dipped in a half-bow. "Only let us return together."

"If you give me some peace, I'll just be a few moments."

They passed a stylite, a holy man who lived atop a tall column five times higher than a man's head. Pilgrims dropped offerings of food and water into the basket at the bottom of his perch, hoping for the effectual prayers of the saint above them. Rika knew she'd never get used to the odd assortment of beliefs in the great city, but at least the broad base of the spire provided a good windbreak for Al-Amin.

"Wait here," she ordered.

The teachings of Islam were a blur of rules and rites to her. Christians in the great city squabbled among themselves, sometimes in bloody argument, over which doctrine was heretical and which was orthodox. She could make no sense of their constant disputes. The gods of Asgard were a distant memory. She was sure they couldn't hear her prayers this far from the North. So she made this weekly pilgrimage to her own private shrine, high on the Acropolis amid the myriad of statues dedicated to the now defunct gods of Rome.

She walked on to visit Mars with a growing disquiet in her belly. It was the same every time—the shortness of breath, the tightness in her chest. She felt hollow as a gourd, stripped bare, and so light and brittle, she might shatter. At the slightest gust, the tiny pieces of her would scuttle away with the remnants of autumn's dead leaves. Sometimes she almost wished it would happen, just like that.

Rika looked up at the statue. The set of his broad shoulders, the tilt of his head, his calm steady gaze, his mouth . . . it was so like Bjorn, her vision tunneled the first time she'd seen it.

Abdul-Azziz insisted she wear the *bourka* in public.

This was the only time she felt grateful for the way it shielded her from prying eyes. The veil covered her completely and she viewed the world through thin gauze stretched over part of her face. The statue's unsmiling features filled her view until her tears made the image waver. Then she pressed her forehead to the cold marble base.

"Oh, Bjorn," she sobbed. "Where are you?"

What little Rika knew had been pieced together from snippets of overheard conversations. Jorand had come to Ornolf with an armband and a sword, the significance of which she never learned. But she did hear that Bjorn had been arrested. By the time Ornolf and Jorand returned to the barracks the next day, Bjorn's trial was over. He'd been found guilty and handed over to the civil authorities for punishment. The military didn't want to execute a foreign member of their corps themselves. That sort of thing dampened recruitment, so Bjorn's punishment was left to civilians.

Somehow in the transfer, all records of Bjorn the Black, Northman and convicted murderer, were mislaid. Ornolf greased as many palms as he could, trying to find Bjorn's trail, but all they had was conjecture. Perhaps he had been consigned to a galley and was chained to an oar somewhere on Middle Earth's great inland sea. He may have been sold to a wealthy widow and gelded; late-made eunuchs reputedly were still able to sustain a rock-hard erection far longer than an intact man, without the troubling aspect of conception to bother with. Or Bjorn could have been summarily garroted and his body dumped in a cesspit outside the city gates. There was no way to know for sure.

Miklagard had swallowed him whole as surely as if he'd stepped into a bog, but Rika clung to the belief that he yet lived. She was sure that her heart would re-

fuse to beat in a world where Bjorn was dead. Though
it twisted her insides to come there each week, the few
moments she spent weeping at the feet of Mars were
the only ones in which she felt truly alive.

Bjorn watched the shadow on the wall and scratched a
line in the stone when he thought it had reached its
peak for the day. The sun didn't vary as much here in
the southlands, but in this crude way he'd still been
able to mark the winter solstice and follow the change
of seasons. He'd kept a tally of the days as well, but
they depressed him.

At least the nightmare had ceased to plague him.
He'd only had it once, and shortly upon waking, he realized the terrifying apparition of Jormungand was
closely connected with Gunnar's symbol of entwined
serpents. He was astounded he hadn't reached the
conclusion before, but then again, he'd never had so
much idle time just to think. From that startling insight, Bjorn began to think back.

Maybe it was his near-drowning with Rika in the
turbulent waters of Aeifor that sent his mind wandering down a long-forgotten trail, but another part of the
nightmare began to make sense as well. A memory too
painful to accept crystallized in his mind.

He'd told Rika that Gunnar had saved him from
drowning on that distant day, but he knew now that
wasn't true. His brother had pushed him into the fjord
and held his head below the choppy water. Bjorn was
alive only because he grabbed his brother's arm and
threatened to pull him in as well. He'd scrambled back
into the coracle by climbing up a startled Gunnar's
arm. Then as a matter of survival, Bjorn altered the incident and swore a grateful fealty to his older brother.
In time, he'd even convinced himself of the revised
event. Since Fenris the Walker had all but confessed
that Gunnar had paid him to kill their father, Bjorn re-

alized the dream had been trying to tell him that Gunnar had murdered their father.

His childhood oath had kept him alive because it made him useful to Gunnar. Now it curdled Bjorn's stomach like rancid goat milk, and if he'd been in Sognefjord, he'd shrug off the last of Gunnar's hold on him like an ill-fitting cloak.

Unfortunately, he wasn't in Sogna.

Sleep was now a welcome respite, because his waking hours were nightmare enough.

The window in his cell was too high for him to see out, but it did grant him light, and sometimes when the wind was right, rain as well. When that blessed event occurred, he stripped out of his rags and let the torrent wash away the crust of filth he'd learned to live with.

Once a day, the slot in the door opened to remove his nightsoil jar and leave a trencher of moldy bread and vile-tasting water. Whether the jailer was forbidden to speak to him or unable to, Bjorn never knew, but he went for months without the sound of another human voice.

He started talking to himself, realizing he did so, but unable to control it. He carved the *futhark* on the walls of his cell, desperate to keep his mind active. Privation, he could deal with. Madness, he feared more than Hel itself. In the isolation and silence, he felt himself teetering on the brink, threatening to slide into insanity.

Then a kind of miracle happened.

Bjorn glanced over to the corner. His miracle got up off his knees and dusted the dirt from the front of his ratty cassock. The prison was so overcrowded the jailer was forced to house another inmate in Bjorn's small cell. He was sure it had saved him from raving lunacy.

"Still praying, Dominic?" he asked.

"As long as I'm still breathing, my son," the little priest said.

"Is your God going to get us out of here?"

"I don't pray for that." Dominic's sharp eyes were bright with intelligence. "I pray for your soul. I would that God will release your spirit from its bonds."

"Why don't you tell him to get my body out of here?" Bjorn said as he settled against the wall to let the light hit his face. The warmth soothed him and for just a moment, an image of Rika flickered in his brain. In his mind's eye, he saw her leaning against an obelisk of some kind, tears streaming. He shook himself. If he were going to imagine her, why couldn't it be a more pleasant phantom? "If your God sets me free from this prison, then he'll be welcome to my soul."

The priest's face beamed with a gap-toothed grin. "God is relentless in his pursuit of us. If that's what it takes to woo you, Bjorn, I'm sure the Almighty will see you free."

Bjorn shook his head. "Woo me? You make your God sound like some kind of ardent lover."

"So he is." Dominic nodded. "The first lover of us all and when we least deserve it."

A god who loved for no reason. The priest's beliefs didn't seem rational to Bjorn. No wonder they had locked Dominic up.

"Well, my gods seem content to let me stay right here, so I'm willing to give yours a chance," Bjorn said. "I've tried them all, even Loki, but either they can't help me or they don't care."

"Or they are too small," Dominic said. "From what you have told me of the gods of Asgard, they exist only inside creation. God is separate from the created world and yet he holds it all together. Beyond all that is, beyond what we believe or think we know, beyond even divine revelation, there is God."

It was easy for Bjorn to see how Dominic had run afoul of the local religious leaders. His God was too big for a man to get his mind around, to big to control through appeasement, and far too big to be crammed into a religion.

"Maybe so," Bjorn allowed. "But you have to admit my gods are more fun at a feast. Take Thor for instance. Now there's a god a man can sit down and share a horn with." Bjorn slapped a hand on his thigh and launched into an old drinking song.

> *"Ale I bring, thou oak of battle,*
> *With strength blended and brightest tunes,*
> *'Tis mixed with magic and mighty songs,*
> *With goodly spells, wish-speeding runes."*

"I know just the shop, my lady," Al-Amin said, all trace of whining about the cold gone now from his pleasant alto. "It's next to that spice merchant from Persia. The pistachios are always of the highest quality."

Rika nodded numbly. She always felt drained after her visit to the Acropolis, but she needed to see the statue of Mars. She didn't understand it, but Bjorn felt closer to her there, as if she could somehow form a connection with him for those few moments. She wondered whether he could feel her love for him still. It was a fanciful notion, but one she needed to believe.

Rika and Al-Amin walked past the Hagia Sophia, the high-domed Church of Holy Wisdom. Ethereal song floated out to them sung by smooth voices, disembodied and bloodless. The drone of plainsong was much admired. It was considered deeply spiritual and pure, but Rika missed the full-throated singing of her homeland. The raucous timbres heard in a longhouse were often unpleasant, but they were always full of life.

She could almost hear them now, earthy and bombastic.

*"Less good they say for the sons of men
Is the drinking oft of ale."*

"Allah be merciful, what is that dreadful sound?" Al-Amin looked around, trying to locate the source. "All that growling! It sounds like a big dog is being butchered alive."

The voice rolled over her again.

*"The more they drink, the less they think,
And end up on their tail!"*

Rika gasped. She knew that voice. She was sure of it. Bjorn had sung that song for her one evening on the island, as they huddled around their little fire. It had a long string of verses each more ribald than the last, presumably as the company became drunker with each round.

"It's coming from that building there," Rika pointed to a fortress across the square. "What is that?"

"The prison, my lady," Al-Amin said.

"We must go there." She nearly broke into a trot. "That voice belongs to . . . a countryman of mine. I will not see a Northman languishing in prison if I can help it."

"It's not seemly for a woman to visit there," the eunuch complained. "You should tell the master and he will see to it."

She wheeled around and fisted her hands at her waist. "I'll go with you or without you, but either way, I'm going. If there's one thing I've learned in Miklagard, it's that anything can be bought for the right price. Now tell me, how does one secure the release of a prisoner here?"

Chapter 35

Bjorn plodded down the dim passageway, hands and feet bound in irons, with the jailer before and a guard behind. He hadn't been out of his cell since he arrived and the wonder of being able to walk more than a few steps before turning around was almost more than he could bear.

"Pity there isn't time to clean him up," the jailer said. "She might pay more if he looked better."

"I don't know." Bjorn heard the guard behind him spit on the fetid floor. "I've heard tell some of these randy women like 'em dirty. Big one, isn't he?"

"I expect that's why she wants him." The first man broke into gales of laughter.

"If she wants a big fellow, why don't you get that Nubian and let her have her pick? Maybe she'd take 'em both."

"I suggested it, but the lady has very particular tastes. She wants the one that was caterwauling, and this Northman's the only one who bursts into a singing fit from time to time." The jailer scratched his head, sending his resident lice scurrying.

"Won't be no trouble selling him, will there?"

"No, I conveniently lost his records when he first came. A big bald man came snooping around once, but I told him we didn't have any new prisoners. I figured on putting this one out on the dock for the slave auction this spring. They always bid up the prices in the spring, but this lady looks to have the coin to beat whatever I'd get later."

Bjorn listened to them discuss him as though he were a bull to be brought to market without so much as a ripple of concern. His life seemed to be happening to someone else since he entered this private annex of Hel. Not caring one way or the other what new horror came to him was his only defense and he sheltered behind studied indifference.

He was shoved into the jailer's office with a rattle of his chains.

"Here now," the guard said, sliding a long club under Bjorn's chin and forcing him to raise his head. "Let the lady have a good look at you."

Blinking in the light, Bjorn tried to get a look at the lady as well, but she was swathed in the folds of her silk *bourka*. He could tell nothing about her except that she seemed to be tall for a Byzantine. The woman's hand came up to her chest and she fell back a step or two. He must smell worse than he thought.

She, however, was scented with jasmine so sweet, it made him feel faint. Months of privation sent his senses spinning. The prison was a miasma of offal and the acrid stench of fear, but this woman's fragrance was a reminder that his world had not always been so. He could have dropped to his knees and licked the sole of her perfumed foot in gratitude.

Her eunuch dickered with the jailer over his "fine" and, after much haggling, reached an agreement. The smooth alto voice was somehow familiar, and Bjorn frowned, trying to place him.

The Arab's house.

It was Al-Amin, though it was obvious the big eunuch hadn't recognized Bjorn. He'd carried Rika into the house and left so quickly the eunuch hadn't had time to mark him, though Bjorn remembered Al-Amin well from the time he'd come to Miklagard as a boy. The Arab's servant hadn't changed much. Bjorn looked down at himself. Tattered rags, crusted with filth, down a good forty pounds. He ran his bound hands over the scruffy beard and mustache covering his face. It was no great surprise that Al-Amin didn't know him. He barely recognized himself.

The woman. He suddenly remembered that her jeweled hand was pale. He looked back up, trying to penetrate the armor of the bourka. She was tall by Miklagard's standards. It had to be Rika. Her clothing was shot with silver threads and gold coins dangled around the edges of her gauze peephole. A wealthy Arab's wife. She could have anything she wanted.

And now she wanted a pet Northman.

"Make your mark here," the jailer ordered him with a leer. He pointed to a line on a piece of parchment that would exchange one kind of imprisonment for another. "The lady will pay your fine and you'll work it off as her slave."

"No," Bjorn said. The jailer frowned in surprise, but Bjorn cleared his throat and repeated his refusal. If Rika wanted him, she'd have to pay dearly. Dominic's coming was the only thing that had kept him sane. He couldn't forget his friend. "I'll only sign if she'll take my cell mate as well."

All the way to the Arab's house, Dominic praised his God in extravagant terms. As they entered the square fortress, he turned to Bjorn.

"Remember your bargain, my son."

"What?" All Bjorn could think of was Rika under

the fluttering veil ahead of him. Rika, whose slim ankles he'd glimpsed as they walked along. Rika, doe-eyed and languid in his arms on the island at the base of Aeifor.

"God has released your body from prison as you requested," Dominic said. "I believe you offered him your soul in exchange."

"Shall I fit them for your service, my lady?" Al-Amin asked.

The veiled figure nodded and disappeared into the shadows of the house. Bjorn's gaze followed her, longing and loathing competing in his heart. She'd made her choice months ago and it wasn't him. How could she expect him to be grateful to her now? To serve her? Part of him railed in defiance and another part was satisfied just to breathe the same air she breathed.

"That's just the trouble, Dominic," he said. "I'm afraid my soul has already been claimed elsewhere."

Rika was shocked by the change in Bjorn's appearance. He was so thin and pallid. But when his eyes blazed with rebellion, demanding she release his cell mate as well, she knew his spirit was intact. A hot bath, good food, a little sunshine and he'd be back to himself in no time.

And if in the meanwhile, he had to bear the indignity of being her slave, well, that turnabout satisfied her sense of justice. After all, he'd made a thrall of her without a qualm, she reminded herself.

Helge was laying down again when Rika returned to her suite of rooms. The old woman fussed and fluttered around Rika when she was up and about, but Helge had been more tired of late. Her advancing years were no doubt weighing on her slight frame. Rika hadn't the heart to disturb her.

As she lifted the *bourka* over her head, Rika felt a twinge of uneasiness. It was clear that Bjorn had suffered already. The thought of him being degraded in any way made her insides squirm. And yet, hadn't she been suffering when he found her mourning over Magnus's body? It had made no difference to him.

But that was before they loved each other, before they'd found that they were both walking around in pieces, yearning for the wholeness only the other could bring.

No. She had to stop this. She'd tell Al-Amin to release him and that would be that. She started back down the winding stairs to the lowest level.

Loud bellowing came from one of the rooms near the stables and all the fine-boned Arabian horses jerked and stamped in their stalls at the unnatural sound. Rika quickened her pace.

She saw Tariq, Sultana's eunuch, come out a door, laughing and dusting off his hands. The cry was feebler now, almost incoherent.

"What's happening in there?" she demanded.

"Only what you ordered." Tariq inclined his head toward her enough to avoid insolence, but only by the barest of margins. He still sported the scant facial hair and upper body strength of a late-made eunuch. "Your new slaves are being fitted for your service."

"But why all the noise?"

Tariq's smile was unpleasant. "The big one objected. It was all we could do to get him strapped to the table. But do not trouble yourself. This will pass. Unreasonable passions will fade and he will soon be biddable as an ox. One gets used to being a gelding."

Rika hoisted her skirt and ran, knees and elbows pumping.

"Do not fear," Tariq called after her. "Al-Amin is skilled with a knife. They almost always live."

Rika burst into the small room. "Stop, oh, stop!"

Bjorn's cell mate knelt in the corner, eyes closed, lips moving, but Bjorn was naked, strapped spread-eagle to the long table in the middle of the room. His head lolled to one side and his eyes were glassy. An awl pierced one of his ears, preparing the lobe to receive the ring that would mark him as her servant. Blood ribboned down his cheek. Al-Amin stood over him, knife in hand.

"What are you doing?" she demanded, rushing to Bjorn's side. A cord had been cinched around the bag of his seed. Rika fumbled with the knot and managed to hopelessly foul it.

"Fitting him for your service, my lady," Al-Amin said calmly. "If you remove the cord, he will bleed to death before I can cauterize the wound."

"No, you're not going to cut him," she said. "Give me that." She snatched the knife away and worked the point under the cord, taking care not to nick Bjorn.

"Do not distress yourself, mistress. He will feel very little pain," Al-Amin assured her. "I always give the men I unmake poppy juice to dull the senses."

That explained the spittle drooling from Bjorn's lips. She sliced the cord and cupped his bag, relieved to her bones to feel the thump of his heartbeat still drumming through it.

"My lady, this is most unseemly," Al-Amin said, his lips pressed together in censure.

"Do not presume to lecture me." Rika glanced around the little room and spied a pile of gauze. She retrieved some and covered Bjorn with it. "I didn't order this."

"But, my lady, these men cannot attend you if they are intact," Al-Amin argued. "It would bring shame on my master's head."

"I have always suspected you do not truly serve me with your whole heart, and now I hear the truth from your own lips," Rika said. "You are still loyal first to Abdul-Azziz."

"No, mistress," he said. "My very breath is yours. But I have been with this house for more than half my life. Old habits and old loyalties die hard."

Rika felt her expression soften. "I understand, Al-Amin, and your loyalty does you credit. You asked me to trust you, and now you must trust me."

"But this man—"

"I owe a loyalty to this man as well," Rika said. "I know him, you see. It will be hard for you to understand, but I was once his slave."

"Mistress!" The whites showed all the way around his black eyes. "Since he was once your master, he will not be able to serve you. He will surely try to violate you if he is not gelded."

"He never violated me when I was his slave," she said without a blink. "He will not do so now. Al-Amin, I have tried to understand your ways. I wear what Abdul-Azziz asks of me. I study with the imam, though in truth, he seems more concerned that he will be polluted by being in my presence during my monthly courses than he is about teaching me. I am trying to accept your customs, but this is not my way. It can never be my way."

A mist passed over Al-Amin's eyes and Rika wondered for a moment whether he sometimes wished there had been someone to stop his emasculation years ago. Someone to lay a hand over his genitals and say, "No, not him. Not this boy." Al-Amin was fiercely loyal to the house of Abdul-Azziz, but despite his protestations of indifference, did he sometimes wonder what it would have been like to have his own house? His own woman? Children?

The moment passed and Al-Amin's eyes cleared. He tossed a glance at the little priest, still kneeling in the corner. "I assume since you didn't really intend to buy the other one, you will allow him to serve you in the stables." His expression was all business.

"Very well," Rika agreed. She handed the knife back to Al-Amin.

"Good. Then that one will remain untouched. But if this one is to serve in your apartments, then it must *seem* as though he has been altered, my lady."

"I understand," she said. "What are you proposing?"

"Only that he be seen coming to me to doctor a wound in the groin area," Al-Amin said. "A burn should do it. If I burn him, just here," the eunuch ran a fingertip along Bjorn's inner thigh, "that should be sufficient." He turned away to heat the flat of his knife.

Rika's gut twisted at the thought of burning Bjorn. She could just release him, set him free to return north with Ornolf in a few weeks. But her heart was greedy for him. She'd lost him once. She couldn't bear it a second time. He could serve in the stables alongside the cell mate he seemed to care about so much. But then she'd barely be allowed to even speak with him. That would be intolerable.

Al-Amin turned back, the blade glowing red. He bent over Bjorn, gripping his leg to hold him still as he lowered the knife. It would be quick. Bjorn was drugged. He would feel very little pain now, but afterward . . . she knew that of all wounds, burns were the most excruciating. Rika grabbed Al-Amin's wrist.

"No," she ordered. "Let him serve with the horses. I'll not see him hurt."

"As you wish, my lady," Al-Amin said, with his habitual graceful half-bow.

Sultana was taking her ease in the vine-covered pergola when Al-Amin and the other new slave carried the unconscious big man to his new room adjoining the stable. The horses nickered restively as they approached. Rika followed after, to be certain her new slaves were properly housed, Sultana assumed.

"Apparently, she only had the big one cut. Pity about the poppy juice. He made some interesting noises before it took effect," Sultana said as she clicked her long nails on the arm of her chair.

Tariq nodded. "The Norse cow is blood-thirsty, isn't she? She wanted to watch."

Sultana narrowed her eyes as her gaze followed Rika's retreating back. "I begin to understand her."

CHAPTER 36

Nearly a month later, Rika watched from her window as Bjorn led a mare into the courtyard. The horse's coat gleamed, and she sidestepped skittishly, eager for a romp. Bjorn held her head steady for Torvald to mount.

"When do you expect Ornolf and Jorand back in the city?" Rika heard Bjorn ask.

"Maybe not for another week or so." Torvald leaned down to stroke the mare's neck. "But I'll ride to the docks every day to see if there's word. If he'd known you were here, Ornolf would never have run down to Thessalonica."

"Do you know if Jorand gave him the sword and armband?" Rika leaned forward, straining to hear, all the while keeping herself out of sight. She didn't understand the urgency in Bjorn's voice over a sword and armband. He'd never been that consumed with trade goods before.

"He did, months ago," Torvald said. "But with only Jorand for a witness, it wouldn't hold up before the

Lawspeaker. Now that we have your word too, we can take it to court."

"We're a long way from a Lawspeaker and I have a feeling my mistress"—Rika winced at the bitterness in his tone—"won't free me to go north when Ornolf leaves. Talk to her, Torvald."

"I'd like nothing better, Bjorn," the old man said. "But she still wants naught to do with me. I lost all right to tell Rika what to do a long time ago. So much time wasted, so much pain." Torvald's voice drifted off, and then he shook himself. "The ramblings of an old man," he said with disgust. "Always wanting to re-do the past and knowing it can't be done."

"It's not only the old who want that, my friend." Bjorn swatted the mare on the rump. He stood, hands fisted on his hips, as Torvald's mount trotted through the big double doors. Rika thought Bjorn glanced toward her window before he turned and strode back to the stables, but the movement was so quick she couldn't be sure.

Helge padded softly up beside her in time to see Bjorn disappear from the courtyard below. "I know you're set to marry the Arab, Little Elf, but I wish it were different for you, so I do." The old woman's eyes watered, rheumy with age. "The jarl's brother, he's a fine lad."

"So he is," Rika agreed, wiping away the tear that trembled on her lashes. "But wishing changes nothing." She heard a swish behind her and knew Al-Amin had entered with the breakfast tray she and Helge shared.

"Al-Amin?" she called. "I'd like to go riding."

"Riding, my lady?" Al-Amin set down the breakfast tray.

Helge lifted the silver lid. "Och! You forgot the oranges," she scolded. The old woman had become accustomed to the eunuch's presence and was even

emboldened to boss him around herself when Rika
was there to back her up. Rika thought Al-Amin tolerated Helge much like a sturdy Akbash guard dog ac-
cepts a yapping Maltese, a vague annoyance but
something to be endured for his mistress's sake.

"In the North I frequently rode horseback, and I'd
be able to get around the city better than on foot,"
she said.

"I shall order a chaise for you, my lady," he offered.
"Surely that is more in keeping with your station."

"But it is not in keeping with my will," Rika said.
"You will ride with me, Al-Amin. See that the Northman rides as well. Two servants in attendance should
surely be enough to remind everyone of my 'station.'"
Since the household still believed Bjorn had been
gelded that first day, his accompanying her on a ride
would occasion no comment.

Al-Amin's eyebrows shot up, but something in
Rika's rigid posture warned him that further argument
would be fruitless. "As you wish, my lady."

Before the morning sun rose high enough to turn the
air sultry, Rika and her escorts rode out the double
doors. The men both trailed her and when she glanced
back at Bjorn, he failed to disguise his scowl. When
she motioned him forward, he sullenly nudged his
mount into a trot to come even with hers.

"Al-Amin has no Norse beyond a word or two, so
we may speak freely. Have you nothing to say to me,
Bjorn?"

"And what would my lady have me say?" His eyes
were brittle dark holes as he gazed at her. "She has
only to make her wish known and whatever words she
wants will pour out my mouth."

"I would have thought a thank-you might be appro-
priate." Rika looked away from him, his stare making
her uncomfortable.

"Ah! *Ja,* thank you for making me your slave, Rika."

"You made me yours quickly enough," she fired back at him.

Bjorn nodded grudgingly. "And all you lost was a little hair. Do you expect me to be grateful that you force me to watch you start married life with another man?"

This conversation was not going as she'd hoped. Her heart was so full of what she meant to say to Bjorn, but all they seemed able to do was jab at each other.

"I meant you owe me thanks for freeing you from that Hel of a prison, and . . . for other things." She wasn't sure he was aware how close he'd come to being gelded. Even days later, she sometimes woke in a panic, dreaming of Al-Amin standing over his bound body with a knife.

"Well, there is that. Dominic told me that you intervened before Al-Amin made a soprano of me. I suppose that does merit a hearty thanks, even if the whole household still believes me a eunuch." Bjorn's crooked smile did not suggest he was especially grateful. "But I just figured you plan to have use of my cock in the future when you weary of waiting in line for your husband's."

She whipped her arm over and struck him hard across the mouth. The force of the blow made her shoulder ache. "You are the most hateful man I've ever known," she said through clenched teeth.

"Thank you, my lady." He bobbed his head at her in mock deference.

Rika wheeled her mount around and drummed her heels into its flanks. She bolted down the street, forcing pedestrians to scatter before her. Al-Amin and Bjorn spurred their horses to follow.

"If you upset my lady again," Al-Amin said to him as they pounded down the street, "I won't take just your manhood next time. I'll have your life."

CHAPTER 37

Rika dressed for dinner carefully. She'd become accustomed to the ethereal, flowing style of the *palla* worn by high-born Byzantine women. The loose robe was comfortable, even sensually pleasing to wear, while draping her figure with flattering folds. Abdul-Azziz was lavish in his gifts and had chosen rich fabrics in colors that suited her.

Each evening when Abdul-Azziz was at home in the city, he invited Rika to dine with him. He seemed enchanted by her Norse stories and had been astounded when she bested him at chess. She knew that after she retired to her suite, he always summoned one of his wives or concubines to his bed. There was much gossip and tittering about his sexual preferences swirling through the harem and tallies kept of who had been called on how many nights. But Rika was the only woman who shared his meals.

At first, Rika was sure it was because he wished not to offend his trading partner, but lately, she'd read something else in his hooded eyes. Something dangerously close to desire. She still hadn't committed to Islam, and therefore to Abdul, but he pressed her to do so with more fervor.

"Did you enjoy your ride today, Little Elf?" Helge ran a silver comb through Rika's hair. It was still shorter than usual for one of her station, but the old woman had a knack for arranging it, tucking the curling ends in an elaborate upswept style that disguised the lack of length. "You weren't gone long."

Rika bit her lip. Bjorn was insufferable. He was crude and hateful. How could she ever have thought he loved her if he was capable of treating her like that? She decided to ignore Helge's question by posing one of her own. "Helge, why would someone repay a kindness with anger and harshness?"

"Oh, it'd be a wise person who knows why anyone does anything, so it would," the old woman said, smoothing down a belligerent red lock. "But I have found that lots of times, anger is just a way to release pain. Especially with menfolk."

"Really?"

"*Ja.* It makes them say and do things they wouldn't if they were in their right mind," Helge said. "Take your father, for instance. He was pure wild with pain when your mother died. It made him do something he's regretted all his life."

"It wasn't my fault," Rika said stubbornly. Helge was never very subtle about working a conversation around to her favorite topic. She'd made no bones about the fact that she wanted peace between her old master and her new mistress and lost no opportunity to try to persuade Rika to forgive Torvald.

"Of course not, lamb," Helge crooned. "But you might bear in mind that pain makes men stupid. All men."

So Bjorn was in pain, was he? Did he think she wasn't? Hadn't she suffered more pangs than a damned soul in Niflheim not knowing whether he lived or died?

She walked to her window. Bjorn was in the court-yard below, forking off a load of fodder from the stack of hay and disappearing into the stalls with it. In his month of servitude, he'd regained some of the flesh his time in prison had stripped from him. The muscles in his bare back rippled as he worked. His powerful stride made her knees give just a bit.

Perhaps pain was making her stupid as well. But was it goading her to commit the ultimate folly? Perhaps it was time she found out.

"Al-Amin?" she said softly. She hadn't seen him in her suite, but she knew he was always there, hovering behind a doorway in the shadows, waiting for her to need him.

"Yes, my lady?"

"I wish the Northman to serve at supper tonight."

"But my lady, he has not been trained for gentle indoor service." Al-Amin's tone indicated that he thought Bjorn barely housebroken and, like a stray mongrel, the barbarian criminal might very well soil the expensive carpets.

"Then please see to his education—and quickly," Rika said. "He told me today that the other servants in the household still believe you gelded him, so there's no impediment to him serving on the upper floors. He's reasonably intelligent. I'm sure you're up to the task of instructing him in serving at table."

Al-Amin frowned and lowered his voice. "My lady, do you think it wise?"

"Probably not," she admitted. "But it is my wish."

"Remember," Al-Amin whispered to Bjorn furiously, "to serve with grace, one must strive to be invisible. Offer the plates from the left, and then stand to the side to wait for direction. And keep the master's cup iced and full without being told."

"Hmph!" was the sullen retort. Bjorn hefted the tray

of braised lamb and vegetables and stepped from behind the stone lattice. He slid the fine plates in front of
Rika and the Arab, and then stepped to the side. He
seemed to have done it correctly because he felt invisible, even in the ridiculous baggy trousers the eunuch
insisted that he wear. Neither of the diners so much as
glanced his way.

Rika's silvery laugh grated on his ears, as he refilled
Abdul's cup with iced juice. For one unworthy moment, he wished for a bubbling kettle of poison to offer the man. But then he reminded himself that his
misery wasn't the Arab's fault. It was Rika's.

"And what Northern delight have you prepared for
me tonight, my pale flower?" Abdul asked.

Bjorn balled his fists at his sides.

"A maidensong," Rika answered, a slight shake
sending the glittering shards of gold across her forehead twinkling in the lamplight. "A love story, if you
like."

"Ah! That sounds like what I'd most enjoy." Abdul
sipped at his juice, his gaze riveted on Rika's animated
face. She was performing for an audience of one, Bjorn
noted, with all the skill of the skaldic art, every nuance,
every expression and gesture perfectly controlled.

"Then listen and you shall hear the tale of Ragnar
and Swanhilde . . ."

A pair of doomed lovers, Bjorn finished for her in his
mind. He longed to cover his ears. How could she tell
the Arab the same story she'd first used to beguile him
all those months ago? That sweet night when he'd first
stolen a kiss from her rushed back to him unbidden.
He'd been marked by it from that moment forward.
How could she make him stand by and watch her tell
that same maidensong to another man? For the first
time, Bjorn came close to hating her.

He shut his eyes, but the sound of her voice went
on, low and seductive, spinning the web of her tale

with the callousness of a she-spider who intends to eat her mate once their coupling is finished.

". . . a *berserkr* cry escaped his lips and Ragnar raised his knife. But Swanhilde leaped up to grab the blade from him just before he could plunge it into his own heart."

Bjorn's eyes snapped open. Rika was changing the story. A skald never changed the story. The lore of the Norse people was a sacred trust to be handed inviolate to the next skald till the end of time. He listened, wide-eyed, as she went on.

"'Forgive me, my love,' Swanhilde cried. 'I didn't mean to cause you pain, but you have been a long time gone and I had to know if your love for me was still true.'"

Had he imagined it, or had Rika glanced at him, just for a flicker of an eyelash?

"Ragnar gathered her into his arms. 'Forgive me as well,' said he. 'I will leave you alone no longer. Let us away to our Northern fastness and forsake this sorrow.'" Rika's voice had a little catch in it.

Bjorn swallowed hard.

"And so they did." Rika made a sweeping gesture to cover the direct gaze she shot Bjorn's way, one brow arched in question. "And ever afterward, Ragnar and Swanhilde drank deep from the horn of love to the end of their days." She slid her gaze back to the man at her side before Abdul-Azziz could mark the exchange.

The Arab clapped his hands together. "Well told," he said. "And how delightful that it ended in joy. In truth, you had me on edge, believing that the lovers would be forever parted. It is so often the case in tales of love, is it not?"

"Frequently, in the old stories that is so," she conceded. "But once in a while, true love must win out."

"Surely it must," Abdul said, and then he frowned down at his plate. "Where is our fruit?"

Bjorn turned abruptly and strode out of the dining room. He vaulted down the stairs, taking them two at a time, to the kitchen below.

Al-Amin met him with a scowl.

"Don't worry, my friend," Bjorn said, his heart light enough to greet even the eunuch with good cheer. "I haven't disgraced you yet. I just need the fruit."

When Bjorn saw the melon halves an idea burst in his mind. "In my homeland, sometimes the cook carves designs in the rind to make the food more appealing. Let me show you." He picked up the fruit and went to work making a series of slashes all around the outside of the half-circles. He was sure that they formed no discernable pattern that Al-Amin could distinguish.

Al-Amin's frown told him he didn't think Bjorn's carving was an improvement.

When Rika noticed the runes sliced into Adbul's melon rind, she sputtered with helpless mirth and had to feign choking to cover her amusement. Bjorn had carved the symbols for *pea-balled troll* into the fruit's thick skin.

As she sipped her juice slowly, she eyed her own melon. The message was clear, but dangerous.

Bathhouse moonrise.

CHAPTER 38

"You summoned me, my master?" Al-Amin had hurried back to Abdul-Azziz after escorting Rika to her rooms. This was the first time the master had called for him since he'd been given to the Northern bride.

"Yes, Al-Amin," Abdul said as he lounged by the low table. "You have been with me as long as I've been in this city and know my mind as well as anyone. Now, I would know yours. How do you find your new mistress?"

"I would not presume to speak, my master." Al-Amin inclined his head ever so slightly.

"Then I command it."

The eunuch breathed a sigh. The master's request was highly irregular. "My lady is kindness itself, a pleasure to serve." He remembered with fondness the way she indulged his predilection for pistachios, but knew the master didn't want to hear about that. "She is quick to grasp our ways and eager for instruction, being possessed of a fine mind. The imam says she is an apt student of the Q'ran for all that she seems not inclined to decision yet. Such deliberation surely indicates purity of spirit and determination. She is unlike any woman I have ever known."

Abdul nodded. "If you had but one word to describe her, what would it be?"

An image of Rika with her hand protectively over the barbarian's manhood flashed in Al-Amin's brain. He met his master's eyes squarely. "Merciful."

"Then she will balance me well, for I am not known for that quality. She has been a surprise from the beginning, a fountain of unexpected delight. Rika is possessed of many gifts if not great beauty," Abdul said. "But beauty is not necessary to breed exceptional sons." He pulled a scroll from his billowing sleeve. "I received an accounting today of my oldest son's latest exploits in Cordoba. Kareem shames me with his gambling and laziness. He squanders my wealth and wastes the opportunities I've given him."

"Kareem is young yet, my master," Al-Amin said.

"He's old enough to be a fool." Abdul crumpled the scroll in his fist. "I want you to summon an imperial scribe first thing in the morning. I intend to draft a new will dispossessing Kareem in favor of the son Rika will bear me."

"This is highly unusual." The position of the first-born was nearly sacrosanct.

"I am unusually upset with Kareem," Abdul said. "When I listen to Rika speak, I can see the son she will give me. Intelligent, strong, not given to dissipation. Once your mistress sees my intent, she will convert, won't she?"

"Forgive me, but her conversion seems to be a matter of principle, not profit." When Al-Amin saw his master's scowl, he hastily amended, "Surely this expression of my master's favor could not fail to impress my lady."

"Good. Then see to it. Make preparations for the marriage to proceed with all speed."

"A thousand pardons, my master," Al-Amin said with a deferential nod. "But we cannot plan the ceremony until the Northman Ornolf returns to the city. My sources tell me he and his traveling companion set sail for Thessalonica last month. Surely, he would consider it an insult if he found the marriage finalized without his presence."

Abdul-Azziz' frown deepened, but he waved Al-Amin away. "Make inquiries. Find out when we can expect Ornolf's return."

CHAPTER 39

From the roof garden, Rika watched the moon rise over the great dome of the Hagia Sophia. Her skin tingled, prickling at the slightest breeze.

The whole world felt different. She'd known it from the moment she changed the story of Ragnar and Swanhilde. Something in the very fiber of Midgard had also changed. Her fate was not immutable any more than the maidensong was immutable. She could decide. She could choose her own future, for good or ill. It wasn't in the hands of the gods of Asgard or the life-weaving Norns. She wouldn't be a victim of Gunnar's schemes any longer. Her life was finally in her own hands, where it belonged.

She slipped through Abdul's apartment, skirting his private room, grateful for the rhythmic huffing and moaning of the newest and youngest concubine to be added to the harem. "The Wailer," she'd overheard Tariq name the girl. He wasn't far wrong. Such loud, overblown passion had the ring of theatrics to Rika's ears, too overly dramatic not to be feigned.

As she glided silently down the curved staircase to

the courtyard, she knew the risk she was about to take. The master of the house could lie with as many different women as he wished, but if she and Bjorn were caught alone together, nothing would stay the hand of Abdul-Azziz. It was worth her life, she decided, just to feel the blood dancing in her veins again.

"My lady." Al-Amin's whisper startled her. "It is late for you to be about."

She put a hand to her chest and willed her breathing to sound normal. "The ride today has given me some pain in muscles I have not used of late. I thought a long soak in a hot bath would do me good."

"As you wish, my lady." The eunuch fell into step beside her, his bare feet making no sound on the stone walkway.

When they reached the bathhouse, she stopped him. "I wish to be alone. Please see that I am not disturbed." She raised a brow at him. "Not even by you."

He blinked at her, but refrained from arguing. Al-Amin nodded and turned his back to her, setting himself to guard the only entrance to the bathhouse.

Rika tiptoed into the cool marble building, her heart pounding, both hopeful that Bjorn was waiting for her and terrified that he might be.

A small oil lamp flickered at the edge of the bath. The deep pool was filled with scented water, rose petals floating like tiny coracles on the smooth surface. Ferns draped toward the shimmering liquid. Wisps of steam curled in the wavering light. The bath was a whole world, a fjord in miniature.

Her gaze darted around the room. She didn't see Bjorn anywhere. Was he crouched in the garden, stopped by Al-Amin's formidable presence? Was this his idea of a joke, a punishment for enslaving him, to lure her here and sneer at her privately? She sighed. He'd prepared this beautiful bath for her. That was

something, at least. She would enjoy what she was offered.

She shrugged off her *palla* and stepped into the
pool, letting the silky water caress her calves, her
thighs, her belly. She let the water close over her head
completely, delighting in the warmth. When she
breached the surface, the breath she drew was heady
with the scent of roses. She floated toward the edge
where she could sit on the submerged ledge.

Rika leaned against the side of the bath, arms spread
wide, her head resting back on the cool marble floor.
She closed her eyes, trying to still her body's rebellious
complaint. The bath was a sybaritic delight, but oh,
how she wished Bjorn had been there waiting for her.
Every bit of her skin screamed for his touch. She
longed for his kiss. And in her secret place, she ached
for him with a hollow throb that would not be stilled.

The rustle of fabric made her open her eyes. Bjorn
stepped out from behind one of the columns ringing
the bath. He'd been there all along.

He opened his mouth to speak, but she put a finger
to her lips and motioned toward the door. Bjorn nodded in understanding. Then he unwound the sash at
his waist and let the baggy trousers fall to the floor.

The lamplight kissed his body, licking over it in wavering pulses. Rika saw that even though he had regained flesh, she was able to count his ribs. The place
in his thigh where the branch had stabbed him was
still indented slightly. That old scar writhed on his
right side and a new one was slashed across his chest
in an angry red line just above his nipples. She yearned
to press her lips to it, to take away the hurt. Her gaze
traveled the length of his glorious, battered body and
she saw that he was ready. She drew a ragged breath.
A bead of moisture glistened at the tip of his erection.

Bjorn lowered himself into the bath and pushed
across to her. When he drew near, she reached for him,

but he caught up her hands and held them fast. He leaned toward her and her wet breasts strained against his chest, skin pressing skin, yearning to join with him as one drop of water is engulfed by another in a merging so complete there would be no separation without total annihilation.

His mouth was by her ear, his breath sending a warm shiver of delight down her neck.

"One of two things will happen now," he whispered. "Either you will scream and whoever is outside the door will come in to kill me and I will let him."

She inhaled sharply.

"Or you will let me love you." He nuzzled her earlobe. "And we will somehow leave this house together when Ornolf returns. For by the gods, Rika, I will not take you by halves. I won't stand by and watch you wed another man. You will be mine or I will be dead." He pulled back to look into her eyes. "Choose."

"I won't scream." Her voice was just a breath.

He covered her mouth with his, all the hurt, all the longing of the months apart distilled into one purifying kiss. Rika slid off the ledge and pressed herself against him. They slipped beneath the water, rolling together, like a pair of sea otters coupling in the surf, only surfacing for lack of air. Bjorn shook his head like a hound coming up out of the water and Rika bit her lip to keep from laughing aloud.

Then suddenly, all amusement faded from his eyes, replaced by smoldering desire. He cupped her face and covered her with kisses, her eyes, her lips, her neck. His hands slid down her back and his mouth found her breasts, suckling the stiff peaks until they ached.

Rika ground herself against him, feeling his swollen shaft slide over her belly and between her legs. She gasped when part of him entered her, but he pulled back.

"Please," she whispered. "I'm burning up."

He grasped her bottom and lifted her. She wrapped her legs around his torso as he teased her with his stiff phallus.

"I'd see you melt first, my love," he mouthed into her ear.

Bjorn set her on the edge of the pool and eased her to lie back on the cool marble. Rika arched her spine as his hands, those blessed skillful hands, slid from her shoulders, across the mounds of her breasts, past her navel and down to spread her legs. She surrendered to him completely.

When she felt his mouth on her, she thought she'd die of bliss. Then the waves of pleasure focused and coiled in ever-tightening strands. The tension building to unbearable heights in her body was only exceeded by her need for more. When her release came, her whole being shuddered and she bit the inside of her cheek to keep from crying out.

She couldn't imagine feeling more ecstasy. And then he entered her and she knew she was wrong. There was more.

His mistress was overlong at her ablutions, even if she was soaking tired muscles, Al-Amin thought. Despite her orders not to disturb her, he felt he'd be remiss in his duties not to check on her well-being. He was adept at slipping unobserved in and out of places, a quality that made him doubly useful as an extra pair of eyes for Abdul-Azziz. His mistress would never know he just sneaked a peek to satisfy himself of her safety.

What he saw shocked him to the soles of his bare feet. Oh, it was not the first time he'd witnessed the act of love. The master often felt that an audience enhanced his performance, so Al-Amin had stood a silent watchful vigil, stomach queasy, while Abdul-Azziz brutally deflowered a virgin purchased for his amusement or savagely rode a randy concubine.

But Al-Amin had never seen two bodies joined in tenderness, sinuous limbs moving as one in a slow dance of torment and promise. He'd never seen the look of trust and wonder between a man and a woman. His mistress and the barbarian were lost, their eyes locked on each other as the moment of exquisite joy wracked them both at once and they strained against each other in one last spasm of rending and binding.

Al-Amin slipped away, ashamed. He'd had no idea. Something so intimate, so sacred was not meant for another to see. When he thought of his mistress submitting to the master's rough appetites, he shuddered.

My lady loves the barbarian, Allah help her, Al-Amin thought. As he resumed his guard, he puzzled over whether he could help her as well.

CHAPTER 40

"So with the armband and the man's sword, you think you have enough evidence to sway a Lawspeaker?" Rika asked, threading her way on horseback through the throng of foot traffic. Bjorn had told her about Fenris's dying confession. It was yet another reason for them to leave this cursed city and head north as soon as possible.

"*Ja,* with Jorand's and my testimony both, it should be enough to convict Gunnar of murdering our father," Bjorn said, nudging his horse closer to hers. "The nine-year sacrifice will be held at this summer's solstice. If we can reach Uppsala by then, a court will be present."

Neither of them had said it aloud, but Rika was sure Bjorn wondered, as she did, whether Gunnar had slated Ketil as one of the sacrifices in the sacred grove. A man who would murder his father couldn't be trusted to keep a secret promise to a woman. Still, going north was dangerous for Bjorn.

"And what of your oath to Gunnar?" she asked.

"We both know it's already in tatters." He met her

gaze with a quick tender smile before carefully guarding his expression. He tossed a glance back at Al-Amin, who trudged on a bay gelding behind them. "The eunuch might not understand Norse, but he is always watching. Last night was a foolish risk."

"And yet I would not take it back for the world," she said, her voice husky.

"Nor I," he admitted. "But we must not be alone together again until we have quit this place. It is too dangerous for you, my love."

"As oath-breaking is dangerous for you."

"It's hard to feel bound to the man who murdered my father," Bjorn said.

Rika looked at him sharply. Hadn't she once blamed Bjorn for Magnus's death? And here she was, more tightly cinched to this man than any oath could bind her. He was seared on her heart and she would never be free of him. Nor did she wish to be. The old skald's death would forever pain her, but Bjorn bore no guilt in it. She realized that now. Even when she'd told him she forgave him at Birka, a part of her heart still held a bit of smoldering resentment. Now even that tiny flame was forever extinguished. Magnus had brought her and Ketil to Hordaland. Bjorn had led the raid. Another hand held the ax. Who was to say which choice caused the tragedy? It just happened. And now they must move on.

"I'll risk the consequences of oath-breaking to see justice done," Bjorn said, his voice stony as flint. "Besides, Gunnar has plundered Sogna long enough. You know there's no limit to his ambitions—and he'll stop at nothing to realize them."

"I don't think it will be a problem for me to leave," Rika said. "I'll just tell Abdul-Azziz that I can't convert to Islam."

"It will not be so easy as that." He shook his head. "The Arab will take it as a personal affront. And besides, you haven't been marking him closely if you think he will just release you. Trust me, I know better than you what a man is thinking. His interest in you is not just for cementing trade ties anymore. That jackal wants you."

Rika shifted in the saddle uneasily. "If that's true, it's only for novelty's sake, I'm sure. He's amused by my tales, nothing more. He made his preferences very clear."

"Unless I'm much mistaken, he seems to have changed his mind." Bjorn's mouth hardened into a grim line. He dropped behind her as they neared the big double doors of the house.

Bjorn took charge of their mounts while Rika and Al-Amin climbed the winding staircase to the third floor.

"I'm back, Helge," Rika called out when she reentered her suite. There was no answer. She pulled the *bourka* over her head. "Helge?"

A muffled moan came from the old woman's small chamber. Rika dashed toward the sound with Al-Amin at her heels. Helge lay abed, her face ashen, her lips a rictus of pain around blue-tinged gums.

"Oh, what's wrong?" Rika dropped to her knees by her friend's bed.

"Little Elf," she breathed. "I feel myself going, so I do. It's sorry I am to leave you, lamb."

"But you were fine this morning—"

"*Ja,* I was. I felt that well myself, so I nipped down to the bathhouse for a quick soak." Helge's tongue flicked out to wet her dry lips. "When I came back to the apartment, someone had left us a tray of sweetmeats, and you know I don't hold with most of this foreign food, but I do dearly love those sweetmeats." She rolled her eyes toward Al-Amin. "Best you throw the rest of them out."

"Helge, what are you saying?"

The old woman's thin frame was wracked by a convulsion and she couldn't speak.

"She means that my lady has an enemy within the house," Al-Amin said woodenly. "The food was poisoned. I will see to it immediately."

Before he could turn to go, Helge reached out a clawed hand and grabbed his wrist. "Watch her for me," she rasped.

The eunuch nodded solemnly. "Depend upon it."

Rika's throat constricted. "Oh, Helge," she said and then dissolved in sobs.

"There, Little Elf, don't take on so," her voice was thin, already disembodied. "I was there when you opened your eyes, so I was. Now you're here to close mine. It's fitting."

"What will I do without you?" Rika realized how she'd come to depend on Helge, even to enjoy her chattering and scolding. It had been nice to have someone to fuss over her, someone to . . . mother her. Magnus had been wonderful, but Rika had never known a woman's gentle care till Helge came to fret and coddle her. And now, the old woman was dying because Rika had attracted a deadly foe. "I'm so sorry. This is all my fault." Rika buried her face on Helge's bony chest.

"Hush, child," Helge said. She laid a thin hand on Rika's head. "I'll not have you thinking that. But if you would make an old woman happy, there is something you could do for me."

Rika raised her face to look into Helge's pale eyes.

"Forgive your father, lamb." Her chest tremored with a suppressed spasm. "Not because he deserves it, even though he does. The punishment that man has laid on himself over the years was far more than you could dish out for him, so it was. Forgive him for yourself."

"Helge, I—"

"Don't let the root of bitterness take hold of your heart, Little Elf." Her voice drifted to a mere whisper. "It's stronger than Yggdrasil once it takes a firm hold and it'll only tear you apart piece by piece, like a root rips through rock."

"I'll try." Rika forced the words out of her throat.

"That'll do, lamb." Helge breathed deeply, pulling Rika close to her heart again. Rika felt the old woman patting her hair in slow, feather-light strokes. Then Helge rested her bony hand on Rika's head. *"Ja, that'll do."*

Her old friend fell silent and it took Rika a moment to realize that Helge's chest no longer rose and fell. Tears pushed at her eyes, stinging, demanding to be released. There seemed not to be any air in the small room. Rika gasped, then collapsed in ragged sobs and wept for Helge.

After she cried herself out, she felt Al-Amin's hand on her shoulder. Her gut churned and she felt her ears burn. Grief turned to anger. "Who has done this thing?"

"I shall try to find out, but it will be difficult, for such a one who could lay a trap of this kind is also capable of covering all trace of blame." Al-Amin sounded weary.

"Once I tell Abdul-Azziz, he will be furious," she said with surety. "It was someone in this house, you said. The hospitality of Abdul's household has been compromised. He'll force the truth from them."

"He would try, and no doubt someone would confess to the crime, but I promise you, my lady, it would not be the guilty party. Such things are arranged for a price and the family of the confessor would reap the benefits, but we would be no wiser and you no safer." The eunuch leaned down and covered Helge's body with a fine linen sheet.

"Then what can we do?"

"Do? We do nothing, my lady," Al-Amin said. "Your safety now lies in subterfuge. The death of an old woman will cause little comment and the killer will wonder whether the poison went astray, but he or she will not know for certain. By not raising an outcry, we will not put them on alert. They will think themselves safe to try again and, trust me, they will assuredly try again."

"So far, you give me no comfort," Rika said, wiping her eyes with an end of the sheet.

"But we will be on alert, my lady," Al-Amin said. "You will eat nothing that I myself have not prepared for you. I will accompany you at all times." He gnawed his bottom lip for a moment, then gazed at her with a directness that unnerved her. "There will be no more late-night baths."

Panic flooded through her. Al-Amin knew. But when she met his eyes, they were an unreadable blank slate.

"Agreed," she said.

"In this household, you may trust myself and the master. I know you have little to do with him, but I'm sure your father, Torvald, would see to your safety as well." Al-Amin ticked the names off on his fingers. Then his features drew up into a grimace of distaste. "I suppose we may also rely on the barbarian and his friend, that little Roman priest."

"I'm sure we can," Rika agreed.

"All others are suspect," Al-Amin said. "Please be guided by me in this, my lady. I would see you safe and, to my mind, only one thing will accomplish it."

"What is that?"

"You must leave this house, my mistress," he said sadly. "You must return to the North. I believe it is in your mind to do this thing, is it not?"

"You know me well, Al-Amin."

The eunuch sighed. "Then I will help you, my lady. I have but one request."

"By now, you know that I can deny you very little."

Al-Amin rubbed his hands together quickly. "I have always heard that the North is very, very cold, and undoubtedly no pistachios will grow there, but when you go," he smiled at her sadly, "please take me with you."

Rika threw her arms around Al-Amin's neck. "Of course you will come and we will buy you new clothes, very warm clothes. Perhaps you will learn to love hazelnuts just as much as pistachios."

Overwhelmed by her display, he let himself pat her back stiffly. "And now, my lady, we must see to Lady Helge's final resting. Shall I arrange for her to be interred in one of the mausoleums or would you prefer she be buried outside the city gates?"

"That is not the way of the Norse people. We do not leave our loved ones under the ground to become food for worms," Rika said. "Neither do we keep them in stone boxes to molder and decay. We send them to Paradise on the wind with dignity and with fire."

"My lady?"

"Send for Torvald," she said decisively. "I need to speak with . . . my father."

CHAPTER 41

Compromises had to be made. In accordance with Abdul's customs, Helge's funeral was a rushed affair. In the North, her body would have been interred in the cold, black earth for ten days while graveclothes were fashioned and suitable belongings assembled. In a frigid climate, the old woman's body would darken, but not decay, in that short length of time.

But Islam decreed a quick disposition of a dead body, so Helge would be sent off in the clothes she died in. Rika conceded that the rich silk was certainly fine enough. In Sognefjord, a soul boat would have been specially constructed to bear Helge's remains to her reward, but Rika had to settle for Torvald purchasing a small coracle from a boatwright in the Harbor of Theodosius.

"Your devotion to a servant is striking," Abdul-Azziz said, as he walked beside Rika in the small procession. His tone told her he also found her devotion unnecessary. Ahead of them, Bjorn, Torvald, Al-Amin and the priest bore the slight burden of Helge's corpse on a flat slab of wood as they marched slowly toward the harbor. In their other hands, they each carried a lighted torch.

"She was my friend." Rika clutched the armful of evergreen branches closer to her, inhaling the fresh clean scent. It cleared her head. In the face of death, the living always took refuge in enhanced delight of the senses, she realized.

She was grateful for the way the *bourka* shielded her from the stares of the curious. She'd heard the cacophonous wailing of paid mourners, trailing caskets in funeral processions through the city. It seemed false to her. Her grief was private and not the subject of public display.

The *bourka* also allowed her to gage Abdul's expressions unremarked. The Arab was clearly ill at ease. She knew he considered this ritual thoroughly pagan. Muslims, Christians, and Jews alike all held burning a body abhorrent. Nonetheless, a crowd of onlookers fell in behind her to see this unusual and, to their minds, spectacular barbaric custom.

When they reached the Harbor of Theodosius, they walked to the farthest point on the spit of land where the small boat was secured. Bjorn and Torvald gently settled Helge into the swaying craft.

"We have no *godi*," Torvald whispered.

"I will serve," Rika said, pulling off her *bourka*. Abdul-Azziz started to object, but she silenced him with a look. "It is necessary," she told him. "We have no Norse priest, so a skald will have to do."

Rika bowed her head, recalling the rite to her mind. In that moment, she realized that she truly no longer believed in the gods of Asgard. They were pale stories, alternately amusing and terrifying tales fit for nothing more than warming a hall on a cold winter's eve. But Helge had believed, so Rika would declaim the rite with all the passion of the faithful. It was the last good thing she could do for her friend.

"In our time of grief, we call upon the gods." Rika lifted her arms skyward. "Hear, All-Father Odin. Give ear to us, Thor the Thunderer, and spurn not our tears, Freya, Lady of Asgard! We ask you to receive the soul of this Helge, one whom we have loved." Her voice crackled with emotion. "She shall be sorely missed."

Rika put a curled fist to her forehead, her right breast and then her left in the prescribed gesture to invoke the trio of deities. She felt hollow as she did it.

"She who is truly worthy shall return in time to her own people. We know full well that our friend Helge is the worthiest of the worthy. May her soul find peace and joy and the best of company in the Shining Lands. This we pray. So mote it be!"

"So mote it be," Bjorn and Torvald murmured in unison.

Rika slipped the amber hammer over her head and knelt to tie the leather straps around the dead woman's neck. It seemed fitting that the little amber talisman should venture into the next world with Helge. "Take this hammer of Thor, beloved one. May thy soul be so protected wherever thou travel."

When she stood, she saw Torvald's lips press into a tight line, but he nodded his head in agreement. He stooped to slip a golden coin of Miklagard into Helge's cold hand as Rika continued.

"Take this coin of the realm, beloved one. May it give thee good fortune and passage to the Land Beyond." As Rika declaimed the rite, she gave an evergreen bough to each member of the party assembled. Only Abdul refused to take one, his furrowed brow making it clear that he wanted nothing to do with this incomprehensible ritual. She supposed she could have spoken the rite in Greek instead of Norse, but she was doing this for Helge, not for him.

"As the tree is ever green, may thy soul live forever refreshed," Rika said as she laid her bough across

Helge's body. The other mourners followed her example. "Behold thy soul boat, dear friend. May thy journey between the worlds be swift and free from peril."

Rika nodded to Bjorn and he stepped forward with his torch to light the dry kindling beneath Helge's body. The other pallbearers dropped their torches into the coracle as well, to speed the burning. Bjorn untied the craft and shoved it into the waves, where it bobbed and dipped, floating farther from the land. A wind whipped over the sea and the flames roared upward, the licking fire assuring Helge's soul of a speedy passage.

"So now let us be joyous," Rika said with tears streaming down her cheeks. "For the soul blossoms as a red flower. It flies as a white bird. Our good friend has gone to a far better place and, if we too are worthy, we shall meet her again in the Shining Lands." Rika wished she could believe the words coming out of her mouth, but the deadness in her heart told her she did not. "So mote it be," she whispered.

She watched the burning vessel till the last of its blackened spars sank beneath the waves. When she turned to go, Rika was stopped by a hand on her shoulder. It was Bjorn's friend, the little priest named Dominic.

"May I add my poor prayer to your ceremony?" he asked respectfully.

Rika nodded, not sure what Helge would have made of it, but she was intrigued enough to allow it.

Dominic bowed his head.

"Jesu, Lover of our souls," he intoned. "We commend to your care the spirit of the woman Helge. Judge her not by her deeds or her creed. None of us will pass into Paradise by that measure. But with your own grace cover her and receive her, for all we poor mortals can do is walk by the light we have received and trust that the Judge of all the earth shall do rightly." Dominic raised his eyes and smiled. Then in halting Norse he added, "So mote it be!"

Rika smiled back at him, her heart strangely lightened by his simple prayer. "So mote it be!"

As they walked back along the banks of the River Lycus to the home of Abdul-Azziz, Bjorn nudged Torvald in the ribs. "Did you see?" he asked.

"*Ja,*" Torvald answered softly. "And we had better make our plans for tonight."

Bjorn nodded.

Before the funeral party had left the harbor, on the distant swells of the Sea of Marmara, Bjorn and Torvald had recognized the shape and sail of the very ship they'd hoped to see. The *Valkyrie* was returning to Miklagard and would be tied up in the Golden Horn by nightfall.

CHAPTER 42

Torvald left the house immediately after the ceremony to meet the *Valkyrie* and forestall Ornolf. If the big balding Northman returned to the Arab's house, the question of Rika's conversion to Islam would be forced to a head and the noose around her would tighten all the more. Rika tried to accompany her father to the harbor, but Tariq stopped her at the big double doors.

"The master feels you should remain in seclusion for a time," Sultana's eunuch said, "mourning being best observed in privacy. He also requests you refrain from riding as you have done of late. Since you are seeking to acquaint yourself with our ways, I am surprised that Al-Amin did not instruct you in the unseemly nature of such behavior."

By her side, Al-Amin bristled at this slighting remark on his mistress's conduct.

"By the master's orders, if you wish to go abroad in the city, you will make use of a covered chair or a cart and driver in the future." Tariq's smile was oily and ingratiating. "I am considered a driver of exceptional skill and my mistress wishes me to offer you my services in this regard."

Rika thought she'd sooner mate with a snake.

Torvald hugged her briefly and whispered, "Don't despair. We'll think of something." His thin lips curved into a shy smile as he added, "Daughter."

He hadn't dared call her that before.

Rika and Al-Amin retired to her chambers. She peeked from time to time from the window of the room that had become her prison and watched for some sign of Bjorn or her father.

Her father. How odd to think of Torvald like that and yet he was. To honor Helge's dying request, she'd made peace with the old man.

Torvald had buried his face in his hands and wept. "How can you forgive this old fool? I'll never forgive myself."

"But I do," Rika assured him, wiping away tears of her own. Helge had been right. That small hurt that never quite went away was finally stilled. Magnus's place in her heart had not dimmed one jot, but Rika found that she also had room in it for this man as well.

The sun was already sinking when she saw Torvald return.

"Al-Amin, please go to the stables and see what my father has learned."

"Mistress, I would not leave you alone."

"I'll bar the door and admit none but you," she promised.

Rika paced and fretted until he returned. In furious whispers, Al-Amin told her the plan that Bjorn had devised to get them all out of the house of Abdul-Azziz.

"But I do not like this, my lady," he complained. "It is too risky."

"Bjorn is right. We must go in stages," she argued. "If we all tried to leave together it would surely cause an uproar. There's no other way to get us all out of this house safely."

Al-Amin stiffened into an erect posture. "Then I will stay behind, my lady."

"No." Rika's eyes widened. "Abdul-Azziz will know you have assisted in my escape." From the time she'd spent with the Arab, she knew he could be charming, but beneath the polished exterior, a hardened core of tempered steel was barely submerged. His wrath would be terrible.

"I would not leave you alone," Al-Amin said. "How can I trust your care to that barbarian?"

"That barbarian was entrusted with my safety for the long, weary journey here," Rika assured him. She thought of Bjorn leaping after her into Aeifor. No matter what, he'd see her free. But even if their plan failed tonight, at least she'd die with him. It was enough.

A short while later, she watched as Al-Amin and the little priest led her horse to the big double doors.

"My mistress wishes me to sell it since she has displeased the master by riding," he explained to Tariq, who continued to guard the entrance. "If you don't let us pass immediately, the hostlers will have closed up shop and the horse buyers will all be in their cups for the night."

"And it takes two of you to sell a horse?"

Al-Amin rolled his eyes at the other eunuch. "I am an accomplished rider as you well know, but I'm no groom. The day I stop to shovel up horse manure in the street is the day I curl up my toes," he said with affectation.

Tariq laughed and swung the doors open wide. Al-Amin minced past Sultana's eunuch with Dominic leading the gelding after him.

"Two away," Rika whispered. Three souls left.

*   *   *

The link boys cried in the streets, offering to light the way for well-born traffic through the dark city for the price of a small coin. Rika heard Torvald call to one of the urchins in heavily accented Greek. She looked out the window in time to see her father slip out the double doors. Tariq bolted them behind him. Even though she stayed well in the shadows, she didn't miss the direct glare the eunuch sent toward her window.

"Three away," she said softly.

"Rika, will you not eat?" Abdul entreated through her door.

"Not tonight." She leaned against the portal, her heart hammering. "It is the custom of my people. I must fast for my friend." Despite Magnus's teaching, the lie came swiftly to her tongue. In the North, funerals were as good an excuse as any for a people devoted to food and drink. Feasting and drunken stupor were more common than fasting to celebrate a life gone by. "You must excuse me for a brief time."

"Tariq tells me that Al-Amin has not returned," Abdul said. "Do you wish someone to attend you? Shall I send one of the other eunuchs?"

"No," she said. "I'm used to Al-Amin. He'll be home soon. Doubtless, he has had difficulty finding a buyer, but I wanted to sell the horse immediately since I had displeased you."

"Thank you, my northern blossom. Your respect for my wishes is commendable." His voice was edged with impatience. "But I want to share my new plans with you this evening. Surely the servant's death has already occupied too much of your time. Can I not persuade you to join me?"

A flicker of movement, a shadow wavered by the crack at the bottom of the door. "Please honor my customs, just for tonight," she added placatingly. "I couldn't possibly be merry company. And I wish to give my full attention to your plans, but at another time, I beg you. Tomorrow, perhaps."

"As you wish." His tone told Rika that those words had not often passed his lips.

She pressed an ear against the door, holding her breath, listening for his retreating footsteps. When she was satisfied he was gone, she expelled all the air from her lungs and wrapped her arms around herself to still her tremors.

Rika propped a chair under the latch. Then she blew out the lamp and sat in the gathering dark, waiting for the house to grow silent. Abdul-Azziz ordered music with his *nattmal,* and she squirmed through the squeals and twangs that his musicians produced. She knew Al-Amin didn't appreciate Norse songs, so it didn't surprise her that she found the Arab's music just as incomprehensible.

She moved a chair to her window and positioned herself to watch so she wouldn't be seen. Tariq had been replaced by another of the eunuchs, but this one looked no less formidable a guard. There had always been someone at the big double doors, but today was the first time she'd been denied passage. Did Abdul suspect something, or was he truly just concerned for her safety and reputation, as Tariq claimed?

The lamps went out in the master's dining room and a swaying candle lighted Abdul's progress around the veranda to his suite of rooms wrapped around the stairwell. If only there was another staircase! The only way from the third floor to the courtyard wound through the master's apartments. Rika admitted to herself that she'd been extremely lucky last night to pass through them undetected. No doubt the Wailer's loud moaning had helped. Abdul-Azziz rarely asked for the same woman two nights in a row, so Rika knew she and her friends couldn't count on that noisy distraction again.

Abdul's many bed partners were nothing to her since she would never join their ranks. She wondered how differently the Wailer's sounds might affect a woman who cared. Like the different perceptions about what made music, might the Wailer's sounds be not a cause for amused indifference, but for despair? The keeping of a concubine in the North was not unknown, but she never expected to encounter the situation personally. Rika spared a moment to pity Sultana and the others. If any of them truly loved Abdul-Azziz they must die nightly, she decided. How could a woman live like that?

The lamps in Abdul's suite were extinguished. No sound but the nervous twitter of a few night birds and the patter of the fountain came to her ears. Whoever shared the master's couch tonight was either less vocal or less moved. She watched the empty courtyard, her body tensing, waiting for the signal to unbar her door.

The moon rose and trekked across the sky. Still there was no movement in the courtyard. Why had he not come? Bjorn had fought in battles. He'd led raids. No doubt he knew more about the timing of this sort of thing, but the waiting was fast jangling her last frazzled nerve. She stopped knotting her fingers and buried her face in her hands, near tears.

One of the peacocks that strutted through the courtyard scuttled from under a bush and cried out. Its alarm made her look up. She saw a figure disappear into the stairwell.

Finally! He was coming and they would steal up to the roof garden together. Bjorn was carrying the stout rope they'd use to lower themselves to the street level from the roof. Then she and Bjorn would make their way to the Forum of the Ox, where Torvald would be waiting with the horse. From there it would be a quick trot to the Harbor of Theodosius, where Torvald had told Ornolf to have the *Valkyrie* waiting, ready to sail the moment they arrived.

Rika only had to brave the dark corridor from her door around to the stairs where she would meet Bjorn. They would creep up to the roof garden together. She slipped Al-Amin's servitude documents into the pouch at her waist. She intended to give them to him the first chance she got. She glanced around the dark room that had been her home for the last half year. There was nothing else she wanted to take. She moved the chair and eased her door open.

The door flew back at her with unexpected force. It knocked her against the wall, her head slamming the stone and leaving her dazed. Rika's vision tunneled for a moment and she felt rough hands on her, thrusting a cloth through her teeth to gag her. Then she was shoved to the floor. The assailant fell upon her, his weight pinning her down, both her hands locked in a painful grip.

Just enough moonlight shafted in the open window for her to make out her attacker. She looked up into Tariq's snarling face.

CHAPTER 43

"Going out for a stroll, are you?" Tariq's voice grated her ear. "I think not tonight."

He ground a knee between her legs. "You're not going anywhere. I made sure of that. You see, I told the master I suspected the death of your servant had unhinged your mind, so he needed to keep you safely within these walls."

Rika struggled under him, trying to scream, but the gag effectively stopped most of her voice. Tariq's strength was amplified by cruelty. He gathered both her wrists into a one-handed grip and rucked up her tunic with the other.

Rika tried to knee him, but he struck her on the temple with his fist. Stars exploded before her eyes.

"You can't expect Sultana to stand by and watch you and your bastards displace her son Kareem."

Rika's brows knit together. What was he babbling about?

He pressed himself against her and Rika was shocked to feel the hardness of an erection against the inside of her thigh.

"Oh, yes," he said, obviously reading the surprise in her eyes. "The stories about late-made eunuchs you've no doubt heard are all true." His face twisted into a sadistic snarl. "But the only pleasure left in it for me is the pain I give to you."

He grabbed one of her breasts and twisted her nipple so viciously, tears sprang to Rika's eyes.

"Oh, yes, that's goo—" Tariq's voice was cut off as his eyes widened, then glassed over. Suddenly his body lifted from hers and dropped beside her. Bjorn stood over him. She saw the glint of a blade as he withdrew the point of his knife from Tariq's ribs. He wiped the weapon clean on the eunuch's baggy trousers.

"Are you hurt?" he whispered as he helped her out of the gag.

"No." She sprang up into his arms, the last remnants of fear still making her tremble. She buried her face in his chest and inhaled him deeply.

"Come," he ordered and shepherded her toward the door. Before they reached it, the portal swung open again. This time it was Sultana, carrying a lamp.

"Help!" She yelled down the hall. "Tariq has violated the Northwoman!" Evidently she was unwilling to wait for an examination to discredit Rika and would even sacrifice her own henchman to do it. Then Sultana peered into the room, her eyes widening as she saw her eunuch dead on the floor and a big Northman approaching her, knife in hand. Sultana dropped the lamp and bolted down the corridor, true terror punctuating her screams this time. "Murder!"

Bjorn slammed the door shut and braced it with a chair.

"We'll never make it to the roof now. What do we do?" Rika asked.

"Change of plans." He strode to the window and looked down into the courtyard. Lamps were being lit all over the house and men were running up the stair-well. "They'll be at the door soon."

Bjorn slipped the coil of rope off his shoulder and tied it to the metal balustrade outside the window. He jerked at the rope to make sure the knot was firm, then tossed the length of it out the opening.

"Climb onto my back and hold on." He hunkered down.

Rika hitched up her tunic so she could wrap her legs around his waist and clasped her arms around Bjorn's shoulders, taking care not to choke him. He put the knife blade between his teeth and swung a leg over the railing. He hooked one of his calves around the rope, then hand under hand, he lowered them down.

"They've broken through," Rika cried when she heard the door give way above them.

Bjorn let the hemp slide through his fingers and Rika knew he was burning his palms. They plummeted in a controlled fall downward, landing in a tumble at the bottom, but both of them sprang up. Bjorn grabbed her hand and they sprinted toward the big double doors. Rika's ankle sent darts of fire up her leg with every step, but she gritted her teeth and strove to keep up with him.

The eunuch guarding the double doors had un-sheathed his sword, probably at the first cry of alarm, but he was no match for a trained *tagmata*. Bjorn feinted and rushed in over the guard's slashing down-stroke, plunging the knife into the eunuch's jugular. Blood spurted in a red fountain from his neck, and he was dead before he hit the ground.

Pounding feet flew back down the stairwell now. Bjorn grappled with the brace that barred the doors and threw them open, taking the brace out with him. Once he and Rika were outside the house, they pushed the doors closed and Bjorn wedged the heavy timber against them.

"We haven't much time," he said as he grabbed her hand.

A clatter of hooves on the stone street made Bjorn pull her back into the shadows of the house. The horseman stopped at the doorway and dismounted. It was Torvald.

"What are you doing here?" Rika asked, as Bjorn shoved her onto the horse's back.

"You were late. Thought I'd see if an old man could lend a hand." Torvald pulled his sword from its scabbard. The wooden doors trembled with the force of a blow. The household of Abdul-Azziz was fully roused and had found a makeshift battering ram of some kind. "Better get going. That door won't hold long, but this is a good defensible position. I'll give you as much extra time as I can."

Bjorn clasped forearms with the old farmer, now turned back into the warrior he'd been as a youth. Then Bjorn vaulted up onto the horse behind Rika.

"No, you're coming too," she wailed to Torvald.

"Not this trip, Daughter," he said. A smile split his face, the first true smile Rika had ever seen on the old man's features. "I have another destination in mind. Take care of each other."

The crack of splintering wood jerked all their heads toward the door. Years seemed to slough off Torvald and he straightened his still broad shoulders. The pain-numbed look of a *berserkr* stole over the old Viking's face. Bloodlust glinted in his pale eyes and his nostrils flared.

"Yah! Get on with you!" Torvald slapped the horse's rump and it lurched to a gallop.

"Father!" Rika wailed.

Behind them she heard the door crash in pieces and Torvald's battle cry split the night in an eerie, feral howl.

CHAPTER 44

Rika wasn't sure which was louder, the clatter of the horse's hooves on the pavings or the frantic thumping of her own heart. Her fingers clenched convulsively around the horse's mane and she clamped down firmly with her thighs on the rolling shoulders of the beast. Bjorn's arm around her waist steadied her, but their headlong flight through twisting alleys stole her breath away.

"Yah!" Bjorn bellowed and the horse laid back its ears and stretched out its neck in a full gallop across the Forum of the Ox.

Rika heard the beat of other hooves behind them. Her gut churned. Torvald was dead then. He'd never have let them past him otherwise.

"They're coming!" Rika yelled. She and Bjorn leaned forward as one and the horse beneath them responded with more speed. But the animal was carrying twice the weight of the pursuers' mounts and, with each pounding step, they lost ground to the household of the Arab.

Bjorn jerked at the reins and they turned sharply

into a dark lane. In that slice of a moment, Rika glanced back to see a pack of horsemen, Abdul-Azziz in the lead, his face twisted in fury like a hot desert wind bearing down on them.

The path was steeper now and the stench of fish guts told Rika they were nearing the harbor. When they burst out of the lane onto the wooden planks of the wharf, the horse hooves' brisk clack turned into muffled thuds. At the end of the long pier Rika spotted the *Valkyrie,* Jorand lighting their way with a torch.

She heard Abdul-Azziz shouting, but the words were caught by the wind. When they reached the ship, she tumbled off the horse, half falling, half being dragged by Ornolf and was bundled onto the waiting vessel. Bjorn pulled out his knife again and slashed the ropes binding the craft to the dock. He shoved her off and then made a running leap into the *Valkyrie* as she surged away from the pier.

Jorand, Al-Amin and the priest were already positioned at the oars. Bjorn joined them and they heaved away while Ornolf manned the steering oar. Rika stood in the prow, grasping at the sides of the ship to steady herself, delayed panic making her shake like an aspen in the wind.

Zzzt! The air around her buzzed with sharp droning sounds like a swarm of angry bees. Arrows sliced through the water around them and one lodged in the long neck of the *Valkyrie*'s prow just finger-lengths from her hand.

"Rika! Get down!" Bjorn yelled between strokes.

She huddled below the curve of the hull, listening to the spat of arrows against the wood. The Byzantine guard had been roused against them. She'd known Abdul-Azziz was powerful, with highly placed contacts throughout the city, but she never dreamed he could mobilize the authorities so quickly.

The air was thick with shouted orders and Abdul's

outraged bellowing. The stinging missiles stopped peppering the Valkyrie. Since they seemed out of arrow range, Rika peeked over the side of the ship. They were making steadily for the narrow mouth of the Harbor of Theodosius. On the shore she saw a group of guards boarding a heavy Greek vessel, while another sprinted for the harbor entrance. At the end of the land spit, men began turning a ponderous wheel, gathering up the wet links of a heavy chain.

"They're closing off the harbor," Rika shouted back to Ornolf. His grim face told her he'd seen it too.

"Toss over the cargo," he growled. "Lighten the ship."

The Greek vessel headed for them, so the rowers couldn't be spared for even a moment. Rika heaved every crate she could lift into the black water, the gold and silver that would have enriched Sogna finding its rest instead in the warm depths of the harbor. Bales of silk and cachets of rare spices bobbed in their wake. Ornolf left the steering oar long enough to hoist the heavier loads. The now trimmer *Valkyrie* surged away from the other ship.

Rika watched the men on the Greek vessel fumbling with a bulky mass. She couldn't tell what they were doing until a torch was lit. Then she gasped. She'd come to the harbor with Al-Amin one day and watched the demonstration of the formidable weapon that secured the safety of Miklagard. It was the scourge of pirate vessels and enemies of the Byzantine Empire all over Middle Earth's inland sea. They called it "Greek fire."

The long arm of flame snaked across the water at them, igniting a silk bale in a fiery blast. The *Valkyrie* was just beyond range, but that would end when her hull met the harbor chain ahead of them.

"We're trapped," Rika said softly, her gaze finding Bjorn. He was still hauling at the oar, his breath com-

ing in hoarse grunts. Her heart swelled with love for
him as tears gathered at the corners of her eyes. He'd
tried so hard. If she must die, at least it would be with
him, and in this last blaze their ashes would be joined
forever. She would ask for no more.

"Rika, get to the stern," Bjorn ordered. She scrambled past him, resting her hand on his shoulder in a
last loving touch for just a glancing moment. "On my
mark, everyone leave your oar and make for the stern,"
he called out.

Rika saw the chain pulled taut at the waterline, the
metal glinting in the light of the Greek fire. The flame
hissed toward them again, its sulfuric breath a whiff of
the Christian hell. The heat of the blast blistered her
arm and she cringed away from it.

"Steady," Bjorn said with icy calm. "Three more
strokes. One." He heaved the oar forward and then
strained, dragging it back through the water.

"Two." The four oarsmen leaned in concert to put
the combined force of their strength toward propelling
the *Valkyrie*.

"Three! Ship oars." After one last heave, they
tucked the oars into the craft to reduce the drag and
the men rushed to the stern. The added weight in the
rear raised the prow and the *Valkyrie* surged forward
under her own momentum.

The shallow draft of the hull let her slide over the
chain a little more than half of the *Valkyrie's* length
before she ground to a halt, prow dripping above the
waterline.

"Forward!" Bjorn ordered and they all scrambled toward the prow. The *Valkyrie's* figurehead dipped toward the water as her stern lifted. "Jorand, with me."
Bjorn positioned himself at the rear oars and together
with his friend, he flailed at the water, trying to lurch
the hull over the chain. The Greek ship bore down on
them and Rika could see the soldiers scurrying to

rearm their weapon. This time the flames would incinerate them like a goose on a spit. Her heart sank to the soles of her feet.

Ornolf grabbed an oar and wedged the blade against the chain, pushing at it with a groan. Al-Amin snatched up the last oar and shoved on the other side of the Valkyrie as well. In jigging fits, the ship shuddered over the chain, first in agonizing finger-lengths, then as the fulcrum shifted along the hull, she lurched in longer slides until the *Valkyrie* broke free and plowed the water, gliding away from the chain.

Fire from the Greek ship blazed toward them, stopping to dance along the chain at the waterline, forming a man-high wall of crackling flames behind them.

"Up oars," Bjorn shouted. He and Jorand hoisted the sail and a fair wind filled the cloth. The *Valkyrie* lifted, buoyant and light, running before the wind like a fleet hind outpacing her hunters.

Even once the harbor chain was lowered and the fire extinguished, the pursuit was over. The ungainly Greek ships could never overtake the sleek Norse craft.

Rika collapsed in Bjorn's arms, shuddering sobs of relief wracking her frame. He smoothed her hair with his hand and clutched her to him.

"Don't cry, love," he whispered. "We're going home."

CHAPTER 45

Al-Amin proved to be a poor sailor, but after Dominic nursed him through a week of sickness, he tolerated the surging motion of the *Valkyrie*, if not with grace, at least without complaint. The trek up the D'nieper was even more arduous than the wild ride down, despite the fact that the *Valkyrie*'s shallow open hold rode empty of cargo. Bjorn, Jorand and Ornolf were constantly rowing, aided by Al-Amin and Dominic as their stamina improved. They fought against a current that was punishing at times and mildly annoying at others, but always dragging at them, trying to pull the *Valkyrie* south to the Black Sea.

Since Rika didn't have the strength needed to row, she insisted that Bjorn teach her to guide the ship by means of the steering oar so when one of the five men was allowed a break from rowing it was a true respite, not just a change of duty. No one could spare much breath for conversation, so Rika was often left with her own dark thoughts.

She mourned the loss of Helge, feeling the lack of a feminine companion all the more keenly in this company of five men. And she often wept silently for Torvald, for that sad, broken man who'd made a terrible mistake, one that haunted him all his life, but Rika felt he'd atoned for it with his final sacrifice. She hoped his tortured soul was at peace.

She fretted over Ketil's fate. Her brother had dreamed of being sent to the sacred grove, just as he'd dreamed of her trip to Miklagard. Now that she knew Gunnar had tried to kill Bjorn as a child and had succeeded in murdering his own father, she was sure her gentle brother was not safe. Rika counted the days till the summer solstice in agitated fury. They must reach Uppsala before the Blot, the nine-day feast honoring Odin, before the rites began and the slaughtered victims gathered on the spreading limbs of the grove next to the mighty temple.

There was never a time for her to be alone with Bjorn and they felt the lack of privacy keenly. A stolen kiss here and tender glances there were fast becoming not enough. Finally at the base of Aeifor, Bjorn called a halt to their progress.

"If I don't marry this woman right here and now, I'm going to burst," he exclaimed once they made camp.

"I don't know how you can rightly do that, nephew," Ornolf said. "Our snares and fishing will feed us, but they'll provide no wedding feast. We've no *godi* to chant the ceremony. There's no way for the two of you to marry properly just now."

"If I may," Dominic said, a thin smile on his lips. "I can marry them. All that is required is that they convert and be baptized and they can be man and wife by the setting of the sun."

"Agreed," Bjorn said. "Your God has taken pretty good care of you so far, my friend. Rika, will you take the sign of the Christ in order to take me as well?"

She hugged him fiercely. Her Norse gods were distant and unreachable entities. She'd lost her trust in the court of Asgard long ago. What little she learned of the Arab's Allah hadn't moved her to faith. The bloody wrangling between the Christians of Miklagard left her distrustful, but the need to worship something still burned in her. She'd even managed to assuage the urge with her weekly pilgrimage to the statue of Mars. All people, it seemed, recognized the need to acknowledge a higher being. It saddened her that they all disagreed so on the who and the how.

She turned back to Dominic. The little priest was a good companion, brave in danger and uncomplaining in hardship. She knew Bjorn credited the man with saving his sanity while they were imprisoned together. If a person were defined by whom or what he chose to worship, Dominic's character spoke well for his God.

"I'll agree to anything that makes me Bjorn's wife, but I know very little of your Christ," she admitted.

"Then consider this your introduction to him." The priest smiled. "If you are willing, you shall know him better hereafter, I assure you."

Ornolf scowled at Dominic, his glare tinged nonetheless with grudging respect. The priest had bent Bjorn to his will finally. It was something few Northmen had managed. "That's a coercive way to spread your faith, isn't it?"

The little priest spread his hands before him self-deprecatingly. "People of the North are so stubborn, I will take my converts however I can."

Rika and Bjorn waded into the D'nieper with Dominic and listened without comprehension as the priest intoned the baptismal rite in Latin. The thunder of Aeifor's fall pummeled their ears, but the roaring of the blood in her veins sounded even louder to Rika. After they were thoroughly doused both by the spray of the cataract and their baptism, Dominic led them in the marriage rite. When they climbed dripping out of the river, they were, happily and finally, husband and wife.

CHAPTER 46

Torchlight blazed over the settlement of Uppsala, casting wavering shadows against the mighty temple that housed the giant statues of Odin, Thor and the stiff-phallused Frey. The reek of putrefaction in the air told Rika that the sacred grove already hung heavy with the bodies of slain victims. The Blot had begun.

Over the course of nine days, nine male offerings of different beasts were ritually killed each night, their throats cut and the blood drained from their carcasses, collected for darker use by the *godi* later. The blood of the sacrifices was necessary for the working of *seid* craft, the secret and often sinister magic of the Norse priesthood. Then the bodies were hung to rot from limbs of the ponderous oaks next to the temple, their slow decay thought to purify that sacred place.

Rika couldn't bear to look. She squeezed her eyes shut for a moment and sent a brief prayer skyward to her new God that they weren't too late, that she wouldn't see her brother's body swaying in the breeze.

"We're in time," Bjorn said beside her. "No men yet. But this is the night. If Ketil is destined to go to the trees, we have only until the moon reaches its highest point."

Rika sagged against him in a confused tangle of both relief and panic, then she straightened suddenly. "Look! There's Surt." Rika stretched out her arm to point at the Sognaman thrall across the crowded compound.

They sprinted to Surt and found that Ketil was indeed the offering from Sogna, one of the nine slated for the Blot, as they had feared. Surt led them to a special hut where the future victims were kept under strict guard. The nine were fed and housed as befitted those destined to meet the All-Father very shortly. Any earthly wants, from rich food and drink, games and music to visits from an accomplished whore, were granted them as they waited for death.

"Sister!" Ketil's broad face broke into a beatific grin. "I knew you'd come. Dreamed it," he slurred. Ketil hiccupped softly as Surt refilled his horn with sweet mead.

"Oh, Ketil." Rika bit her lower lip. He'd never had a head for drink, but she supposed that Surt felt it was a mercy to send him to his doom slobbering drunk. She knelt beside her brother and kissed his cheek. A tear slid down her own.

"Told you not to cry," Ketil said as he smoothed the tear away with his fingertips. "Knew I'd see you again . . . at the place with the big trees." His face crumpled in anguish. Evidently, Surt's brew wasn't potent enough to erase his predicament from even Ketil's simple mind.

Bjorn stooped to lay a hand on Ketil's shoulder. "Courage, brother," he said. "You will not go to the trees this night. My oath on it." Bjorn's grim expression left no doubt in Rika's mind that he'd do whatever was necessary to keep this vow. Then he straightened. "Stay if you wish," he whispered to Rika. "I'm for the Lawspeaker."

"Then I'll come with you," she said.

"I'll stay with your brother, if I may," Dominic offered. "Giving comfort in time of distress is my business."

"Looking for another convert, priest?" Ornolf crossed his arms over his chest.

"Wherever I can find one," Dominic said unabashedly.

Rika hugged Ketil briefly. "I'll be back soon," she promised. "We will leave this place together, brother." One way or another, it would be true. Either she and Bjorn would see Ketil freed, or they would all die this night and leave the bonds of Midgard forever.

Flanked by Jorand, Ornolf and a totally bewildered Al-Amin, Bjorn and Rika strode across the compound to the Jarl of Uppsala's longhouse. The raucous sounds of feasting and drinking spilled out into the warm night.

Bjorn burst through the door and scanned the long room through the haze of smoke from the fires. He spotted Gunnar, whispering into a serving girl's ear and then laughing, with Astryd glowering beside him. Ornolf pointed to another man, seated beside Halfdan of Raumarike and some of the other jarls. It was Domari, the Lawspeaker.

"The Law demands justice!" Bjorn bellowed above the din. "Hail, Domari, keeper of the Law."

One by one the knots of conversation hushed around them.

"I seek your wisdom and know you will hear my cause." Bjorn strode forward, confidently mouthing the time-honored request for the Lawspeaker's intervention.

"Who are you, and what is your complaint?" Domari stood ram-rod straight. Despite his sixty winters, he was a powerfully built man with a shock of silver hair brushing his shoulders.

Bjorn waited until the hall was quiet. "I am Bjorn the Black of Sognefjord, and murder has brought me here." He turned slowly to glare at Gunnar. "I charge my brother, Gunnar Haraldsson, with the murder of our father, Harald of Sogna, one-time jarl of that fair land."

"Oath-breaker!" The word exploded from Gunnar's lips as he leapt to his feet, pointing an accusatory finger at Bjorn. "This man has sworn fealty to me, and he dares slander me before this company on our holiest of nights!"

"Is this true?" Domari asked.

"*Ja,* I am Gunnar's man," Bjorn admitted. "But hear my evidence against the Jarl of Sogna first, and I shall answer for my oath-breaking hereafter."

"He admits it!" Gunnar roared. "Why should the Lawspeaker trouble himself with the words of an oath-breaker?"

"Sit down, son of Harald," Domari ordered, narrowing his eyes at Gunnar. "Your father was my friend and the Law seeks the truth. Let us see if there is any here that needs concern us. Speak, Bjorn the Black."

Bjorn did a slow turn, meeting as many of the eyes that were riveted on him as he could. He wished for Rika's gift, for her facility with words and the ability to send images to her listeners, but just the bald facts plainly told would have to suffice. In spare strokes, he related the story of his fight with Fenris the Walker and the big man's dying confession.

"A fanciful tale," Gunnar interrupted. "My brother has been bewitched by that woman," he glared at Rika, "who styles herself a skald. No doubt she has concocted this fantasy."

"I am Jorand of Sogna, son of Orn. I was witness to this fight." Jorand stepped forward. "It happened just as Bjorn the Black said. Fenris confessed as he lay dying and named the man who gave him a silver armband as the one who struck Harald of Sogna the fatal blow. I do not think a man will step idly into the next world with a lie on his lips."

"Bjorn the Black is Jorand's captain," Gunnar said. "A man will say anything for his captain's sake."

"It is true that he is my captain and I will add to that. Bjorn the Black is also my friend." Jorand's voice filled the hall. "But I am not oath-bound to him. My words are my own, and upon my honor, my testimony is true."

"This armband you speak of, do you have it with you?" the Lawspeaker asked.

"We do," Bjorn said. Watching the blood rush from his brother's face made Bjorn's gut churn with a thrill, an anticipation of victory. He clamped the feeling down. He was sure his brother was not finished yet. Ornolf presented the armband for Domari to examine.

"I am Ornolf Bloodax," he said. "I gave this armband to my nephew, Gunnar Haraldsson, on his wedding day. Entwined serpents are the device Gunnar had chosen for himself. You'll find there is an inscription on the inside." He fingered the runes and then left the band in Domari's hand as he turned to eye Gunnar. "I was sad to see it again in Miklagard and to hear that it had purchased the death of my brother."

"A man can lose an armband," Gunnar protested to Domari. "Besides, surely you see that this is just a case of jealousy. Second sons must stick together. Isn't that right, Uncle?" Emboldened by the Lawspeaker's silence, Gunnar strode forward. "All they have is the word of an oath-breaker, the lies of his admitted friend, and a long-lost piece of finery, which I will claim again as mine. The rest is no better than a tale to frighten children on a winter's night."

Domari frowned down at the armband. "Is this all?"

"No." Bjorn drew out the Galata sword and held it up in the flickering light. "This is the sword of Fenris the Walker. As you can all see, it's a fine blade, but it has a flaw." He ran a finger along the flat, careful to avoid the razor-sharp edge. "The sword of my father, Harald of Sogna, left a nick too deep to grind out. This blade left a similar nick in my father's steel as well." He narrowed his eyes at Gunnar. "Come, brother. Draw our father's sword and let us see if the faults are a match."

"Only to send you to Hel, little brother," Gunnar roared. He whipped out his sword and slashed it down on Bjorn in a deadly arc. Bjorn met the blow with the Galata.

At a signal from the Lawspeaker, men leaped to grab both Bjorn and Gunnar's arms and immobilize them.

"Let no blood be shed in this house," Domari said. "The Jarl of Sogna has chosen trial by combat. So be it. Prepare the *holmgang* and let the challenge begin before another torch burns itself out."

CHAPTER 47

"I want you to leave now," Bjorn said to Rika as he hefted the light wooden shield. Two others lay at his feet for use when the first was shattered by a blow. "Take Jorand and steal Ketil away during the confusion. Then all of you make for someplace safe."

"And where would that be?" Rika asked, as she eyed Gunnar across the *holmhring*. The jarl had a good thirty pounds on Bjorn. "There is no place in all Midgard for me without you. Either we all leave together or none of us do."

The *holmhring* was nearly finished. A large cloak had been pegged to the earth with three concentric squares etched into the dirt around it. Ropes were strung from hazel poles at each of the four corners of the outer square, enclosing a fighting area only twelve feet across on each side. Bjorn and his brother pulled their tunics over their heads. No mail or hardened leather was allowed. According to the rules of the *holmgang,* once the three shields of soft linden wood were destroyed, a man's only defense was his sword.

"Besides, you need Jorand as your second," she said.

Bjorn frowned. "You are a thoroughly disobedient wife."

"And likely to stay that way."

"Rika, please—"

She pressed her fingertips against his mouth. "No, love. I can't desert you. Don't ask it of me." An ache centered in her chest. Bjorn was still well under his fighting weight, and she knew he was exhausted from the breakneck pace they'd set trying to make it to Uppsala in time. Gunnar was sleek and rested, the firm muscles in his chest and arms standing out in stark definition under his smooth skin. Despite everything, Rika forced a smile. "You can take that pea-balled troll any time."

Bjorn bent to her, his lips lingering over hers. When he pulled back, Rika saw his soul shining in his eyes, radiating love for her.

"You warned me," he said. "We've lived quite a love story, haven't we? A maidensong holds as many dangers as pleasures, you said."

"So I did." She wrapped her arms around him, burying her face in his chest. "But I didn't know at the time that the pleasures would be well worth the risk."

He chuckled. "Ah, Rika, they are indeed. I do love you, girl." Bjorn ran a hand over her head.

"And I you."

"In the winters to come, remember me," he whispered into her ear.

"In the winters to come, we will tell our maidensong to our children and our children's children," she said evenly. "They'll never believe it's not a skald's tale. You must win, Bjorn. I'll not forgive you if you don't get me with child."

Bjorn nodded, his crooked smile deepening the dimple in his cheek. Then his dark eyes hardened and he turned back toward the *holmhring* to face his mortal enemy, his brother.

"This combat is enjoined to determine the guilt or innocence of Gunnar Haraldsson in the matter of the murder of his father, Harald of Sogna," Domari said, his deep tone ringing into the night sky.

The moon had risen over the treetops, but Rika wouldn't let herself think about Ketil's fate when the silver disc reached its zenith. She focused on Bjorn and prayed. If Dominic was right, if this new God did indeed love them, she prayed he would show that love right now.

"The right of the first blow belongs to the Jarl of Sogna," the Lawspeaker said. "Let the *holmgang* begin and let no man interfere."

Bjorn and Gunnar both struck their shields with the flat of their swords and stepped onto the cloak. Bjorn flexed his knees, preparing to meet his brother's strike.

Gunnar raised his arm and, grunting with effort, crashed his sword down on Bjorn. The shield absorbed most of the blow, but it cracked down the middle. Only the leather strap around Bjorn's forearm stopped it from falling to ground in pieces. He tossed it aside and Jorand lofted a second shield to him.

Rika caught herself tensing and holding her breath. She forced air in and out of her lungs, willing her heart not to leap from her chest. Across the *holmhring,* she saw Astryd, her face shimmering with hate. If Bjorn lost, Rika knew Astryd expected to take her as a drudge once more.

Bjorn brought his heavy sword down on his brother, but Gunnar's shield glanced the blow to the side, leaving his protection still intact. It was Gunnar's turn again.

There was no strategy to the *holmgang,* no method for winning other than brute strength and endurance as the combatants exchanged blows. Bjorn staggered back a pace under the brunt of an attack, one of his feet leaving the cloak.

"He gives ground!" The shout went up from all the

onlookers and Bjorn scrambled back onto the cloak ready to continue combat. To let both feet leave the cloth-covered area would invite the shameful cry of "He flees!"

Rika closed her eyes, a knot in her throat making it difficult to swallow. She couldn't bear to watch. The sound of splintering wood, the low grunts of exertion, and then the clang of steel on steel made her open her eyes again.

She gasped. All three of Bjorn's shields were in tatters, but Gunnar still had one left.

"You should have left it alone, little brother." Gunnar's face stretched into a macabre smile. "The winner takes all in the *holmgang,* you know. Of course, all you've got is that little redhead, but don't you worry." Gunnar swung his sword in a wide arc, an easy swing, just toying with Bjorn. "After I finish you, I'll go watch the sacrifice. Then I'll take care of the skald for you. And when I'm tired of her, I'll pass her around to my men."

Rika felt Al-Amin crowd close behind her. The eunuch rested his meaty hand on her shoulder. She shivered. However much Al-Amin might try, he wouldn't be able to protect her from Gunnar if Bjorn fell in the square. But if Bjorn died, the flickering lamp of her soul would wink out with him. She would cease to care what happened to her anyway.

"Doesn't it bother you that I'll have your whore?" Gunnar said tauntingly, trying to goad his brother into a poor stroke.

The muscle in Bjorn's cheek ticked, but he still didn't move. Rika knotted her fingers together and gnawed her lower lip.

When the blow came, it was so fast, Rika's gaze could barely follow it. Bjorn feinted toward Gunnar's remaining shield, then slashed upward to meet his sword squarely. The lengths of steel rasped against each other toward their hilts as Bjorn stepped into the swing.

And suddenly, the nicks in the sharp edges caught and held fast like a pair of stags whose antlers were locked. Gunnar's eyes flew wide with surprise. Bjorn jerked back and wrenched the sword from his brother's grasp. The blades were still frozen at right angles, but both of the pommels were in Bjorn's hands. Rika gasped. In all her life, she'd never seen anyone disarm his opponent in the *holmhring*.

Gunnar stood like a statue, stunned, with his shield arm hanging at his side. Bjorn didn't bat an eyelash.

"The next blow belongs to the Jarl of Sogna," Domari said.

"Canute, a sword," Gunnar yelled to his second.

The big blond Viking spat on the ground. "A man in a *holmhring* is allowed three shields, but only one sword."

"Why, brother?" Bjorn's voice was a whisper. "It would all have come to you eventually. Why did you have to kill him?"

"Harald could have lived another twenty winters. Why should I wait for what's mine?" Gunnar's eyes went icy and he screamed at his brother in a *berserkr* rage. Then he slammed his remaining shield into Bjorn, who impaled it on the tip of one of the swords.

"Winner takes all, as you say," Bjorn said coolly, as he stepped toward Gunnar. "I'll settle for your life."

The jarl staggered back.

"He gives ground!"

There was no mercy in Bjorn's dark eyes. Gunnar stumbled backward again, trying to escape the arc of death the locked swords would unleash.

"He flees!" The crowd shouted when both of Gunnar's feet left the prescribed fighting area.

The words seemed to stiffen Gunnar's drooping spine and he stood straighter and stepped back onto the cloak. A faint whiff of urine, the smell of fear, swirled around him, but he stood to face Bjorn.

Bjorn swung the swords to one side, preparing to bring a final slashing stroke across his brother's unprotected middle. But he stopped, frozen, his chest heaving as if at war with an unseen foe.

"No," he said, driving the points of the blades into the ground instead. A confused murmur rustled through the crowd.

"I have taken the sign of the Christ. I cannot kill a man in cold blood, not even one who deserves it. But Lawspeaker Domari, the outcome of this combat is clear. My brother is guilty of murdering our father." Bjorn turned and walked to the edge of the *holmhring*. "I leave his fate in your hands."

"Bind him," Domari ordered and several men seized Gunnar. The Lawspeaker turned back to Bjorn. "You may think your act of mercy not so kind after all, Christian." Domari's lip curled with undisguised loathing.

"Gunnar Haraldsson, you are found guilty of the crime of patricide," the Lawspeaker intoned. "The penalty is well known. You will meet your death on the wings of the blood-eagle."

All the color drained from Gunnar's face. His living lungs would be ripped out through his ribs while he gasped for air. It was terror enough to melt the bowels of a braver man than he.

"Damn you, little brother," he hissed through clenched teeth. "Finish me."

"Once more will I ask the Lawspeaker to hear me," Bjorn said. "I am no longer Odin's man, but my brother follows the Old Ways. On this holy night, let him offer himself to Odin in the grove both to honor his gods and to pay for his crime. Let Gunnar Haraldsson be the sacrifice from Sogna."

The Lawspeaker narrowed his eyes at Bjorn, seeming to consider his words. Odin's victims were usually thralls. A nobleman going willing to the grove would increase the prestige of the temple and please the priests.

"So mote it be!" Domari's voice rolled over the crowd as Gunnar was led away to replace Ketil. "In accordance with the law of the *holmhring*, Bjorn the Black is heir to all that was Gunnar Haraldsson's. From this moment, you are Jarl of Sogna."

A cheer went up around Bjorn. Gunnar had made many enemies. Only Astryd shrieked her rage and bolted from the ring, away from the direction her husband was being dragged.

"Now to the matter of oath-breaking," the Law-speaker said, his voice solemn as befitted the seriousness of the offense. "A man's word is sacred, not to be lightly given, and not to be gainsaid once it is spoken. Oath-breaking is a crime I am loath to tolerate. According to the Law, Bjorn the Black, you should be banished from the North for three years. But your brother broke faith with your father and with you and with all the people of Sogna. Your offense is mitigated by his crime. Therefore, I command that instead of banishment, you will confine yourself to Sognefjord for three years. Lead your people well and if you raid beyond your realm during that time, you will answer to me."

Rika ran to Bjorn and threw her arms around him, relieved by the Lawgiver's unexpected mercy and comforted by the steady thump of her husband's heart.

"Jorand, you'll help me, won't you?" Bjorn asked.

"I thought I already made it clear tonight," the young man said. "I'm not your sworn man. You can't order me about, even if you are a jarl. I think I'm for a voyage, a three-year-long one perhaps. And what will you do with yourself for the time of your confinement?"

Bjorn looked down at Rika. "I've a mind to build a keep with a high tower for this saucy wench."

"A fastness on a wind-swept crag overlooking the sea?"

"Just so."

"Ah! So once your three-year sentence is up, when you go viking, I can watch for your ship in the fjord?"

"You know my mind well."

"Then you know nothing of mine if you think to leave me, Bjorn the Black," she said. "I've had enough parting from you to last a lifetime. Unless you want to meet Ragnar's end, you'd better stay home and tend the fields."

Bjorn swept her into a tight embrace. "How about if I stay home and tend my wife?"

She kissed him deeply. "Even better."